...

Blue Moon

NARGIS & COMER,
I'M SHOWING YOU MINE. HAHA!
IT WAS A REAL PLEASURE MEETING
YOU BOTH!! ENJOY BLUE MOON,
AND ALL MY BEST, COMER, ON YOUR
AMAZING ACCOMPLISHMENT.

Ron Ehrens

MY BEST! REh

...

McKenna Publishing Group
Indian Wells, California

Blue Moon

ISBN: 0-9713659-2-X
LCCN: 2001097525

First Edition
10 9 8 7 6 5 4 3 2 1

Printed in the United States of America

All my thanks and love to my wonderful wife, Julie, and our beautiful children, who make me happy to be me every day. To the dozens of my friends, family and co-workers who read the manuscript and encouraged me throughout, thank you.

I also owe a great deal of thanks to Cornell Shaw for his talent in designing the cover art. And, a special thank you to my friend Dee Castrellon for her invaluable "free-lance" editing, and to my agent, Ric Bollinger, for his unending faith.

For Alex and Bailey

Book I

"The expulsion from the Garden of Eden
is the beginning of life as I know it."

Frank Orrall
Poi Dog Pondering

1

Like a calf one day becomes a nice filet, I was sent off to Hebrew School for three hours every Sunday morning to be the good little Jew I am supposed to be. I was taught the Hebrew language, of all goddamn things, and to read from right to left, and that, even though my birth certificate very clearly states, "Chicago, IL," I was actually from Israel. I didn't even know where that was, but assumed it was in the Big Ten with the other I states, like Indiana and Iowa.

My Sunday morning education was a Swiss Army knife of Jewish tools and information that I felt were about as useful as the Swiss army. My classmates gobbled it all up and went home with fanciful stories to tell their parents, who in turn filled them up with far too much self-esteem. I went home thinking God didn't even have to get out of bed on Sundays.

Back then, I couldn't think of a more boring or useless way to spend time. Fortunately, I've grown up, and my thoughts on religion have evolved immensely. Now, I realize I hated it because it sucked.

I only mention it because one of my significant flaws, and it's really never had an upside, is that I've always felt the need to objectively analyze everything rather than simply follow the pack. To me, there's something awful about being a stereotype. The thing is, though, your stereotypical politicians get elected, your stereotypical ass kissers get promoted and your stereotypical good little Jew happily goes to temple on Sunday morning and gets to be life-long friends with every other Jewish person on earth. There are even wonderfully cutesy terms to describe this last phenomenon, like *The Tribe* and *Jewish Geography*, and I am fast losing membership in each. The point is that enthusiastically embracing membership in whatever group you happen upon appears to be working for the population in general.

Then there's me. I have a talent for feeling and acting like an outsider in the midst of even the closest of relationships. In college, I joined a fraternity, but didn't live in the house or go to a single meeting. In my career, I have worked at a company for years and still refer to them as they, rather than we. In my family, I too often think about them in my head, rather than simply feeling them in my heart. In my love life, which is an awfully generous term for it, I can date a girl for months while knowing she has characteristics that will never qualify her as a kindred spirit, thus dooming the relationship to a series of missteps as I try unsuccessfully to let her down easy.

Theoretically, when you tend to question and see through the phoniness of every relationship and every institution you're involved in, it should lead to an intense devotion to the things that truly appeal to you. Right? I believe that's true. I believe when I meet the right girl, for instance, I'll be so foolishly loving and devoted and obsessive, she'll need to beat me off with a hockey stick. The only two possible results will be true storybook love, my personal preference, or a restraining order. However, through no lack of effort, I've failed spectacularly to find my soul mate, or perhaps more accurately, I could name one or two who had stunning resumes, but it happened before I had game enough to do anything about it.

I love meeting women. I've actually gotten much better at it, and I feel like it's the one true scorecard for where I am in life. It's true that there's an entire class of girls who think I'm from Mars, but since there's virtually no overlap between their needs and mine, this has pretty much worked in my favor. However, I've gotten to the point where apparently I am somewhat attractive to a certain select segment of the population. This has mostly been a train wreck.

Sadly, this has been my typical relationship. It starts off with incredible innocence, excitement and possibility until it peaks in, give or take, the third minute. Even then, after the good times, if they still want to go out with me, we date several times with vague hopes that we can make it work, though I've usually decided by that time that they aren't soul mate material. However, in case my intuition is wrong, which has never actually happened, and because it comes with occasional opportunities to have sex, this phase is still essential. This is typically followed by several months of tripping over myself because I feel guilty for going out with someone who I've decided won't be the One. And if they aren't the One, why should they be with me when Mr. Right may be at the other end of the bar? I'd feel terrible if I were the cause of them not meeting. I mean it.

While Ms. Not "the One" is actually listening to something I'm say-ing—because she hasn't grasped the concept yet that it doesn't matter what I was saying because she's not "the One"—or is mentally drawing one of those police witness sketches deciding if I might look better with a goatee or a nose job or top hat, or *something,* they could miss that the future father of her children is just right over there ready to pay for her alcohol, and talk about things she cares about and buy her more alcohol and compliment her hair when he really wnats to say, *"Jesus,* how much more is it going to cost me before I see you naked"...and, what were you saying, oh God yes, we have a lot in common, and, are you kidding, yes, it was, it *was,* fate that brought us together...and they soon begin the mating process that will provide them offspring who will be loved and adored by all of their class-mates because the test will be graded on a curve. It could easily happen.

While I'm truly sincere about this, you'd be surprised how few women are eternally thankful that I'm so concerned for their well being that I'd break up with them out of the goodness of my heart. I've found this self-less gesture is never quite viewed as the win-win I had envisioned. On the other hand, I'm very (very!) familiar with how much it sucks to be rejected. So not only do I feel too guilty to stay with them, I feel too guilty to break up.

I'm one of the worst breaker-uppers of all time. Seriously, there a SPED class. I once decided in the cab home after the first date that this particular girl wasn't *it.* She didn't have *it,* she didn't get *it.* But she was sweet, and we had a decent time—and she had just been let down hard by the last son-of-a-bitch she had dated—that I just couldn't break up with her. This was going on for a year, and I kept feeling worse and worse about it. So, I finally decided to break up with her on, of all days, our anniversary. I think, actually I more just imagine, that two people being in love is as good as its gets in this world. So it just felt all wrong celebrating a day in honor of us being together. So the ambassador to love and goodwill that I am, I chose to relieve her of her girlfriend responsibilities just prior to our big romantic dinner. Despite the poor choice of timing, I was probably doing the right thing to get out of this one-way relationship. Right? Any-one?

The thing is, when I tried to end it with her, she started sobbing un-controllably, like someone sobbing uncontrollably or something, and tell-

9

ing me how this kind of thing always happened to her and that she hated herself, and that sob, sniffle, *guys*, sniffle, sob, *suck*. I felt so bad, I ended up telling her we'd work it out and that, of course, we should stay together, and—*where the fuck did this come from*—why don't we go visit your parents for the weekend.

For nearly six more pathetic months this went on, until I blatantly made plans to go for a boondoggle weekend with the fellas on—see if we can spot a trend here—her birthday. She broke up with me, and, if it can be considered progress or therapy in some small way, I'm pretty sure she now hates me more than her.

My name is Seth Gold. I'm thirty-three years old. I've failed at love so often, so spectacularly and so consistently, I reached a point in my life where I actually tried to make myself believe that if I can't make myself happy being me, I needed to try to be happy being someone else. Looking back on it now from the straw hut bar from which I sit, swaying almost religiously to *No Woman, No Cry*, I'm at a loss for any other explanation for Shulie Cohenberg.

2

I met Shulie in late January at Four Farthings, one of my favorite taverns in Lincoln Park on Chicago's north side. That night I had met my buddies, Craig, Fishy and Rags at Fishy's place and Craig was keeping the mood light and airy by providing details of how his latest girlfriend had tossed him overboard again. The news, Craig just springing it on us like that, came as an enormous and unsettling surprise to no one that had ever met him. Craig's problem was that his relationships were always a candle in the wind, and that he had a really, really little wick. He combined being hopelessly needy, attractive to the hopelessly needy and a master, really, at meeting their short-term needs. They'd then stick around as long as it took to say thanks, without giving the door enough time to hit them in the ass.

It was for the third time by the same girl, and this time, I thought to myself, it had a hint of finality. She told him she was a lesbian. It had drained the life out of the poor guy, and now he was draining the life out of us. Fishy, desperate to get Craig out of the mood he was in, had bribed him with free drinks to go out with us. And so Craig finally agreed, his inability to turn down anything free overriding his nearly suicidal disposition.

So, after a couple of cold ones at Fishy's, we walked the six blocks to the bar with a wonderful sense of purpose and confidence and camaraderie.

Okay, not exactly. Craig walked as if he was having trouble keeping up with his shadow. Rags, who had recently decided that there was a much higher form of life at the club scene than the pub scene, was asking, "Why the hell are we going to the Farthings?" I suppose he was thinking that, as guys, we'd talk it over and pour our hearts and souls into it until we came to a consensus.

"Jesus, shut the fuck up," said Fishy, helpfully. He had gotten there first and spoken for the group.

"Screw you. I'm just saying it's not my type of crowd."

Rags was moaning because he was suddenly into dancing to dawn with some ethnic bimbo with fake boobs, lamé pants, and a glittery halter top. Probably because of her personality. At my age, if I haven't achieved my objective by 3 a.m., it's probably not worth happening. To him, he needed that time before dawn for alcohol, desperation and a glittery halter top to team up and decide he looked good enough in black. Then a drink. A dance. And as consciousness faded, who knew what kind of meaningful relationship might blossom.

"What kind of crowd you looking for?" Fishy asked, egging him on, as if he cared.

Rags ignored Fishy and said to me, as if I cared, "You hear what I'm saying Goldie, man, I'm looking for a girl that's…more…you know…."

As Rags looked to me for just the right words to say alive or fun or reckless or out there, Fishy and I pitched in to help him out with, *"Lonely?" "Artificial?" "Brain dead?" "For hire?"*

"Fuck off."

Fishy and I laughed and gave each other a low-key high five, dissing Rags being too easy to get worked up over. Fishy, though, had concerns of his own. "If it's a sausage fest, we're gone." It was the same thing he'd said prior to going to every bar we've ever gone to. If a bar's patrons on any given night consisted of more than two percent men, Fishy condemned it as a sausage bar and thought the city should do the same. It was nothing more than an excuse for not getting any, though no one wanted to publicly come out in favor of a bar needing more guys. Privately, I didn't feel that any bar featuring just the four of us was going to attract a wide and varied assortment of beautiful women for us to choose from at our convenience, but publicly I provided my complete solidarity on that point.

Fishy was a really good looking guy with a Tom Cruise look that the rest of us envied, though his stature and repore with the guys never seemed to translate to the opposite sex. There were, in fact, starting to be rumors that he must by gay to be that good looking and that unsuccessful. I wish I was good looking enough for people to wonder that. I wonder if anyone does. In any case, I had no reason to think the whole sausage thing was a cover up, but maybe the reason he noticed all the sausage was because that's what he was looking for.

I dropped back to see if I could help with Craig, who looked thoroughly defeated and was walking hunched over with his hands buried in his coat and wearing a ski hat that looked ludicrous, though I had to admit that I was fucking freezing without one. Even though he had at least twice as many clothes on, he seemed way colder than the rest of us. The chill of the night had descended not only on his skin and bones, but you could almost picture it settling like the January dew on his thoughts.

"Hey," I said to Craig, watching the mist of the cold air I was breathing out, thinking it'd be pretty cool if the smoke actually spelled out "Hey."

He didn't respond and I was unable to translate the smoke signals from his breathing. He didn't look up. If he knew I was walking next to him, he didn't acknowledge it.

"Bud, you gonna be okay?"

"What?" I thought I heard. His head was still buried in his chest and it could have been him talking or his coat.

"You alright?" I asked, trying again.

"Huh?"

That seemed too complicated to respond to, so I switched paths. "Have you called her?"

"Who?"

"*What?*"

"Huh?"

Okay, good talk. "Jesus, Craig, who the fuck do you think?"

"Oh." He shook his head in comprehension, but didn't say anything.

"Hey, asshole, have you called her?" *No wonder she said she became a lesbian.*

"Uh," he finally said, "yeah."

Progress! He was really opening up to me. "That's good, right. There's still hope," I said, patting him on the back, gently though, because he was pretty fragile.

We walked a little farther, and since I had come so far, I pressed on, making the mistake of asking, "Did you leave a message?"

"Yeah, man…twelve." He actually said the word twelve, it seemed, condescendingly, as if the experts had determined that was the appropriate number of calls to make to win back someone who's dumped you multiple times before proclaiming herself a lesbian. I only mention it so you know it's not eleven or thirteen.

"Okay, that's, uh, good, I'm sure," I said, trying, without success, to throw any encouragement into my voice whatsoever.

I looked at him walking in as close to the fetal position as you can be while on two feet, and then started and stopped asking the next question a few times before I finally asked, cringing, "Any word?"

Either he or his coat mumbled, "No."

Oh, the humanity. I grimaced in pain and hoped the police weren't going to find out about this anytime soon. "You know, Craig, I'm not really buying the lesbo thing, pal. I think she'll come around."

He slowly looked at me, seeking any trace of sincerity or hope, and I tried my best to give him all the appropriate body language short of a thumbs-up.

He held my gaze and I felt compelled to give him the best possible spin I could, "I think she sees something in you that brings her back, you know. She probably just hasn't figured it out yet, right. That takes time or something or whatever, okay, but once she gets it, she'll…"

His small smile was meant to stop me, I think, before I said something too entirely lacking in credibility. He, like I, knew that I was very likely full of shit, but I think he appreciated the effort. I patted him on the back again to show that I really did care.

Then, though, I made the tactical error of looking over at Rags, and whatever the fuck his problem was, I really didn't care.

"This scene bores me to death," I heard him say under his breath, intended for me, as if he was placing the entire night under protest. I needed a beer.

Frankly I'd had enough of Rags. He was an actuarial for a living, a condition he'd brought on himself by taking something like seventeen tests to become that boring. Seriously, I think he did it to have something to bitch about. I wanted to tell him that if he really wanted to have some fun, he and his work pals could figure out precisely the odds of being bored to death, but I wasn't in the mood to get drawn into a conversation with him. Instead, as we turned onto Cleveland Street I rushed past him to get to Lincoln and Cleveland, where the bar was.

Instead of heading into the bar, though, I hailed the first cab I saw heading south down Lincoln Avenue. When Rags caught up, wondering where the hell I was going, I gave him $20 cab fare and told him to go where he wanted to be. Life was too short for that shit. A debilitating sort of confusion came over him, as if he was entirely unable to decide if what he really wanted was to go to another bar, or just complain about this one. Instead of waiting for him to decide, I opened the cab door and shoved him in. As the cab raced away to go make Rags someone else's problem, I turned around and looked at Fishy and Craig standing together. They were both still staring at Lincoln Avenue, at the spot where the cab had been, as I walked past.

These were my boys. My fellas. My troops. If it weren't for them, I'd probably have some really cool friends. Actually, I'm kidding. If it weren't for them, I wouldn't have any friends, at least not to hang out with on a Saturday night in the neighborhood. I had a lot of friends from college that were all married at that point and living in the burbs, and wanted to live vicariously through me if I had more to offer them. As it was, they were busy making babies and mortgage payments and trips to Disney World, as if someone would actually pay to do that, and were ready to re-admit me when I got a similar life. I couldn't even picture it.

In any case, we had arrived at the bar and my pals had successfully elevated my spirits to the point that I wanted to physically harm the next person I met who had friends they actually liked. Fishy, who tended to be our vocal leader, gave us a much needed pep talk, "Alright, ya losers, we're here. Try not to scare 'em away. And, Jesus, Craig, you gonna take off that fucking hat?"

With that, the bouncer waived us in without checking our IDs, and we arrived to the warmth and welcome of the crowd and wove our way to a near optimal spot standing only three or four deep from the center of the bar. I felt comfortable at Four Farthings. It was all browns and greens and high ceilings, and whatever, there were babes in every direction you looked.

We ordered a round of drinks, taking the time to make our initial evaluations. Fishy leaned over and said, "Lotta dudes here tonight."

"Stop looking at the guys," I said back.

Four Farthings was packed with a somewhat older crowd than the hordes of twenty-two year-olds with the folded-bill, turned-around baseball hats drinking cheap beer from plastic cups that predominate at many of the other area bars. The Four Farthings' crowd ranged from a few week-ends to a few years away from a similar lifestyle until many of us came to the sudden realization we could no longer put it away like we could in college. Or perhaps that members of the opposite sex were no longer providing positive reinforcement for conversations including, "We were sooooo wasted last night." I'd guess most of this crowd had found it's taken until next weekend to recover from last weekend, and decided to hang with the relatively more mature crowd at Four Farthings. That, and, as I mentioned, the babes.

I'm not really proud of this, but I'd gotten really good at scoping an entire bar for prospects in a matter of seconds—just in case the future love of my life should show. During one such reconnaissance mission, I had noticed Shulie and two friends enter the bar, and with some almost miraculous timing, score a round table and some chairs near the front door. One of her friends was an exceptionally cute blonde girl. The other girl, as was Shulie, clearly from the aforementioned *Tribe*. For some reason (the cute blond), I kept tabs on their group, and even pointed it out to Fishy, the only other one of us even in the game.

So, when Shulie started walking up to us about two beers after they walked in, I saw her coming. As she worked her way through the crowd, I briefly noticed the reaction of her friends, who were leaning forward, smiling expectantly like high school cheerleaders watching their friend go talk to the new guy, their hands clasped, tucked between their breasts and the tabletop, to follow the action. At least the blonde was, I may have been speculating about the other one.

Shulie was olive-skinned, wide-eyed, round-cheeked, and, with a closer look, emanated with an unpretentious beauty, and I sensed, a desire to get what she was looking for. All in all, it was not a bad combination to be walking toward you on a Saturday night as your buzz was just beginning to move up its life cycle. Fishy and I stood there, watching and waiting, unsure if she was coming to talk to us, and if so, to him or me, and if him, *what the hell*, he's probably gay.

But for whatever reason, I sort of knew it was going to be me. So, as she walked up, it may not surprise you that the first thought I had as this very attractive, and I'm not kidding, she was *really* attractive, girl introduced herself to me was…what the fuck kind of name is Shulie? I later learned it was Hebrew for How Jewish Can I Get.

16

"Hi," she yelled looking up at me with a bright smile.

I did the old chin nod, the sly smile, the old once over, and then "Hello," giving her one of those non-committal looks that are sometimes necessary to try to get a girl to think you're cooler than you are.

"I'm Shulie."

"You *are?*" I asked, without much tact, but probably not loud enough for her to hear over the crowd or the Edwin McCain song playing from the jukebox.

She nodded her head toward the table her friends were at and shouted, "My friend says you were here last Friday night. Are you a regular here or something?"

Wow, I had been spotted last week by one of her friends. Which one? Which one! Little fireworks started going off in my head. Please, be the blond! I strained to look over there and suddenly these two women from the Amazon were in my way. Move! Standing right between us. Jesus, fucking move! I twisted and turned and tried to stand on my toes, but they were like the great goddamn wall of China. Finally the giraffes moved, someone must have thrown a basketball the other way or something, and I was able to make eye contact with, goddamnit, not the cute blond. Apparently the other friend fell just below my radar last Friday. She smiled at me, and I nodded briefly as if to thank her for the referral.

Turning back to Shulie, I answered, "Yeah, you know, pretty much." Turning to face the bar, I raised my arm above the crowd to signal the bartender and called out, "Hey doc, the usual and one for my friend!"

I caught his attention long enough for him to shoot me a "what the fuck's your deal" look before continuing his effort elsewhere to keep up with the demand for $3.50 "specials" on Sam Adams. I knew I'd have to go to a different bartender next time to have any chance for him to pick my order out of the crowd.

"He has no idea who you are or what you drink?" she asked, kind of amused.

"Nope." I said smiling apologetically and she chuckled. Kind of an affecting little chuckle at that. "Will you buy me a drink?" she asked undeterred.

After following the conversation, my friends quickly scattered and I wondered if they were already assuming I'd be leaving that night without them. I considered that possibility a progression in my life. I had spent a good portion of my years so utterly unpopular and unhappy that I don't have a single high school moment I'd want to share with you. If high school's supposed to be a defining time of your life, it is only to the extent that when I have a bad day I wonder if I'm really still that insecure, scrawny, four-eyed, four-inch afro-wearing nobody I had been. And, not to date myself, which ironically I was forced to do quite often back then, did they not have hair conditioner in the late seventies, or had just nobody told me? And I fucking hate the word *introvert*. To be called that and be too defenseless to do anything about it causes a fair amount of rage in me even now. Anyway, I was getting more evidence to the contrary, and felt that way less and less, but I still chalked up the fact my friends were assuming I'd get this girl as another step up my personal development ladder. In any case, regarding the drink, I figured what the hell.

"What the hell," I yelled. "What would you like?"

"How about a glass of Mogen David?" she yelled back.

Mogen David? I laughed out loud, while briefly scanning the crowd to see if anyone had heard and now had us pegged as the Jewish section of the bar. Mogen David is a really horrible sweet red wine that forced on us at all Jewish holidays. "That's great," I finally said, "You're joking right?"

"Uh huh," she said, with kind of a proud smirk.

"Cute."

"Thank you."

Hmm. Maybe this girl really had potential. Unless the Mogen David crack was just some Jewish bonding secret code, or worse, she was just checking to make sure I was Jewish, too.

"No really?" I asked, this time with a smile, giving her the benefit of the doubt.

"I'll have a Rolling Rock."

Unable to just casually beckon to the bartender for two Rocks, I was finally able to get the other bartender's attention. It took a full scale effort to break through (for you youngsters: shoulders squared to the bar, eyes focused and alert, cash waiving like a fucking madman), but finally, thankfully (before having to give up and ask the more appealing Shulie to help me out here), I managed a triumphant, "Two Rolling Rocks, in bottles."

"Thanks for the beer. What's your name?"

"Seth." We clinked bottles as she somewhat pleasantly invaded my personal space. "So, Shulie," I asked with a smile that probably looked like I was really enjoying her company but was actually more that I still couldn't say Shulie with a straight face, "who are you here with?"

"My friends, Hannah and Jennifer. Jennifer, over there is the blond. She's here to meet her boyfriend." *Crap.* "Hannah's only out for a couple drinks." *Whatever.*

"So, they're your friends from work."

She hesitated and then asked, "Was that a question?"

"Um, no."

"Why do you say that?" she asked, the early eagerness fading from her eyes.

"This is going to sound bad considering we just met, but if I had to guess, I'd say that you probably have no friends who aren't Jewish."

"*What?*" she asked and I knew I had lost all the goodwill I had built up by buying her a beer and being Jewish.

"No really, be honest, your cute blond friend, Jennifer, is just an acquaintance you'll never talk to again once one of you leaves your current job. Hannah, though, is a nice Jewish girl that you'll always hang out with, probably invite to your wedding, and if all goes well, carpool your kids to soccer practice in your minivans."

"That is so not true. I have friends who aren't Jewish." I could almost see her trying to think of one.

"You do? Really? That you call to do stuff with on the weekend? Not from work?"

"Yeah, I do, and that's none of your business." *None of my business? How old are we, nine?*

"Name one?" Okay, I was getting a bit juvenile myself, but I couldn't really think of a way to prove my point to someone confronted with a truth they won't admit.

"*No.*" She answered irritated, not exactly disproving my point.

This conversation was deteriorating rapidly. I was afraid the next thing I might say is that my dad could kick her dad's ass. Instead I tried to resort to reason. "Okay, let me ask you this, Shulie, why did you pick me out of a crowded bar to talk to?" To answer for her, she was obviously just going for the Jewish guy.

"I have no idea," she said, answering for herself. She turned to leave, but then she stopped and looked back at me, looked me right in the eyes and asked me something that was a lot less childish than it sounded, "Who do you think you are?"

Whether she knew it or not, and I've often wondered if maybe she somehow did know, it was a question I had been struggling with. I wasn't expecting someone else to point it out for me, and it somehow hit me in the heart and I felt shaken and cold and alone. I just looked at her, hoping the answer would come to me. Nothing did.

"I'm outta here. Thanks for the beer." The word asshole at the end of her sentence was understood, but left unsaid.

"Hey...I'm sorry," I called out lamely to the back of her head as she exited to the safety of the other side of the bar, the word sorry falling off a cliff.

And I was. I'm not one for playing games. I was only being a prick because, I don't know, sometimes I'm a prick. Maybe more so lately as I've developed opinions of my own. I mean, I don't think I used to be like this. In fact, really the only nice thing people used to say about me was that I was a nice guy, which I always felt translated fairly snugly to *loser*. I'm mostly not that same guy anymore, and I'm mostly proud of that, but, as it relates to continuing the self-improvement, I made a mental note to not always say every fucking thing I'm thinking.

My buzz, which just moments before had been my best friend, had now turned dark and hard against me. My head hurt with the frustration of not being able to find the right girl or any form of contentment, and the gnawing feeling that it was possibly, partially, my fault.

Meeting women has been as joyous and uplifting experience as I've had, but more and more it's mostly felt like a game where people make quick judgements and complete dismissals in a matter of moments. I'm probably more guilty of this than anyone, though it works both ways. I've been dismissed by, in my early years, one hundred percent of the female population; and in recent years, just less than that. I was maybe getting too cynical, and needed to remember to be a regular guy, not bar guy. But that, I knew, was just a small part of it. The larger question was Shulie's. I was sure she was asking why I couldn't just accept who I was supposed to be. Considering she'd only known me a few minutes, it was a pretty damn astute question. I wish I had the answer.

My buddies had vanished, no doubt in search of greener pastures, because it's always the bar's fault if they don't get laid. I looked over at Shulie, having known this girl about as long as it takes for a Polaroid instant photo to develop, and I got a very sobering picture of myself. I felt nothing but alone, my spirit for the evening's possibilities long gone, and in any number of ways, rotten about the incident with Shulie. I turned to the bar and ordered three Rolling Rocks. On my way out, I gave one to Shulie and one to each of her friends and Shulie my business card with an "I'm Sorry. Seth" note on the back.

She gave me the same sort of non-committal glance I had given her earlier, and we looked at each other a second in silence before I walked back out into the cold night to go home.

3

I was working for a mutual fund company, and had just routed for approval a letter I had written to sweet-talk parents into sending more money for their kid's college fund. I had a talent for that. In fact, my marketing letters were more often than not coming back with kudos from our company president—who wasn't accustomed to handing out praise. The response rates were also steadily increasing, which I only mention because I'm sure it's fascinating to the general public. Writing an effective letter isn't so hard as long as you focus on what the customer is getting, rather than what you have. This is particularly true if you don't have jack. In this case, what we didn't have was a one-year investment return on our most popular mutual fund of more than two percent. However, having learned from the best in my Jewish mom, I could muster up a great sense of guilt if the shareholders even considered not adding to little Timmy's college fund. Thus ruining his life.

Having a bit of insight can go a long way. It may be my primary offering as an employee. However, I've found that those who get ahead the quickest do so based on how well they remember long-winded facts to support their claim that, "We've done that and it doesn't work (asshole.)" If your voice carries, that's also a very good thing.

Me, I've already forgotten what I had for lunch and I didn't have to close the door to my office no matter how personal a conversation I may have had. On the other hand, the good voice, useless facts types—though they could talk loudly about every program anyone has ever run (and why it didn't work, asshole)—are generally completely void of meaningful insight, and despite rising through the ranks, couldn't develop a winning strategy to sell a football coach the other team's playbook.

I'd worked for nearly three years at Wright Star Mutual Funds, where I was in charge of our direct mail, our customer database and our web site. Overall, I guess, things weren't going too bad. Despite my shortcomings, which, as far as I knew, were mostly obvious just to me, I had come down the mountain with a series of monumental declarations, such as, "You know, we may want to follow up with people who have asked for more information," and "Gee, it may be a good thing to personalize our marketing approach," and "Hey, let's not mail to the losers." Not that anyone considered me to be Moses or anything, but I was slowly building a bit of credibility for my ideas. I was hoping it was enough to sell my latest bit of insight.

The powers that be, along with the brown-nosers, had this opinion that we should focus on the quote unquote sophisticated investor market, the people who read the *Wall Street Journal Money* section before the sports section. I had a different view. Mine was that no sophisticated investor would ever choose Wright Star among the twelve thousand other mutual fund options. You can imagine how popular I was.

What we needed, I was convinced, was a niche market of unsophisticated would-be investors. Those pre-novice investors who have a vague notion that they should be investing, but have no clue how to do so, have never read the business section and who think no-load means needing a laxative. Yet despite their complete lack of financial knowledge, they still hold down valuable and well-paying jobs. You know who you are. In any case, I have a fund idea and marketing plan for you, and if I had a more resonant voice and remembered useless information in mind-numbing detail to impress others in meetings, you might already be investing in it.

I was just convincing myself, again, of how I could turn around the company's fortunes if they would just listen to me, when the phone rang.

"Oh my God, you're at Wright Star, why didn't you tell me? I'm at Capricorn!"

"Who is this?"

"Shulie!"

"Shulie? Shulie! Hi, hi, um, how are you? Jeez, no kidding? So, you're at Capricorn? Wow." You can be honest, I sounded like an asshole.

"Yes, I work at Capricorn," she said, "do you believe that?" Capricorn Funds was a direct competitor of ours and only a few blocks away. "So, what do you do?"

"I'm Database Marketing Manager," I answered, knowing how much chicks must dig that.

"I know. That's what your card says. What does that mean?"

"I'm in charge of our direct mail. I try to understand our customer base and then target offers to best meet their needs."

"Oh…cool," she said generously.

Remembering our last conversation, I said, "I guess we didn't get around to talking about our careers last time we talked. I like to take things one step at a time, you know. I find it's always better when step one is to make wild-ass, insulting generalizations when you first meet someone. I hope you don't take that the wrong way."

"What, that you're a schmuck?"

Laughing, I replied, "Okay, I hope you *do* take it the wrong way."

I could almost see her match my smile on the other end.

"Actually, my friends and I thought you were kind of cute when you walked out with your tail between your legs like that."

"Shulie, that wasn't my tail."

That cute chuckle again. "What's that? Step Two? Do you have like a twelve-step program?"

"You've seen my infomercial." I was kind of enjoying that we were both apparently in on the same joke. As I mentioned, my relationships usually peak in the first three minutes, and glancing at my watch—given the brevity at our first try at this—I still had another good minute or so on the clock.

Rising to the occasion, she asked, "You mean, 'Twelve Steps to Pissing Off Women'?"

"Yep, that's the one. Shulie, look how much you might have to look forward to."

"I might? What, are you asking me out?"

Seth, buddy, no, no, no! "Um, yeah. We can talk mutual funds until we're giddy." *Oh.*

"Yeah, okay. I mean how could I pass *that* up? What'd you have in mind?"

"Are you free Saturday? We can meet at Sedgewick's at eight. Maybe catch a bite later?"

"Sounds fun."

"Hey, Shulie," I asked getting a hint of seriousness in my tone, "have you considered having your breasts enlarged?"

"What?!"

"I thought I'd get Step Three out of the way now. I'm just kidding. I'll see you Saturday."

She was laughing as she hung up.

I sat there a few minutes looking out my thirty-second floor office at the Chicago skyline, which I adore. On nice days, and I vaguely remembered the last one being the previous October, I could see the John Hancock building to the north, the Chicago River to the west and north, and even clear to Lake Michigan. Even on a cloudy day, it was a glorious view of visionary architectural styles, and, just as my eyes had, my mind had left the building.

So, what was that about? You were there. She clearly sort of liked me. Right? My theory was that I was the most eligible Jewish guy in her current Rolodex—perhaps there was a Bar Association meeting out of town or something. Girls like her, actually most Jewish people I know (including some of my best friends), revel in their Jewishness. They've probably even rationalized that brown eyes and dark curly hair look better than blue eyes and blond hair. I guess that works for me, because damn, I'm no Matthew McConaughey. The whole thing made even more sense if she'd recently gotten out of a long relationship, perhaps some sort of rehab or witness protection program, or simply didn't get out much.

The question I was struggling with, though, was what the heck was I thinking? Have we not gone down this road before? I bet you a dollar I could have told you a half a dozen or more things about her at that very second. Every one of which, for good or bad, rubs me the wrong way. They are each an indication of a way of life that I was born to and expected to participate in. However, through whatever set of social circumstances that led me to be this way, I see it as, at best, limiting, and at worst, selfish. As with almost everything else, I view Jewish society as an outsider. The insiders—and the ones I know are all insiders—studiously make sure it stays that way by maximizing their Jewish relationships and activities, and their very Jewishness, and minimizing (or ideally completely eliminating) their non-Jewish relationships and activities. That way they can stay in their comfort zone. Because the group so faces in, they exclude all other people and their ideas, and their world becomes very small. Inside, in their little isolated space, they can act as ridiculous and annoying as they want, and there's no one to tell them they're being ridiculous and annoying. That's fine for them, I guess, and the rest of society may be okay with it, but it just doesn't work for me.

I could have given good odds that Shulie went to either the University of Illinois or the University of Michigan. She joined that school's cutest Jewish sorority. The next time she considers the possibility of marrying a non-Jewish guy will be the first. She's certainly from Northbrook, Highland Park or Buffalo Grove. She summered at Camp Chi. Her dad gave her the car she drives. She probably still lives at home. Her boss is Jewish. Despite what she may say, she doesn't plan to work after marriage. And though she looked quite nice in her jeans when I saw her at Four Farthings, she was more of a leggings and oversized sweatshirt kind of gal. Oh, and I knew that when I next saw her, she'd be wearing a black leather jacket, which must have some sort of religious significance (if I went to Temple I'd know), because it's pretty much a staple. None of this makes her a bad person, but was I really ready to renew my membership in *the Tribe*? To try to fit in where I've always been welcome, but never comfortable? To wear bad sweaters to Bulls' games?

Yet, there I was asking her out just like that—not even a half-way evaluation date like a weekday lunch—but a full-fledged, alcohol-influenced Saturday night. I mean I obviously felt like seeing her again. She seemed to be smart, funny, and attractive, and I was enjoying talking to her. But maybe there was more than that. Was I undergoing some life change? I'd dated such a procession of *shiksas*, and antagonized my mom for so long, that the thought of dating someone she'd actually like had kind of a strange appeal to it. I mean, after all, what good had any of the previous relationships done me?

The biggest payback I could give her for all the things she's done to raise me would be for her son to have a nice Jewish wedding, under a *huppah,* excuse me, breaking the glass that signifies the wedding party is that much closer to the holiest of all Jewish wedding traditions—the sweet table. Seriously, the wedding band playing a little *Hava Nagila,* so my uncles could hold hands and squat and kick out their legs, dancing in a circle of my clapping relatives like we were a bunch of brainless Russian peasants, might make up for a lot of past behavior.

It didn't all compute. I mean going down that path kind of meant admitting that, all along, I was the dysfunctional one rather than all the people I'd dissed for so long. The fact that my thoughts were even leaning in this direction was revealing, and very, very disconcerting. I wasn't sure if it was a sign of maturity...or desperation.

4

There I was at Sedgewick's, early even, eating some popcorn, nursing a beer, taking in the crowd and watching college hoops on ESPN. For those of you keeping track at home, I was wearing an oversized white button down Abercrombie shirt, that does a nice job of dressing up and dressing down at the same time, Levi's and some Cole Haan black boots that I frickin love.

I saw her coming toward me as she walked across the bar. She was wearing a very stylish waist-length black leather jacket, blue jeans, and black patent leather low-cut Doc Martens. Though she hadn't strayed too far from the manual, she did look pretty damn good as she smiled while shaking some snow out of her hair.

"Sorry, I'm late," she said with that same bright smile as when I first met her, "Whattya drinking?"

"I just sat down myself. I got a Honker's Ale. What can I get you?"

"I'll have the same."

I ordered two Goose Islands and some more popcorn from the waitress as Shulie took off her coat and grabbed the barstool across from me. She was wearing a somewhat tight white turtleneck sweater, and I made the happy mental note that there was no need for any breast enhancement surgery.

"Nice seeing you again. You look really nice," I offered, hopeful that I wouldn't continue to use the word nice in every sentence. I was determined not to ask the standard top twenty questions about Shulie's life right away to avoid the irritation that I was correct in all my preconceptions, so I started with what I'd been thinking about before she arrived, "Okay, listen, I was just thinking. I don't want to be tempted to make the same mistake of making premature judgements about you, forcing me to sulk out of here pathetic and alone. Therefore, I'm not going to ask you where you live, what you drive, what your dad does, where you went to school, what sorority you joined, what's your favorite mall or where you went for summer camp."

"Um, nice seeing you too," she said with a smile, grabbing some popcorn.

"So what does that leave?" I asked, making the mistake of not knowing the answer in advance.

Shulie glanced down at the table, grinned and said, "The popcorn's pretty good." I was really starting to like her quick wit.

"Yeah, not bad," I replied smiling and thankful for the temporary reprieve.

We got our beers. Since I had effectively killed what could have been an entire date's worth of conversation, I needed a new approach quick. I struggled with this for a few long moments before coming up with, "Tell me about your last great relationship."

This was the turning point where she might decide I'm oddly cute—and worth opening up to—or, you know, from Mars.

"My last great relationship. Hmm." She took a few moments, and then said, "Okay. I can't believe I'm going to tell you this, but there was this guy Marco in college."

"*Marco*? Not Josh or Jeremy or Solomon or Abraham?"

"Good thing you're not rushing to judgements."

"Sorry, I'm sorry. Tell me about the Italian Stallion. I'm sure mom and dad were thrilled to death. I bet mom couldn't stop bragging about it at Mah Jong."

"Actually, I never told them, though I always thought that would've been fun. Marco was a tight end for the football team. And boy if that wasn't truth in advertising. He was in my Poli Sci 101 class freshman year, and I had just finished dating Jeremy—who was friends with Josh, Solomon and Abraham—in high school. He sat next to me in lecture one day and we made fun of Professor Mothballs. He was, I don't know, a little rough around the edges, but was pretty funny and had a smile I couldn't get out of my mind. Not too long after that we ended up studying together…mostly me helping him get through the class. What?"

I must have been smiling at her. "Nothing. Go on, this is great."

"We started showing up at some of the same parties and ended up drawn together. After one of them, and too many glasses of that punch from garbage cans you guys always use to get we unsuspecting girls drunk, I found out he had something else I couldn't get out of my mind. Not like Jeremy, if you know what I mean." Unfortunately, I knew what she meant.

"I bet he didn't spend three dollars on me, but I had a great semester."

"Only a semester? Sounds like Romeo and Shuliet. What happened?"

"Cute."

"Thank you." This was kind of fun.

"I don't know. I mean I was in college and free to do whatever I wanted, and it felt great to be a rebel. At first, I loved hearing about his Italian heritage and family—there were like forty of them in his immediate family—and it was kind of a novelty to meet his friends. But, you know, he wore a crucifix all the time, and was from a strict Catholic family. It kind of started to bug me. After a while, it seemed like we were from two different planets. That's horrible, isn't it? Anyway, I joined the sorority and he went off with his buddies to go strip cars and meet the Pope or something, and that was kind of that."

"Strip cars and meet the pope?" I laughed at her self-effacing view of Italian people. "And that was the last great relationship you had?"

"Yeah. I thought about that time in my life quite a bit since then. That was what I wanted at that time." She hesitated, thinking for a second, and said, "I'm convinced it was the last time I got exactly what I wanted from a relationship." She said it with no bitterness or sorrow. It was just something she had come to realize. I liked that she was the kind of girl that would realize something like that.

Sedgewick's has a pretty good menu of bar food, and I was getting hungry. "If what you're looking for is fried cheese or a quesadilla, I can provide you exactly what you want in this relationship."

"My hero," she mocked, chuckling, "maybe I'll be talking about you in a few years."

We ended up splitting some potato skins. She also ordered a Chicken Caesar Salad, and I went healthy (and kosher) with a small bacon, sausage pizza.

After taking an energetic gulp of her beer, she asked, "So, how about you?"

"Mine was also in college. She was a Jewish girl named Debbie Levitts. She lived in my dorm sophomore year, and I had a bit of crush on her all year. I knew she liked this pretty boy from the dorm, who ended up in my fraternity. Actually a good guy. He was always in big demand, and I don't think they ever hooked up.

"The last week of school that year, we ended up at a party at my frat. Pretty boy was getting cozy with someone else, and I noticed her bumming as she watched them leave together. I went over to her, gave her a beer, tried to get her to think about something else. I asked her to dance…it was *What I Like About You* by the Romantics, a pretty fun song back then, which helped. She was still mostly somewhere else, but I hung out with her on the couch most of the rest of the night. Maybe she knew that she'd have spent the rest of the night lonely and miserable and what the hell, hanging with me was marginally better than that. Anyhow, she started smiling a bit more and more as the night progressed. I walked her back to the dorm and we kissed at the end of the night. To me, it was wonderful. Maybe I was being a little opportunistic, so I didn't try to take it any further that night, but it just felt full of promise and possibility.

"We talked a few more times that week and had some great conversations. We even took a walk together around campus the last night that year and near the end held hands. It was nice, you know. We kissed goodnight, exchanged phone numbers and addresses of where we'd be that summer and promised to stay in touch.

"So, that summer I wrote her a letter. You don't know this yet, but I'm far more entertaining in writing than in person."

"Really?" she asked with a smile.

"Yep, and better looking."

"Hmm. I'll have to get your email address." She was quite the little flirt.

"Yeah, if I could figure out a way to consummate a relationship by email, I'd never have to leave the house." I said it laughing a little more enthusiastically than normal, conscious of trying to mark the nice moment we were having.

"Anyway," I continued, "she wrote back, saying she loved my letter. I could tell she did, because she even tried heroically to be funnier than she was. Inspired, I sent her off another letter, which was longer and funnier. She wrote back and that continued all summer. I was really looking forward to getting back to school. I mean, I didn't know what this all meant to our relationship, but it had to be good, right?"

"Don't keep me in suspense. What happened?"

"I called her the first week I arrived, left a message with her roommate and she never called me back."

"Oh my God! You're kidding?"

"Nope. Apparently she knew where my head was going to be and decided there was a big difference between getting good mail—and remember how cool that was in college—and otherwise lowering her standards."

"And *that* was your last great relationship?"

I thought back on that time for a moment. "Yeah. It was only me who got hurt, and I could sort of keep that pain to myself because no one knew anything about it. Besides, I learned a very valuable lesson."

"What?"

"That someday I should devote my life to direct mail."

She laughed out loud just as the food came. The waitress gave me an attaboy look.

Our stories bonding us together nicely, she looked at me and said, "Failed relationships make me hungry. Let's eat." We both wore the dopey smiles of a date that's going really well.

We had more beer, talked work, music and the Bulls, and I pretty much avoided my usual landmines. I also had done a good job of not finding out her life story, but when she let out a boisterous, and rather drunken, "Yes!" when Michigan made a last second hoop to win their game, she let that wolverine out of the bag. I had gone to Indiana University, and we both further reminisced about our college days, and I managed to show rare discipline by not pointing out that I always hated Michigan.

We even caught a late set down the street at a jazz club, and with the snow lightly falling, I walked her back to her car parked on the street. Maybe it was that I hadn't yet found out all the stuff that I didn't want to find out, but the night had turned out to be very enjoyable.

Under the snowflakes and yellow glow of a streetlight that gave the moment a Norman Rockwell feel to it, we had a *really* nice kiss.

I told her, "I think this may be the last great relationship I've had."

She smiled, happy with that, and put her hand on my chest and said, "Email me," looking up at me out of the corners of her eyes. She kissed me again, got in her car, and waived as she drove off. As she did, I noticed on her license plate holder that she had bought her car in Highland Park. As I walked to the corner to grab a cab, I wasn't gonna let that get me down.

Though I couldn't see it because the sky was filled with clouds producing a pretty snowfall, I knew the moon was full. I only knew because it was the second full moon in January, making it a blue moon. The news stations were making a big deal about it being a banner year for blue moons. It was the first blue moon in nearly three years, and there was going to be another one in March. There hadn't been two blue moons in a year in almost thirty years. I was bummed I couldn't see it. I've always been drawn to the light of the moon, particularly during some of the more searching moments of my life, for inspiration or direction or meaning. I wondered what it might be telling me as I embarked on this possible new relationship with Shulie. In my heart, as I stared up at the night sky that night, I felt for certain the blue moon was a sign of change. That Shulie, the blue moon and I had gathered that night for a reason. But it was a sign hidden by the clouds, so there was no telling where it might lead.

5

Checking my emails that Monday, I was interested to see a new email address join the party: scohenberg@capricorn.com. I opened it first.

Seth,

I promise, if you send me nice letters, I won't not call you. Thanks for the other night.

S.

P.S. Looking forward to seeing how good-looking you are in writing.

I saved that and deleted most of the others before running to maybe the biggest meeting of my Wright Star career. I was going to present my big new mutual fund idea to see if I could get a piece of the budget pie, or if we were going to launch another ridiculous me-too fund with an arcane name like the New Horizons Small-Cap Global Value Fund or the Old Horizons Floating Prime Rate Interest Municipal Fund. Funds that should come with a warning, "If you even know what we're talking about, you probably know better than to invest in Wright Star."

I came complete with charts and graphs and even a few people I had recruited to also argue in favor of the new Wright Star New Investor Fund.

The one person at this meeting who mattered was our company president, Jonathan Thomas. He's an extremely bright guy—way smarter than I am—and I have a ton of respect for him. Unfortunately, he has a tendency to see himself as the target market. In my view, compared to JT (as he's called around the office), the target market, like the electorate and the people you'd see when renewing your driver's license, are a bunch of idiots. No offense.

He's in the top percent or so both in smarts and I'd guess in income. My job was to convince him that people like him are already invested elsewhere, that none of our funds are selling, and that even if he can't relate, the uninformed investors—particularly the affluent twenty-five to thirty-five year-olds—are our biggest opportunity to find a niche we could build on.

My charts showed how this generation was the most investment-oriented generation ever, wanted control over their lives and their futures and were being completely ignored by every other mutual fund company. I had profitability analyses, a marketing plan, promotional concepts, and arguments in favor of thinking long term, and some of these were even in color.

I was very prepared, very into it, and it was progressing nicely. JT was giving me a lot of "rights" and "uh-huhs" as I made my way through the presentation.

Then I made the mistake of casually mentioning that, based on some research that had been done on this group, I had even come up with a slogan of, "Take Control of Your Future, Have More Fun". Oops. That sort of set him off. He had just read something on how many baby boomer marketers, thinking they could relate to the GenX market and could connect with them, had failed miserably. He brought up Sprite's 'Obey Your Thirst' campaign, which he personally hated. How could we expect to know how to do it successfully? And had I factored in the cost of hiring someone who could do it right?

I didn't particularly agree with his assessment of the Sprite campaign— he thought they were telling GenXers who they were, while I thought they were making fun of the stereotypes of GenXers in a way that got under their cynical, collective radar—but he asked good questions. I was about to embark on the almost impossible argument that I thought I had nailed the insight that would allow us to connect to this group. That after all I was *in* the target market and that I could connect with our audiences on much tougher, less intuitive concepts than this.

However, sensing the shifting winds, the good voice/useless information types, including the empty suit head of marketing, went on a rampage about how some so and so had tried it and it didn't work (asshole) and that we could get to profitability sooner with the Shooting Star Mid-Cap Emerging Growth Focused Sector Fund, or some other fucked up thing. While I had done the numbers and knew my fund wouldn't see profitability for a few years, I knew it would be the only way for Wright Star to bring in NEW shareholders. Investores they could grow with, as opposed to continuing to squeeze the blood out of their existing shareholders, and I say 'existing' on faith, because with their current demographic profile, many were on life support, at best.

But from there it was effectively over. Since JT seemed to be leaning the other way, no one wanted to stick their neck out to disagree with him. Besides, the fund that would be profitable sooner was a much safer, lowest common denominator choice. It would also fail.

I got a few conciliatory, "Maybe just not the right time, buddy" sentiments, but my remaining pleas, like, I was beginning to think, the rest of my tenure at Wright Star, would come off as futile.

I sulked back to my office. I could clearly see the future of our company in a fund like this, and others like it I had ready to pitch once this was successful. It was also going to be my breakthrough and my legacy at Wright Star. At that point, I could only envision more of the same average funds to dying markets. Though I had presumably lost my quick ticket to V-P, my job was safe, and I still provided a lot of value. Thing is, I wasn't sure my heart would be in it anymore.

I needed someone to talk to and who better than my new friend across the river at Capricorn Funds. I re-read her flirtatious little email that morning, smiled and replied:

Here's some nice letters:
S H U L I E
Let me know if you're free tonight.

Seth

All right, all right, it was lame. But I had a disconcerting morning and was looking for maybe a better evening. Also, frankly, I have this personality flaw where I'm never really comfortable having the upper hand in a relationship. That comes from my high school and early college years when girls were for fantasizing about, maybe even reaching for, but not actually getting. I'm still not sure how to act if I like them and they're the reachers. In cases like that it doesn't seem to matter how much upper hand I'm given (look at her email for example), I manage to give it right back.

In any case, she seemed pleased with me and we arranged to meet for happy hour at Rivers, in the Chicago Mercantile Exchange Building. It's on the Chicago River in the west loop, about midway between our two offices. In the summer, it has a large patio overlooking the river that gets a big after-work crowd. Since it was early February, though, we had to settle for the inside bar, which can get a little obnoxious, and a lot smoky, with the trader crowd. Rivers, besides its sizable, and rather loud bar area, also has an up-scale restaurant. The restaurant kind of has two personalities. During lunch-time, it's as crowded and noisy as the happy hour bar, but at night, is sub-dued, well lit, and much less crowded. I figured if all was well after drinks, it'd be nice to show her I could go beyond potato skins for dinner.

She looked terrific once again. We both commented on how grown-up we looked in our work suits. We kissed, though, it was quicker and less comfortable than Saturday night, likely because we were a) sober and b) starting to act a little like boyfriend and girlfriend.

It's only a slight overstatement to say that all Jewish girls have dark curly hair (many, of course, have dark *straight* hair, and scientists have re-cently uncovered natural blond hair on a Jewish woman from Shaker Heights, Ohio), but Shulie's dark hair had wonderful, round bouncing curls that looked like glistening sliver moons. Her curls complimented her big, round eyes and high cheekbones with round dimples. Her face, for all its round features, was angled nicely and the overall effect, if seen from a distance would not be judged as round. From where I stood, her face with its olive skin, lit well at Rivers, was definitely growing on me. I decided to ask if she'd like to skip the bar and have dinner with me in the restaurant.

She said to hang on a second, made a call on her cell phone, put her arm through mine and said she'd be delighted to.

6

"Who'd you call?" I asked after we were seated by a fortyish, tall, elegant guy with perfect hair, a goatee and all black clothes. It wasn't that the restaurant was all that trendy, but he appearred to be the permanently single assistant manager guy, who lived in a loft in a converted warehouse, couldn't afford a car, dressed nicely and fairly regularly got some action from the young waitresses or after-hours crowd. In any case, he seemed happy enough with life, his attitude was good and he made Shulie and I feel like we were at home.

"Home," she answered. "I just wanted to let mom know not to expect me for dinner. It's the least I could do, I feel like enough of an imposition still living there."

"That's thoughtful," I acknowledged as I considered whether it was the right time to go down that path. I figured I'd have to sooner or later. "So, you live at home?"

"Yeah."

I waited for a second for some elaboration that wasn't forthcoming. The waiter came by and we ordered drinks.

Since she didn't want to talk about it, I needed to know. I asked, "Are you going to fill me in on the life and times of Shulie Cohenberg?"

"I already told you about the best relationship I ever had."

She was certainly being more reserved about some other part of her life, so I guessed, "I get the feeling I'm now asking about the worst relationship you ever had."

She looked at me, sipped her red wine and flickered enough of a smile to let me know I was right.

We had a little bit of a stare down, and she finally said, "Alright. The quick version of a long story is that I was going to be engaged…"

"Going to be engaged?" I wondered out loud, interrupting her, "Isn't that one of those things, like virginity, where you either are or you aren't?

"Thanks, Seth, you're helping a lot," she said, smiling.

"Sorry."

"Anyway, yeah, you'd think so, huh?" she answered more quietly now. She looked into my eyes, I think, to gauge how much she wanted to tell me. "He did ask and I did say yes."

"I have no personal experience here, but I think that counts."

A smile came and went as she thought back on it. "It was very romantic, Seth, in a rowboat in the middle of this pristine little lake in Wisconsin. It was a gorgeous September day. Can you imagine how happy I was? Everything was perfect. The weather, the breeze, my hair," she said with a quiet laugh, "except for maybe one minor detail. The ring. He was a lawyer and just starting his own firm, and said he had picked out a ring—and that I'd love it—but that he had plowed all his money into the firm, and couldn't really afford to buy it yet."

"Uh oh."

"I know."

"You should have jumped in the lake, swam to shore and left his ass in the rowboat the second you found out."

"That's what my friends said, but then again they measure a guy in karats, if you know what I mean."

"I meant because he's a lawyer." We smiled at each other's jokes.

"Turns out you're right. At the time, though, I wanted to be understanding and supportive…after all, Jack, that's his name, kept telling me it was for us…for our future." The statement was dipped deep in sarcasm and it wasn't hard to tell it was getting more difficult for her to talk about.

The waiter had brought a second round of drinks, and Shulie took more than a sip of her wine, taking her time starting again. I waited, taking an occasional sip of my Absolut and Tonic, taking her in over my glass. I'm always attracted to people's problems, and between that and her pretty face in the soft lighting, she definitely had my attention.

"Over time, Seth, I started having these doubts. I was starting to wonder if there was ever even going to be a ring. I finally brought it up a couple of months after our, you know, *alleged* engagement. And, what do you know, he said he had just ordered it and it was being worked on. I was really excited and started wondering how he'd plan to give it to me. I waited a week, and nothing, so I brought it up again. He said the jeweler had made a mistake and it would be a little while longer. Okay, I guess, that's possible. Then, when I asked again, it was finished, but needed to be appraised, and that would take thirty days. *Thirty days?* Who the hell was appraising it, Lloyd's of London? So, I was dealing with all of that, and not too well, to be honest, when I found out I might have another problem.

"Jack had a party at his apartment, his friends, my friends, whatever. I'm having a good time and at some point I realized I haven't seen Jack in a while. A friend of mine, Matthew, pulls me aside and says he doesn't know how to tell me this, but that he just saw Jack all over some girl he had invited to his party. Seth, I went numb. I had planned out my whole future, and all of a sudden, my perfect little life went black.

"I made my friend promise not to tell anyone what he saw and I left without telling anyone.

"I just felt ripped apart. Confused, pissed, everything. I was a mess. I didn't return his calls or his hundred emails a day. My parents, though, had known Jack's parents their whole life from temple. They really liked Jack. They started working on me, making excuses for him. They said that I couldn't leave him based on what someone else saw. Maybe Matthew had another agenda; maybe he had a thing for me. Maybe it just looked worse than it was. All of it was possible, I guess, but I've known Matthew my whole life and he's a pretty real guy. I had set him up with a friend of mine once, and he's never been anything but grateful and trustworthy and genuine to me.

"I just wished that I had seen whatever it was that happened myself. You know, maybe my parents were right. Could I really throw away my whole life, as I had planned it in detail, based upon someone else's account of what may or may not have happened? Looking back on it that was wishful thinking, but I was ready to believe that to ease my humiliation and to go on with the life I had planned.

"I agonized over this, but finally decided to give him the benefit of the doubt, *but* only if he was serious about us. I put him to the test. I called, and without mentioning the night of his party, gave him the ultimatum that he needed to give me the ring by Hanukah. He could tell I was serious about this. He had one week. He promised he would.

"My parents were having the family over for Hanukah to exchange gifts. Jack was supposed to be there and it was going to be the night to get the ring. I thought it'd be really special getting it in front of my family and sharing the moment with them."

"Instead," she said, "he just never showed. No call, no explanation, *nothing*. *That's* what I had to share with my family."

I closed my eyes and could easily picture Shulie surrounded by her family, basking in her moment. I reached for her hand as she struggled to keep herself under control. It was still too fresh for her and I realized she meant *that* Hanukah. Just over a month before! Something else came together for me, and I felt horrible for being a prick in the bar that night. It was probably the first time she had gone out, and I could envision her coming up to me as the first attempt to start her life again. No wonder her friends were on the edge of their seats.

"I'm sorry, Shulie," I said. For everything, I meant, but didn't say.

"Thanks Seth."

All I could think of to say at that point were bad cliches, but I finally offered, "It can't be much consolation, but it's better you found out before you married him."

"Yeah, I know." She hesitated, holding my gaze as if she was looking into my heart. I squeezed her hand lightly, and she went on, in an almost tortured voice. "Seth, it was bad. Really…bad. I cried and beat myself up most of the time, hating myself. On really bad days, I almost felt that he had picked me out for this, that the whole thing was intentional. That there was something about me that made him pick me to do this to.

"But mostly—and this was even worse—I thought, I really did think he loved me, and that the feelings I had for him were real. That I loved him. You know, for him. And that made it harder to just walk away. I'd ask myself if anyone was going to love me like that again and was I going to find someone I felt that way about again? Was that my big chance? There were days where I wanted to just let him back in, to try again. In the end, though, I must have had a reservoir of self-worth somewhere inside me, because I started to understand that it wasn't my fault. It was all his. I didn't deserve any of that. I'm so glad I found that strength, because, you know, the jerk even had the gall to start calling me. He'd cry and beg for me to reconsider. It was pathetic."

She laughed, which, I think, slightly won out over a cry.

"He came over with a ring one night, if you can believe that. But I had turned the corner—maybe just barely—and realized I was better than that, and deserved better than that. And, you're right, he probably did me a huge favor by fucking up before I invested my life in him. I told him where he could put that ring, but," she said while looking out the window," I kind of wished I had taken it and thrown it in the river or something."

Again, I didn't know what to say, so, shaking my head, I just said, "Jackass. You do deserve better."

"Jackass," she agreed.

Fortunately our dinner came, allowing us to regroup and focus on something else for a second. She had ordered bay scallops with tortellini and I got the goat cheese ravioli. Both looked excellent.

We ate quietly for quite a while, and then figuring we both wanted to change the subject, but lacking the words for a smooth transition, I said, "Jeez, enough about you. Let's talk about me already. Me, me, me."

She laughed. "Please. Let's do. Um, so how was your day?"

"Well, I didn't get robbed at gun point, or get forced to go to a country music concert, so I can't complain too much, but otherwise not so good."

"What happened?"

I told her about the new fund idea and the meeting earlier that day. Shulie worked in HR at Capricorn and was a terrific listener. She also happened to think my idea was great.

"You know," I said, "it really feels as if my career at Wright Star was like a train platform where I could have gotten on the express or the all-stop. I think the express just sped by me."

"Seth, I think it's their loss. It sounds like your idea is just what Wright Star needs. In fact, I'm thinking that maybe Capricorn might be interested in hearing your ideas."

"Really?" Hmm, I was just looking for sympathy, I hadn't thought of that.

"Yeah, the guy who's our V-P in charge of marketing sounds exactly like the guys who killed your fund idea. I had always thought he mostly got ahead because he's tall and has good hair. But, come to think of it, he also has a booming voice and, from what I hear, is king of the rally killers in meetings."

"Wow, the guy has it all."

"Meanwhile, though, our funds are bleeding money, and he's starting to lose a lot of points with the big guy."

"Mr. Merchant." I had heard of him. Gary Merchant was an innovator in fund advertising in the eighties, and got quoted in the press a lot. According to JT, who was not a big fan of Gary Merchant or Capricorn, they were both still relying on past glory.

"Seth, what would you think if I were to set up a meeting with you and him? I don't know if you've heard, but there have been some rumors of our parent company, Justice Financial, really starting to put the heat on him. I think he might be pretty receptive to what you have to say."

I thought for a second, and let her know, "If it's clear that it's an interview for the V-P of Marketing job, and not just one of those informational love fests, where he takes my idea, I go back to Wright Star, and he promises to be my best friend forever."

"We have a pretty good repore. I'll talk to him about it. Clarify what you're looking for. Obviously, it would be kept from Mr. Good Hair. What do you think?"

It was heresy for a Wright Star person—a JT person—to interview at the hated Capricorn. On the other hand, I recognize my limitations. In that I rely so much more on my ideas, rather than on the ability to present them or play internal politics, I needed to be closer to the top. I needed to stamp my own ticket, to implement my own ideas, to be less reliant on other's approval, to not be so average any more. I looked at her, and said, "Let's do it."

"That's great, Seth. I'll see what I can do and let you know."

I thought about it and nodded my head, feeling pretty good. Things were starting to feel kind of right. The two of us, maybe this opportunity. Who knows, maybe it was even meant to be. We ordered an incredible raspberry white chocolate dessert. As we shared it, I told her that I was glad she gave me a chance after my wonderful first impression, especially after all she had just been through. She said the first impression wasn't *all* bad, and that it meant a lot when I apologized on my way out.

After dinner, we had to walk in different directions to catch our respective trains, so we headed out to the patio to say goodbye. She stood at the rail overlooking the river, which hadn't frozen over yet. It was windy and cold, and the mostly full moon high in the sky looked down on us through thin passing clouds. I put my arms around her from behind, which helped fight the cold. The moon reflected on us as I reflected on it. Thinking of it as a metaphor, so much of my life had been on the dark side, but the bright side was so near and so bright if I could just get there. I turned Shulie around, and probably startling her, looked into her eyes and gave her as hopeful and intense a kiss as I could ever remember.

I took off my glove, and slipped off my ring. It was a silver band that I wore on the wrong finger in a last ditch effort to still look young and anywhere near the cutting edge. I gave it to her, and said to pretend it came from Jackass. With the moonlight illuminating her face, she looked at me and smiled. Then she tossed it into the river.

We stood there a moment, watching the ring float away, as if we could see it.

"Thank you, Seth." She caught my eye, I touched her face and she gave me a hug.

As I watched her walk across the bridge, it dawned on me that maybe I *was* changing. And, more to the point, that's exactly what I needed to do. As if reading my thoughts, she turned around and waived at me with a big smile. I smiled back, held up my hand and watched her walk away.

7

I lived on the third floor of a brownstone building near Armitage and Halsted in Lincoln Park. I had been renting for eleven years, which reminds me not to get a financial planner or they'd ream my dumb ass.

I always figured I'd buy a place after I've met the love of my life so that we could pick it out together. It just seems like kind of a big decision for me to make solo. What if I had to pick out curtains or cabinets or something? Maybe I'd be okay for awhile, but then they'd ask what kind of counter top I'd want, and I'd run away crying. It's better to wait, though who knew it would be this long.

I lived with my cat Ed. Ed's like 107 years old in dog years. Ed had lost the ability to do all but eat, sleep, poop and get cat hair on my black clothes, which come to think of it, doesn't make him that much different than any other cat. I got him at the urging of a former girlfriend, who's shedding, like Ed's, was also messy.

The brownstone has four apartments. On the ground floor were two Chicago Bulls' cheerleaders. They had just moved in last October. One was named Roxanne Fanelli, the other, Tina Marie. Really. Like the rest of the Luvabulls, they were perfectly suited for the job in that they were (as the saying goes) good from far, but far from good. They did, though, have world class bods to go with their world class hair, and all in all, I figured they would be welcome additions to the rooftop sundeck that summer. I had met both briefly and found both to be very pleasant.

Though Craig and Fishy had practically begged me one night to invite them up for beers to watch a Bulls' away game—thinking they'd do leg splits after each every basket?—my game plan was to not do anything that might get me in trouble with the guys I pictured them dating, the Marcos of the world, or their larger, scarier brothers.

As I walked in the building, I saw Roxanne. She had her Bulls' gym bag over her shoulder. "Hey Roxanne. Practice tonight?"

"Yeah, I don't think this season is ever gonna end."

"Well, at least they had the good sense to get rid of Michael and Scottie, so they won't be in danger of making the playoffs."

"Thank God for that."

Wow, she really was rooting for them not to make the playoffs. It was a bit confusing. What was the motivation? I think her real job was a school teacher. Did she really act like a mindless, peppy bimbo for the, what, twenty bucks a game? You had to give even the Spice Girls, and the boy bands, credit for doing it for the money. What did Marco think of this? I'd have to give this more thought. In any case, I just said, "Have a good night."

"Yeah, you too, Seth."

The second floor belonged to a couple of guys from the aforementioned pre-Four Farthings crowd. Their door was perpetually open and they had an extra refrigerator with a keg of Bud Light. A lot had happened to both my career and perhaps my love life and, not ready to hang out just with Ed, I decided to have a beer with the boys.

"Fellas."

Bob and Javy (pronounced Hah-vee, but his actual name is, no lie, Javier Javier) gave me a "Goldie" in stereo, like I was Norm walking into Cheers.

Bob threw a thumb in the direction of the fridge and I went and got a beer.

Bob was like 6'6" and 250, which, from what I heard from Javy, he'd been since the third grade. Bob had been a star baseball pitcher (with most little leaguers afraid to even step in the batter's box against him) and football player until sustaining a knee injury in a drinking incident in college. Now he had a long blond ponytail and big bushy goatee and managed to look sensitive and scary at the same time.

"Hey Goldie, be honest man, what do you think of this?" He started strumming an electric guitar and singing an early-REM-like song he had been writing. He owned a towing company, which fit his look, but was really a talented guitarist and singer.

"What is that," I asked, "the gay national anthem?"

"You've heard it before, then, haven't you?"

Luckily Bob, who was very straight, had some wit to him and didn't have to resort to putting my face through a wall.

"Course when that song comes on at Man Hole," I said, "the guys race back *into* the closet."

"Not you, Goldie, you're out to stay."

"I had to get out of the closet, Bobbo...I saw Javy fucking your mother in there and I almost yalked."

Javy is as good-natured as they come and also *really* good looking. Not that Bob doesn't do all right for himself occasionally, but he's had a lot of time for practicing his guitar while Javy satisfied one of his many female fans. He was enjoying our little conversation, until Bob and I got up and started beating on him. He managed to push me off, but the Chicago Bears, especially the Chicago Bears, would've had a hard time even nudging Bob. Finally, Javy says while clinging to quite possibly his last few breaths, "I didn't know it was your mother, man, I swear, get the fuck off of me, I thought it was the laundry chute, the hole was so big."

Bob fell off him laughing so hard, and with a crash so loud, I thought Joe, the owner of the building, would evict him on the spot. Javy and I laughed so hard we nearly cried.

Bob, gasping for air, said, "Goldie, we've missed you man, where you been?" and gave me a manly bear hug that I hoped hadn't cracked any ribs.

After taking a few moments to recover, I replied, "The usual spreading of misery, you know. Speaking of which, Bobbo, you'll be interested to know I may be dating a new one." Our main topic of conversation, besides our favorite B-movies on Cinemax, was my pathetic, but apparently very entertaining love life.

"Who's the unfortunate victim?"

"You won't believe this, but she's actually a member of my people."

Bobbo seemed stunned. "Get the fuck out of here! Isn't that breaking one of your Ten Commandments? Thou shalt not ever date a Jewish girl; thou shalt never root for the Cubs or Notre Dame or ever vote for anyone with an "R" after their name; or watch the Grammy's if they give shit to Celine Dion or Mariah Carey; or wait in traffic if you can pull in the right lane and pinch in front of the left lane like an asshole; or eat green food; or see a movie with anyone from the cast of *Steel Magnolias,* or vote to convict anyone of shooting someone in the NRA...there's no fucking way you're dating a Jewish girl."

Apparently Bobbo was paying attention. And yes, I was dropped on my head as a kid, and became a White Sox fan, despite growing up on the north side. "The other nine are in tact."

Javy said, "I thought you can't deal with Jewish girls."

"That's not exactly true, we just haven't co-existed well in the past. When I was younger, they didn't want me. When I developed a little, I didn't want them."

"Well that explains it," Bob proudly declared, "you're just trying to get them back one at a time."

"I'm not trying to, but with my track record, it's a distinct possibility, Bobbo."

"What's her name, so we can identify her to the authorities after you get done with her?"

"Shulie."

Bob snorted as he laughed, "Shulie? What the fuck kind of name is Shulie?"

"Hey, man, don't be making fun of my people."

"I'm sorry, there, Goldie, I know how sensitive you get about that."

"Thank you."

"Speaking of which, shouldn't you be running off to temple or eating that kafarcta fish?"

"It's gefilta fish, you big dumb shit. Speaking of going to temple, Sportscenter's about to start."

As we had done many times before, we very reverently watched Sportscenter on ESPN before I called it a night and went up to check on Ed before passing out.

I was struggling with getting the keys in the door, when, as is too often the case, "my buddy Joe," the landlord, opened his door to talk life and women. Two subjects he felt somehow qualified to discuss.

Joe is in his late forties and holding up quite nicely if you like big, flabby, hairy guys with large breasts. It was a magnificent physique he managed to keep up despite smelling like an ashtray from across the hall and through the door.

Joe was the kind of guy that wouldn't stop by to fix anything unless he had heard me come in with female companionship. Then he'd stop by unannounced and see if everything was working okay.

He either had vague hopes of seeing my date dancing around the apartment naked, as you can imagine so often happened. Or he'd decided that my dates needed to know there was a big, fat, hairy option available after their relationship with me invariably ended. Come to big, bad, Joe, baby!

I can only imagine what a well-oiled machine Roxanne and Tina's apartment was. I knew he had, more than once, called after nine at night to check on them, and had even sent Tina flowers. I know because I could actually hear Tina, from two floors above, shriek with terror and a possibly permanent case of the willies when the flowers came and she read the card. Judging by the fact that Roxanne and Tina still wanted to live in that apartment, I can only assume that their rent had been cut to next to nothing—Joe's Luvabull discount in full effect—or that the Marco-like guy had already planned a hit.

As if he wasn't already impressive enough, one night when I mistakenly let him in my apartment to sit on my furniture, Joe casually, but proudly, mentioned that by trade he was an embalmer. Talk about a brush with greatness. Jesus.

I had a feeling that if I'd also offered him a beer, I might have found out that he's having fantasies about Tina as a big blue cadaver.

"Seth, buddy, what's the good word?"

"Joe, buddy, the word is sleep and the sooner the better."

"Been on kind of a cold streak lately, haven't you?"

Hoping to spare Shulie, and thinking again that I needed to hang a rope from my bedroom window to gracefully sneak in my dates, I said, "Sure am, Joe, not a thing going on, but thanks for noticing."

"Seth, I keep telling you, you need to listen to your friend Joe. I've been around the block a few times, and if there's one thing I know, it's women."

I would've guessed beef jerky, actually. Take that any way you will.

"Here's the deal," he said slapping his belly, as if to emphasize how irresistible women must find him, "you need to make yourself available when the ladies have needs—anticipate their needs even—but still play it cool and hard to get. You end up looking heroic—like their fucking knight in shining armor—and *that's* when they start wanting you," he said with a wink and a lovely hacking cough. The cough—which nearly made him double over—was not enough to curb his pride in the profundity of his words, as if he'd just figured out the whole damn meaning of life. I pictured him probably writing it down and then, unable to find a single flaw in its logic, looking for an opportunity like this to trot it out. Thank God I was able to benefit from it.

"Wow, that's interesting Joe. That's really…interesting. And this is working for you?"

"I'm telling you, man, I should write a fucking book."

A book? What, I wondered? *The Erogenous Zones of a Corpse? The Myth That A Women's Sexual Peak Occurs Before Death? When They're Blue, I'm Not?* I took a deep breath and just said, "Go for it, Joe, buddy. I could use all the help I can get."

"That's what I'm here for."

I waited for him to stop coughing, then put my hand on his shoulder and said, "I'm lucky to have you as a landlord. I mean it. I'm getting fucked on rent and my faucet won't stop leaking till I get a date, but I get all the free fucking dating advice I can get. You're the best. I gotta get some sleep, Joe. Talk to you later."

I heard, "Listen to what I'm telling you, man, and you'll start getting the babes," as I closed the door behind me.

I was wondering if I even knew anyone normal anymore.

I went straight to bed without turning on any of the lights, saving me from having to think about how lax I'd been with the household chores lately. If I were going to entertain Shulie at home any time soon, I'd probably have to hire a cleaning service.

As I laid in bed, I saw a happy vision of Shulie's face in the moonlight. I wrapped that thought in the covers with me as I went to sleep.

8

I had to go to Boston for the next two days to discuss our web site plans with Wright Star's parent company. Calling in for my voice mails on Wednesday, I got the message that Shulie had good news about Mr. Merchant. I left her a message back that I'd call from home when I got back.

Like Chicago, I found Boston to be a city of great urban neighborhoods, with pubs, flower shops and corner grocery stores adding to the overall quality of city life. Unlike Chicago, whose neighborhoods (at least the north side ones I've lived in) are stocked with twenty-two to thirty-five year old college graduates, Boston's streets are filled with college students. They're everywhere. With its high number of body piercings per capita, it would be easy to look down on that whole group. But Boston, it felt to me, was, not only on average, but in spirit, kept younger by its students. I had lunch with two forty-something professionals who spoke fondly of being a waitress and the other of being a bartender, with each saying they could still be happy doing that today. Looking at each of them, I saw people much younger than they were, and I assumed the city in which they grew up and worked had a great deal to do with that. If so, kudos to Boston for that. In my role at Wright Star, I don't often get the opportunity to travel, though it's something I enjoy. To me, there's something about capturing the spirit of the people, and the city, that I get into. Flying back to Chicago, I wondered if staying in one place means missing everything else.

Climbing the stairs up to my apartment after my trip, I poked my head in to say hi to Bob and Javy.

"Goldie!" Bob greeted me. "Hey, man, Javy must be banging a Ticketmaster chick, because he came home with six free tickets to the Alanis Morissette concert. Why don't you and Shulie come with us? It's this Friday night at Metro."

"Cool! Sounds like fun. I dig Alanis Morissette. She's bitter like most of my ex-girlfriends. I'll ask Shulie, but count us in. Thanks, man." I slapped

Bobbo five. "And thank Javy for me! That was so thoughtful of him to have sex with some babe so we could all go to the concert. What a great guy."

I got a Bud Light on tap and headed upstairs. I was kind of worn out from the travelling, but even I was freaked out by how my place looked in the light.

With a date in two days, I had to bite the bullet. It took several hours of scrubbing dishes and floors and toilets and moving piles around to less obvious places; but in the end it looked, if not anal, at least presentable. I even found Ed.

I gave Shulie a call around ten, hoping it wasn't too late.

Her mom answered in a sing-song, removed-from-reality voice that sort of startled me, "Hel-lo." It was like reaching the very top of a roller coaster and then starting back down.

"Hi, this is Seth. Is Shulie home?" I had the brief thought that this must have been what it was like to talk to girls in high school, if girls in high school would've talked to me.

"Se-eth, oooh yeah! Shulie mentioned you the other night. What's your last name, Se-eth?"

"Gold, mam. Seth Gold."

"That's a Jewish name, no?"

"Mam, excuse me?"

"I was just wondering if Gold was a Jewish name."

"Um, yes it is, mam."

"What temple do you go to?"

"What temple? Ah, Temple Baruch Atah Israel."

"I haven't heard of that, is it in Skokie?"

"Yes, mam. It's very small and the congregation is mostly Hassidic. My father, he's a doctor, saved the rabbi's life once and they let me in. It's quite an honor."

"Soooo, your father's a doctor!" she repeated, as if to throw open her arms and say I love you like a son already. *Sooooooo, yah fawtha's a doctah!*

"Yes, mam, Martin Gold, he's a very famous neuro-surgeon. He only works on Rabbis, and is always flying to Israel and Jewish communities around the world saving Rabbis' lives."

"How fascinating. That's wonderful, Se-eth. You must be ver-ry proud."

"Very."

"So, where's your family from, Seth?"

Oh my God! I should just send her my itemized tax return, and detailed family tree tracing back to Israel and get it over with. "Um, mam, may I speak with Shulie?"

"Oh, I'm sor-ry, I'll get her. It was a pleasure talking to such a fine young man." *Son.*

"The pleasure was all mine, mam." I waited for what seemed like an eternity.

Shulie was flustered. "What did you tell my mother? She was going on and on about you and your rabbi-saving father, and this temple she never heard of in Skokie."

"Um, I wanted to make a good first impression. You know how important that is to me."

"Unfortunately, I do. What the hell did you tell her?"

"What she wanted to hear."

"Seth! I can't believe you just made up all that stuff to my mother. What's she going to think when she finds out the truth?"

"Maybe that she shouldn't judge people based exclusively on how Jewish they are."

"Seth, that's…"

"No, I'm serious. She just decided I was a very fine young man without knowing a damn thing about *me*. What kind of bullshit is that?"

"Why are you getting so pissed?"

"Shulie, what if I said I wasn't Jewish? She probably would have said you weren't home, that you were on a date with, I don't know, Ari Goldsteinbergfeld, or something. Why is the fact that I'm Jewish or not so important? I don't get it."

"I don't want to get into it, Seth, it just is. I'm going to tell her the truth and when you meet her, and I hope you do, you better apologize to her."

"Yeah, okay. I'll apologize to her. But I hope she gets my point."

"Well, don't count on it," she said, though she had lightened her tone considerably.

"I know. I have a Jewish mom, too."

"Does she like you?"

"Not so much." We both laughed.

"Listen, I called for a couple reasons. First, because I happen to have my finger on the pulse of the Chicago social scene, I scored two Alanis Morissette tickets for this Friday night at Metro. Friday's Valentine's Day. It'll be a blast. Wanna go?"

"Alanis Morissette? Aren't you a little old for that?" Ouch.

"Too old? No, you don't know me yet. I'm very immature for my age. I was thinking we'd skateboard over there. So, do you want to go?"

"Sure, I'd love to. But maybe the next week I'll take you to see Neal Diamond. That'll be easier on your pacemaker."

"That'd be lovely and he's such a nice Jewish boy. Your mom will probably spring for tickets."

"Hey lay off, Mister."

"Sorry. We'll have a good time Friday night. I'm looking forward to it."

"Me, too. I was wondering if you were planning to ask me out on Valentine's Day."

Since, to be honest, I hadn't thought about it before getting the tickets, I did the only thing I could, mumble incoherently and move on.

"Hey, I also called because I got your voice message. You said you had good news for me?"

"Yes! I talked to Gary and told him about some of your marketing ideas and your new fund idea and he totally wanted to see you."

"He did? That's great. Did you explain that I'd only do it if I was being considered for the V-P of Marketing job?"

"I did, and after thinking about it for maybe ten seconds, he said yes. This is just my opinion, but I think if he had someone with ideas he could get behind—actually any ideas at all—he'd be happy to escort Mr. Good Hair to the door."

"Well, that's interesting. It sounds promising. Are you going to set it up?"

"Yeah. Gary mentioned that, besides him, he also wants you to interview with my boss, Larry Freedman. Also with me. He said to try to do it early next week."

"I'm going to interview with you? Don't be too hard on me."

"Depends if you behave between now and then."

"Uh oh, I'm in trouble. I'll check my planner tomorrow and we'll set a time. Thanks Shulie, really. I'm kind of excited about this."

"Me, too. It'd be neat if you get it. I think it could be great for you, and it might be fun to work together."

"Hey, Shulie, did you tell him I'm sleeping with you?"

"Seth, you're *not* sleeping with me."

"I hope to by then."

"Really? Well, don't count on it," she said again. "Good night, Seth," she whispered sweetly.

"Good night, Shulie," I said, rather than make a continued plea based on the admittedly weak premise that I had cleaned my apartment.

9

Thursday morning I got to work to find I was deluged by emails in the two days I was in Boston. It only bummed me out because I didn't have time to read the dozen or so jokes I received from my buddy Gary, who's a photographer, which meant he worked about nine days a year and made twenty grand more than me. In his considerable free time, he'd devoted his life to passing on email jokes. God bless him. As far as I'm concerned, email is the single greatest technological development of my lifetime. By simply targeting the appropriate jokes to the appropriate people (my database marketing skills finally paying off), I can keep dozens of relationships going simultaneously without ever having to think of something to say. It's a beautiful thing. And on the occasions I actually feel compelled to use my own words, I can be as clever as hell because I have as much time to think of a response as I want. It's roughly the equivalent of a phone call where I could get away with something like, "I have a feeling I have a charming, clever response to that—that you're just gonna love and quite possibly want to sleep with me—but I can't think of it right now. Can I get back to you next Tuesday?"

My inbox was also overflowing, which reminded me that it was nearly time to throw out the bottom half of it. On top of the pile were the legal department comments regarding my mailing to get people to add more money to their kids' college fund accounts. Since this mailing had a great deal of potential to persuade investors to actually send money, legal was very suspicious. The returned letter had so much red writing, I had trouble making out the copy they were referring to.

The legal department at most mutual fund companies, including Wright Star, is known affectionately as the Sales Prevention department. They ensure that you aren't allowed to say anything that would contribute to someone wanting to invest with you. Then, even though you haven't said anything, you still have to add legal hedge that basically says you didn't really mean what you didn't say.

The general rule of thumb for legal hedge on marketing materials is that it must be at least twice the length of the marketing portion of the letter and once read, the potential investor should no longer have any desire to send money or ever leave their homes.

Here's a representative sample of the kind of copy I had to add to all marketing materials: *"This shameless sales pitch by our overzealous marketing department must be accompanied or preceded by a prospectus. The prospectus was written by a bunch of lawyers you'd be likely to kill if you met at a party. Because we understand that you have no life, please read the prospectus carefully before investing. Of course, past performance is no guarantee of future results. Share price and investment return will vary, so you may have a gain or loss if you sell shares, unlike burying the money in your back yard, which, if you haven't considered it, completely eliminates the risk of investment loss. It's important to ask yourself if you really want to risk your future and hard earned money by sending it to us. The only advice we're allowed to give is please don't send money!"*

I sold my soul once again and made all the changes legal requested, though I did draw the line at their attempt to make the hedge a larger font size than the letter copy. I tried not to think about that *this* was how I used my writing abilities, signing someone else's name to a letter than I wrote and the legal department massacred. I had taken some writing courses in college, and liked who I was when I was writing. I vaguely considered becoming a writer, but since that involved confidence I lacked at the time in having something worthwhile to say each and every day, I never seriously pursued it. Despite how easy it had come to me, I let it go. On days like this, that path not taken seemed to take joy in mocking me.

The rest of the day was spent fighting a losing battle to get any Information Systems Development support at all. We're lucky at Wright Star in that we recently hired a new IS manager who has greatly streamlined the IS project request process. It is now much easier to find out that my project is so far down the list of priorities that when archeologists discover my request in like the thirtieth century, they'll think, "Hey, that was a pretty good idea, too bad it was never implemented." Previously, it had taken much longer to find this out. On most of my projects, I'm now asked if I've considered Y3K ramifications.

You'd think that, as a Database Marketing Manager, the company would recognize the importance of making available to me someone who knew how to program something, even his frickin' VCR. That hasn't turned out to be the case, and I'm working on a new strategy of just remembering everything there is to know about our customers. And doing predictive statistical models in my head.

I've recently begun to wonder if I'm not, in fact, in charge of every facet of the company that no one gives a shit about. While there are many conferences and business papers out there extolling the benefits of customer-focused, personalized marketing—enough so that I was hired for this purpose—I'm still pretty much the freak who always wants to take away advertising dollars from the lofty goals of increasing awareness and building our brand. Despite much profit and (mostly) loss analysis to the contrary—provided by yours truly—advertising, with the rationalization of brand awareness is still king at Wright Star. In my view, a company the size of Wright Star trying to build brand awareness might as well be spitting into the wind. It's much more effective and profitable to target mailings based on our customer's needs. These aren't points anyone argues with me, they simply say, "You're right" and then keep doing what they were doing. It's the same with the web site. It's clearly the wave of the future, and I was put in charge of our site to make it the personalized, interactive method of communication it can be. On the other hand, I was given a budget that I could use for this purpose, or to buy a Happy Meal. I think I'm going to go with the Happy Meal because of the cool toy.

As someone who has the fatal flaw of not being much of a corporate cheerleader anyway, my disappointment regarding the new fund idea was making me question everything else. I've been thinking about it, and I'm not pumped.

Maybe I was just having a bad day, but I couldn't help asking myself some questions like if I really do have a talent for writing, why am I wasting my time and ability on marketing letters trying to sell funds that people don't want, with copy I don't even recognize after legal gets done with it, signed by someone else?

And, do I really want to continue to fight these losing battles for marketing approval, systems' support, and some semblance of sanity from our legal department?

With these thoughts going through my mind, I picked up the phone and called Shulie with the days I was available to interview at Capricorn. I also had the inspired thought to call a flower store in the neighborhood and send her some roses to arrive on Valentine's Day.

10

We were all to meet at seven at Bob and Javy's place before the concert. When I arrived downstairs, only Javy's date, Alexa, was already there. Apparently Javy's deal with the Ticketmaster girl—the one that netted these tickets—only included one night's "service charge," because there was no chance *this* girl worked in a ticket booth. Turned out Alexa was an international fashion model. If you don't mind my saying so, "WOW". Where did Javy meet people like this? Was there some sort of web site with a special password where beautiful women referred Javy to each other? Alexa was magnificent in an other-worldy kind of way. I typically like the girl-next-door look, but even in her All-American blue jeans, white v-neck tee-shirt and jean jacket, this was not the girl next door. Still I had to check my natural inclination (as a heterosexual male talking to a girl that didn't fit on a scale of one to ten) to be too overtly flirty with her. After all, I had a very attractive date of my own showing up, and besides, I don't even fantasize on that scale.

I joked with her and Javy for a few minutes. I was wearing tan jeans, an untucked tee-shirt and a corduroy pullover shirt that, as far as I was concerned, Jim Morrison would've worn had he been going to see Alanis Morissette and not, you know, dead. Javy and Alexa good-naturedly gave me shit for my attempt at a grunge look. I might have been more defensive about it, had I not realized she'd probably been to concerts with, like Eddie Vedder before, and how do you compete with that? She laughed when I said, "You're right. I'm thirty-two years old and have a white-collar job. I'm going upstairs right now to change into my golf shirt, penny loafers and wrinkle-free Dockers. I'll be right back." She said she was just kidding and that I looked very cute in my corduroy pullover shirt. *So there.*

I asked Javy and Alexa if I could get them another round, and went to the kitchen with Bobbo to get the beers. We joked about how Javy was really scrounging for dates lately. Probably have to put an ad in the classifieds soon—single Hispanic male looking for sex on the other twelve days a year.

While pouring another beer, I asked Bob who his date was. I wasn't surprised to learn it was Darlene. I had never met Darlene and I'm sure she was very nice, but she was from this over-done, mall of a suburb called Schaumburg. Based on the little that Bob had told me about her, she sounded like all the reasons city people make fun of Schaumburg. They had met at Excalibur, a huge bar in a tacky part of Chicago that was developed for the purpose of giving suburbanites a place that wasn't too hard to find, where they could meet other suburbanites and think they were cool. The night they met, Bob had been attending a friend's bachelor party on one of the bar's upper floors. The bar itself is three or four stories high. As he left the bachelor party, he looked down at the dance floor, from like hundreds of feet above it, and immediately spotted Darlene. That gave me a pretty good indication of what she might look like. Bob made his way down the dance floor, they met, and since they had dated a few times. I think Bob really liked her. He had bought her three different presents for Valentine's Day, and I could tell he wanted that night to go especially well. I hoped he had a good night.

As we headed out with our beers, Darlene showed up, and folks, was worth the price of admission. She had hair that could've been declared a suburb of Schaumburg. It was a spectrum of colors, ranging from dark brown to a near-neon white as it moved farther from the equator. So much hair spray was used I could envision the hole in the ozone layer getting larger as she got ready.

While the large hair was the feature presentation, there was so much more to enjoy. She was wearing a leather-like—if I had to venture a guess, I'd say plastic—pair of white pants that the Army Core of Engineers must have helped her get on. Luckily for her, the manufacturer, probably DuPont, had the foresight to make a matching leather-like cropped white jacket that was equally fitted and, not to be judgmental (because that's so not me), just as cheesy. It's buttons were undone, most likely to allow breathing, and it revealed a tight sweater, interwoven in a way as to be mostly see through to her hot pink bra. The cropped sweater shirt also never traveled south of her navel, revealing a belly that could've used a few more sit-ups. I wouldn't call it a beer belly exactly, but I had the feeling that if she saw Alexa's tummy, she'd be rushing to put on more clothes. I hoped so anyway. She also had the vision to tie it all together with hot pink four-inch spiked heel shoes that perfectly matched the bra. I wondered if it was the bra salesman or the shoe salesman who did the nice cross-sell job, but there's certainly going to be an Employee of the Month prize in that guy's future. In any case, the overall effect was spectacular. I wish you had been there.

Bobbo, though he could surprise you with his sensitivities for a guy his size, was mostly a simple guy with simple needs. He missed most of the subtleties and cynicisms of city life. Though he lived in the city, I always felt he was destined for some semi-rural suburb, its name boldly emblazoned on a water tower, where long stringy blond hair, bad mustaches, Harley clothing and pick-up trucks predominated. It'd be the kind of place I wouldn't live in for anything. On the other hand, the thing is I was sure he'd be happy there, especially with a girl like Darlene, and I truly envied him, and wished him that happiness.

He was generally pumped that she'd do the full get-out get-up for him. Not seeing what the rest of us could barely believe, he showered her with compliments. Even through all the make-up, I believe I could tell that she was blushing.

Shulie arrived a few minutes after Darlene. Bobbo wasn't the only one flattered at his date's outfit for the evening. Shulie, dressed in all black, looked damn hot if I may say so. She had on a short black skirt, with black leggings, and under the black leather jacket, had on a sheer, moderately see-through long-sleeve black blouse that subtlely revealed a sexy black bra, and some not insignificant cleavage. Woof.

"Hi! You look amazing," I said, as if seeing her for the first time.

"Thanks, Seth. You look kind of cool yourself."

I was glad to hear that because I was starting to feel a bit underdone myself.

I fidgeted a bit longer, than took her coat, and introduced Shulie to Javy, Alexa, Bob and Darlene. It had to be a lot to take in at one glance.

Darlene, as bubbly as her outfit, was the first to make Shulie feel at home. "Oh, I just love that outfit, hon, it must have cost a bundle. Where did you get that blouse? You're an angel, look at you."

I wasn't sure how Shulie might handle that compliment, but apparently she showed some tact and the two of them retreated to the couch to talk about it, as I went to get more beers. I'd have to remember to get all the details of that conversation. I imagined the next line of Darlene's questioning being something like, "You have really great boobs, hon, are they real?"

Alexa also got up to get a beer. As I was pouring from the keg in the extra refrigerator with my cup angled *just so*, because, as I mentioned, I'm a college graduate, she asked me about Shulie.

"So, is that your girlfriend, Seth?"

"Well, I don't know. We just met a few weeks ago. We've gone out a few times. It's been good so far."

"She's very pretty."

"Yeah, you know, she really is." She gave me a very genuine smile that a lot of companies would pay a lot of money for.

"Do you like her?" It was asked in such a sweet and gentle way that I found my mind fighting over what to concentrate on. I wanted to focus on where she was going with that, yet it was hard not to get lost in her unbelievable beauty. I was getting the feeling she—the person, not the supermodel—was someone I'd like to know. There was an unmistakable sincerity in her demeanor that just felt warm.

"You mean, do I like her, like her?"

"Yeah, I mean, tell me to shut up if I'm prying into areas I don't belong, okay, but I had a good feeling about you guys—both individually and together—and that you were meant to meet each other. Sorry, sometimes I get these feelings about people and, I don't know, I was just wondering if I wasn't too far off."

I smiled, heartened both by the compliment to Shulie and me, and because I knew exactly what she meant. "That's really nice to hear," I said. "You know, I believe in that kind of thing. That sort of knowing before you know thing."

"Right. That's right. I mean it feels like I can meet someone and it's like taking a picture of their soul." Her hair, parted on the left, lay like silk down her right shoulder. Talking to Alexa was like staring at a Monet. Except more than just being a feast for the eyes, it was as if you could also hear the water lillies reflecting on what it's like floating in the bliss of the pond, gazing up at the simple beauty of the Japanese Bridge, existing in perfection, reflecting serenity. The picture and the words, fully absorbing, were fighting to a draw. Just as Monet painted the exact same garden scenes at Giverney over and over again, like every day he saw a different beauty there, Alexa had a beauty, inside and out, that I didn't think would ever get old or faded. I wondered if others saw what was inside her.

"I'm the same way with people," I said, "I usually know that I'll like or not like someone way before I have a tangible reason to feel that way. And invariably, that feeling turns out to be right on target. There was this one girl in college who I saw from across the dance floor. I don't know what it was, but I kept looking at her and looking at her and I knew—I just absolutely knew—that she was the girl I had been searching for. It was almost as if there was a floodlight shining just on her. We went out for a while, and had some great nights, at least for me, and she turned out to be everything I expected. It didn't last very long, because she didn't ultimately share my feelings, which I also suspected from the start. But, the point is when it's someone I like, there's a glow about them I can feel. When it's someone I don't like, they might as well be x-rays, glass houses, the wind. I see right through them. I see what they're really about."

"I know," she said, her voice trailing off, reflecting, I thought, some distant sadness. "In my business, believe me, I know a lot of x-rays." For just a moment, I thought I saw her eyes trail her thoughts elsewhere. Selfishly, I wanted her eyes back, so I asked something I'd often thought about myself, "The good news is that the opposite is also true, though, don't you think? The less you can see through someone, the more layers someone has, the more you're attracted to them."

"Are you kidding? Have you seen anyone like that? Where's my coat?" she joked and her smile lit me up. "You know, Seth…this is…I've never really been able to talk to anyone about this. I guess I knew I could with you."

I filled with pride, realizing I was bonding with the best looking person on the planet, and probably shedding layers of my old self on the linoleum as we spoke.

"Seth?"

"Yeah?"

"I've got to ask you this. Do you think it's a good to be like this? For a while it kind of felt like a gift, you know, but I think I'm coming to realize that it's not doing me any good."

"You're right, Alexa. It sucks. I mean look at Darlene. She's so transparent, she's a ghost, but Bob doesn't see that. And I bet he'll be happier than I'll ever be. I've ruled out so many people so quickly, I'm now looking for someone with characteristics I don't think I'll ever be able to find."

Her resigned smile told me she knew exactly what I meant. When her eyes registered again on me, she quickly and quietly confided in me, "It's kind of why I'm here with Javy tonight. He's a good guy and all, but obviously, this is only going to be a one night thing. Seth, since I haven't been able to find what I'm looking for, tonight I'm just looking to have fun, you know."

"I understand, Alexa, and I think that's great. I do. It's too easy for people like us to stay on the sidelines, waiting for the right one, making fun of everyone else. But, sometimes, even when the game's not real, it's good to mix it up a little. To remember what the game is like, just for fun. Because, it ain't easy finding what we're looking for, and sometimes, I think, it's too much to ask to have to wait that long."

She looked right at me, with a curl of her lip under a perfect row of upper teeth and for a moment I struggled to read her expression. Then, as if attached to a dimmer switch, her spirit lifted, her eyes regained their light. She seemed profoundly grateful for my understanding, for my knowing, for my acceptance of what she was doing. It dawned on me that the moment somehow had more significance than I realized. It became fairly obvious that she was coming off some recently painful experience. My guess, thinking about it later, was that perhaps she was starting to feel lost, adrift, out of control, lacking a plan, questioning who she was...all those things I had been feeling myself. If so, I may have helped her feel like she wasn't lost—just on a small detour—and that she wasn't alone.

It was as touching a moment as I could remember when she touched my cheek before straightening the collar of my Jim Morrison shirt with both hands. It was thank you and I'm glad we met in a way words couldn't touch. It was our new club. Alexa, the real person, who happened to be a work of art, and me.

"So, Seth," she asked with a sudden look of embarrassment, as if to say, 'I wanted to know about you and here we are talking about me,' "what about Shulie?"

I thought I'd better hurry back to possibly save Shulie from Darlene, so I quickly replied, "She's one of those people I would've completely dismissed in the past, just because she's comes with this whole Jewish lifestyle I'm not sure is for me. The thing is, I'm tired of being detached and disconnected. I'm really trying to change, you know, to be more accepting. People like me—like us, don't you think—have a hard time just fitting in with everyone else's expectations, right? We see through too much of the bullshit that goes with that. But, *if* I can do that—you know, change to fit into their game—then maybe the game will become real for me. I'm not sure if I can, I'm not even sure if I'm even right, but I'm thinking it may be the best chance I have to be happy. In the meantime, I like her, you know."

She put her hand to my face. "I really hope you find what you want."

"Thank you, Alexa. I hope you do, too." Her smile felt like a kiss. It was a very nice moment.

We both took very deep breaths, which made us both laugh. She tipped her head towards the living room and I led her back. Slipping into my comfortable spot on the sidelines, I stated the obvious, "Quite a group tonight, huh?"

She rolled her eyes, put her hand on my back and said, "You got that right."

I know I've never thought this about anyone before, but if Alexa weren't so amazingly beautiful, she'd be someone I'd really like. As it was, I wasn't in her league and, nothing against her except for her astonishing looks and the kind of people I'm sure she attracted, but I didn't think I could play in that ballpark. In any case, it was very refreshing to find proof that not all stereotypes are true, and that there are happy surprises to be found. I didn't think I'd ever see her again, except in some magazine, but I really hoped she'd meet the right person and find the same elusive happiness I was seeking.

I gave Shulie her beer and sat down next to her. I gave her a kiss and said happy Valentine's Day. I meant it and I hoped it showed.

Shulie and Darlene had just finished their conversation about their favorite stores at the mall. Since Darlene's tastes ran more towards Kohl's, Hit and Miss, and the softer side of Sears, Shulie must have shown incredible skill finding some common ground.

Darlene was proudly telling a story of how a bouncer at some suburban club had complimented her shoes and how great that was because the shoes were "only $14.99, sweetheart, if you can believe that," when Bobbo, in a beautifully impromptu moment, grabbed Darlene, put her over his

shoulder and set her down in the middle of the room. They started dancing wildly to a party tape Bob had put together. Alexa pulled Javy up to join
them, and after giving Shulie enough time to at least get half her beer down,
we were all out there acting silly and whooping it up. Bob danced with the
finesse of a hammer, Darlene's dancing looked like it needed to be treated
medically. Javy was effortlessly cool, in the way that the good looking don't
need to try as hard or be as good. Alexa danced like someone used to, but
not affected by, the spotlight. It was graceful and contained, yet child-like in
its enjoyment. Shulie's dancing became looser with beer and adrenaline until
she finally let herself go and became part of the music, the moment and
me. The seductive movement of her legs and chest and arms—the giving
up of that for the moment—became something that no longer rose to a
conscious thought for her. I was proud of her for that. For my part, I'm
told I'm a decent dancer, though I'd be afraid to look in the mirror or a
videotape for fear of the dreaded white man's overbite.

I found myself looking at the night as through a lens. Six of us, most
of whom had never met before, somehow grouped together in an apartment in Lincoln Park in Chicago dancing and singing as loudly, and as
poorly, as humanly possible. Like it was the most important thing in the
world. In a city with so many apartments just like that, our dance floor was
a snapshot of a time just before change, like a picture at graduation or a
soldier saying goodbye to his parents before boarding the bus. There was, I
was sure, a story that had led Alexa to this spot. Her night, it felt to me, was
a catupult between an old life and a new. Bob and Darlene—the hammer
and the epileptic fit—I pictured together the rest of their lives. The night
would always be theirs. Shulie and me, struggling to find the balance between who we were and who we wanted to be, trying to make us work. I
couldn't picture it, yet, not like Bob and Darlene, but the night felt like an
open door to walk through together. Even Javy, who was a local theatre
actor, had stunned me earlier by mentioning a girl in California he wanted
to see again. I don't think he'd ever even considered a second date.

A snapshot. A time before change. A launching pad. Looking back,
our wonderful time that night was all those things. But you can't stay in a
snapshot. A rocket needs to take off, to go where it's going. Luckily, Shulie,
a few beers behind, noticed we should probably head over to the concert.
Our rocket heading into the night. Our futures beginning.

11

We were a rocket, but we still needed a cab. We all poured ourselves into one cab and arrived at the show about four minutes before it started. We ended up in the last row of seats in the balcony, and were just getting our fifteenth round of beers, counting Bob and Javy's place, when the lights went down and Alanis appeared.

Fitting with the joyous mood of our little group of misfits, Alanis kept the party rocking. We did a *YMCA* kind of dance thing to *Hand in My Pocket*, sang along to the dirty parts of *You Oughta Know*, were mesmerized by the stark beauty of *Thank U* and appropriately enough, Alexa even grabbed me to dance during *See Right Through You*. With an arena-size set-up at the clubby Metro, her band had the seats literally shaking, which I hope explains the fact that during *You Learn*, while dancing on my balcony chair, I lost my balance and went tumbling with such grace to the floor that I'm surprised they didn't stop the concert to find out what the hell was happening up there. Bobbo, obviously more concerned that I was embarrassing him in front of Darlene than that I potentially had neck and spinal injuries, looked down at me and immediately yanked my up by my corduroy pullover shirt. Thankfully, Shulie and Alexa had picked that song to use the ladies room so I still clung to the possibility of getting some later that night, if I wasn't, in fact, paralyzed. Ultimately, I think I escaped the neck and back injuries, but wasn't so sure I wasn't going to need hip replacement surgery.

I stuck to dancing on the floor after that, and mostly behind Shulie, so I could use her as a walker to stay upright and to hide my occasionally wincing pain. Aside from the near death experience of my fall, it was really a fun date. Shulie and I danced and sang and joked and had a great time together. My preconceptions about her aside, most of which, by the way, were turning out to be true, we seemed to complement each other well. Thinking back to my conversation with Alexa, and her promising intuition about the two of us, I was becoming more convinced I was doing the right thing.

The concert ended despite Bob and Darlene cupping their hands to their mouths and providing some incredibly determined "WOOOOO"s for Alanis to come back out. Alexa and I joined them, to the amusement of Shulie and Javy, and we continued to give it the best we had until the house lights came on. Alanis must have known we all had better things to do.

Despite the February cold, we hailed three separate cabs home so we could make our yes/no decisions about staying over that night in the privacy of each other and a cabbie named Achmed, or someone else who's name sounded like a noise you might make if you had a cold.

Comically, all three cabs arrived simultaneously outside our building, and the six of us reunited out on the front porch. I was happy for everyone involved that we were all going to have the Valentine's Day night we wanted. We all said our goodnights outside Bob and Javy's door. Alexa kissed me goodnight, and whispered, "Good luck." I hugged Darlene, did some backslapping with the guys, and Shulie and I headed up to my place. I could hear Joe opening his door, and I shoved Shulie in the door in the nick of time.

My place wasn't very big, and I could pretty much do the whole tour standing in front of the door. It had hardwood floors throughout and had nice moldings around the windows and entryways that provided it its character. To our right, as we walked in, was the living room, which had the television, a couch, a recliner and a fireplace. It opened into the room we were standing in, which would've been a dining room if I had a dining room table. Since the need for formal dining didn't come up much at my place, instead it contained my stereo, a piece-of-shit entertainment center, a large plant on the floor near the windows, and, well, nothing else. I called it the ballroom. Just to the left of the door, was my bedroom and beyond that the kitchen. Through the kitchen was the back deck, which was like heaven in the summer, but just snow and ice and wind and cold now, so I dropped it from the tour.

I grabbed a blanket from (don't say anything) under my bed and grabbed a few big pillows from my couch and set them in front of the fire. I got the fire going and went to the kitchen to grab a bottle of Bailey's and a couple of glasses. On my way, I turned on the CD player, and the current disk in the rotation was a David Gray CD. It seemed to fit the mood, so I left that on.

When I returned with the Bailey's, Shulie was petting Ed as she sat in front of the fire. I settled in as well.

"This is nice," she said.

"It is."

"Thanks for the flowers at my office today. They were beautiful. Everyone kept popping their head in my office to see who they were from."

"What'd you tell them?"

"Some Hassidic guy. Dad's a neuro-surgeon. Treats only rabbis."

"Cute."

"Thank you."

After a few nice moments watching the fire, I said, "You know, I'm a little surprised this is happening…I mean I wouldn't have been able to predict something like this before meeting you…but everything with us, I don't know, feels right. I feel like you're making me better, maybe making me feel happy, even."

"It's been good for me, too."

She kissed me and gently took my glass and set it down.

I took off my Jim Morrison shirt. She kissed me again, pulled off my tee-shirt and kissed my neck as she rubbed my arms. Twelve years of going to the gym all felt worth it at that very moment. She looked up and gave me a devious little grin before undoing my belt and jeans and pulling them down around my ankles.

Between the fire and my raging hormones, my body temperature reached about 160 as I helped her out of her sexy black clothes. While I'd guess the general population looks better in clothes, Shulie was an absolute vision as her dark skin shown in the firelight. She's about 5'5," and trim in all the right places. Her stomach was toned, her arms strong and her upper leg muscles had a nice, noticeable definition to them. I kissed her legs and started moving up, past her thigh, to her stomach and up to the swell of her breasts. Ahh. I could've spent about a week exploring there, but remembering I wasn't the only one who was supposed to be enjoying this, I moved on, continuing to move up from her neck to her pretty face. I put my hands gently through her hair, which she seemed to like, and even threw her head back, going with the moment. Then I rubbed her cheek slowly with the back of my fingers, looking in her eyes as if to somehow communicate that this one meant something to me. Her eyes smiled back at me and we kissed slowly and passionately as our lips and tongues moved together. Still kissing, I rolled on top of her and our bodies became one.

We were going slow, just past the feeling out stage, working towards a rhythm and just hitting our stride, so to speak, when (and this is so like my life) the David Gray disk ended and, of all things, the goddamn Johnny Mathis Christmas album started playing.

We both tried unsuccessfully not to laugh and lose our momentum, but she put her hand over her mouth, started giggling and then blurted out, "What the hell is that? Are you just doing this to antagonize me?"

For a moment I forgot how to talk. Then, finding my breath and the English language again, I stammered, "Of course, not, Shulie. I guess I haven't listened to my stereo in a while."

"Why would you have Christmas music?" *Oh God. C'mon, let it go.*

"I don't know, I, uh…it must have been an ex-girlfriend's." *Fuck.* Realizing that's not an ideal conversation to pursue while having sex with someone for the first time, I tried to quickly change the subject with the first thing I thought of, "Sometimes, it's appropriate. You know, like now."

She gave me an incredulous look, "I'm afraid to ask, but how is it possibly appropriate now?"

I realized it was too late. I was locked in. There was no getting around it. All that was missing was the countdown. I took a second just to remind her that we were, in fact, still having sex, before responding, "Well, my chestnuts are roasting near an open fire."

I was ejected so fast I feared that NASA might send a team to study how they could duplicate that action on *their* next space launch. As was not uncommon with my sexual partners, she started laughing uncontrollably. Apparently, I'm a riot during sex. It was going on long enough that I briefly considered turning on Sportscenter.

"Um, why don't you change the music?" she finally let out, between fits of laughter.

I got up to do that, pulling my boxer shorts up but leaving my pants still around my ankles. Thinking it was charming, I hopped across the ballroom to the stereo, making a mental note to get my hip replaced the next day. I put on a Marvin Gaye disk (ever since college, *Let's Get it On* has always been successful for me) and hopped back—well, at least most of the way back, before tripping on my pants and falling more or less on my face. Had I gotten a few feet farther, I'd have made it to the pillows, which might've helped break the fall. She broke out laughing again. I was starting to feel like I should go on tour with this stuff. She finally looked at me for a long moment, just shaking her head and smiling. I think she decided right then and there that she either a) loved me or b) should get a tax break because this was the most charitable sex she was ever going to give.

I managed to get re-situated and we finished our glasses of Bailey's. Fortunately, from there, we were able to eventually regain the mood, and proceed without any further injury or insult.

If having sex for the first time is like a right of passage in a relationship, one that reinforces the feelings you may or may not have for someone, I think, after all was said and done, we were more entwined in each other than we were before. Despite the possibly major medical bills I'd be facing (just kidding), our first try at this was, I think, as it was meant to be. Especially on Valentine's Day. It felt, for me, a lot more like making love than having sex. It's a feeling I've felt too few times in my life.

I held her in my arms for a long time, as the light from the fire and the moonlight shown on us. I kissed her forehead and I wondered if, maybe, I wasn't beginning to see the brightness, despite myself.

Alanis sang that night while I was falling off my chair, "You *live*, you *learn*." Those words rang in my head that night as I lie in bed next to Shulie. The question I had was could I live, learn, and *change* who I'd been? I was beginning to hope like hell I could.

12

Shulie met me at the reception area and we made a show of very formally shaking hands. She escorted me to Mr. Merchant's office, and just outside his door, with no one looking, gave me a quick peck on the cheek and whispered good luck.

Gary Merchant had puffed up a bit from the ads I had seen, but he still looked distinguished in his gray, pin-stripe suit and dark hair with graying temples. I'd say he was in his early fifties and he looked the part of the CEO. He greeted me warmly and I felt comfortable talking to him.

"Shulie tells me good things about you. Let's get straight to the point, Seth, how can you help Capricorn?"

I liked his straightforward approach, mostly because it allowed me to dive right into a speech I had semi-prepared.

"Well, sir, the way I see it, everyone in the mutual fund industry does the same thing, and they're all doing it wrong."

"Really?" he said, possibly insulted, but intrigued. "Go on."

"Depending upon how you look at it, there are, what, seven to twelve thousand mutual fund options for investors. Mutual funds have become commodities, and all mutual fund companies are trying to scream louder than the next guy with ads proclaiming that their performance is better, or that their portfolio managers are smarter, or—and I love this—try harder. That's bull, if you don't mind my saying."

"Go on."

"I think it was J.P. Morgan who said the stock market will fluctuate. No secret, right. So, by its very nature, the performance of all twelve thousand or so mutual funds will fluctuate. All those people chasing the best performance will eventually get burned by buying when the price is high, and they'll compound their mistake by selling when it goes down.

"What we have here are hundreds of fund companies all saying the same damn thing to attract investors who will split as soon as performance nose-dives, as it will. It's all product-focused, mass marketing, and it's a losing game."

"Go on."

I went on. I went through Database Marketing 101. I told him about insight. I talked about creating niche investment products that met customer's life-style needs. I told him that he'd no longer have to scream louder than the next guy, competing solely on fund performace to the same stagnant group of investors that everyone else was trying to get. I gave examples of funds and markets. I gave him a new way to compete and win. I had him. Trumpets were playing, employees were doing the wave, and I could see the light bulb going on in his head.

"Seth, you've really thought this through. You know what, in many ways—actually quite profound ways—you're right. It isn't quite as simple as you put it, but the old model isn't working. On the surface, your alternatives make a lot of sense. I need to give this more thought, because we're not talking about small changes here, but I have a gut feeling you're on to something. Listen, I appreciate your time, and I think we may be talking again soon."

He was a busy guy, and I figured I better not blow the sale by asking the questions I had prepared for him, so I just said a stout, "Thank you, sir."

He brought me back to Shulie's office, shook my hand, and was quite gracious in his compliments to me in front of Shulie. He said he looked forward to talking to me again. Shulie gave me a look that said, "Way to go."

We went into her office, closed the door, and I locked it without her noticing. Walking behind her, I couldn't help recall the rear view from the other night. I think I felt the beginnings of a little stiffie, if you must pry.

Still standing, we kept up our pretense at formality. "Mr. Gold, thank you for coming in today. It sounds like it went well with Mr. Merchant. I can tell he likes you. I just have a few questions for you today."

"You're welcome, Ms. Cohenberg, I am excited about this opportunity." I added, "Can I ask a question before we get started?"

"Of course, Mr. Gold."

"Call me Seth."

"Of course, Seth."

"How long is this interview scheduled for?"

"We have a half-hour, I believe, before you're scheduled to meet with my boss, Mr. Freedman. Why do you ask?"

"Because I was thinking this…" and I lifted her up, put her legs around me, kissed her and said, "Tell me more about this position."

As usual, up to the challenge, she responded, "This position is a challenging one, but it has it's rewards."

"Hmm," I asked while kissing her mouth and face, "is there another position for which I'd be better suited?"

She grabbed me and we made, I have to tell you, rather exciting love on the floor behind her desk. I didn't even have to tell her how much I enjoyed that position.

Afterwards, we stifled laughter as we helped each get our clothes back on correctly. I needed a glass of water, or maybe the Chicago Fire Department to put out my fire, but she got me some water and we settled down for the last portion of the "interview".

"So, Mr. Gold, ah Seth, do you have any more questions?"

"How are the benefits here?"

She tried hard not to, but she started laughing again, as did I. "We can put together a pretty exciting package for some people. We want our most special employees to be very satisfied."

"I see that. Well, thank you, Ms. Cohenberg, I like your interview style."

"You were a good candidate."

"Thank you."

I have to admit that sex, at any time, means I'm fast asleep in a matter of minutes, but since I was kind of pumped by both of my interviews, I felt I could rally my way through this next one. I asked her how I looked.

"Great," she lied. We kissed and she opened the door to bring me to her boss' office.

Her boss, as I may have predicted earlier, was also Jewish, and I wondered how much of a factor that played in Shulie getting her job.

Larry Freedman was smallish, maybe five-foot-nine and probably not more than 160 pounds. He was graying and slightly balding in back, but with his gray and silver nicely maintained goatee and wire-rim oval glasses, was managing to age gracefully. He was also dressed impeccably.

We shook hands, and with his hand on my back, he guided me to sit down next to him on the same side of the desk. In an interview, especially since my voice doesn't particularly carry, I think that kind of proximity can work to my advantage.

"So, Seth. I've looked at your resume. It's very impressive."

"Thank you."

"Where are you from Seth?" he asked, causing a neural alarm to go off.

"I'm from Skokie, sir."

"Did you go to Niles North or West?"

"I went to Niles North." Oh shit. I knew where this was going and I didn't like it.

"Niles North, huh? What year?"

"I graduated in 1983."

He was thinking through his catalog of Jewish who's who. "1983, let's see. Do you know Danny Herzon?"

"I don't recall, actually."

"The Herzon's are good people. Danny's daddy, Michael, is our family dentist. Danny's now in New York. He's senior editor of *The Jewish Times*."

"Great."

"You say, 1983 at Niles North. Oh, you must know, Lisa Gomberg. I'm pretty sure she went there sometime around then."

I hated high school, and have pretty much completely blocked it from what was a rather weak memory to begin with. I may have sat next to her in every class I ever had but I had not even the foggiest recollection of Lisa Gomberg. In fact, I never know these people.

I lied, "I think she may have been a year or two younger than me. My brother probably knows her better."

"Yeah, could be. She's a real sweetie. Her folks go to our temple. Good people. Lisa's now married to an orthopedic doctor in Northbrook. They have two kids. Really cute."

"Oh, that's great. Good for her."

"And you went to Indiana University. Great school. How about that Bobby Knight, what a schmendrick, huh?" I was going to answer, but he had more important questions for me. "Hey, do you know Sherry Bernstein? She was an A E Phi at Indiana, or David Israel, I believe he was in Sigma Alpha Mu?" I opened my mouth to answer, but he had begun rapid-firing

Jews at me. "…or Larry Rubin…oh, or Myra Rabinsky…or Linda Goldstein …or….or….or…"

I tried to pick out names and recall if I ever heard of them. David Israel? I was actually in the SAM house, but as apathetic as I was, except for my pledge class, I couldn't pick too many of the rest of them from a police lineup.

Rubin? Rabinsky? Goldstein? They were all named Goldstein as far as I was concerned. I had no clue who Sherry Bernstein was either, but, lacking anything to satiate Larry's need for me to know these people, I figured I'd go with that. "Sherry Bernstein, yes, I remember her! What…a…great…girl. Oh God, Sherry. Yeah, she was dating this one guy from the basketball team—what was his name—Duane or something, I think. He was a 6'4" black guy (I whispered black as if I was afraid some 6'4" black guy might be eaves dropping in the hall), didn't play much, and then got kicked off the team for something—drugs or grades, I don't know—but I remember the poor thing got pregnant her sophomore year, and her friends kind of knew it was Duane's. I heard—she once told me— that she loved him, you know, but they weren't quite ready for that, and then Duane transferred somewhere. She ended up having an abortion, and her folks never knew about it. Lucky for her. Sherry Bernstein, wow! So, how is Sherry these days, anyway?"

I don't think I could exaggerate how much I enjoyed watching the color drain from Larry's face. He was stunned, absolutely floored. He looked like he needed to grab onto something and finally found the rails of his chair and held on for dear life. He stammered, "She's fine, I think. We're not really that close with them." He was nodding his head a lot as if to indicate we didn't need to talk about it anymore. I had a feeling he'd be steering clear of her folks for now on.

"Well, if you see her, tell her I say hi. It's great to hear these names again."

"Um, yeah, okay."

He fumbled around a while, the entire recovery precious, but finally got back on track. There were, strangely enough, no more Jewish Geography questions and he began to progress through the rest of the interview.

He was, I was beginning to notice, very touchy-feely, and I could have been wrong, but it felt like he was looking deep into my eyes when I was answering questions. Even though it's an interview 'don't', I started trying to avoid eye contact as much as I could. I couldn't shake the feeling that Larry, who didn't have a ring, might've wanted to have the same kind of interview with me that Shulie did. He was polished and professional, and I got the feeling that's the impression he left in public, but I bet Sherry Bernstein wasn't the only one who'd be embarrassed in temple if old Larry told all.

The interview ended and he put his arm around my shoulder to walk me through the door. I was praying he wasn't going to slap me on the ass, as if I had just scored a winning touchdown, or knew the entire Jewish population of my alma mater.

I had planned to change into my casual clothes in their men's room, but instead practically ran to Shulie's office, told her I'd call her later, and left the building as soon as my little feet would take me. When I returned to my office, I closed the door, changed clothes and called Shulie.

She was anxious to get my thoughts. "So what'd you think?"

"I know I want a second interview with you."

She ignored me, and asked, "I mean with Larry?"

"Well, we spent the first twenty minutes playing Jewish Geography."

"Oh my God. Did you let him have it?"

"Me. Of course not, not that he realized anyway."

"Seth, what am I going to do with you?"

"Interview me again."

She also ignored that, which I think she was finding was an effective strategy. "What'd you say to him?"

"That some Jewish girl I apparently went to college with had dated a drug-using black basketball player who knocked her up and that she had to get an abortion so her parents wouldn't find out."

"You're joking, right? Tell me you're joking. Please."

"Well, I could tell you that, but I figured this was the only way he was going to stop asking me about every Jewish person who has ever come within five hundred miles of me. By the way, you'll be happy to know they're all doing fine, Shulie, and they're all *really… good… people.*"

"Jesus, Seth, he was just trying to bond, you know. I don't know. I really wish you'd get past your Jewish-phobias, or whatever they are."

Clearly, this bothered her, and it wasn't really fitting with my theory that I was going to have to change the old Seth if I hoped to find any sort of happiness some day.

"Listen, I'm sorry, Shulie. I've been this way for a while, it's just something that bothers me, but I'll try, you know, for your sake. Actually for our sake. I think you and I may be worth it."

She sounded surprised. "Really? You think that?"

"Yes, I do."

She took a second and said, "You're gonna drive me nuts someday."

"Just keeping things interesting."

"Uh huh. So, after you played your little games with Larry, how was the rest of it?"

"Shulie, are there any rumors floating around the office about Mr. Larry?"

"Excuse me?"

"Any whispers about old Larry's office being a closet when he finally comes out of it?"

"What?!"

"Shulie, I thought the guy wanted to take me behind his desk, and interview me the way you did."

"NO WAY," she practically yelled.

"Way, babe."

"Oh my God." When she recovered a little, she tried to come up with other explanations. "Maybe," she offered, "it was your imagination. You were coming off the interview with me, your ego was probably raging out of control. You may find this hard to believe, but not everyone wants you."

"Really? Is that true? Tell me you're kidding," I joked. "Well, maybe you're right. Maybe Larry is just one of those hands-on, touchy-feely, penetrating eyes types. I guess I can see how that could be misunderstood. Is he that way with you?"

"Touchy? Well, no, not really," she said weakly. I could imagine cartoon doubts starting to race through her mind.

"Shulie, he's never patted you on the back, or touched your arm on the way back from lunch, nothing?"

"Oh God," was all she said as it sunk in.

"Uh huh."

"So you had quite a day of interviewing then, didn't you, stud? How'd it go with Gary, did he dress up like a woman and sing show tunes for you?"

I laughed out loud. "You're pretty funny, kiddo."

"So far, with you, I've needed every bit of my sense of humor. Really, how'd it go? It seemed like he liked you."

"Yeah, I think it went well. If nothing else, I gave him some things to think about. Do you think he'll discuss the interview with you?"

"Hard to say. If he decides to go with you, he would need to fire Mr. Good Hair, and probably even have to sell it to Justice Financial. I'd think he'd want to keep that as confidential as he can until he was ready to move. I'll see what I can find out, though."

"I see what you mean. Let me know if you hear anything. So, are you doing anything this weekend? Want to get together?"

"Sure. Maybe we can see a movie on Saturday."

"Sounds good…city or burbs?"

"You know what, I think it's time you apologized to my mom. Let's do the burbs and we can have dinner with my folks before the movie. I want them to meet you, to see that you're an asshole just some of the time. If you're good, I'll go back to your place."

"Flattery and bribery. It just might work. Pick the place and time and let me know, okay?"

"Will do. Bye Seth." She gave me a kiss.

"Bye Shulie."

She called on Saturday morning and said we were all set for dinner at a restaurant called the Bagel Place at a mall in Skokie, and for movies at the mall afterwards. This sounded very much like my future if Shulie and I stayed together. I shuddered at that thought, but figured if I could get thrown to the wolves like that and survive *their* game, maybe I could pull this off after all.

13

I arrived at the mall on time at five-thirty, parked and was walking up when I saw Shulie get out of her dad's car. He was dropping off the family in his Lexus. I hoped to God he worked at the Treasury Department or something, because his vanity plates said, "MAKN DOH". I resisted the urge to puke my guts out right then and there, which would make my second impression with her family only slightly worse than my first.

Mr. Cohenberg drove off, and I caught up to Shulie and her mom just outside the restaurant.

I gave Shulie a polite kiss on the cheek, and greeted her mother, "Hello, Ms. Cohenberg, it's a pleasure to meet you in person."

Shulie said, "Mom, this is Seth Gold."

She extended her hand, and said, "So, this is Seth Gold? Nice to meet you, Seth Gold, I'm Estelle Cohenberg."

"Hello, Ms. Cohenberg."

"Would it be so bad to call me Estelle?"

"Listen, Ms., ah Estelle, I'd really like to apologize for my behavior on the telephone that night I called for Shulie. It was terribly inappropriate, and I hope you'll accept my sincere apology. My dad isn't really a surgeon who operates only on rabbis."

"What, you think I should *be* that lucky? Quite a sense of humor my Shulie says you have. Sometimes you don't know when to turn it off, no?"

"That's, unfortunately, sometimes true. I'm very sorry."

"What? Stop apologizing. It was funny. Listen, you gotta be able to laugh in this life, no?" And then she let out a, "Ha, ha, ha," like some sort of duck with pneumonia, to prove to me she thought I was funny. I put my hand over my mouth so I wouldn't laugh out loud at the duck snort. Shulie saw me and punched me in the back, hard, as she followed me through the revolving door into the Bagel Place.

When we were inside, I said, "Thank you, Ms. Cohenberg, for being so understanding. You have a lovely daughter, and I see where she gets her good looks."

I admit it wasn't the most sincere compliment I've ever handed out, but I felt like I had to be extra charming to get out of the hole I started from. She was shorter and stockier than her daughter. She looked as if she might be on an exercise program at the gym, or something, but was fighting a losing battle with age and a few too many bialys. Her hair I could only describe as 'coiffed'. She had clearly spent several hours at a beauty shop recently, and asked for everything they had.

"Thank you, Seth." *Se-eth*.

Apparently, the Cohenbergs were regulars, because despite a huge crowd of Jewish people waiting for tables (and this is not an undemanding group), we were seated almost right away. Had I been the host, I might've been somewhat discreet about the whole thing, to avoid raising the ire of the waiting crowd. Instead, the hostess, a heavy set Jewish lady named Ida practically yelled, "Es-telle, my love. So good to see you again. You look darling, look at your hair. Dotty does such work, oy, a magician is what she is, I'm telling you. Come on, dear, I have a table for you over here."

I had my head more or less buried in my hands—to ward off the evil glances we were getting as Ida escorted us to our table—when Ms. Cohenberg introduced Shulie and me to Ida.

Ida was practically beside herself. Possibly literally, because she sounded like she was asking herself questions. "Oy, have you ever seen such a beautiful couple? What wouldn't I give to look like you kids" I thought she was going to pinch our cheeks or call over a photographer. "So, when's the wedding?"

I thought she was joking, so I replied, "After we find out if Shulie's pregnant."

Luckily, Ms. Cohenberg missed that as she entered the booth ahead of us (my voice doesn't carry, as I mentioned, and it was no match for the crowd at the Bagel Place), but no such luck with Shulie, who punched me even harder. This was turning out to be a painful relationship.

Ida, not knowing what to do with that, pretty much threw our menus at me and started kibitzing with some of the other patrons. Adam's braces, Josh's grades, Daniel's Bar Mitzvah. Oy, have you ever seen such beautiful, talented children?

We sat at a booth, as Mrs. Cohenberg said how much she loved Ida and the Bagel Place. Apparently, she and the girls ate there four or five times a week. From out of the crowd emerged Mr. Cohenberg.

He was a smiling, effervescent guy, and said loudly, "Seth, I'm Irving Cohenberg, damn glad to meet you. The food here sucks, Seth, but there's so many Jewish people here, I feel like I have an excuse to not go to temple on Sunday."

Laughing, I said, "Pleasure's mine, Mr. Cohenberg."

I was still holding the license plate thing against him, but I could see where Shulie got her wit, and likely why she could put up with me.

We ordered—Estelle's bagel having to be toasted *just so*—and started getting to know each other.

Mr. Cohenberg started, "So, Shulie tells me you're also in mutual funds."

"Yes, sir, I'm Database Marketing Manager for Wright Star Funds."

"Really, that's interesting." Then realizing he had no clue what that meant, asked, "What the heck does that mean?"

Unable to think of a way to make it sound interesting, I just answered, "I send the junk mail."

Shulie stepped up for me, evidently so her parents wouldn't think I was a mope unworthy of their daughter, and said, "Seth decides who gets mailed what and tries to tailor the marketing messages so that it's more relevant and interesting to the reader. He's talented and has a lot of great marketing ideas."

Irv said, "I understood what he said."

Unable to resist, I casually added, "Shulie interviewed me the other day for a job at her company."

I gave Shulie a smile, and she kicked me under the table. I could have dressed as a goalie and still gone home with injuries.

Estelle, possibly concerned that I'd be seeing her daughter all the time, asked Shulie, "So you may be working together? Wouldn't that be so hard, you'd always be on top of each other?"

I was smart enough to let that one go. I didn't think I had enough insurance. But not taking any chances, Shulie quickly answered, "We'd be working in different departments, and I think Seth would be great for our company." She glared at me from the corner of her eye and I just gave her an innocent look like, 'That's what I would've said.'

The food arrived. Everyone else had ordered breakfast, even though it was dinnertime, so I got Eggs Benedict, which isn't exactly kosher, but not until after Irv ordered a ham and cheese omelet and bacon. What a guy. Estelle made the waitress take the bagel back because it wasn't quite done enough, asking, "You'd think they'd know how to make a bagel?" We all agreed.

Irv, Shulie and I were just about to eat when Estelle spotted her friends Mort and Lois Bloom in line. She enthusiastically beckoned them over. Lois was wearing a highly ornamental jogging outfit. She looked fit and tan. Mort looked just tan.

Estelle asked why they weren't in Florida.

Lois explained that they were in for their granddaughter's first birthday and immediately whipped out pictures. The baby was photogenically challenged, I think our table would all agree, and we all sat there with nothing to say, until Estelle said it'd be great to have grandkids.

Mort talked about how they couldn't wait to get back and that he couldn't imagine anyone living in this *facachta* cold anymore. "The wind, the snow, you can have it." He made a gesture like get away from me with that, already.

"Oy," I somehow felt compelled to offer to the conversation. Everyone agreed.

Estelle explained for my benefit, as if I needed help with the concept, that they were snowbirds and hated the cold.

Thinking I had to say something, I said to Lois, "It looks like you're ready to jog back to Florida."

She looked at me as if I had just stepped on the grass of her condo, which, for the uninformed is a third-degree felony in condo Florida. Many unsuspecting vacationers have actually served time in condo prison.

Estelle helped me out by saying, "Please, you should see how Lois stays in shape. She's the talk of Coral Springs West. She walks five miles a day (I'm guessing this has never been independently verified) and she swims, and the energy she has, oy vay, she puts us all to shame. How she does it, I don't know. And, what, she's been president of the condo board for three straight years. I'm telling you, this girl's a real goer and a doer."—goah and doah—"If there's something she wants done, she goes and does it."

Lois beamed with pride while I wondered if she ran for board president on the *goer and doer* platform. I felt bad for the poor candidate who ran against her on the *sitter and vegetator* ticket.

Estelle asked about her kids. One daughter had successfully married a doctor, but the other, who had the ugly baby, was a concern.

"So the party, tomorrow, is at their tiny little house. Mort and I don't care, you know, we'll…make…do (uh huh), but God only knows where they're going to put everyone. It's not even catered. This guy she married, first of all he's not Jew-ish (she whispered this confidentially as if she was saying he had can-cer), and he's a policeman of all things, and can't even buy her a decent home. Oh please, don't get me started, I don't know what she sees in this guy." She said this whole thing while smiling, as if saying really nasty stuff about someone doesn't count if you're smiling.

Mort added, "And they never visit."

"You have got to be kidding?" I blurted out, louder than I would have liked, but luckily without laughing. I could only imagine how eager Officer Friendly was to drop everything, and spend his hard-earned paycheck visiting his loving inlaws.

Just the same, we all agreed it was a real shame.

They continued to smile and bitch (kafetch for those of you following along in Yiddish) about the cold and the wait and the policeman until they finally got a table.

"They're sweet," Estelle concluded, as she returned her toasted bagel a third time.

I took advantage of the lull between guests to ask Mr. Cohenberg about what he did for a living.

"Mr. Cohenberg, I noticed your license plates, are you in banking or investments or something?"

"Banking, schmanking. Seth, even better. I own a chain of bakeries in Highland Park, Deerfield and Buffalo Grove. You know how much Jewish people love dessert? I add extra sugar to everything, and they're lined up out the door."

Relieved that the license plates weren't nearly as obnoxious as I had previously feared, I said, "I'm sure my family has helped. We typically have a three to one dessert to people ratio at our family gatherings. And they're all chocolate. I once had to break up with a girl who actually brought a cherry pie over to Rosh Hashanah dinner. Poor girl, I think she's still in therapy."

Irv chuckled. He was my new best pal.

Estelle finally accepted her bagel, though I had a hard time believing that the waitress didn't just keep bringing the same damn bagel out until Estelle convinced herself it was ready.

We finished our breakfast, at dinner, and I think I pretty much passed the audition, except I was forced to admit that my family didn't belong to a temple. I did lie and say I tagged along with my Jewish friends to their temples on the high holidays, which seemed to make Estelle feel more comfortable. The truth is I'm one of the few Jewish people on earth who goes to work on those days. It's not like I wouldn't rather take the day off, but I'd feel guilty if I did (which, I admit, is a weird manifestation of having a Jewish sense of guilt.)

Thinking about it now, I'd certainly take the day off for the Jewish New Year, Rosh Hashanah, for example, if there were drinking and football involved, like on that *other* New Year (the one with the better advertising agency.) I could definitely see going to a New Year's Eve party, then with a hangover, watching the Matzoh Ball Soup Bowl game on TV. But, no, nothing. No one has asked me yet, but I just think it's a missed marketing opportunity. I can only speculate that at the root of it is that no Jewish mom would let her kids play football. "Oy, you could get hurt and have to go to the doctor. Forgetaboutit. Better you should be a doctor!" Suffice it to say there are no games, no parades, plenty of doctors and I go to work.

As we were leaving the restaurant, it seemed like there was a general level of good will, and I actually even asked the Cohenbergs if they'd like to join us for a movie. Luckily Estelle said, "You kids run along and have a good time."

They hugged me and Shulie and we headed in the direction of the theatres.

"So," I said, breaking the silence, "that was nice."

She tried to figure out if I was joking or not.

"I think they liked you. You and dad bonded."

"It's not hard for guys to bond. We have to make a showing of conversation in public, but we know that under different circumstances we could watch an entire football game, not saying more than 'getcha a beer?' and be great buddies. I think Irv and I could watch a game together."

"Guys are Neanderthals."

"And your point is?"

She seemed tense about the whole night, and maybe as a nervous reaction, she laughed.

I asked how I did with mom.

"I think you may have charmed her a little, but I'll see what she says next time I talk to her. It's not hard to read her."

"Find out if she thinks I'm a goer and a doer. I want to be that." I laughed, but Shulie wasn't sharing the entertainment value of my new favorite term.

I stopped her, outside of Pottery Barn, and gave her a kiss. It was meant to reassure her that even if that whole dinner scene gave me the creeps, it didn't take away from what I thought about her.

Maybe reading my thoughts, she asked if dinner was really that bad.

Divulging my thoughts on that would have meant having to evaluate our whole relationship and my fucked-up psychological profile. I didn't want to get into how I thought *she* was great, but that I was still trying to convince myself that I wanted to, or could, fit in with Jewish society, to the possible exclusion of everything else. To me, it wasn't about being Jewish, or not so much in my case, as it was about whether I could change who I was. Sometimes, when I was just with her, I thought I could. Other times, like that night, I wasn't so sure.

I just said it was fun and her parents were sweet.

"Come on," she said putting her arm through mine, "let's 'go' to the movies, and then I'll 'do' you at your place." Her joke seemed forced, but I figured it was my reward for not making a scene. I wondered if this is what Pavlov had in mind. For the dog's sake, I hope not.

14

It had been over two weeks, and I hadn't heard anything from Capricorn. Shulie had heard rumors of an increase in the number of closed-door meetings and conference calls Gary Merchant was having with his bosses from Justice, some unknown consultants, and her boss, Mr. Freedman. This could be a sign of almost anything. I hoped it wasn't a sign of the two of them dressing up and singing show tunes. Just kidding. Actually, I was getting more anxious to hear from them. My work at Wright Star had begun to seem more pointless and my main motivation became to not make it obvious how unmotivated I'd become.

Shulie and I had gone out a few more times and things were progressing nicely I think. As we were becoming more of a thing, I had given her a lot of thought. I had to admit to myself that Shulie wasn't someone who made my heart beat fast, or who'd invaded the recesses of my heart and soul, as I'd experienced once before in college, and thought was the greatest thing in the world. There was no one thing I could point to and say if she was different in that way, I'd feel stronger about her. I guess you just feel that heart and soul thing or you don't. That I didn't was a little concerning. On the other hand, she was clever and beautiful, much more giving than demanding, and our personalities kind of fit together. She made me laugh and truly enjoy my life. Overall, I don't know, I felt lucky to be with her. I recalled the Groucho Marx line that he wouldn't want to join any club that would have him as a member. It's pathetic, but I actually lived that way much of my life. I had so little self-esteem, I almost resented the few girls who wanted to go out with me. I'm not that way anymore, but I'm still just insecure enough to still be grateful that a pretty girl like Shulie would choose me. Who the hell knows, maybe the fact that this relationship made more sense in my head than anywhere else was the sign of a stable, mature relationship. In any case, when we were together, it seemed to be working.

My thirty-third birthday had been on a Friday in early March. Not wanting to give her time to buy me anything, since that can be a very un-comfortable thing when you've only dated someone a month, I called her late that morning to see if she'd like to spend my birthday with me. She chastised me for not telling her sooner, but definitely wanted to be with me on my day. We had dinner at Geja's Café. It's below street level, and its brick walls and curtains strategically and romantically divide the floor into pseudo-romantic hideaways. Candle lit tables also add to the ambiance. It featured fondue, a great wine list (which only makes it that much more embarrass-ing for me to order White Zinfandel) and one of those live flamenco guitar players you'd probably want to shoot if he stayed at your table even ten seconds longer. It was sort of a cliché romantic date place, but trying to successfully dip your food into the fondue pot made it kind of fun and playful. Dinner was topped off by dipping strawberries into chocolate, and we made a game of watching each other eat our dipped strawberries. For me, this was not only very fun, but a great prelude to sex. Though, come to think of it, what the hell isn't?

We had finished our bottle of wine, and the chocolate-dipped straw-berries, and, though I can only speak for myself, I couldn't have been any more in the mood. Wine makes me horny and sleepy, so by definition I'm working with a short window of opportunity. Just before leaving, though, Shulie caught me completely by surprise me by reaching under the table and handing me a little gift bag.

"What is this?"

"I ran out at lunch. It's your birthday present."

"Shulie, I purposely didn't tell you until this morning so you wouldn't do this."

"Whatever. Shut up and open it."

I showed good manners by opening the card first. She had handwrit-ten, "Can't wait to go to the Neil Diamond concert with you, if you can still handle it, old man. Hate you, Shulie."

We had just started saying I hate you as sort of a pre-I love you baby step. Sort of like training wheels or, for that matter, white zinfandel.

I looked at her and said, "I hate you, too."

"Go ahead, open the rest."

I dug around in the bag's confetti, and pulled out a CD. I laughed out loud when I saw it was the Neil Diamond Christmas album. She added to her joke by saying, "If you're gonna have Christmas music in your apartment, it should at least be by a Jewish guy."

"Who could possibly argue with that?" I asked. "Oh, hey, look at this, it's got some of my all time favorites, 'Jingle Bells, Schmingle Bells', 'Oy, Holy Night', and look at this, 'I Got News For You, It's Gonna Be a White Christmas, Already'."

"Easy there, bud," she warned, though she was laughing. Then, unable to resist, she added her own, "Rudolph, the Big-Nosed Reindeer."

We both laughed. "That's good. This is really great, Shulie. I'll play it all the time."

"Just saying thanks is enough. Really." She laughed, pointed to the bag and told me, "There's more."

I dug through the confetti and pulled out a tiny wrapped box. I opened it up and alternately stared at her and it. She had gone out at lunch and picked out a sterling silver ring for me to replace the one she'd tossed in the river. It was also engraved with the initials S D G (heart) S J C

"I can't believe you did this. I love it. How'd you know the size?"

"Actually, I had to guess, try it on."

I put it on the ring finger of my right hand.

"That's amazing, it fits perfectly."

"Like me." She gave me a sweet smile, which was illuminated nicely by the candlelight.

"Like you," I agreed. "Hey, look at the initials, SDG and SJC. What is that, the Self Deprecating Guy and Some Jewish Chick?"

"I really do hate you."

"Come on, let's get out of here." I had to get home before my window closed.

We went back to my place and she gave me another birthday present. Wink wink. I also gave her one, when by some gift from God, I was able to come back for more. Not bad for an old guy.

We spent the rest of the weekend being kids "in hate". That Saturday, we went to my gym together, then leisurely read the newspaper while having a late breakfast at Salt & Pepper Diner. We then explored the city like tourists. We went on an architectural tour, and visited a couple of the lakefront museums, the Shedd Aquarium and the Planetarium. I hadn't been to either since field trips in like third grade. At the planetarium, while looking at pictures of various phases of the moon, I told her what I was think-ing that night holding her at Rivers; that the bright side of the moon seemed so near and so bright if I could only get there. I told her I felt with her I was getting closer. She looked up at me, and with her eyes and smile even brighter than the picture of the moon we were looking at, she gave me one of those long, hot get-a-room kisses. At the aquarium, we watched the dolphins swim, and then outside had a snowball fight. We dried ourselves off in front of the fire at one of the downtown hotel's lounges while we drank hot buttered rums. We ended up having dinner at Four Farthings, where we met, which has an excellent restaurant attached to the bar. This visit was far more successful than the first, and we joked about how we could maybe tell the kids one day the story of what a jerk daddy was to mommy when they first met.

The next day, I moved my mattress in front of the TV and fireplace, and we never left bed, or even got dressed, except to stoke the fire, take that any way you will, until our order of Chinese food arrived that evening. Unfortunately, though, the weekend was wrapping up, real life was beckon-ing and Shulie had to head back home. At the door, she kissed me and said, "Happy Birthday, Seth."

I caught her eye and said, "Best ever. Thank you."

After she left, I put my mattress back in my room and began my typi-cal routine over the last few weeks, since the downfall of my Wright Star career, of dreading Monday.

But that Monday morning, as if nothing could possibly go wrong on my birthday week, I got a call from Larry Freedman at Capricorn. They wanted to make me an offer. *They wanted to make me an offer!* My heart started racing as it started sinking in. He asked if I'd be free to have lunch with Gary the next day to discuss the terms of the offer.

"Yes, of course. Larry, that's great! Just to clarify. This is for Vice-President in charge of Marketing?"

"It sure is, Seth."

I closed my eyes and said a silent thank you. "I'll see you at noon tomorrow, then."

I closed the door to my office and did a brief victory dance around my desk. The significance of the moment hit me like a ton of bricks. Wow, I was going to be Vice-President of Marketing at a fairly major mutual fund company. If they were going to hire me, obviously they intended to put my ideas to use. In many ways they were entrusting me to turn around the entire company. It was heady stuff, and I was feeling absolutely exhilarated. You know what else it felt like? It felt like, officially, finally, I was no longer the guy I was in high school. For the first time ever I considered going to my next high school reunion. I put both arms in the air, as if I had hit the winning home run, and pumped my fist into the air. "YES!!!"

That next day, I went over to the Capricorn's office just before noon. Shulie had a huge smile as she again formally greeted me in the reception area. She rode the elevator up with me as I went up to Mr. Merchant's floor. She gave me a quick peck on the cheek and wiped some lipstick off my face before the door opened. When I got to his office, he said, "Seth, let's go have lunch."

We got a booth at one of the deli's near their office. "Seth, I guess you've heard from Larry that we would like you to come on board?"

"Yes, he called yesterday. I'm very excited. I think we'll be able to accomplish some great things."

"I agree. That's why we'd like to bring you on. Let me get you up to speed on what's happened since we last spoke…" He did that, apologizing for taking so long to get back to me, and explaining the steps he took to come to a decision and fire their current V-P of Marketing.

"So, here's the deal," he continued, "this year my plan is to really ride the portfolio managers to see what we can't do to improve our fund's lackluster performance. Marketing is yours. I'm planning to provide you the budget you need to introduce two of your new fund ideas. If successful, we'll do the same the next year. We have a good group of people, but I'll be counting on you for big things this year."

I was going to say that I was up for it, but thought that might sound corny. People who get to that level, it seemed to me, always knew what to say. I hoped I wasn't in too far over my head. I just solemnly nodded my head, which I hoped translated into, "I fully understand the stakes, and am confident in my abilities to meet and exceed your expectations," rather than, "I feel like a three year old right now."

"Larry will go through the offer with you, but I think you'll like it. It has a base salary that will be significantly more that you make now, but I believe in paying for performance. If your fund and marketing ideas work, and we'll set realistic goals for each year, you will make a very good living. You'll also get a personal assistant and a corner office."

"Thank you, sir, I look forward to earning your trust and making us both look very smart."

"That's what I want to hear, Seth." We shook on it, finished our sandwiches and headed back.

I went back to Larry's office to talk through the details of the offer.

He laid out the salary and bonus structure for me, and it was awesome. If all went reasonably well, I'd more than double my current compensation. Figuring it might look unprofessional, I resisted the urge to jump up for joy. I barely heard Larry as he went through the rest of the details, though I did notice when he put his hand on my knee to congratulate me.

Just for show I told Larry that I'd consider the offer overnight and get back to him in the morning, though I didn't think I was kidding anyone with that little charade.

Afterward, I asked to speak with Shulie. She closed the door. I told her the offer, which she already knew, and we literally danced around her office.

So, that night, for the third time in the last four nights, we went out for a really nice dinner to celebrate. This one was at Café Spiaggia, in the One Mag Mile building, overlooking Michigan Avenue. It was also classy and romantic, and we mostly discussed fantasy ways for me to spend my paycheck. Maybe I'd even buy a place if she'd help me look for it. I was in seventh-heaven and wanted to tell everyone I'd become someone. I told the host, the waiter and total strangers on the street that I was the new V-P of Marketing at Capricorn. No one, of course, gave a shit, but they seemed entertained by my enthusiasm.

Even though it was a Monday night, I really wanted Shulie to stay over. She said she wanted to, but said she didn't have a change of clothes. So, after dinner, feeling like Mr. Upper Tax Bracket, we went to Bloomingdale's just before it closed and I bought her an outfit and shoes that we picked out together.

We got to my place and made love again, which I think put the number of times we'd done that in the last four days in triple digits.

I wiped her hair from her forehead and told her I had so much to thank her for. I had met Shulie only six weeks ago, and look what had happened in my life. I had suffered a career setback, but there she was to help me get my dream job. I was a lost, jaded single guy who probably caused most of his own problems by being overly analytical and cynical. But there she was to be my motivation and reward if I could just be more accepting, and more tolerant of others. She was there to show me that if I could just try harder to fit in, rather than going with my own, more comfortable agenda, these good times would continue. It again seemed very Pavlovian and very enlightening. I knew my old agenda hadn't exactly provided me any positive reinforcement. If I needed to be like Mr. Pavlov's dog to find some sort of contentment, then "Bow, wow, baby." This development had also opened up a number of other possibilities. For one, my parents were going to absolutely love her. They'd be so surprised and relieved the first time they met her, I couldn't imagine the evening ending in anything other than a prolonged group hug. Then, there were all my Jewish friends, who were all married to the Jewish girls they had met in college. As a single guy, it was difficult enough to stay close with them. But, this was especially true since I tended to date girls their wives had nothing in common with, and had no desire to try to build common ground. I could now be one of the guys, without the disapproval of their wives. I realized that I needed to start the Shulie world tour soon. There'd be much rejoicing, I was sure.

For the first time, I think, ever, my life felt damn near whole. Things were good. They were really good, and in my mind I had her to thank for all of it. Perhaps I just got too caught up in the moment, but before I knew it, I looked her in the eyes as she lay next to me in bed and blurted out, "I love you."

15

It was certainly a moment, but not one that changed everything and sealed our fate. She whispered, "I love you too." I don't know if I was reading too much into it, but it seemed to be with just the slightest hesitation and uncertainty. She wasn't, I was quite sure, saying "I love you and I want you forever, you're my everything." Just "I love you." I let it go—she said she loved me, and no one I'd ever wanted to, had said that before—but I'd find out over the next few weeks that I was still under evaluation.

That next morning, I had to give my notice at Wright Star. However, since it wasn't something I was looking forward to, I put it on hold so I could make a few calls to gloat and revel in my good fortune. My first call was to my mom.

"Mom, it's me."

"Hi dear," she said, excited that I called. "What's going on?"

"Well, I just wanted you to know that your son is V-P of Marketing at Capricorn Mutual Funds."

"What? You are? Congratulations! I didn't know you were interviewing."

"Yeah, I interviewed with them about two or three weeks ago."

"And they offered you the job?"

"Uh huh." (This is where I get asked every question she can think of—even if she knows the answer—as sort of my punishment for not calling more often. It's also the start of her assuming that I hadn't thought this all the way through.)

"Are you sure you want to leave Wright Star? I thought you liked it there?" *Here we go.*

"Mom, did you hear me? V-P! Vice-President. IN CHARGE OF MARKETING."

"I just meant that you like the people you work with now, and the president is a nice guy, right? What if they're not nice at the new company?"

"I've met the president. He seems like he'll be good to work with, and he's giving me a lot of space to do my job. If I don't like the rest of the people, I'll fire them."

Since I don't think my mom actually listens to most of what I say anyway, she ignored my joke, and pressed on, "So, you'll have a lot to do then, huh?"

"What?"

"It sounds like a big job."

"Yeah." *And your point is?*

"They're going to expect a lot from you."

"Yeah…"

Then maybe realizing that didn't sound like she had a hell of a lot of confidence in me, said, "Well, I guess that's good, right?"

"Mom, what do you mean you guess that's good? It's really good. They entrusted me with their entire marketing effort based on the strength of my ideas. They're doubling my salary. I get a personal assistant and a big corner office. I can make people call me sir, for chrissakes. It's REALLY good."

"You don't have to get mad."

Ahhhhhhhhhh.

"I'm not mad." Then trying to take the agitation out of my voice, I said, "Really. I'm just calling to tell you the good news."

"So, you think you're doing the right thing?"

"Yes, mom, I do."

"Well good. I hope so, and I'm proud of you." This was where I wanted her to eventually arrive, though I could tell she'd spend the next half-hour worrying about this on my behalf.

"Thanks, mom. Hey, something else. I met a new girl I'd like you and dad to meet."

There was no enthusiasm in her voice whatsoever, "Who is she?"

"Her name is Shulie Cohenberg."

From nowhere, a spark of interest. "That's a nice name. Is she…"

"Uh huh. What do you think about that?"

"I want to meet this one."

"I thought you might. Are you free Saturday? We can come over for dinner."

"I think we have plans, but I'll break them. Come over around 6:00. So you like her?"

"If you have plans, we can do it another…"

"No, don't be silly. Saturday night, and don't be late. Do you like her?"

"Yes, mom. I think she's great. You'll like her, too. See you Saturday. I'll call dad."

I called my dad and got the same 'Congratulations…are you sure you're doing the right thing…we're proud of you' reaction about the job as I got from my mother, though with fewer questions. Also, my dad's too nice to have disliked any of the previous girls I'd brought home, but he was noticeably excited when I mentioned I was bringing a Cohenberg home. Finally a nice Jewish girl. I was sure he'd immediately called my mom to begin to speculate about the delicious possibilities. I'm not so sure my mom wasn't already thinking in terms of places to have the rehearsal dinner.

Next I called some friends, whose reactions were more along the lines of, "Hey cool, let's get drunk." I planned three separate drinking nights for the next week.

Then, I figured it was time to talk to JT. Not only did I respect JT, as I mentioned earlier, but I also like him a lot. He had shown a great deal faith in me, and had even given me a thirty percent increase in pay last year to match an offer I got from one of my vendors. I felt that in some ways I was letting him down by leaving, especially since he seemed to have some sort of personal rivalry going with Gary Merchant. And though my analysis of the situation told me that all my activities were relegated to the margins at Wright Star, I was quite sure I'd have to prepare for JT's argument that all my responsibilities were cutting edge and the future of our company. It wasn't worth arguing these points with him, but it wasn't going to make our conversation any easier for me. In the end, though, neither he, nor I, could argue with the fact that I had to do what's best for my career. Unless he'd offer me the same position at Wright Star—and even then it wouldn't be the same because JT would still make all the marketing decisions—this was a good career move for me.

I knocked on his door, and though he was on the phone, he motioned for me to have a seat. When I closed the door before sitting down, he knew something was up and seemed to hurry through the rest of his call.

"Hi, I need to talk to you about something."

"Uh oh. What is it? You're not leaving are you?"

"Well, I did get a job offer that I think is too good to refuse."

He seemed visibly upset—which I thought was generous of him to allow me to see—and I had to make sure all my points in favor of leaving were lined up and ready to go.

"With who?"

"You won't like this, but Capricorn offered me the job of V-P of Marketing."

"Don't tell me that," he said, half-kidding.

"I know. I hate to do that to you. I've always really enjoyed working for you. I mean that. I know you and Gary have a thing, but believe me, it's nothing personal."

"Did they contact you?" He wanted a reason to lash out at Mr. Merchant.

"Well, no, not really. As luck would have it, my new girl friend works there in HR, and I was telling her about my marketing philosophies and fund ideas and she thought Gary Merchant would be interested in talking to me. I made sure it was in the context of a job interview for the V-P job, and when they said it was, I talked to them. He seems to be really interested in going forward with one-to-one marketing and my lifestyle fund ideas. He's giving me an increased budget and the go-ahead to implement my ideas, and, you know, the big corner office, and the whole deal."

"Seth, all the things you've been doing—maybe they haven't gotten enough attention—but that kind of thing is the direction of the company. When you got here, we didn't even know how to measure results and we mailed everybody everything. We now have discipline and focus in what we're doing, and you deserve the credit for that. You also have the ability to see things from a customer's perspective in a way we've never really done before. Even with all of our budget demands—with all the things we're trying to do, and with the increased accountability we have to hit our profit margin numbers—your area has grown every year. I planned to continue that. You really are a big part of what I want to do here."

"I appreciate the kind words, but I think Capricorn is offering me more than that."

"Seth, if we could match the compensation, would you stay?"

"I'd have to think about that hard, but it's nearly double."

His mouth almost hit the floor. "What?!"

"Yeah. The offer I got, if I can meet some very attainable goals, will be double what I currently make. I don't think I can even ask you to do that."

"I don't think I can get that done with our current budget structure. I wonder how the hell they can?"

"Well, they did let go the current V-P, who had been there a while, to make room for me. That must account for most of it. The rest is performance-based, so if I don't produce, they don't pay."

"For us, it would be all an incremental increase."

"I know, and I'm not asking you to do it. I really think this is my opportunity to shine. To be the man. Here, you're the guy, which is as it should be, but Gary Merchant is giving me full responsibility for marketing and I think it's too good an opportunity to pass up."

JT thought for a second. He's a smart guy and also wouldn't talk me out of something that was in my best interest. "You know, Seth, there's been some talk of some conflict between Capricorn's management and their parent, Justice. You should try to find out as much as you can about that. I'm only bringing it up because you want to make sure you're going into a stable environment, if there is such a thing. I tell you what, I'll see if I can find out anything."

Shit, I hadn't thought much about that, and I didn't need anything raining on my parade. I said, "I guess you never really know when you step into a new situation. I'll see what I can find out. If you find out anything let me know. But for now, I'm giving you my notice. As sort of a measure of my appreciation to Wright Star and to you, I told Capricorn that I'd give you three weeks. Does that sound good to you."

"Well, I don't think we'll be able to find a replacement that quick, but I do appreciate you giving us the extra week. I know you don't have to do that."

He shook my hand, said he really hated losing me to the "scumbags" at Capricorn, but that he sincerely wished me well.

On the way back to my office, even though I wanted to tell everybody else at Wright Star, I remembered that I still hadn't accepted the offer. Back in my office, I called Larry and said I'd thought about it, and decided to accept. He made a pretense out of sounding relieved and excited to hear that (as if I was really going to say, you know, I need three times my salary or it's not worth my time.) I told him I that was going to give three weeks notice and that I'd start April 5[th,] and just to tweak him a little, I added, "Just after Easter weekend." I knew he wanted to say, "You mean just after Passover," but restrained himself. "That should be just fine. I'll get you all the paperwork, so you can get a head start on that. Welcome to Capricorn, Seth."

From there, I got to tell all my peers and co-workers, who were excited because it meant several more happy hour events before I left. It was looking like I'd spend most of the next three weeks drunk, but what the hell, it's not like anyone would expect any work out of me.

I spent the rest of the week alternately researching Capricorn and Justice, making personal phone calls and otherwise generally fucking around. I'd typically been more of a stay in my office and work kind of guy, but now I was Mr. Social, bopping around to everyone's office to make sure I wasn't the only one not being the least bit productive. I learned more office gossip, and backbiting, than I had in my previous three years. It was good stuff, spiced with affairs I had no idea about, and petty internal hatreds. Duly educated, in the future, if I wanted to keep in touch, we could talk about the employee soap operas rather than the boring internal politics. I also made sure there would be good showings at my going-away events. The previous record had been four events in this one guy's goodbye week, but he was popular with everyone and was moving out of state. I figured if I had three, that'd be a respectable showing.

That Saturday night, Shulie and I met at my parents' house. I was relieved to find they had decided against literally rolling out a red carpet down the driveway, or putting out rose petals for Shulie to walk on. I arrived before she, and when I walked in my mom gave me an enthusiastic kiss. They were both bubbling over with anticipation and peppered me with a few hundred questions about Shulie and my new job (in that order.) They went through so many questions, so quickly, they even started asking about Ed. I said he was studying for his Bar Mitzvah and sent his best.

Shulie arrived about fifteen minutes after I did as I had told her to do, so she wouldn't have to endure both solo. My parents lined up at the door to greet her, just barely giving her room to squeeze into the room. They couldn't have been more excited had the President dropped by for dinner, even if the President was Jewish.

Shulie and I sat together on a love seat and my parents sat on an adjacent couch and asked most of the questions they had just asked me. They were apparently happy with the initial returns and my mom even offered us a beer, which if I recall correctly, last happened never. We're far more of a dessert than an alcohol family. This provided a nice contrast in culture to most of the girls I'd dated, who if their family remembered to eat at all, it was considered either a victory in their fight against alcoholism or just a bad party. Most of their parties were good. Anyway, I gratefully accepted, while Shulie joined my parents in having wine. I was also relieved that my parents didn't opt to break out this bottle of red wine that had been given to them on the day I, their first child, was born. It was meant for really special occasions, and since this had to be the most special occasion since my Bar Mitzvah, I'm fairly certain they considered it.

We sat to eat and the lovefest continued. My dad even knew her brother's wife's dad's friend's brother's dad's wife, or something, from their Jewish bowling league. This wonderfully exciting bit of information had been successfully gathered from some Jewish Geography that they all appeared to enjoy very much. And, joyfully, our parents even both had tickets to the same opera series. I could envision them figuring out a way to sit together at the next one to work on baby names. Coffee talk at the table went on for what seemed like hours. I'm someone who prefers reclining whenever possible, so I've never been good at prolonged sitting around the table. I got up several times to put away dishes and provide hints that I'd rather move back to the couch, but to no avail. I probably should have just turned on the TV and laid down on the couch for all they needed me in the conversation. Once, I returned to the table to find they were discussing family illnesses and tragedies, a favorite topic, and I knew this could last well into the night. I've often thought that if my parents and their friends could set up bleachers at the Highland Park Hospital ER, they'd get season tickets and never run out of dinner conversation. For them, reading the obituaries was similar to me reading the sports section.

At about nine I thought I was out of the woods, when my mom got up to get dessert. Actually, four deserts. After all, there were four of us and we each needed our own. I had some chocolate cake and some coffee, because I had come way down from the initial buzz I got from the three beers I'd had earlier in the evening. When Shulie excused herself to go to the rest room, my mom told me she thought she was beautiful and sweet. My dad just gave me a proud, fatherly thumbs-up. I smiled and thanked them. There was something to be said for contributing to their happiness. Then there was kind of a lull in the conversation. They kind of both had silly, grinning, faraway looks, and I can only assume that they had begun to simply wait for the wedding.

We said good-byes and there were hugs flying everywhere. My parents even hugged each other, because, I guess, they had so many more hugs left in them. It was beautiful.

We left her car at my parents, and drove together back to the city. She seemed to be very happy with her new best friends. "So, do you think they liked me?" That could've been rhetorical, but I answered, "A lot more than they like me. I'm surprised they didn't ask you to marry me. I'm pretty sure they had a ring."

"Seth, they're sweet. You shouldn't make fun of them so much."

"They are sweet. And I'm glad they like you." I looked at her and smiled. She reached up and gave me a kiss on the cheek. If she had seen her future that night, she had no problems with it.

16

Shulie had decided it was time I met her friends. Originally, they had wanted to meet at some lame place in the 'burbs, but I put up a bit of resistance, and we ended up agreeing to meet at Hi-Tops, a sports bar across from Wrigley Field. Hi-Tops is *the* place to watch the NCAA men's college basketball tournament, which had just started the day before and, as luck would have it, both Indiana and Michigan were playing that night. I was pretty sure I wasn't going to like her friends, so having the IU game on would be a nice reason to ignore them.

Hi-Tops has several thousand TVs, a life size Michael Jordan crashing through the lower floor ceiling, and some of the best Buffalo wings in the city. During big sporting events, and there was none bigger than this considering the still raging alumni enthusiasm of most of the area's residents, it crams in probably three to four times the number of people the fire marshal would allow, if he could get in to find out how many people were there. I had a drink with Shulie after work at my place, and we got to Hi-Tops sooner than her group of friends. I had some friends in line and we managed to get inside in about fifteen minutes. We even got a table with some other friends of mine, and fought like hell to get and save six seats for her friends. Our table was situated between two giant screen TVs, and Indiana was playing on one, and about an hour later, Michigan's game was going to start on the other. If IU won, Michigan lost and her friends didn't show it'd be a perfect night.

Though Indiana's basketball team was doing its part by winning at halftime, her friends finally got in, and if I had to make a guess—based on the nearly hour long continuous stream on bitching about the drive downtown, the parking, and the people in line—I'd say they weren't entirely happy.

I was introduced to her friends Robin, Tracy and Deann. Since their winter coats were all some combination of shearling, black leather and fir— I could only presume they had even more expensive coats to wear when not going to a sports bar—their dates/husbands spent the first fifteen minutes trying to find someplace appropriate to put their coats. After some animated negotiations, they eventually settled on the manager's office. Their dates were David, David and David, or maybe David, David and David, it was hard to keep them straight. Robin was sort of round, on the short side, and with straight black hair. She wore, to my taste, too much makeup; which if I can be honest, didn't do anything to hide the fact that she was short and fat. On the other hand, to her credit, the fact that she resembled the great pumpkin did nothing to detract from her feelings of self worth. In fact, she bossed around her David, a balding dentist, like he was put on earth to make sure she was always comfortable. I liked her immediately. Let me know if my sarcasm is too subtle and I'll come right out with it. Apparently Shulie and Robin had been friends since grade school, and their thing was to whisper secrets to each other, which I don't find annoying at all. Still too subtle? Robin immediately was in Shulie's ear to tell her something about someone, which they both found amusing and I couldn't have been happier.

Since Robin completely ignored me—which I didn't take as a thank you for risking my life to save her and her friends seats—her David, who I felt bad for because he seemed like an okay jellyfish, did shake my hand to introduce himself. Since it was halftime, I started asking him about his dental practice, but a beer had spilled in the vicinity of our table and Robin immediately made David rush off for a mop or something. Her voice was so loud and shrill, I nearly got up to help him.

Shulie's friend Tracy, on the other hand, was a babe. Oh, man. A real knockout. Her David, who I think was her fiancé based on the fact that she was wearing like a seventy-five karat diamond engagement ring, was also a very handsome guy. I'd have probably liked her if she weren't the biggest bitch on earth. And I mean that with no offense to the other bitches out there, because now I like each of you more than I did before. She reminded me of girls I knew in high school. When I got to college, I met some really attractive women, who, though they didn't want to go out with me, were very sweet about it. That had never happened to me in my high school. I just thought it was understood that if you were pretty, you were bitchy—in the same way that two plus two equals four. You didn't stop to think about it, it just was. Apparently there was a handbook for Jewish high school girls or something. But enough about looking forward to my high school reunion.

Tracy's renovated nose was so far in the air, it looked like she was trying to sniff the Michael Jordan guy stuck in the ceiling. I thought if MJ had to listen to her whining conversation too much longer he'd manage to extricate himself down to the floor—still in his Bulls uniform—shake his head at how horrible of a person she was and with his basketball in hand, head out into the cold night to go get stuck in the ceiling of some other sports bar.

The only thing I liked about Tracy the Bitch is that she also ignored Round Robin, which I felt was fairly poignant. Shulie, Deann and Tracy's David were the only ones she condescended to talk to. Apparently that was enough for Shulie because Tracy the Bitch and Shulie my Girlfriend were thick as thieves.

Tracy's David, was, I learned, a sports agent. His whole look was slick and polished. He had teeth so large and white it made me a little nervous. He wore dress slacks and an obviously expensive gray mock turtleneck shirt under a black blazer. He also sported a very thick gold bracelet, because that is so cool. He and Shulie had been friends in their days at the University of Michigan. He had gotten his start while attending law school at Michigan, where he befriended some of the guys on Michigan's basketball team, guys who were now celebrities in the NBA.

Being a sports fan, this seemed like an interesting path to pursue. I learned the heartwarming story of the Michigan basketball guys getting him great seats to their games, his scalping the tickets to the highest bidders and then splitting the money with the players. From there, he kept in touch with the guys—mostly it appeared because he'd shared his cocaine with them—and after passing the bar, became their agent when they entered the pros. He had thus made a very nice living, but enough about the American Dream.

What I thought was really great was that he wasn't driven by the money. Judging by the rest of the conversation, what he really lived for was suing people for no apparent reason, and complaining persistently enough at meals that the bills would get comped.

He bragged about how he insisted that one of his star players "sue the balls off" the public school district that the player's deaf child could not attend because they didn't offer a program for deaf kids. This, despite the fact that the player made $12 million a year, and was not planning to send his kid to public schools in the first place. He'd won this action, thus saving the school district the trouble of buying the new computers they had budgeted. "Great story," I uttered.

David had also sued for punitive damages, on his own behalf, because his BMW 'smelled funny' after a valet parking attendant returned his car to him. He proudly declared that the restaurant had to go bankrupt as a result, and that "really the car didn't smell that bad," and was mostly a result of the garlic and onions in his doggy bag. He got a big kick out of this story, and my goodness, I was just so happy for him.

He talked about various free lunches and frivolous law suits as if they were his children, which was very charming. He had just finished with this tearful and joyous, "This is my life and don't you just love me to pieces" story, when I looked at my new pal in disbelief and said, "Ow, shit!"

That's because Shulie, who had been following this conversation and my visceral reaction to it, saw where I was going to be in a second, and practically ripped my arm out of the socket, pulling me off my bar stool so quick and so far, I thought I'd have to wait in line again to get in. "What the fuck was that for?"

"I need a beer."

"They have waitresses, you know."

"Seth, I don't know what you were going to say to David, but he's a friend of mine, and I don't need the two of you beating the crap out of each other in the middle of a crowded bar."

"First, it'd be me beating the crap out of him, and I was just going to…"

"What, tell him how much you admire his entrepreneurial spirit?"

"I might have phrased it differently, but something like that."

She put her hand on my arm, and trying to sweet talk me, said, "Seth, I don't think it's asking too much for you to be nice to my friends."

I ripped my still sore arm away and said, "I'm going to watch the game."

Rebuffed, her tone turned a little nastier as she sneered, "I would like a beer."

I just sort of threw some money at her and watched the rest of Indiana's game more or less by myself. The game, as did my night, got more miserable after halftime and IU blew their big lead and lost. After that, still trying to ignore her friends, I tried to focus on Michigan's game. Deann, who had also gone to Michigan, started watching the game with me. We talked and laughed about a few things and I was surprised to find she was rather likable. She was cute and friendly and had an easy smile, and, unlike the rest of her friends, I could tell why Shulie liked her. As the night wore on, though, I came to appreciate what an obnoxious, full-of-himself prick her husband David was. He was also almost comedically ugly. When I had a chance, I asked Shulie what she saw in him. Shulie said, "She thinks he's cute."

"She must be very deep," I said, incredulous. It became crystal clear when Shulie went on to describe him as a trader and from one of the wealthiest families on the North Shore. He wore one of those button-down long-sleeve shirts with the polo player that makes the statement, "I have no real taste or style, but I want everyone to know I have money." It was also bright orange, which I only mention because it was bright orange.

Before talking with Deann, I'd pretty much ignored him, but I'd since noticed his entire rap and persona were intent on letting us know he had more money than the rest of us combined. I wished I could've been more helpful as he lamented over if he should upgrade from his Porsche to a Ferrari, but then I didn't know if he'd still be able to afford his private plane. He must have had to seek help elsewhere, because his cell phone was used so often I wasn't entirely sure if it could even be removed from his ear. It was depressing that an otherwise attractive girl with some nice qualities would choose this asshole. She couldn't have sold out anymore had she been a crack whore on North Avenue, no offense to them.

Michigan went on to win their game, making me a big oh-for-three on my perfect night. I was so down, I didn't even enjoy my wings. This was fortuitous, I guess, because the Davids teamed up against our poor waitress, dissecting every line item on the bill for so long that the wings and a number of other items were suddenly on the house. As the Davids high-fived each other, I grabbed Shulie, pulled the waitress aside and gave her a $50 tip because I was sure she'd be otherwise stiffed, and got the hell out of there.

Outside the bar, an agitated Shulie tried to get into it with me. "Seth, you can't..."

She looked really pissed, but I just cut her off, "Shulie, don't talk to me right now."

She thought better of responding at that moment. I think she considered going back into the bar to apologize for my behavior, but the line was even longer, so she walked silently along side me until we got a cab back to my place.

When we got to my apartment she said, "You owe me an apology. You couldn't have been any more rude to my friends. They didn't do anything to you."

"They didn't even acknowledge me, except for Deann and one of the fucking Davids."

"You were predispositioned to not like them. You weren't even going to try."

"I was trying as hard as I could not to fucking lose it. How can you be friends with those people? Jesus, Shulie, one's the wicked bitch of the north shore; one's a gold digger who's basically just a whore, and let's not forget the fucking round mound of sound who redefines the term high maintenance. The only thing I enjoyed is that their men deserved them. That was the most obnoxious, pompous, self-important group of people I've ever had the misfortune of having to spend an evening with, and I was fucking embarrassed to even be part of that table. I just kept looking at you and thinking, here's this beautiful, special girl that I'm crazy about—in love with—and she's friends with the Jewish Horror Picture Show. Those people made me nearly physically sick, and I can't help it, but that's how I feel." I just looked at her and said, "Listen, if you want to go home, I'll understand."

"Do you want me to?"

"No, of course not. If you were like them, believe me I'd never, ever, ever have gone out with you. But you're not, and I love you, and I want you to stay."

"I love you, too," she replied so softly I could barely hear it.

Obviously, we had some issues. However, at that moment, though it could've gone either way, neither of us was willing to give up what we had. It happened to be her time of the month, which fit the evening like a glove, so we couldn't fool around, but I held her like I was trying to hold onto what we had until we both fell asleep.

17

Over the next two weeks, Shulie and I did our best not to talk about the night out with her friends. We went out with some of my married Jewish friends from college one night and everyone had a good time. Girls who hadn't talked to me in years were now pumping me for details and, since I was now one of them, planning double dates. The guys were now pumping me for details on my sex life, and since Shulie is kind of a babe, planning double dates. She was made to feel welcome by all, and just as she did after meeting my parents, she seemed to go home with the feeling that if that was part of sharing my life with me, she was fine with it. I wished I could say the same regarding her friends and family.

We also hooked up with Fishy, Rags and Craig one night. Since there was a bit of a competition for who was gonna get me, the girl or the lonely pathetic guys, it wasn't the most comfortable night out I ever spent. Shulie's behavior was commendable, though, probably because at some point she decided that if we were ever together I'd have no reason to ever see them again.

My last day at Wright Star was going to be Thursday April 1, because Friday was Good Friday, a day off at Wright Star. That Thursday also happened to be the first day of Passover, and my mom had already called a week and a half ago to make sure Shulie and I would be there. We agreed to do the second night of Passover at Shulie's house on Friday.

I started my last week by ensuring there'd be at least one event in my honor by bringing in cinnamon rolls from Ann Sather's restaurant on Monday. On that Tuesday, there was a goodbye lunch with the marketing department where I'd had a few beers, and that Wednesday, we had scheduled a happy hour goodbye at Rivers. I made sure they didn't invite the whole world, just the people I liked, but it promised to be a good turnout. Shulie agreed to join me for that.

That Tuesday afternoon, after my lunch, JT stopped by my office to chat.

"Seth, got a second?"

I quickly closed the game of computer solitaire I'd been playing, and, damnit, looked about ready to win, and said, "Sure."

He closed the door, sat down, put his feet up on my desk, and asked, "So, you been working hard?"

He was joking, so I played along and said, "Oh, sure. I'm exhausted."

His normally easy laugh was mixed with some concern.

"Listen, I debated whether to bring this up with you, but I decided I should and you could decide what you wanted to do with it."

"Okay," I said even more quietly than usual. This was ominous.

"Well, I made some calls, and found out the word is that Justice Financial, whose stock has been sucking, is fed up with Capricorn's performance dragging them down. They're also not enamored with Gary Merchant in particular. They think he's a loose cannon, and too full of himself. The perception, and perception can be everything, is that he's lost his marketing touch. It's one of those, 'what have you done for me lately'. My source didn't know how this might manifest itself, if, in fact, it does; but he'd heard some rumors of a possibly imminent shake up." JT took his feet off my desk and sat up to perhaps emphasize the seriousness of the point he was making, and said, "Perhaps a sale or maybe even a change in management at Capricorn."

I looked at him as if I was looking at my devastated trailer after a tornado. I could feel a major headache coming on.

"Seth, you know me, and you know I'm not just saying this to prevent your leaving. I like you, and I'd never do that to you. But, Seth, if I was you, I'd have some very real concerns."

I hadn't used my brain in nearly three weeks, and with the beers I had at lunch, wasn't entirely ready to start. In general, I try not to focus on negative possibilities, but I couldn't shake the one unthinkable thought I had—no Gary, no dream job.

As if reading my mind, JT said, "I'm sorry. This has to be tough to swallow, and I know how much that a job like that could mean to your career. The thing is, though, and I'll just lay this on the table for you, I need to know what you want to do. I got really lucky and have a candidate for your position ready to go. He's from Target Funds, and talks like you do about personalized marketing. If you decide to stay, the job's yours. I'll even give you a $5,000 raise as a way to ease your disappointment. But, if you say you're going, I'm going to offer him the job tomorrow. Once I do, I can't go back on that. It's just way too messy, and I don't want to go back on my word." Jeez, how quick life moves on without you.

"I understand. So, I have until tomorrow to decide?"

"Yeah, I don't know what else I can say. I'll push him off until after lunch. Could you let me know by noon?"

"I don't know if I'll know the answer by then, but, yeah, I'll let you know one way or the other. Thanks, JT, I appreciate what you're doing for me."

"You're welcome, and I hope you make the right decision, whatever that is." He smiled and walked out.

After he left, I got my coat and went for a walk. I needed to think. I went downstairs and stepped into one of those double-digits-below-zero wind-chill days that give Chicagoans such character. Despite two scarves, a snow mask, and earmuffs—when the weather is like this, fashion is meaningless—I made it only about a block. I ducked into a Starbucks, ordered the biggest size of their caffeinated coffee of the day, and tried to think of how to even think about this.

How much could I gamble on my dream job?

Once the caffeine started to kick in, one thing I realized almost immediately was that my attitude was similar to one of an out-manned football team. Recognizing the unlikelihood that they'd win using conventional means, they go for it on fourth down, run trick plays, blitz every down. The thinking is that the only chance they have of winning is to try to get lucky with some of their gimmick plays, because, hell, they weren't going to win anyway. Tracing back to my high school days, I've always lacked the confidence that I'd ultimately succeed doing things the same way as everyone else. I saw myself on the edge of success, and I've always been afraid that the "same as everyone else" route wasn't going to be good enough for me. As a result, even though I'm quite sure the smart thinking on this would have been to play it safe, take the five grand raise and work toward the next opportunity—be it at Wright Star or not—I found myself leaning the other way. If I turned down a one-hundred-percent increase in salary and the job that would allow me to do all the things I believed in, would I ever get that opportunity again? This job was there for the taking. If I didn't take it, I knew nothing like this would be promised me.

By the time I finished my coffee, I was pretty sure I knew what I was going to do. I got back and still shivering from the cold, called Shulie. "Hi. Listen, have you heard any rumors about a shake-up at the top of Capricorn?"

"Well, I heard they were firing the old V-P of Marketing and hiring a handsome new one."

"Don't joke around." I was pretty sure I'd never said that before.

"Why, what have you heard?"

I told her what JT had told me.

"Oh, my God. Are you having second thoughts about accepting the job?"

"Well, yeah. Wouldn't you?"

"No. They're just rumors. And look at the source. He's probably just jealous that Gary's stealing you away."

"I don't think that I believe that. You haven't heard *anything* like that?"

"No, I'll talk to Larry and see if he has, though. Okay?"

"Okay. Yeah, thanks. Maybe I'm just freaking out for no reason, like this is too good to be true."

"I think you're overreacting. And, it's not too good to be true because you deserve it."

I wasn't convinced about either of those statements, but I just replied, "Thanks. Let me know if you hear anything. Call me tonight, okay?"

"I will and Seth, don't worry."

Oh, sure. It was only my entire future at stake. "I'll talk to you tonight."

That next morning, armed with no new or useful information, I knocked on JT's door.

"Hey."

"Seth, come in."

His office was very low-key for a top exec. I looked around as if for the first—and for that matter, last—time. There was no couch, no showpiece desk, no pictures of himself with dignitaries. Just a lot of pictures of his new baby boy. In fact, the office and desk were the same size as every other office. I liked him more for that. I sat in one of the two chairs facing his desk.

"Well, I've come to a decision. I decided yesterday afternoon, and even though it was excruciating, I never changed my mind. I look at my future here, and I see three or four people behind you, but ahead of me. And they're the kind of people I can't compete with. They all remember way more about everything than I do, they say all the right things, they play golf with the right people, and they're always in your office. I can't say that I don't have more good ideas than that whole group combined, but they're the kind of people who've always been promoted instead of me. And I can't change to be like them. It's not me."

"Seth, you've got to give me more credit than that for evaluating talent. I can't say you would or wouldn't get the next promotion, but I'm your biggest fan. You offer the kind of thinking that I'm never going to be able to replace. I'm not looking for bureaucrats or yes people. Believe me, no one disagrees with me more than you." He smiled at that, as did I. He paused for a moment to give his next thought more emphasis. "No one will ever get promoted based on how often they come into my office or who they play golf with. I'm looking for people who can make Wright Star the great company it can become. I'd really like you to be a part of that."

"JT, I appreciate all that. It's nice of you to say. But, I'm sorry. I'm basically tired of being average. In fact, I'm *afraid* of being average. The Capricorn job gives me the opportunity of a lifetime. I can't turn it down. I just can't."

"So, that's your decision then?"

"Yes."

I was getting choked up, and was glad that JT simply said, "Well then I wish you luck."

We shook hands, and I told him I'd stop by to say goodbye before leaving the next day.

I wish I knew that I had made the right choice. I could've used a couple of reassuring signs. Like that JT had a garish office that I suddenly found myself resenting, or some insincerity in his words. I generally believe in the inter-relatedness of good or bad things. Now, at the last minute, absent any of those signs, I wondered if I wasn't making a mistake.

That night, JT stopped by for a few drinks at my goodbye party, giving it special significance, not just because he decided to expense the tab. I asked if he had offered my job, and he said it was offered and accepted.

"Well, then," I said, "there's only one thing to do...have a drink."

He smiled and, maybe a first in Wright Star goodbye party history, JT bought us two kamikaze shots. We clinked our shot glasses, toasted my future, and went bottoms up. I said thanks and he slapped me on the back. If he was just trying to show me what a good guy he was and that I'd miss working for him, it was working. Again, I hoped I had done the right thing and worried that I hadn't.

I left work for my party at around four-thirty, and Shulie showed up around six. Since no one I worked with knew her, she became quite an attraction. Not long after I kissed her, sat her down next to me and got her a drink, the women I worked with swarmed her individually or in groups. She was charming and witty throughout, and I got many compliments on how pretty and smart and sweet she was, from both the guys and the girls. I was proud to be with her. Once again, I was struck by the divide between how we seemed so well matched when we were together, but how it seemed like we were from two different worlds when we were with the rest of Jewish society. Unfortunately, though, it seemed like the latter was getting harder to ignore. It was a subtle change, too subtle to even talk about together, but she seemed more reserved in her happiness about our relationship. Several weeks ago, she had let herself go and lost herself in the wonder of our great new relationship. She'd since started to hold back just a little bit back, and I realized I had slipped backwards into another evaluation phase, like I was on parole or something.

Between that uncertainty and the fact I had desperately rolled the dice hoping to come up big with the Capricorn job—and the fact that drinks were free, and some of my closer work friends were staying out late with me—I got nice and toasty drunk.

As I was leaving the bar, I looked up in the clear sky at the full moon. It was the second full moon in March and the second blue moon of the year. The last blue moon came as I started going out with Shulie. I wondered what changes, or new phases of my life, I might be entering into with this blue moon. With my new job beckoning, I figured that was the next phase of my changing life. I figured wrong. I had no way of knowing as I walked home from the train that night that this blue moon was bringing with it much larger changes than that.

114

18

The blue moon was still lighting up the sky as the calendar turned to Thursday, April First. A lot in the old Franklin Planner today. This was my last day at Wright Star. It was the first day of Passover. It was April Fool's Day. And, it was the last day of life as I knew it.

Normally I read the paper on the way to work, but last day and all, I figured I'd bring the paper inside my apartment and read it with a leisurely cup of coffee. I'd get to work when I got to work.

I started, as usual, with the sports section, and read about the Bulls losing again, and that night's NCAA tournament matchups. Frickin Michigan had won again the Saturday before and were playing again that night in the Sweet Sixteen. I frowned thinking about how that might bring some enjoyment to Shulie's evil friends.

I don't usually check out the horoscope, but with so much going on, I looked at that next. I wished I hadn't.

Today is a troubling day for you. Be cautious in your moves or you could get burned, and in a big way. If there's ever a day where you should consider not leaving your house, this is it. By the weekend, things will be very different, and you'll feel like you're out of the rat race. The question is can you really escape or will you still be a rat.

I did a double take, but that's really what it said, stopping just short of predicting I'd get hit by my train. I was thinking it might be some sort of April Fool's joke, but the other signs' horoscope prognostications seemed normal enough. I was just convincing myself that this zodiac stuff had to be garbage—with a batting average only slightly better than the weather guy on the news—when I heard a violent crash in the living room.

I rushed in to find that Ed had fallen off the table he had been laying on, and eerily, was laying on the floor. I was stunned motionless, not having any experience in what to do if your cat falls off the table like a brick. Then I remembered that Tina, from downstairs, was a nurse. So I ran down the stairs, and banged like hell on the door. Tina answered the door wearing only a long thin tee-shirt. She had no bra on, and though I hate to admit noticing under these circumstances, I could see her large breasts were still in motion from running to the door.

"Seth, what is it?"

"Tina, you're a nurse, aren't you? My cat, Ed, just fell off a table. He's not moving, and I'm freaking out. Would you mind? I really need someone to come tell me what to do."

She started through her door, then looked at herself, and said, "I'll put some clothes on, and be right there."

I got back to the apartment and Ed was still laying there. He had this look of confusion on his little face. I briefly wished that if this was it for old Ed, that I could see his expectant expression one more time, as if I were going to give him a treat or pet him or let him cuddle with me.

Tina bounded through the door, and ran up to Ed and me. She looked at him and felt around on his chest. She looked at me, and touching my arm gently, told me what I suppose I already knew.

She just said, "I'm sorry, Seth."

Ed had moved on to somebody else's apartment in the sky. Tina guessed that he might have suffered a stroke. And then added, maybe to ease my mind, that it had to be too quick for him to have felt any pain. She hugged me, which was nice of her.

I asked what I should do with him now. She said to call the city and they'd send someone. She waited with me while they did. I put Ed in his bed so he'd at least look comfortable, and petted him for the last time. I poured Tina some coffee and told her some Ed stories—like how he'd once fallen in the toilet trying to get a drink; and how he'd sometimes jump in the refrigerator without me noticing, and one time I found him in there an hour later licking the butter—that made us both laugh. Ed was a good guy. I wasn't one of those pet freaks who is always in touch with their pet's emotions or signs their cards, "Love Ed and Me," but he required almost no maintenance, was universally loved by every date I ever brought home, and when the fellas were over, was somehow kind of one of the guys. In spirit, anyway, he'd be having a beer with us. Now that he was gone, I was surprised to realize that I was going to miss him. I hope he didn't resent having to live his life with me.

After Ed was taken away, I thanked Tina and she gave me another hug. I'd like to joke about how silly it was for her to try to ease my pain over the passing of an eight-hundred-year-old cat, but I *was* feeling some pain, and it was a sweet gesture for her to be there for me.

It was ten-thirty by the time I showered, dressed and was ready to head to work.

When I got there, I had twelve voice mail messages—well wishes from vendors, people asking about happy hour, JT asking where the hell I was and then the message from Capricorn that would change my life.

It was from Larry Freedman, and he wanted me to call him right away; that it was urgent. After Larry's message, there were six calls in a row from Shulie. Each sounded more worried than the last, though neither she nor Larry gave me any clue as to what happened. I just knew, goddamnit, that it wasn't good.

I braced myself and called. "Seth, thanks for calling," he began, before stammering out, "Um...we...uh...had some stunning news today. Justice Financial Company, who as you know is our owner, announced the consolidation of their two mutual fund subsidiaries, Capricorn and American National Funds. I'm sorry to tell you this, but they decided to let Gary Merchant go. The combined company will be run out of ANF's office in Denver. So far, no one else has been let go, but who knows what will happen. We're all quite worried, as you can imagine."

I don't give a fuck about you. "Larry, what does that mean to ME?"

"ANF made a subsequent announcement that they have instituted an immediate hiring freeze until they can evaluate the situation. That applies to anyone not on the payroll as of today."

I was near panic. "So, let me get this straight. You're taking back your job offer? I fucking quit my job yesterday, and they already hired my replacement, and you're telling me you can't offer me a job?"

"Seth, I understand your frustration and anger. We're so sorry, obviously this isn't what we had in mind when we offered you the job. I did talk to their HR director about you, and I think I'll be able to get you a severance package, probably two weeks. I'm really sorry about this Seth."

"I can't believe this," I said out loud to myself.

"Seth, again, I'm sorry. Give me a call early next week, and I'll let you know about the package we can offer you."

I hung up and practically ran to JT's office. He was in a meeting in the conference room and I asked if I could interrupt him for a minute. It was an inappropriate request, but he saw the look in my face and made his apologies to the group as he headed to his office to talk to me.

"Seth, what's up? Where were you this morning?"

"Oh, my cat died. I had to wait for the city to come pick him up."

"I'm sorry." Then thinking a second asked, "That's not why you pulled my out of my meeting is it?"

I felt like I had been shelled and shaken to the core. I could barely speak without shaking, but I finally managed to stammer out, "JT, the warning you gave me...turns out to be true...J.F.C. decided to consolidate Capricorn and American National Funds, their two fund subsidiaries into one company. They let Gary Merchant go and due to some fucked-up hiring freeze instituted by A.N.F., I'm S.O.L."

"Seth, I don't know what to say."

"I know what the answer is, but I have to ask. Is there any way..." He gave me a look like it was out of his hands, "I'm sorry, Seth. I told you, I won't do that. I can't."

"I know. I had to ask."

"Listen, though, if there's anything I can do to help you, a reference, a referral, whatever, you let me know."

"I will," I said, feeling helpless, "thanks."

"Seth, you're really good at what you do. You'll land on your feet."

"Thanks, JT. This is all so sudden, but I'm not so sure that I'm up for starting over with someone else, trying to prove myself all over again, just to get to where I am now."

"I better get back to my meeting before the natives get too restless, but I think you just need to take some time to put this in its proper perspective, and decide what you want. This is a shocking development, and maybe you'll find with a week or so off, you'll feel somewhat re-energized. Please keep me in the loop, though. I want to help."

We shook hands, and I headed back to clean out the rest of my office. I could feel him looking at me as I walked away. I hated that feeling of pity he had for me. I decided not to tell any of my co-workers. I figured I'd tell them what happened after I was back on my feet. First, though, I called Shulie.

"Seth, where the hell were you? I've been calling all morning."

"Ed's dead. He died this morning. I had to wait for the city to come pick him up."

"Jesus. I'm sorry. I liked Ed. Are you okay?"

"I've had better days."

Silence, then softly, "So, you've heard?"

"Yeah."

She said more to herself, "This sucks. I can't believe this happened."

This was all my fault, I knew; but she had advised me to ignore the rumors, and since I wanted to lash out at the world, I wasn't quite ready to let her off the hook. "Yeah, it sucks a lot."

"Maybe if I had heard something, or not told you to…" She was, I could tell, struggling to not lose it, "…this wouldn't have happened…I'm sorry…I'm…"

I waited for her to regain her composure.

Since I think she'd noticed I hadn't yet said it wasn't her fault, she continued to try to see how much I blamed her, "Seth, do you hate me for this? Do you think this is my fault?"

As pissed and disillusioned as I was, I couldn't keep it up. It was my decision to make and no one else's.

"No. Of course not. Listen, Shulie, I was warned this could happen but I made the decision anyway. Don't beat yourself up, it was all me. Okay."

"Do you want to talk about it?"

"No."

"All right. So, what time do you want to go to your parent's tonight?"

"What?"

"Passover Sedar. That's tonight you know."

"Oh fuck. I forgot about that. Can my day get any worse?" As much as I dislike all the Jewish holidays, to me it's rampant Jewishness out of control, I really hate Passover. Ever since I started dating mostly non-Jewish girls, my mom has started making an even bigger production out of recalling the story of the flight of the Jews from slavery. Every year, we read the four questions from the Hanukah book, and even though I don't particularly believe in this stuff and everyone knows it bothers me, my mother forces me to read from that fucking book. Every year, I get more annoyed. All in all, I was thinking, it should be a perfect end to a perfect day. Even the desserts suck on Passover. "All right, meet me at my place, at

119

say four, and we'll drive over there together."

On the ride to Skokie, I asked her how the changes would affect her job. She said she had no clue, but that Larry mentioned having another opportunity and if it worked out, that he'd like to bring her along. Aside from that, we barely spoke.

We got to my parent's house and everyone was there, my aunts and uncles, cousins, my brother and his wife and child, my grandmother. I wasn't up for that. I could tell immediately that my parents were in a great mood to have everyone, most notably Shulie, over for the holiday. There was gefilta fish, matzos, little appetizer meatballs, chopped liver, and the damn Mogen David—like regular wine, but with sugar—was flowing. In their joy over Shulie, they had completely forgotten my new job, which was a good thing, because I didn't want to talk about it. Shulie melted easily into the conversations, and though I hid in the company of myself, since that wasn't altogether unusual, no one paid much attention to how distant I had become.

We settled down for dinner, and my dad, as was his custom, made a toast about how wonderful it was that we could all be together. He also welcomed the terrific new addition of Shulie, and then while listing all the good things over the past year, he remembered my new job— "and Sethie, got a great new job as Vice-President of Marketing…"

Not feeling in the spirit of the moment, I pretty much killed the feel good of the whole toast, by interrupting it to clarify, "The offer was rescinded. I'm unemployed. Happy fucking Passover."

Mouths fell open. Everyone who'd been happily arguing politics and talking the usual family stuff before the toast, all looked at me with stunned silence. It was a mixture of wanting to know what happened and silently cursing me for ruining the nice moment. Silence, except for my mom and Shulie who reprimanded me for talking like that.

My dad sat down with a dazed look with his wineglass still in toasting position. He recovered only enough to ask me what had happened. I told them about the consolidation of the companies and the letting go of the president who had stuck his neck out to hire me.

My mom asked, "Well, can't you go to your boss at Wright Star and get your old job back?"

Sure mom, it's that easy. "No."

"Well, maybe if you tried."

"I did try, and they've already hired my replacement."

She couldn't resist, "I knew you shouldn't have left Wright Star."

There was nothing I could say that would've been appropriate in front of the whole family, so I just looked at her, and shook my head, like "yep, you're right, I'm an idiot". The biggest problem with my mom, who seemingly knows everything, is that she's usually frickin right.

My dad stood back up, and with a sheepish smile said, "Well, here's to everything else."

I smiled a little, appreciating the little joke to salvage the moment, and clinked my wine glass with everyone. I clinked with Shulie, who gave me a look of concern. I think of what I might say next.

Passover is the eight days observance commemorating, as I mentioned, the exodus of the Israelites from slavery from Egypt during the reign of Pharaoh Ramses II.

My dad launched into the story of how three thousand years ago, Moses warned the Pharaoh that God would send severe punishments to the people of Egypt if the people of Israel were not freed. The warning, like JT's to me, was ignored and the consequence was that God unleashed ten plagues on the people of Egypt that included blood, lice, locusts, bad weather, frogs (don't ask me), darkness, disease, vermin, Michael Bolton, and the slaying of the first born. The name Passover is derived from instructions given to Moses by God that the Jews should put lamb's blood on their door and God's plagues would 'pass over' their homes and condos.

The Pharaoh's army then chased the Jews through the desert. The Jews, being chased and all, didn't have time to fully bake the dough they had packed for the trip, so they quickly baked the dough in the hot sun into hard crackers called matzos. To commemorate the event, Jews aren't allowed to eat bread products or anything with yeast, during the eight days, which explains the bad desserts. My friends don't even drink beer because of the yeast thing, which I think is odd, because if the Jews had just gotten out of slavery and were running through a hot desert, you bet they would've stopped at a convenience store for some cold Bud Light. Or maybe that's just me. Anyhow, when they got to the Red Sea—and this is the kind of thing that gets me disenchanted with religion because there's no fucking way this actually happened—the waves of the Red Sea were parted long enough for them to escape. Then the waves came crashing back down, and drowned all the bad guys who were trying to get them.

The reading of the Passover book was expected of all the children, and not that all the people in the story didn't allegedly have bigger problems than my pending unemployment, I wasn't in the mood.

The reading of the book goes in ascending order of age, starting with the youngest. Since my little nephew didn't know how to read, my teenage cousin was the youngest and read the first question, "Why do we eat only matzo on Passover?"

He then read the answer about the Jews running away in Egypt, and I made a bitter, inappropriate crack that they were running to a semi-annual sale at Neiman Marcus.

The next youngest was Shulie, who read the second question, "Why do we eat bitter herbs at our Sedar?" She read the answer, which had something to do with reminding us of the bitter and cruel way they were treated in slavery. I wanted to ask if that explained their bitchiness throughout the rest of the year, but resisted.

My brother asked and answered question three, "Why do we dip our foods twice tonight?" I could give you the answer, but I won't because I'm against ever double-dipping.

Then, since my brother's wife, Lauren, was older than I, and I wasn't sure she knew how to read, I was next. I glared at my mom, like 'don't make me do this…do *not* make me do this.' "Sethie, will you read the next question?" She asked this with a smile knowing I'd hate that she'd ask, but that, of course, it was okay to say anything as long as you're smiling.

"That's okay, I don't want to deprive Lauren of this honor."

"Yes, but it's supposed to go in order of age. You're younger." She was still smiling, and speaking very slowly so I would grasp the concept.

I smiled back and said, "I know, but I also don't give a shit."

Shulie kicked me under the table. I was definitely in enemy territory here. The thing is, though, none of this means anything to me, and it should be my choice on my level of participation. I've felt that way for years, but my mother insists on making me more Jewish than I want to be. Especially on a day when my career was in flames and my cat died, I was gonna go down fighting.

"Seth. Everyone else is participating, and you will, too." *Yeah, the moti-*

vation of being like everyone else was gonna work with me.

"No, I'm not. It seems to me that religion is a personal choice. I choose not to participate."

My dad, trying to keep the peace, practically begged, "Seth, can't you just read the question?"

"Can't you just respect my feelings about this? Every year we go through this. You know how I feel about it. To force me to do this after the day I've had today…I'm really not in the mood for this."

"It's tradition. You should respect that."

"Why? Every year we read the same fucking questions about the goddamn matzos, to commemorate a story that sounds like total bullshit to me, and you insist I compromise who I am by reading this crap. If you can't respect that I have my own opinions, then screw this, I just won't come anymore. I hate this holiday, anyway."

I sat there for a minute not knowing what to do next, but it became unbearably uncomfortable, and I just wanted to go somewhere and hide. Besides, any further discussion would just make things worse. So, I got up to leave the table, not so much in a huff, as just trying to disappear quietly. My parent's house has a great room, so the table and the couch and TV were in the same room as the dining room table. Everyone watched as I went to lay on the couch, just as my sister-in-law read the fourth question, "Why do we lean on a pillow tonight?"

They all laughed at me for the irony in that question, adding insult to insult. I wasn't amused.

She went on to answer that we "lean on the pillow to be comfortable and to remind us that once we were slaves, but now we're free." Okay, it's a little bit of an overstatement to compare myself to the plight of slaves, but, as I stewed on the couch, I convinced myself that I still wasn't free to have my own views on religion.

As they progressed to dinner, I went in the kitchen to get some matzo ball soup, which my mom does a killer job with. Shulie was apparently intent on ignoring me the rest of dinner, adding to my feelings of being an outcast. And my parents, if they could've called the Cohenbergs to inquire about a trade, certainly would have. Probably would've thrown in some cash, too.

I wasn't hungry after the soup, but with the religious stuff safely out of the way, I quietly returned to my seat. I figured I should at least be mature enough to do that. I sat there quietly picking at my beef brisket until dinner ended.

After everyone got up from dinner, Shulie finally decided to speak to me, but only to say, "I want to go home. I know you've had a bad day, but I don't want to be with you right now. Make some excuse for me, and let's get out of here."

Not exactly wanting to stick around myself, I told my mom that she wasn't feeling well, which, because illness is a favorite topic, led to a hundred questions from everyone. I was able to keep the story straight and we made it out the door.

On the driveway, I caught up to her to find she was crying in the cold night. "Please drive me home."

"Shulie, listen…"

"No, what you did in front of your family was inexcusable. I was humiliated, and I don't want to be with you tonight. And I don't think tomorrow's a good idea either. I want you to drive me home now or call me a cab." She could barely get the words out.

"Okay, okay. I'll drive you home."

We drove in silence to her parent's house in Highland Park. When she opened the door, it was obvious I shouldn't try to kiss her. I just said I was sorry, but she didn't even look back at me as she walked away.

I drove back to the city, wondering if there was any possible way the whole day had been a big April Fool's joke. When I got home and turned on my answering machine to hear my mother crying and saying that I was anti-Semitic and needed help, I knew for sure that the only thing that was a joke was the state of my life.

19

On that Friday—Passover to some, Good Friday to others, Piece of Shit Friday to me—both Shulie and I had the day off of work…actually I did indefinitely. I spent most of the day calling her house without a reply. I finally called at around three and left a message that I was driving out there and needed to talk to her.

On the way, I called my mom and dad and apologized for the previous night. My mom answered. She was clearly tired and drained, and it sounded as if she had just spent a sleepless night wondering where she went wrong with me. There was an edge to her tone which didn't soften until I mentioned I was on my way to see if I couldn't make things right with Shulie.

She took a moment, and then said something she'd obviously given a lot of thought to, "Seth, I had grandparents who I loved dearly, who were persecuted just because they were Jewish. It makes the things you said hurtful and cuts to my heart. They were good, kind, giving people. I try to respect your views, and as a matter of fact, I can honestly say that I shared some of them when I was a girl and sometimes even now. But I regret that I wasn't more knowledgeable and better able to teach my children and instill in them a respect for what they are and where they came from."

There was so much there I wanted to respond to that I couldn't say anything. I finally just said, "Mom….." and then took a very long time to gather my thoughts as I drove. "Listen, the way I think is just me. It's not your fault and you have nothing to regret." I paused and she waited. I could tell she was really listening to me, and that we were finally being honest with each other. I didn't want to blow it. "Also, I mean no disrespect to any of the older generations who suffered through atrocities large and small. I'm sure I'd think differently about things if I had suffered persecution. But, mom, not that I'm an expert or anything, but I have a lot of friends, and a whole lot of ex-girlfriends, who aren't Jewish, so I can sort of see things from different perspectives. Personally, I think that when I poke fun at myself and my culture and don't hide in the protective comfort of Jewish life, any potential bigotry or mistrust goes away. I can still be Jewish if I want to be, but I won't let that define me. So, when I'm talking to my friends, I'm not the Jew, I'm their friend who happens to be Jewish. I really think there's a lesson there, not just for Jewish people, but for all cultures. The more people get together and are open and honest with each other, the less fear there is and the less likely people are to be enemies. You know? I think fear and isolation leads to more fear and isolation. You know what, I don't expect you to understand, but I feel strongly about that."

She took it all in, which was something kind of new for her and I felt closer to her than I ever had. "Seth dear, it takes a lifetime to come to terms with who and what we are and want to be. And over the years, our ideas tend to change and grow. You don't know enough to understand."

"Why don't we sit down one night and you tell me all about your grandparents, okay."

"Seth, let's do that. There's a lot that they went through that you should know."

"Let's plan on it. Hey, can you put on dad?"

"Seth…"

"Yeah?"

"I know you have a thoughtful, loving, caring, giving, and searching heart. And your mother couldn't ask for more."

I was feeling like an emotional bulls-eye with too many arrows having hit me right in the chest. I felt nowhere near whole, but it had helped close at least one large wound. "Mom, thanks for saying that. I appreciate everything you've done for me more than I can say. And again, I'm sorry for last night. It was a really bad day or I wouldn't have lost it like I did."

My dad got on and he also accepted my apology. In the end, the combination of their worrying about me, and the fact that I was on my way to patch things up with Shulie, won out.

Despite the holidays, or maybe because of them, traffic was horrible. There was a light snow and it took an hour and a half to get to her house. I called her when I got on her block and left a message to meet me outside. I waited and she didn't show, so I got out of my car and rang the doorbell. Her mother answered, and said Shulie wasn't home, but she wasn't a good liar and I begged and pleaded with her to tell Shulie I was down stairs waiting for her. Since I think she knew it was the only way I was going to leave before her company arrived, she finally agreed to see what she could do. Five minutes later, Shulie met me at the door.

"Hi. Can we talk?" I asked. A snowflake had landed just below my eye, which, combined with the emotional roller coaster I'd been on, made it feel like I was crying. I was feeling like a shell of myself anyway and the cold wind blew right through me.

She held onto the door, as if for protection, and said, "I don't think I'm ready for that."

"Please, you can't just not ever talk to me." Her mom had been standing there watching over her, and Shulie looked at her, as if it was okay, and her mom reluctantly walked away.

Since she didn't offer, or even say anything, I pleaded, "Can I come in, I'm cold?"

She opened the door, and I walked in. I took off my coat, rubbed my hands for circulation, and followed her to their living room.

She looked strung out, like she had been crying instead of sleeping the night before. She didn't offer to take my coat, so I put it on the side of the chair I sat in.

I was still shaking from the cold when I sat down, wiped the snowflake tear from my face, and told her, "Shulie, I'm sorry. I really am. I called my parents and apologized to them, too."

She didn't say anything, so I kept going.

"Obviously I was having a bad day, you know. The Passover thing is annoying to me every year, but I've never blown up like that. I just kind of boiled over. How many people lose two jobs—one of them their dream job—and their cat in the same day? That wasn't really me. I'm normally not a bitter person, but yesterday was so difficult for me. Here I was on the doorstep of all my dreams, and the door gets slammed in my face. It's like, 'you thought you weren't a loser anymore, but jokes on you, bud, you still are.' You can understand that, can't you? Please."

She seemed physically unable to speak. She finally whispered, "You're not a loser, and you shouldn't ever think that. I understand why you blew up, but..."

She didn't seem to have the words to continue, so to fill the silence, I said, "And I happen to think religion, and how much I choose to participate, is my choice. Just like no one can tell me how to vote or what to eat. No one seems to agree with me on that, but I think it's worth standing up for."

She didn't appear to hear anything I had just said, which at that moment wasn't a bad thing since I'm not sure where I was going with that anyway. But then, "Seth, I don't think you and I are going to work."

What? I understood that she was mad at my behavior the previous night, but I wasn't expecting that. It was like a punch in the stomach. "What are you saying?"

It seemed to be too painful to talk about, so rather than repeat it, she just whispered, "You heard me."

"Shulie, I…" Not prepared for that at all, I just stopped and put my head in my hands to think. I thought about meeting her at Four Farthings, our first date at Sedgewick's, hearing her story about Jack, the ass, at River's. I remembered my birthday weekend and going to a Bulls game together. I remembered dancing around her office when I got offered my dream job at her company. I thought about the first time we made love in front of the fire in my apartment. Suddenly, our fire was gone.

Then, because I had to say something, "I don't know what to say, Shulie, I just had a really bad day and made some inappropriate comments, and you're going to throw away what we have for that?"

"Seth, it's not just that."

"Explain it to me."

"You and I are great together. I've never connected with anyone in my life like I did with you. But almost every time you're with a crowd of Jewish people, you practically break out in hives, you literally can't deal with it. For our sake, I want to ignore that, to pretend it's not like that, but I can't. These are my friends and my family and the kind of people we'd be hanging out with the rest of our lives. If we were together…"

She couldn't finish. I got up to try to hug her, but she pushed me away. "Shulie, I love you. Don't do this. We can work it out. With everything else going on, I don't think I can handle this, too."

"I thought about that. This seems really cruel, I know. I hope you'll understand someday. But, I learned something from both you and Jack. It's that I shouldn't settle for less than what I want. Exactly, what I want. I'm worth it."

I remembered the Marco story about that being the last time she got exactly what she wanted, and realized our relationship had come full circle. Then I had another thought, and even though I knew the answer, I had to ask. "So, what are you saying? *You're breaking up with me because I'm not Jewish enough for you?*"

My tone was kind of accusatory, and I could tell she was debating whether to admit it was true. Finally, she said, "Yes, I guess I am."

It was so comical, yet so completely unfunny, that it broke my heart. I sat there for probably two minutes staring out the window at the snow. It was my last chance to salvage the life I had. I started slowly and then began to build up steam.

"I know," I said softly, "that my inability to want to fit in with *the crowd, whatever the crowd happens to be,* hasn't been rewarding behavior for me. I'm not where I should be in my career, and my relationships all end up in some wreckage of regret. I don't know why I am this way, but I am. The thing is, I realize that and I'm trying to change. I met you and I realized, here's this wonderful girl, and we could have an amazing life together if I could just get past myself." I said the last four words slowly to emphasize each one. "I just need to change, to be more accepting of people, but you know, it takes time. This is new for me, and I think I can do it…I think I can change for you…because I've decided you are worth it."

I had given my summation, and it went to the jury to decide my fate. If she deliberated, it wasn't for long.

She looked right at me, wanting, I think, for me to understand. She spoke quickly and just above a whisper, fighting to get the words out. "Seth, I don't think you can. I don't think people can change who they are. I tried to change, too. I recognize you have these issues and I tried to be more accepting of that. I just think we both are who we are. No matter how much we'd like to be different, no matter how much incentive we have to be different, we can't change who we are. I'm sorry, Seth. I'd like to be there for you…I'd like there to be a future for us…this is fucking killing me…I love you…but I can't do it."

And she got up and ran away. I heard her steps as she ran up the stairs. I don't know how long I sat there, but long enough to be completely lost. At some point, her mom put her hand gently on my shoulder, and I realized I was still in their living room. Her look seemed to be of concern for me and I nodded to her that I appreciated her not adding to my woes. I got my coat, put it on and slowly started for the door. But then I thought of something and stopped to take off the ring Shulie had given me for my birthday—which seemed like a very long time ago. I looked at the inscription, and then set it on the mantle in front of a smiling picture of her. In a series of painful little emotional breakdowns, I had another one. Then I stepped out into the cold night. To what else I was stepping into, I had no idea.

20

Even though I've lived in Chicago my whole life, in my mind when it's April it should be springtime. Birds should be chirping, bulbs should be blooming, the breeze should feel warm, and people should be falling in love. In Chicago, a tough town, we apparently have no use for spring and winter hangs tough until at least May. I tried to bury myself in my coat as I walked down their icy driveway to my car. Night had descended both literally and figuratively. I had way too many questions to try to deal with, so I let my mind, instead, just focus on my surroundings. I drove through Highland Park, and out of a life that, by all indications, I wouldn't ever allow myself to have. I drove through streets of expensive, presumably happy homes. It was the second night of Passover, and all those people who happily accepted their lives for what they were supposed to be, were laughing and arguing and eating in the warmth of their wives and mothers and fathers and brothers and sisters. As I turned right onto Clavey Road, and left onto the Edens Expressway to head south to the city, I seemed to be drifting further out of my body. Everything was becoming surreal.

Leaving Highland Park, I didn't see road signs or bridges or white lines, but images of smiling families and groups of people and the padlocked doors to Capricorn and Wright Star. While Jewish families were celebrating Passover, I realized that other families were gathering to observe Good Friday and to prepare for Easter Sunday. I found myself thinking I wasn't a part of either group; in fact, of any group.

As I drove down the highway, I wondered how many of the other drivers were lost souls, or if they were on their way to join their friends and families. Even though I've driven that highway my whole life, all of the familiar sites seemed to look different and faraway, like I was suddenly a stranger in my hometown. I drove past Skokie, and the house and the mall and the high school where I grew up, and I had the very uneasy feeling of being close to my teenage years, but a million miles away from my family, my friends, and, despite how little time had passed, to Shulie and my former career. In fact, I was feeling like a stranger to my own life. I'd always, at least, had a direction to head in. Now, my car and my body were taking up space, but I had nowhere to go.

I managed to make it to my street and my apartment building. I saw Joe briefly as he entered his apartment across the hall and wasn't entirely amused at the realization that he now had far more going for him than I. I absently opened the door to my apartment and saw all my stuff, but not a thing to make me feel like I was home. I hadn't eaten anything all day, and still didn't feel like it, but in the dark of my apartment, I poured myself a bowl of cereal and slouched over it at my kitchen table. I took a few bites, but it wasn't doing it for me. I grabbed a bottle of Absolut Vodka from my freezer, but there wasn't enough left for a drink. So I brewed a pot of coffee, made a fire and curled up in a blanket to drink a big cup with the rest of the Bailey's I had. I watched the dance of the fire and sat there as close to thoughtless and hopeless as you can be.

I don't know for how long I sat there watching the flames of my useless life or the smoke of my failed dreams, but I must have drifted off. When I got up to see what time it was, the clock in my room illuminated the numbers 3:15. I was just about to get in my bed, when, from out of the blue night, on a night illuminated by a blue moon, a thought hit me.

It took a minute to come into focus, but it was there. Like hundreds of impossibly random puzzle pieces that had somehow come together, it felt like a gift.

Why should I change? Seriously, everyone's different, right? Everyone's got something unique to offer the world. If I constantly felt like I was on stage in a role I wasn't comfortable with, I needed to find a new play. If I was going to be a star, I needed to find the night sky.

It was three-fifteen in the morning, and I actually smiled to myself. I put on my robe, turned on all the lights, and grabbed a pad of paper. I had to figure out what I was good at and what direction to head in, and I was going to do it before the sun came up.

I split a piece of paper into two vertical sections: what I'm good at, and what I'm not. On the left side, I started with what I considered my positive points. I wrote the words *not the same as everyone else.* Then the words *insight and intuition.* Than the word *writing.* Then *some people think I'm funny.*

Then *passionate when I'm on the right track*. Then I circled the word *freedom*. That wasn't a strength yet, but it sure could be.

An idea had already begun to formulate, so rather than bothering with listing all my negatives on the right side of the paper, I just wrote *everything else*.

I was looking at the answer. It was right there staring back at me, beckoning me to go with it. What I needed to do was work on my own, to answer to no one, to rely on only my thoughts and insights and ideas. To be my own person. To take pride in being the unique person I thought I was. *To be me!* At 4:03 on the morning of April 3rd, I decided that Seth Gold was going to become a writer. I was going to write a book—a book with my name and my thoughts and my legacy that no one could take away from me.

I remembered Bruce Spingsteen's *1985 Born in the USA* tour, when he did one of those talking raps before the song *Racing in the Street*. With a sad, lonesome backdrop of music as Bruce walked to the front of the stage, mike in his hand, and sat down on a row of speakers. It was so quiet you could hear every breath and holler of Bruuuuuuce from way back in the crowd. He started into this rap about a failed love—not unlike Shulie and me—where it started off so easy and so good until each other's faults got to be too much, and the girl ended up leaving. It was what he said next, though, that stuck with me. I wished I remembered it exactly, but it was something like, "And I don't know if people expect too much of each other—sometimes I think maybe they do. But to have just one thing, you know—one thing in your whole life that you do, that you do good, that you feel proud of—that's not too much for anybody to ask." It felt like I had remembered that all these years later for a reason. Writing was what I was good at, what I was proud of, what I wanted to do. And, given recent events, if that was all I was good at, then I hoped Bruce was right about it not being too much to ask. Maybe people spent too much time worrying about their weaknesses, rather than taking advantage of the things they did really well.

I looked around my apartment and it all of a sudden felt too small, too confining, too uninspiring for the thoughts I was having. With picture-perfect clarity, it dawned on me that as much as I love the city of Chicago, I needed to get away, to start over. I needed to go to a place where I wasn't

Jewish or not. Where I wasn't unemployed or a former aspiring business-man. Where I could just be a person, and a writer. Where I could go racing in the street. I wanted to go somewhere where creativity could be sparked and freedom would take me for a ride. And I wanted to be where I've always done my best work, by myself.

The thought of it was staggering. I was convincing myself, I realized unexpectedly, that I could go anywhere in the world. Anywhere I wanted to go. I had about $5,000 in my various mutual funds. I also had maybe two weeks of salary coming from Capricorn, and probably 35,000 frequent flyer miles. I went to find my last statement from American Airlines and realized that was enough to go to the Caribbean. The Caribbean! After enduring another Chicago winter, it sounded insanely perfect.

But, where? It probably didn't even matter. But then, for not much more reason than that I loved grooving to the rhythms of reggae music and had always been partial to Red Stripe beer, I wrote on my pad of paper Bob Marley's home country, *JAMAICA!* I closed my eyes and tried to imag-ine it. The warmth and the breeze and the music washed over me like I was there. I was so pumped, I felt like running to Florida and swimming to Jamaica.

It was a quarter to five in the morning. I called American Airlines and when they said I could get a flight, using my miles, at eight a.m., I practically screamed yes.

What the hell did I just do?

My heart started beating faster as I thought about what else I needed to do. My lease was up at the end of April, so I wrote Joe a check for the next month, and a note saying I wasn't going to renew. If he wanted to lease it furnished with my stuff, he could. I'd call him for where to send my security deposit. I put it in an envelope and wrote JOE on it.

Then I wrote a note to Bob and Javy saying I'd leave a key under their mat and they could come and take my TV and stereo and whatever else they wanted. If they didn't want it, I gave them my brother's phone number and asked that they call him to take whatever he wanted. Oh, and that I was going to Jamaica to write a book, and that'd I call when I was famous. I wished them good luck with everything, signed it Goldie, and put that in an envelope with their names on it.

I even wrote Tina a note thanking her for helping me with Ed, and that I wished I would've had a chance to know her and Roxanne better. I ran to all of their apartments and taped their envelopes to their doors. I was practically jumping out of my skin as I ran from apartment to apartment at dawn taping envelopes to people's doors.

Incredibly, it took thirty-three years to accumulate a life's worth of stuff, and I gave it all up or away in under five minutes. My heart was pounding. I'm not sure my brain was still functioning.

In a small duffel bag, I threw a bathing suit, two pairs of shorts, some tee-shirts, some underwear, no socks, my bathroom stuff and, showing my survival instincts, a bottle opener. I also laid out shorts, sandals, shades and the white Abercrombie button-down shirt I'd worn on my first date with Shulie, to wear on the flight. I put my camera, portable CD player, and a CD case with my twelve favorite disks in a camera case, thus answering the question what music I would take if stranded on an island. And I was going to need my laptop to write my book, so I grabbed the case it was in. I also realized I'd need my birth certificate, and after briefly panicking, finally found that. I put the duffel bag, camera case, and laptop bag near the front door. I showered and shaved and got dressed, and it was six a.m. Delirium had moved in, kicked out everything else, and was now giving the orders.

The sun was coming up not just in Chicago, but it felt like in my life. I stood there a minute looking around my apartment at the life I was leaving, taking some mental photographs of the place that had been my home for so long. So much had happened there, much of it really good, but it hadn't led anywhere. I wasn't who I wanted to be. I was nearly overwhelmed with emotion. I took a moment to say a fond and sad goodbye to Ed, and then quickly closed the door to my old life.

As I drove my '94 Saab Convertible through the streets of the city, it felt like a jailbreak. In the early morning before the sun, I was leaving before anyone would realize I was gone. I cranked Ziggy Marley's *Higher Vibrations* as I hit the highway and hit the gas. For once, there was very little traffic and I arrived at the airport in no time. My buddy Craig had always loved my Saab. I left him a message that if he wanted to come to O'Hare to economy parking lot E, row B4, he could have my car. I told him I'd leave it unlocked, and that the he could pop the trunk and the keys would be there under the spare tire. I told him the sooner the better so the parking wouldn't cost him so much, smiling at the thought that it would be like Craig to bitch about the cost of parking even as I was giving him my car.

With other early morning travelers, I boarded the airport train from long term parking to the terminal. As usual I played the game of wondering where were they all headed. It could be anywhere for any reason, and it was one of my favorite things about going to the airport. Business meetings, back to school, family vacations? Maybe off to see a loved one for a weekend in New York or somewhere to say goodbye to a dying relative? People could be headed for an adventure in South America or French Poylnesia. Couples could be on their way to honeymoon in Maui, or to pick up an adopted baby in the Orient. Foursomes could be off for a golf trip in the Carolinas or to horse around in Vegas. The possibilities were unlimited, and they all felt good. Forty-five minutes later I would be boarding a plane to Jamaica, I thought to myself, and suddenly my possibilities were also unlimited.

21

O'hare International Airport was a runway even inside the terminal. The salesman who had tried to grab as much sleep as possible before their early morning flights were now in nearly full run to try to catch their respective flights. No one, though, was going faster than I. Not that I particularly had to rush to get my plane, but almost as if I had no control over my body or my actions, my adrenaline kept pushing me with nearly reckless abandon towards my flight. Toward my flight from everything I'd ever known.

I hustled by the newsstand and remember thinking the *Chicago Tribune* and the *Wall Street Journal* would soon seem completely foreign, and completely useless to me. As I walked through the business travelers going in every direction, I became conscious of the fact I was wearing shorts, while they were all in the work uniforms. I felt different than them already and better for it, though I also thought my legs looked very white in my shorts. That was gonna change. I looked up from my sandles and white legs and saw the sign for my gate. And there she was standing right under the sign.

I couldn't be completely sure from where I was, but it was Shulie. She was wearing a black leather jacket, and seemed to be looking around expectantly. *She definitely looked like Shulie!* Oh my God. Had she come to see me? To stop me from leaving? How the hell did she know? Could she have figured it out?

Since 3:15 that morning, when I started making the fully-thought-out, enormously rational decision to give away all my stuff and move by myself to a remote island where I would have no career, I don't think I had thought once about Shulie. But just about one hundred yards in front of me, there she was, waiting for me in front of the gate. What was she holding…a bottle of Mogen David? It would be just like Shulie to bring a funny peace offering like that. Who was that with her? Was that her blond friend, Jennifer, who had been with Shulie the night we met at Four Farthings? Jeez, I hadn't seen or heard about her since that night.

But they appeared to be together. Did Shulie drag her out of bed and to the airport to show me that she had realized I was right? That it wasn't me who needed to be more Jewish, but she who had to be less? That there were lessons to be learned by hanging around with people of other faiths and backgrounds? That to prove it she was going to start hanging around with Jennifer. I got kind of excited. Partly because Jennifer was a babe, but more so that I could really get behind this new and improved Shulie. Damnit, I was right. She had come around. I had shown her the light. I am unique! I am admired! YES! How did I look? Oh fuck it. Whatever I looked like would be fine after she rushed to the airport at the crack of dawn to stop me from leaving and to save our relationship. I started to run towards her. This would be a great story some day. Maybe I could buy Shulie a ticket and we could take a vacation in Jamaica. Or, what the hell, I could buy tickets for both of them and we could all go. I ran to tell them the good news.

I was nearly to the gate, and her back was turned. Jennifer, the blond, was no longer in sight. I debated how I should approach Shulie for maximum affect. Be overly confident (because this had to be good, right?) and give her a hug from behind. Or play it coy and innocent and walk around her and say a subdued hello. See what she had to say and act surprised. I chose the more subtle approach and it turned out to be the right move.

Mostly because it wasn't her. It wasn't even close. I mean, she was Jewish all right and I'm sure Larry Freedman would have known her…and that she was a really good person…but it wasn't Shulie. Just some Jewish girl with dark, curly hair. What are the odds? And, Jennifer, who, now that I think of it, had never done me any damn good, wasn't there either. That settled it, no free ticket to Jamaica for her.

I found a seat and sat down. I guess it was then that I realized that I hadn't slept at all. Between the lack of sleep and the surreal euphoria of the insane decision I had made, maybe my mind had been playing tricks on me. I buried my head in my hands a moment to try to gather myself. And that's when it hit me that it must have been some sort of sign.

SHULIE. She had meant so much to my life. It was she who showed me a door to happiness. She had changed everything. She had given me an outlet for the love and compassion I had stored up inside me. She had given me a tangible sense of hope, to say nothing of my parents. Sure, she was hurting now, but if I could convince myself we were right for each other, why couldn't I convince her in time?

I was at the gate and could see the board that said Montego Bay. I pulled out my cell phone and saw Shulie's number stored in the memory. First class had just been called to board. What should I do? What would you do? What was real? I briefly considered asking the Jewish girl if she thought Shulie would take me back.

I ended up near the desk and the attendant asked if she could help me. I didn't think she could without explaining the whole damn story, so I just gave her my driver's license and e-ticket information and she gave me a boarding pass. The rows in front of me were being called to board.

I looked at my phone and the name Shulie. SHULIE. If I could just change who I was. If I could just accept who I was supposed to be. If I could just believe that was the right thing to do.

My row was called. Excited and loud vacationers moved toward the door. They were bubbly, all pumped up to be going to Jamaica, and then they were gone. Suddenly the terminal had become quiet and still. I was left outside the gate with Shulie's phone number staring at me in one hand, and my ticket in the other. The ticket said the passenger was Seth Gold. I had an opportunity to find out for sure who that was. To discover my strengths. To believe in myself.

In between two blue moons, I thought I had held the tickets to my happiness. But now, maybe, finally, I was holding the right ticket. I gave it to the attendant and got on board. Ten minues later the plane pulled away. I was on my way to Jamaica.

Book II

Moon Song

"And I fucked up so many times in my life, I want to get it right this time"

Frank Orrall

22

The pilot had welcomed us, the stewardess had insisted we all listen to whatever the hell she was saying, the fasten-seat belt indicator was on, all electronic devices were off and all seats were in their full upright position. There I was sitting on a plane, convincing myself it couldn't possibly be real.

We had taken flight a few moments earlier and had begun to soar over and away from the city of Chicago.

As the plane lifted off through the clouds of my old life and had found the blue sky of my new, I was hoping my spirits would soar with the plane, but, instead, found mostly compelling points in favor of this being just a dream. A flight of fancy, if you will, though I think I speak for all of me when I say I'm not sure why you would. For one, I had to consider the fact that in the middle of the darkest night of my life, in the space of maybe an hour, I had made plans to toss aside my entire life as I had known it—my friends, family, career, the city I loved, the freedom of the greatest country in the world, the opportunity to maybe try again for Shulie, and, oh my God, I just realized, my softball team. In an hour! That's less time than it normally takes me to decide what to wear.

Plus, here I was, very unemployed and majorly dumped, yet my over-whelming feeling was one of barely restrained jubilation. Like the loser dude who had been renting most of the space in my body just hours earlier no longer existed. It didn't seem possible.

Finally, not to be ignored was the fact that not only had I decided to move from my hometown, but also out of the country—to go live on an island in the Caribbean—like that would really be happening to me. Ya, hi, nice to meet you, I'm Jimmy fucking Buffet, going to find Margaritaville. Who hasn't had that fantasy at one time or another, but the key thing is that no one actually *does* it.

Frankly, I was starting to get a little bummed. Not to mention concerned about the appropriate ettiquette when you've discovered you're not really on a plane. At what point do you mention that to the stewardess? And is it appropriate to order a drink first?

On the other hand, I looked around and took in fellow passengers in orange beach wear, or powder-blue tee-shirts that just said, "HAWAII, or brown sandals and black socks, or neon pink baseball hats with Mickey Mouse on them or rose-colored sunglasses bought at a gas station, and tried to recall if I had ever dreamt in color, or black and white trash, before. Either way, if it was a dream, I needed to have a talk with the Dreamworks people about casting and wardrobe. And, speaking of which, if this really was a dream, I'm gonna have to be honest with you here. If this really was a dream, as strange as it may sound, I'd have probably been lost in some Elizabethan-era fantasy. I know that sounds weird, right, but there's something about sipping Chambord and Champagne, nestled in first class between Elizabeth Hurley and Elizabeth Shue, baby, planning a hot tub or nude beach to meet up in later for tropical drinks that seems somehow better than real life.

But since none of my fellow passengers looked remotely Elizabethan, I started to convince myself it couldn't be a dream. But what really clinched it for me was that the gentleman I was sitting next to had life-long dreadlocks and a long salt and pepper beard, and if I'm not mistaken, it's not possible to smell like ganja in a dream. This meant that my flight—literally and figuratively—had to be real, which at the moment was a huge relief, and I was very proud of myself for working through it like that.

Seeing Chicago and Lake Michigan fade into the distance, and now feeling sure that the plane was, in fact, really headed for Jamaica, my mind continued to play tricks on me. I wanted to ponder nothing more than sunsets and rum drinks in coconuts, but I kept having to set my euphoria aside and ask myself, "Did I *really* want to do this?"

To you, the reader, you're like, get over it dude. But to me, it was a big question. I mean, there's a fairly significant difference between taking a few weeks off to re-energize myself and actually moving to Jamaica. Sure, it sounded cool in theory, but I still had something to offer potential employers, and I could still have made a good living, and I could still have met somebody else (or decided to try again with Shulie), and I could still have lived the life that, up until about four hours earlier, I had expected of myself. And, I had to consider the fact that I was going to a foreign culture, to live among strangers, and that I had no idea what the living conditions were like, what the political situation was like, what the attitudes toward Americans were like, even what the currency was. Would you do it?

Plus, the centerpiece of my new life was writing a book for which I had no hint of a story in mind. And getting it represented, published and sold, which can't be a walk in the park for someone who's never published dick. I had no idea, come to think of it, where I'd even stay. Basically, it became clear to me that I had mostly decided to go to Jamaica because I really liked Bob Marley's *Legend* CD. So I had that going for me—a greatest hits album, no less. I almost laughed out loud at what a schmuck I was.

I thought about the fact that I already had a return flight booked at the end of the month. When American Airlines asked when I'd be returning, I booked an April 30th return flight just because I guessed that Jamaican custom's authorities might not let me enter the country without a scheduled return flight home, either as a matter of public policy or as a personal character judgement. And, aside from that, I figured it'd be a good opportunity to clear out my apartment before my lease ended.

In other words, there was no reason I couldn't make it a vacation rather than a move. I could've picked up the phone in the seat in front of me at that very moment and told Joe, my old landlord, not to lease my place and Bob and Javy, my buddies from next door who I had allowed to take whatever they wanted from my apartment, to get their grubby hands off my stereo. I could've gone back at the end of the month to the lost and found of my old life for a job, a girlfriend and renewed motivation.

The thing is, I wasn't finding that plan appealing. In fact, as I thought about it, I found it less and less so. Being my overly objective self, I didn't feel that the goals of business could motivate me any longer. There was too much bureaucracy and too little vision. Gary Merchant, who had offered me my dream job before getting fired from his, had tried to be visionary, and look what the bureaucracy did to him. There'd always be someone over me trashing my ideas or taking credit for them. There'd always be too much insanity in the legal department, inability in the IT department, and instability overall. And besides, what was I accomplishing or adding to the world? It's not like if I wasn't around, no one would be able to find a mutual fund—there'd still be twelve *thousand* of them, for chrissakes. And if Wright

Star's customers were told they'd never get a phone call or mailing from Wright Star again, I think they'd have a big fucking party. And not invite me. Plus, for good or bad, I'm me. There are so few things that truly appeal to me that I get fanatical and obsessive about the things that do. I need to be passionate about what I'm doing. I had that for a while in my career, but it was gone, and I had a feeling, gone forever. I needed a better goal. To me, writing a book, doing what I loved doing, living life on my own terms and getting at least a small bit of immortality was a better goal.

As the captain turned off the fasten seat belt indicator, I moved my seat back and let myself drift into a dream of becoming a famous writer. In my daydream, I had fans, if not critics, who loved me. I was wanted on the talk show circuit. I flirted with Katie Courac, joked with David Letterman, and blew off Oprah. I no longer had to answer to any employer or make myself care about quarter-end profits. I could travel around the world being who *I* wanted to be. If I wanted to write about neighborhoods or people in Boston or London or Provence or New York City, I'd just set my next book there.

Twenty years from now, someone could walk into a garage sale in Chicago and pick *my* book out of literally four or five others in a shoebox and say, "You want how much for that Seth Gold?! A quarter? I'll give you a dime, ya crook, and you're lucky to get that." In twenty years, dimes will be worth so little you won't be able to stop on them anymore, but at least, I, Seth Gold, would have a place in history.

Hell, I'd be an "artist," in a sense, though not in the sense I'd ever call myself that. I'd be someone who was known for creating something all his own. I'd be doing what I was good at. Writing my own book would mean that I became the person I wanted to be.

I was reveling in my little fantasy and a smile must have come over my face. I sensed, before I saw, that Rasta Man was looking my way.

He kept his glance, as if he looked hard enough, he could figure out what was up with the freaky white guy. It became apparent I should say something, so I mumbled, "I was just having kind of a good dream," certain I sounded like an idiot.

"Yes sir, I can see you were in a dream, man," he said with an easygoing, comfortable smile and a funky dialect that sounded like, *Yeh suh, me a see ya inna dream, mon.*

"My name's Seth," I said.

"Nice to meet ya, Seth, call me Alfred." I reached over and shook his hand.

"It's nice to meet you, too, Alfred." Probably a dumb question, I thought to myself, but, "You live in Jamaica?"

"Yeah, mon." I'd guessed he was in his fifties, and he spoke very slowly—probably for my benefit—and with a heavy accent and a dialect that seemed to be all his own. He had a thoughful, philosophical aura about him, as if that was what was expected of him. My intuition told me he might have some sort of leadership or mentoring role in his life. "I come from the hills outside Negril, in an agricultural area, if you catch my drift," he said with a sly smile in his burnt-out eyes. *Me a cum ya da hills outta Negril. Inna agriculcha groun, if ya catchin me drift.* "Where are you going?" *Weh ya go?*

I smiled to let him know I was keeping up so far. "I don't know. I could go anywhere."

"You have friends in Jamaica?" *Ya av frens in Jamehka, mon?*

"No actually, not one. Really, I decided at four o'clock this morning that I'd had it with my life, and that I wanted to live on an island and write a book." Don't think I didn't recognize how stupid that sounded saying it out loud.

"You're a writer then?"

"Umm…well…no…not really." I was building quite a case for myself.

"Ahhhh…you're going to be!" *Ahhhh…ya gaan be!* He said it as if it had life-affirming significance, so I wasn't sure if I was being dissed.

"Yeah." My voice became the equivalent of an embarrassed shrug, as if waiting to get scolded for being so irresponsible.

"*Me se-en*," he declared. "*Whad a ting! Yah disgruntled wid da direction yah a gwan, mon…say nuff arreddi…an ya tink ta see weh anodda path might tek ya, mon…*"

I was digging the way he said stuff, and grateful he continued to speak deliberately enough to keep up with most of it. More than that, he was making what I was doing sound not so completely ill-conceived.

"Yeah, Alfred, I guess that's pretty much it. I decided I did need another path to head down."

A smile formed on his face, creasing his dark skin like the rows in a garden ready for planting. He nodded his head for quite a while and said,

"Dat irea, mon. Dat awrite. No problem." Irea, I knew, meant cool or all right or something along those lines. He seemed to have genuine admiration for my dumbass move. *"Yah suh,"* he concluded, *"cum to Jamehka an cool out yu ed."*

It's cool how you can have everything in common with some people and not relate with them as much as you can with a total stranger from a different world. It seemed like a lesson for people who would only be friends with only a certain kind of person, but enough about my friends and relatives in Chicago. I also liked how cool everything he said sounded. I may be a dumbass, but coming to Jamaica to cool out my head sounded good—or *irea*—to me. Smiling though the apprehension I was feeling, I just said, "Thanks, you know, I hope so." Then, laughing, I added, "My ed needs cooling out."

He laughed with me and asked if I had someplace to stay.

"Yeah, I guess so. It's wild for me to think about this, you know, but I could go in any direction the land goes." Jesus, did I just say that out loud? I mean, I wasn't entirely sure what he was asking because of the funky dialect, and was trying to answer in a broad enough way to cover any possible meaning of his question, but oh man, I could go in any direction the land goes? Stuff like that must be where the term "deep shit" comes from. Trying to gain back some credibility with myself, I said, "I think I'd like to stay on a beach. I don't know a lot about Jamaica, but I heard that Negril is where you can see the sunset."

"The sunset in Negril is the most beautiful *ting* you will ever see, my brother."

I always loved how Bob Marley sang "Every little ting gonna be alright." Daydreaming out loud, I said, "I wouldn't mind drinking a Red Stripe on the beach and watching the sunset tonight. It's sounding like a nice ting to me."

He seemed lost in his thoughts for a moment, and then, like a guidance counselor who had discovered a promising path for my future, accentuated the word should when he advised, "You should go to Negril. It's a good place. You'll have no problem in Negril, no problem." *Yeah, mon, mek me tell ya sinting. Ya shud gwan to Negril. Is a upful place. Yah av no problem in Negril. No problem, mon.*

"Really? I mean, that's great. Why do you say that?"

"Negril is like an attitude, mon. It's a laid-back place. You'll like it very

148

much and they will like you." *Negril like a attitude, mon. Is a ease-up, homely place. Laid back, ya be seen. Yah like it nuff, an dey will big you up, mon. Star, ya like gaan to bed.*

I laughed. What a great expression! How bad could *gaan to bed* be? Jeez, it was one of my favorite things. I mean, he could've said it was like gaan to the dentist or that Americans were considered a food group in Negril. But, no, it was like going to bed. Count me in. I thought about it for maybe two more seconds, and nodded my head and said, "All right, then, Alfred. I'm going to Negril!"

His smile told me he approved. That settled, I worked on getting more specific on my itinerary, "So, do you have any suggestions for where I might stay?"

Probably deciding I needed all the help I could get, he surprised me by offering, "Don't worry. You can come and stay with my family and me. We have a big house in the hills. You can stay as long as you like."

Wow. There was certainly something to be said for easing into a new culture with someone who could show you the ropes, and make sure they weren't around your neck. I stared back at him a few moments, and thought he seemed completely genuine. But I realized quickly I had something else in mind. "That's incredibly generous for you to offer, Alfred, thank you, but I really couldn't impose like that. And to be honest, in my dream, I'm writing my book while sitting on a barstool looking at the ocean, you know. And, I was kind of looking for some alone time, you know....to cool out my ed."

He understood easily and took no offense. "No problem, mon. You have to go for your dream. I tell you what, though, my car's at the airport. You have no ride, so why don't we ride together? I'm going that way and I can tell you all you need to know about Jamaica. I made up my mind and am not going to take no for an answer."

I smiled and took about a second to consider his offer. I had been more than a little concerned that I hadn't really thought about how I was going to get wherever I was going. I knew I didn't want to rent a car and I had no clue what kind of public transportation was available. Getting a ride from Alfred seemed worth taking a chance.

"You got a deal, Alfred. Thank you. Dat sound irea to me, mon." He rolled his brown and red eyes, amused at my lame attempt to talk like a

Jamaican. That settled, Alfred and I talked about the *frens* he had visited in Chicago and the night they had gone out big at the Wild Hare reggae bar, which also happened to be one of my favorite late night places. I guess his friends knew the band, and he told a funny story about how they had partied with the band so much that late in the show the singer tried to stand up on the platform where the drums were, lost his balance, and ended up flailing wildly into the drums. I loved the way Alfred put it, *"It be di opposite of graceful."* I also laughed as Alfred recreated how the drummer had to sit Indian style to hold his drum—*kyarri it ya*—to play the rest of the set, while the rest of the band couldn't stop laughing. I said that I couldn't imagine how much ganja it must take before a reggae singer would be affected like that, and Alfred just said, "Oh, he's a rasta-fake-n, not a Rastafarian." That made sense to me. If you were a reggae singer, you'd want to grow the dreads whether you were a Rastafarian, a Christian or a Jew for Jesus.

The captain announced that we'd be landing shortly in Montego Bay, and as if it was his personal doing, boasted that it was a perfect sunny and eighty–five degrees. Damn the luck. After landing, I breezed through the immigration line. I found out they let you in without a visa if you had a return flight within six months, and patted myself on the back for thinking of such an obscure detail at four in the morning. I grabbed my paperwork and bags, and walked from the fairly modern-looking air-conditioned airport to the bright Jamaican sun.

Trying to take in everything at once, even though it was just a frickin airport, I nearly missed Alfred. He called out to me and I spotted him, smoking something, next to his car in the parking lot. I walked across the lot soaking in the sun and the warmth for the first time in six months. Montego Bay's airport is not far from the ocean, and I could smell the sea waft through the air. I could see palm trees along the roads that overlooked the airport and could feel the soft breeze. I put on my shades and Alfred commented, *"Irea darkers, mon."* Everything seemed cooler here. I remembered the commercial, "Come to Jamaica and feel all right" and smiled to myself. Yeah, mon. I had come to Jamaica, and had no idea what I was doing, but I felt alright.

23

Alfred's car was something called a Nissan Bluebird and made the Altima look like a mini-van. It's A/C went unused, but its radio was tuned to a reggae station—IREA FM—and that kept things cool enough for me. The DJ introduced a song by someone named Beenie Man. Alfred nodded approval and turned it up. Heading out of the airport, through a couple of round-abouts to find the road to Negril, we were both kind of grooving when Alfred passed me a joint somewhere between the size of a Louisville Slugger and Long Island. "*Quality bud, mon. Yah brown up?*" It was a variation of a question I'd get asked several thousand times in Jamaica, as if the answer was the one thing that defined my existence.

I didn't imagine it would help his driving much, but as the passenger, what the hell? "Yeah, mon." I lifted the thing up with two hands and took a hit that swept around my head like a tropical storm. "Jesus *Christ!*" I said blown away and completely out of my mind already. "Are you sure that's going to be enough?" I asked coughing. "What if we run out?"

He laughed his head off as we found the ocean front road to lead us from Montego Bay to Negril. Alfred informed me, "*Negril soon come,*" and to settle back and relax. They drive on the left in Jamaica—if they aren't slaloming around moon-crater potholes, fearless uniformed school kids or aimless goats—which constantly made me feel like I was about to be in a head-on collision. But after that hit, and another, and, well, okay, one more to *cool out my ed*, relaxing was not going to be a problem.

He asked my story, and though it almost seemed like I was talking about someone else, I gave him the highlights. It reminded me that Shulie had broken up with me *the day before.* I felt a tinge of sadness and a sense of loss that I couldn't describe and hadn't quite come to terms with, but it mostly felt like it was a different lifetime and I was somehow a different person.

He listened intently. When I was done all he said was, "My friend, you should be you." *Star, mon, yah should be yah*, and I realized, right there, that's what my whole journey was about. *Yah should be yah!* I should be me. I just looked at him a while, the clarity of his insight gradually taking shape inside me. As those few words twisted through my brain like a water slide, my anxiety turned into resolve and my fear into hope. I just nodded—slowly, at first, and then with a big smile. Alfred and I looked at each other, and he knew, I think, that I'd stopped looking back and started looking to the future I wanted for myself. He smiled to himself.

The windows were down, wind was blowing through my hair, and the reggae sounded great. We were travelling along a winding, insane coastal highway that was in the process of being built, and according to Alfred, always would be. My good mood was in stark contrast to many of the homes we were passing. The living conditions of the locals was sobering, or would have been were it not for Alfred's 747 spliff. You'd be looking at some structure along the road and trying to decide if it was abandoned or not. You'd be sure it was, then you'd spot laundry hanging in the backyard and wonder how people could live there. Other homes would be a riot of vibrant colors, but the size of a walk-in closet.

The road was also spotted with hundreds of tiny wooden shacks that seemed to me the kindred spirit of a child's first lemonade stand. You know how kids—who haven't quite grasped the concept of location, location, location—put up a stand in front of their house, even though no one's walked by their house since the Indians? And so their parents end up buying $32 worth of lemondade. The locations of these Jamaican stands, it seemed to me, appeared just as casually thought out, and business had to be just as sporadic. Inside there'd usually be a single, lonely sole hopeful to sell a Red Stripe beer, or Ting soda, or the appropriately named "Craven A" cigarettes. Unless they sold the occasional Red Stripe for like $800 to the victim of a nearby car breakdown, it didn't seem possible to make a living.

Speaking of breakdowns, we had just rounded a bend in Lucea, pronounced Lucy, a village along the road to Negril, when a truck we had followed into town must have taken a turn too quickly and overturned not thirty yards in front of us. *"Choble, mon! Ya dam lagga head bud."* I assumed the first part meant trouble, and the second didn't sound like an endorsement of the driver's abilities.

I was aware of tires screeching, and a chicken flying and was sure we were going to run right into the back of the truck, but Alfred slammed on the brakes just in time. I was very glad he was driving, because after Alfred's ganja, no way would I have been sure to hit the right pedal. Alfred pulled his car to the side of the road, and we opened the doors and headed for the truck. There were two passengers in addition to the driver, and we could tell right away that no one was seriously hurt, though one had suffered some cuts. We had beaten a group of people to the wreckage, and I was just about to help the drivers out, when Alfred grabbed me. "Stand back," he said holding me back. *Tan tedy.* And then after looking around furiously, commanded, "C'mon, let's go." *Cum ya, gwan.* He practically pulled me back to his car.

"What's up? Shouldn't we help those guys?"

"Those three will be alright," he said, dismissing that thought. Alfred quickly explained that it was a meat truck and we didn't want to be there when the vultures descended for their free parting gifts. *Dos tree be awrite... dis a meat chuck, an a whole eap a people bout dey tiefing demselves a early Christmas present. Gwan be a ugly likkle cuss-cuss.*

There seemed to be people loitering everywhere in Lucea and sure enough, many had descended on the truck and some were starting to pilfer some of the meat. A storefront in the center of town housed the police station and as they arrived to make sure there wouldn't be a free pass for all, a minor melee broke out. Some of the officers were beating off some of the people with their sticks, and I was glad Alfred had pulled me out of there. It didn't take long for the whole scene to play out, and soon we were back in the Bluebird, my heart still racing.

I was a little shaken, but trying not to show it, I asked Alfred, "Why'd you pull me out of there, I could have picked us up some dinner?"

"*No badda. What sweet nanny goat a go ruin him belly.*" I looked at him like, "It's great that you have your own funny little language, but, could you throw me a bone here."

He smiled and clarified somewhat, in his own way, "You shouldn't bother with that, things that seem good to you now can hurt you later."

Appropriately schooled, I just joked, "I thought you meant it was goat meat in the truck."

"That, too." He nodded a smile. If he was embarrassed about the looting of an overturned truck, he didn't show it. He also explained for me,

153

"I'm Rastafarian and I don't eat meat. Also, I have no alcohol, no tobacco, no spices (*sal'ting*.) We only eat *I-tal*, pure, natural food."

"Wow. You know, I'm ashamed to say that all I know about your religion is the dreads, reggae and ganja. Come to think of it, where do I sign up?"

"Be careful what you ask for there, Star. One of the early principles of the dreads is the hatred of all white people, the complete superiority of the black race, and revenge against whites."

Huh?! "Hey…I was thinking, this is good," I uttered, only half joking, "you can drop me off here."

He smiled at me. "No worries, mon. Respect."

Oh, really? I wasn't so sure about that.

Sensing, I'm sure, that I needed reassurance, he continued, "Let me tell you. A thing about Rastafari is that it is vague and broad enough to cover many different beliefs and interpretations. I don't think any one race is superior and another inferior. The Rastafari life grew out of the poverty of Kingstontown, and many blame the white people. They say they are the oppressors, the Babylonian conspiracy, to keep the black man down." He smiled when he added, "Now, we all know that Jesus is black and that white Christian preachers have been perverting scriptures to conceal that fact, but, Star, *mi bredda mon, me think ya cum fi drink milk, ya nuh cum ya fi count cow.*"

I just looked at him and asked with heart felt sincerity, "Alfred, what the fuck are you talking about?"

"I think you and I are brothers." *You and me is bredda.* "I think you come here to conduct your business in a straightforward manner…I don't think you're here to oppress Mr. Alfred." He smiled to let me know he was just being funny.

"Oppress you?! Jesus, Alfred, I wouldn't even know how." We both chuckled, amidst thoughts of how strange it was that the two of us were together.

Mostly as a way to pass time, Alfred continued with his religious lesson, "I believe in one love. *I and I* is the expression Rastas use to totalize the concept a oneness. *I and I* means that God is in all men, so we are one blood, one people. *Praise Jah.*"

"Praise Jah," I cheered, not to be disagreeable. Taking a minute with that, though, I thought about the lyrics to Bob Marley's songs *Get Up, Stand*

Up and *One Love,* realizing he must have been singing about *I and I,* a concept I was finding to my liking.

I said to Alfred, "I like the *I and I* concept, you know, I think it's a nice way to think about the world. One love, one heart, one people. That there's God inside all men. That works for me."

I meant it, too. Religion has somehow evolved into highlighting the petty differences between people and cultures and religions rather than the common goodness—that voice of integrity and conscience—that could bond them together. From my perspective, Catholics and Protestants, believe in, give or take, the same damn thing. I don't get why they're always fighting each other. Course, what the fuck do I know? In any case, finding myself more curious than I'd been about religion maybe ever, I asked Alfred, "If God is in everyone, is there one main God you believe in?"

"Yeah, mon. In 1930, a man named Ras Tafari Makonnen was crowned king of Ethiopia. Took the title of Emperor Haile Selassie I, Conquering Lion of the Tribe of Judah, elect of God and King of the Kings of Ethiopia."

I was a little disappointed with that, to be honest, not necessarily buying Mr. Tafari's qualifications to be God and all, so I just joked, "Wow, he must have had great business cards."

Alfred looked at me like maybe it's not good to joke about everything. "We accept that the one and only true Jah is the late Haile Selassie, the personification of the almighty, and that Ethiopia is the true Zion. Ras Tafari lives on in all the brotherhood of mankind." Then, as if reading my thoughts, joked, "Except for you." I laughed out loud at my Rastafarian comedian friend.

We drove for a little while longer as I continued to consider some very deep, fundamental thoughts about God and religion and the spirit of life. I finally decided, "I mostly like the cool hair."

He laughed. "Yeah, mon! Natty dreads inspired by the Bible, mon. It talk against the cutting of one's hair."

"Really? Cool. Does the Bible also mention ganja?"

"Yeah, mon. Ganja is considered the holy herb. Through the use of ganja, the Rastafarian reaches an altered state of consciousness. In this altered state, the revelation that Haile Selassie is God and Ethiopia is the home of the black mon is realized. The herb is the key to understanding of

the self, the universe and of Jah. It's the transport to cosmic consciousness."

"Well, then, if I'm gonna find religion, I better have another hit."

"Yeah, mon! Respect, mon." He lit it up, which took a while (a blow-
torch might've helped) and passed it over.

I took a hit and toasted, "Here's to cosmic consciousness. I may be a
Rasta man, after all. Praise Jah." He laughed and signaled I should take
another.

"Am I black yet?" I said, before taking a toke, coughing like a nerdy
white guy, and passing it back to him.

"*Chat bout? Child must creep before him walk, mon. It be takin more dan dis,*"
he imparted with a smile before inhaling and passing it back to me for
another hit—because that's just what I fucking needed.

"Tree hit a dis, mon, an me waken up in Zion," I said in a horrible
Jamaican accent, unable to stop myself. He let out a big belly laugh.

There was a study done once that revealed that I'm one of the three
worst singers ever in western civilization. My world ranking is slightly higher
only because apparently there are a lot of really bad singers in *eastern* civilization. I had always said there wasn't enough beer in the world to get me to
do karaoke, but I obviously hadn't counted on Alfred's ganja. Out of the
blue, I felt compelled to start singing the words to Bob Marley's *Three Little
Birds*. I started singing the first verse, just sort of to myself, the song's
simple message…to you-u-u…lifting my spirit in a way far more beautiful
than the way I sang.

Alfred shook his head and chuckled at me, but joined me for the cho-
rus. Unfortunately buoyed, I started to amplify a bit.

*"Singin don't worry bout a ting
Cuz every little ting's gonna be arite"*

We repeated that a few times, getting louder and worse until Alfred
informed me, "*Be needin to cut ya off, der, Star.*"

I was falling into some sort of coma, I think, but figured I should find
out all I could about my new home country, "So, Fredfred, (did I just say
Fredfred?), what else do I need to know bout Jamaica?"

Acknowledging the state I was in, Alfred joked, "Don't take rides from
no more Rastafarians." *Nuh drive wid nuh mah Rastas.*

"Now you tell me. No, really, man, what should I know?"

"Whatyah need to know?" he asked, back in his role as mentor.

At that point, I was barely able to speak, but I figured there were important things I should be thinking about, though none were coming to mind. "I don't know, man, is Jamaica at war with anyone?" The ganja must have helped make this a really funny concept to me, "Like with the Bahamas, those fucking bastards?" He made the mistake of laughing, so I kept going, "Or, the barbarians in Barbados? Or, the commies in the Caymans." For some reason I was quite proud of myself. I'd also used up most of the rest of my brain cells.

"Star, you're pretty funny for a whitie."

"It must be the cosmic consciousness. Alfred, seriously, I don't know, man, what's the currency here, do you have a democracy, is there a sports section?" They were the three most meaningful questions I could think of.

"Let's see. The currency is Jamaican dollars. Whole different thing than US dollars. You get roughly JA$37 to $1 US. We have a democracy and a Prime Minister. Name's Percival Patterson. People call him P.J. Patterson. No war, but much poverty and that can lead to unrest in Jamaica. You can read the news in The Gleaner. They write about many sports, but mostly football, our kind, and cricket."

I looked at him through the fog in my head and realized I had already forgotten everything he just said. I asked him, "Were you talking?"

He shook his head. "You make me laugh."

I closed my eyes and drifted for a few minutes, or hours for all I know, until I heard Alfred say, "Hey, we're here." *Hey, mon, we ya.*

"We ya?"

"*We ya, mon.* The world-famous Negril seven-mile beach. You need to pick out a place to stay. Whattya have in mind, mon?"

"If I had something in my mind, it's not there now."

We started passing some resorts I had heard of, Couples, Sandals, Hedonism II, and I realized I wouldn't be staying at any place like that. "I guess I need to stay somewhere cheap. I just need someplace with a beach and a bar."

"*Ya suh.*"

We continued a few more miles, passing many low-rise resorts and hotels that looked too expensive for me. Alfred told me that no hotel or structure could be built in Negril that was higher than the highest palm tree, though some resorts were working on importing taller trees. On the right side of the road, among many other wooden, hand-painted signs in faded, funky colors, I noticed a wooden, hand-painted sign for a place called the Blue Moon. If the sign was any indication, it was in my price range. I ran the name around in my head and it felt good. I felt a connection with the place, thinking the Blue Moon symbolism had to be somehow significant, maybe even fateful. "Stop! This is it!"

Alfred looked at me to make sure I was serious, and then quickly turned right and wove the Bluebird through its short, winding driveway into the hotel's small paved lot. He said he'd better come in with me to check it out. I opened the door and literally fell out of the car. Alfred came over to get me back on my feet. As he shook his head, amused, I remembered the story about the singer at the Wild Hare. I asked, "You have this affect on everyone, don't you?"

He steadied me and I took some baby steps to make sure I still remembered how to walk. When I got going, I realized I was determined to stay at the Blue Moon whatever it was like. Partly because of the attraction with the name, but also because I knew all my systems were about to be shut down. If I didn't stay here, God knows where I'd end up.

Alfred and I walked toward the beach, and I found myself pleasantly surprised that the place didn't seem bad at all. In fact, through the haze of my buzz, it seemed kind of cool. The main building was a two-story, white stucco structure, with pastel blue trim and some nicely ornamental trimmings. The stairs that headed up to the second floor were painted pink and yellow and above that, on the wall, was a colorful mural of the water of the ocean in orange and yellow showing through tall palm trees and bordered by the blue of the sky. We had parked just outside of the main office, which had paned windows in a brown trim, which seemed apropos of nothing, but managed to provide some eclectic charm. The main building was perpendicular to the beach and appeared to have maybe ten to twelve rooms on each floor. Walking past the main building to our left, on the beach on the south side of the property, the hotel had an open-air, thatched-roof bar with four tables inside and a couple of outdoor round tables under straw umbrellas. Speakers attached to the bar were playing a Ziggy Marley song, which sounded like a personal greeting. In the water, also to the left, was an old wooden motor boat with a Jamaican flag, flapping gently in the breeze.

In my stupor, I found myself drawn to the flag with its yellow diagonal "X" and green and black triangles. I couldn't put my finger on it, but something about it struck me as somehow perfectly Jamaican and I actually smiled to myself. Combined with the music, the Jamaican flag, and the simple walk on the beach, I was feeling at peace with my decision to come here.

The beach had maybe ten lounge chairs placed symmetrically between two large palm trees and several smaller ones. We walked across the beach to the north side of the property. Just past the main building were four small cabins. They each had a little porch with a triangular overhanging ceiling, painted white with the pastel blue trim. I could easily picture spending afternoons with my legs up on the edge of the porch, drinking Red Stripes and typing my book into my laptop. There was no pool, but between the beach and the cabins, down one sidewalk, then another I noticed a small Jacuzzi secluded by the property's vegetation. I took one peek, and like the hotel, I felt lucky to have found it. It was right out of my dream. I was in love with this place.

We went to find the manager, and when we walked into his office, I was surprised to find out was a white guy. He said his name was Dugan and was the hotel's owner. He was welcoming, but spoke too quickly and I got the feeling he was less than completely trustworthy. I introduced him to Alfred, and they seemed to instantly appraise and distrust each other, though in my altered state I couldn't be sure of anything. I asked about the cabins, and Dugan said they were $740 a night. I temporarily panicked, thinking the place wasn't *that* nice, until Alfred had to tell me again that the currency was Jamaican and what the exchange rate was. My condition didn't allow me to do the math, but Alfred told me the summer rate was thirty US dollars a night. I asked about a monthly rate. Dugan said it was $750 a month. Alfred said it was too much and that we should go. Dugan relented and said he'd let me stay a month for $600 US. I asked about a refrigerator. He said he'd put me in a cabin that had one. That seemed good enough for me. I looked at Alfred who nodded his approval. With that, I gave Dugan my card to pay for the month.

Alfred and I walked back to his car together to get my stuff. On the way, I asked him what he thought. He said, "*Keep an ay on dat one, dat man a ginnel, a trickster, but sides dat, everyting cook an curry.*"

"Cook and curry? Is that good?"

"Yeah, mon."

"Cool." I held out my hand to shake and said, "Alfred, really I can't thank you enough."

He said, "This is how Jamaicans shake." He put his fist to mine straight-on, then an upward and downward five using the still-closed fist. *"Do dat an dey will big you up, mon."*

"Cool. Thanks, man," I said, assuming getting 'bigged up' was also a good thing, and not something that might happen, in, for example, prison.

"Star, maximum respect, mon. I wish yah nudding but irea."

"Yeah, you too, man, you too."

"Soon, me ring yah up," Alfred said, *"Yah gwan fe mi ouse. We jooks."*

"Jooks?"

"I and I hangout. Relax."

"Cool out our eds?" I asked showing off, like I was Mr. Coolass Jamaican Guy.

"Yeah, mon," he said with a smile.

"That sounds nice. Maybe we can get some dinner. But I have to tell you, though," I said joking and telling the truth at the same time, "I only eat impure foods."

He laughed. "Rastas make anyting taste irea. You will see."

"Alfred, have you heard the term 'munchies'?"

"Yeah, mon. I heard it from my frens in Chicago." He laughed, before coming up with, *"I and I get red-red wid da ganja, mon, and go from picky-picky to licky-licky! Yeah, mon!"*

"Picky-picky to lickly-licky. That's very good, Alfred. I have a feeling I might be pretty licky-licky at your house."

"Mi tink yah might." He laughed and shook my hand again. *"Cool runnings, mon."*

"Yeah, mon."

I held up my hand to wave as he drove off. I was stoned out of my mind, deliriously tired, and all alone. It was time to start my new life.

24

Negril Jamaica, I would find out, is a very laid back place with few inhibitions and few links to the real world. Dugan, however, seemed coiled and barely in control of himself, not unlike a slinky. He walked me clumsily around the main building to the cabins akin to a baby duck frantically trying to catch up with momma duck and her pack or herd or whateverthehell group it is in which ducks travel. The cabins were off a sandy dirt path bordered by some graceful palms and fragrant hibiscus trees on the other side of the path.

Mine was the first cabin and first room from the beach side, which provided not only a view of the ocean but an unimpeded ocean breeze. Feeling the sea winds caress my skin, I followed Dugan duck into the cabin, momentarily apprehensive about what I might find. I took a cautious look, realizing I really wanted to like it. It was sparse, I had to admit, but seemed at least clean and airy. Though it didn't have air conditioning, it did have a pedestal fan next to the bed, and slats in the windows to allow the gentle winds to do their thing. The wooden walls were painted white, and the two twin beds had white sheets and a thin white blanket. The walls were adorned with no pictures, so the room was pretty much, well, white. The faded tile floor looked like it may have been yellow at one time, probably in the sixties, but more than thirty years later, no discernable color could reasonably be attached to it. Besides the bed, there was a small white nightstand, a folding chair, a wooden dresser, possibly made of cardboard, and a small refrigerator. The dresser used most of its strength to hold up a white lamp and a small vase with fresh flowers that seemed incredibly colorful in these surroundings. They seemed out of place in the otherwise colorless room, but were a nice touch and showed that someone cared. The bathroom was small, and white, and not too obviously gross. Overall, I decided, it could have been much worse.

"So, everything okay?" Dugan asked as if he didn't particularly care if it was or not. His eyes, always indirect, seemed to dart around, like he was playing a video game. He also had a hard time keeping still, as if he had to go to the bathroom or something. I almost offered mine.

Everything seemed fine to me, so, making the mistake of being super cool Jamaican guy again, I answered, "Yeah, mon, everyting cook and curry," with accent and everything.

"Oh, Jesus fucking Christ," Dugan said, not exactly providing me positive reinforcement or the bonding moment I was looking for, "check out the goddamn Patois-speaking Jamaican-wannabe. Take a look at yourself. Yep, see there, you're white. Talk like it."

"Pat–what?" I asked, somehow managing to focus on the only word of that reprimand that didn't make me want to kick the living duck shit out of him.

"Pat-wah," he condescended, shaking his head and drawing out the pronunciation like he was talking to a two-year old, "the local dialect." Then, as if I would have no way of knowing what the word dialect meant, being as incredibly fucking stupid as I apparently was, he felt compelled to further enlighten me, "It's how the Jamaican scumbags talk to each other. It's bad enough when they do it. I think the white people could hold themselves to a higher standard and not talk crazy shit like that, too."

Great, well, thank goodness we white folk have someone to hold us to a higher standard. Otherwise, we'd be all cool and charming like Alfred. That's what I was thinking, but all I said was, "I see your point," being unbelievably generous for me. I'm generally a pretty confrontational person, at even the slightest slight, and it's never been like me to defuse a situation. But I was alone in a foreign country, and either because the ganja had taken my edge off, or because I didn't need to get into it with the owner of the hotel I wanted to stay at, I let it go. I already knew for sure, though, that I didn't—and was never going to—like this creep. I mean, the guy's living in one of the garden spots in the world, lighten the fuck up. And, it's their fucking country, not yours. If they were as ungrateful and uncool as you there'd be no tourist industry and you'd have no hotel. Plus, he reminded me of the Grinch. Like he hadn't really figured out how to make life work for him and was miserable, so he was gonna make sure everyone else was too. I'm guessing his heart and his dick were at least two sizes too small, too. And, as if I needed any more reasons to dislike Mr. Dugan, he

162

wore the collar of his golf shirt up, which, I don't bring up as a social judgement of any kind, but medically speaking, it often makes me want to puke all over the place. Okay, maybe the ganja hadn't completely taken my edge off. But at least I hadn't hit him.

He started asking a couple questions about where I was from and stuff, but I wasn't really willing or able to answer. Luckily he got the hint and waddled away. I was starving, as you can imagine from my ride over with Alfred, but too wiped out to do anything about it. I looked at my watch and saw it was one-thirty in the afternoon. I climbed in bed, completely exhausted, and was out like an American who'd decided to quit his entire life and move to Jamaica less than twelve hours ago. Exactly like that, actually.

When I awoke, it was near six-thirty that evening. I showered, but still felt mostly in a fog, like my body was awake but my mind had hit the snooze button. Walking out onto the beach, the sky, unlike my head, was clear and the night peaceful. I had the sensation of walking into a dream. I looked out over the horizon as the sunlight appeared as a giant upside-down "V," dramatically connecting the sun to the shore, and illuminating the beach almost like Jamaica had laid out an amazing welcome mat for me. I headed over to the bamboo-topped bar, soaking in the warm breeze and sea air. A neatly written sign behind the bar said they served a menu of jerk chicken and "World Famous" cheeseburgers. The thought of eating seemed like a fantasy too good to be true. I opted for the local and ordered the jerk chicken. The concept of jerked food seemed interesting to me, but I decided it wasn't something I wanted to over think. The bartender, Spike, was a friendly guy, with a huge smile and a uniform I'd guess he'd rather not have to wear. Spike took my order, and with a welcoming tone, "Yeah, mon, you want wid or widout di suicide sauce?" Quickly evaluating my life, I went for the suicide sauce on the side. I introduced myself, glad for his friendliness, and figuring I might be there a lot. We talked as I chowed down the chicken. It was really good, or licky-licky as Alfred might say, and Spike wasn't kidding about the sauce.

It didn't take much to get Spike going. He started telling me the history of the hotel and the bar and the boat. Apparently, Negril started getting popular in the late sixties as a haven for hippies. The original owner had been the flower child son of a high ranking officer of the U.S. Army who'd decided to take some of his dad's money and hang in Jamaica instead of fighting in Vietnam. According to Spike, that was the last good decision he'd made. As the hotel fell into disrepair the more mushrooms the guy ate, the more he'd tried to unload the hotel to his guests. He ended up selling to someone so stoned that the contract they'd written that night took many weeks, and many lawyers, to try to decipher what they'd agreed on. The new guy, a former record store owner, wasn't very good at running a hotel, but he had put in a good effort and was able to keep it in business for nearly twenty years. Dugan had acquired it from him, though the details on why he gave it up weren't clear. That was about the only detail Spike didn't know. And, about the only opinion he didn't share was how he felt about Dugan. Like if you can't say something nice, it's best not to slam your boss. Otherwise, he seemed to know everything and everyone and loved to talk. I could tell he'd be the guy to go for the scoop on anything.

He introduced me to his staff. She was a cheerful and very pretty Jamaican girl named Erika. Erika had this thinly individually braided hair that looked like a bunch of short "L"s sticking up in every direction. It looked really cool, though I imagined you might want to be careful if fooling around with her. As they say, it's always funny till someone pokes out an eye. Actually, the more I looked at her, the more I realized she was more than just pretty. She had this natural beauty to her that seemed to extend inside her as well. We shook hands and I got kind of a nice vibe. I was beginning to get a little enamored with her. She asked if I was staying at the Blue Moon and I told her that I was, and that I was really looking forward to my first Negril sunset. I totally was, but I didn't think it hurt to sound like Mr. Sensitive. Her eyes practically lit up. She spoke eloquently and passionately about how spectacular and inspiring the sunsets were in Negril. It was going to be a clear, perfect night, she said, and after my first sunset, I might never forget how beautiful the world can be. She spoke quietly in a very proper English—almost British actually—but in a wonderful accent that made everything sound engaging and sweet. She also swayed to her words in a way that gave them not just meaning, but rhythm. You could actually feel what she was saying. I started wondering what I'd found here. The sunsets weren't the only inspiring things you could find on a beach in Negril.

I said, quite enchanted by her and hoping she'd join me, "Well, then I think I'll order a couple of Red Stripes and find the perfect spot to watch it." I grabbed two lounge chairs from between the palm trees and put them close enough to the water to put my feet in. My mind actually took the time to make an internal announcement that I was about to watch a sunset in Jamaica with my feet actually in the ocean drinking a Red Stripe. If I was groggy when I'd woken from my nap, I'd become fully awake. I did a gentlemanly gesture toward the empty two chairs, and motioned for Erika to join me. She looked at Spike who gave her a what-the-hell look. She brought the two beers over and handed them to me. I thanked her and asked if she'd join me.

She sat down on the edge of her chair as if to indicate it was only for a second. But when I offered her one of the Red Stripes, she relaxed and stretched out in the lounge chair. She seemed a little surprised, but smiled and said with kind of a flirty smile, "Thank you. I don't mind if I do". She had a nice confidence about her, like she was smart about what she did, so she didn't worry about what anyone else might think.

The sun was sitting about fifteen degrees above the water, and an orange path ran from it to the shoreline, looking like a sidewalk to heaven. We clinked the glass of our bottles. Talk about a difference twenty-four hours can make.

From nowhere, the sky produced some pencil-thin wisps of horizontal white clouds above and below the setting sun. I was struck by a wondrous layering of colors. The sky above the clouds was a deep night blue as it presided over the whole show. The next layer, a stubborn daylight powder blue was soft and fleeting. Below that was star of the show, the orange sun, alone in the distance, sending its orange flecks to dance on the water. Between the sun and the water was a wonderful struggle between a brilliant orange and a powdery-white blue, won mostly and spectacularly by the flaming orange. Below that, the water, in calm purple, sat ready to catch the sun. I was sitting in a postcard, drinking a Red Stripe and thoroughly enjoying the show. We sat silently watching it unfold, with the fluidly changing brush strokes of colors and layers as the sun descended and quickly disappeared into the horizon. I may not be the most religious guy in the world, but, wow, kudos to whoever's idea that was.

Erika seemed just as pumped up. She silently clapped to herself. "Isn't it so unbelievable there could be a thing like that?" Try to imagine the accent because I was eating it up. "Seth, I love that I get to see this every night. You will see, it's never quite the same. It keeps finding new ways to move you."

"I don't know if I've ever seen anything more beautiful," I replied in all seriousness. I looked around and, in the dusk, couldn't see anyone else on the beach. The sunset seemed to be just ours. I was never someone that needed to have a lot of friends, but I could always count on them being around if I needed them. Being in a foreign country by myself, I couldn't help but thinking that had I been alone watching something that magnificent, I probably would have felt really small and even more alone. I looked at Erika who seemed to be lost in her thoughts as well, and I said softly, "Hey, thanks, you know, it wouldn't have been the same watching this by myself."

The lighting seemed to attach to her just right and she looked peaceful and sweet as she sat sipping her beer and gazing out at the water. Finally, she said, "It'd be sad if I ever start taking this for granted. I hope that never happens to me."

"Tell you what, Erika, you won't have to watch it alone as long as I'm at the Blue Moon," I offered (not entirely a selfless gesture), extending my hand to shake on it. "Deal?" She took my hand, looking at me, and held it maybe a second too long. "Deal."

She looked back towards the bar, and said, "I better be getting back to work before Spike starts giving me a hard time. I usually don't get off to the last customer leaves, are you going to be around a while?"

"Yeah, I think it might be nice to hang out here a bit. I'll save a seat for you."

"Good. I'll stop by later, and every once in a while to make sure you don't get too thirsty."

"Wow, a really beautiful girl to watch sunsets with and bring me beer, what more could a guy want? If you're not careful, I'm going to ask you to marry me, right here in these two chairs. If all goes well, I won't ever have to leave this spot."

"Just what I need…a lazy, drunken husband to wait on," she said, but I think she liked the compliment.

I laughed. "Good, so, you'll think about it?"

She rolled her eyes and sweetly said, "I'll check on you later."

"Thanks, I'll be here."

Not bad. I was doing all right so far. My first day and I'd already met a couple of people I could get into being friends with. Maybe not a fair comparison, but that had taken about nineteen years back home. I looked up at the sky and was surprised to find the show hadn't ended. There was a calm beauty you never see in postcards as the white sky stood above the calmly shimmering gray water. Maybe an hour after the sunset, as if unable to give up the attention, the orange made a curtain call. This time it was joined on stage by shades of pinks, mauves and burgundies. With the horizon still a tapestry of the softest, prettiest colors it had to offer, a single bright star appeared where the sun had been when I first started watching. Then, as the sky slowly darkened, the single star was joined by a friend, and I thought of Erika. This one was much higher in the western sky. With the coast now scouted out and cleared, stars appeared by the thousands. The stars were the brightest, highest and lowest I'd ever seen. Looking up through the leaves of a palm tree, I knew for sure that I was in paradise.

I sat there with my feet in the water, the reggae from the bar sounding wonderful, getting mesmerized watching the movement of the Jamaican flag in the darkening sky, awestruck that I now lived in Jamaica. The nearly full "bluish" moon, not to be out done, kept dipping in and out of the clouds, as if to check on me. I wanted to yell, "HEY I'M DOING ALRIGHT!" like the moon was a satellite transmitting back to all the people I left back home.

There's always been something about looking out over a body of water that makes you think about your life. Looking at the ocean, my mind drifted until it found Shulie. My first thought was that I had been ready to spend my life with her. She was pretty and sweet and funny, and to be honest, I couldn't think of a single bad thing to say about her. But, I also knew it was always my head fighting for her, *not* my heart. I found it revealing that after all was said and done, of all the different emotions going on inside me, I was mostly feeling relief that I hadn't gone down that path. I wasn't anything against her, either, it was more that I might have become someone I didn't really want to be. Even though I knew I was going to miss talking and joking with her—even on the plane I'd thought of all these smartass comments about the other passengers I'd have liked to share with her to hear her smartass replies—I really felt like I avoided making a big mistake. With benefit of hindsight, it was easy to second-guess the entire relationship. I found it interesting that my mind had led me astray, but my heart had been right on target. Maybe because the heart isn't capable of over thinking things or playing games with you. I decided right then that if I did ever find the right person, I would know it in my heart, and that I wouldn't settle for less. Feeling alone and kind of bounced around, though not sad, I wondered if I ever would. Everything that had happened was all too new to fully absorb I thought, but I hoped I'd come to terms with my emotions. If nothing else, it might provide some clues as to who I really was and what I really wanted. And for all the reggae and sunsets and Red Stripes in Jamaica, and as far away as I was, I guessed before long that real life would find me.

But, you know what? I was going to make reality work to find me, to hide a while longer. I decided my soul searching and introspection and book could wait. I knew what I needed to do and it involved a lot more drinking than thinking. I grabbed my cell phone to call my buddy Walker.

Walker Peters II was probably my best friend, which was interesting in that I always felt we had next to nothing in common. He had lived next door to me in the dorm freshman year in college, and more than anyone, helped make college the great experience it became.

Even then, we didn't agree on girls, or sports, or clothes or music. I was the analytical one, he was the salesman. Where I needed to come out of my shell, Walker couldn't have been more outgoing. While I've tended to think the masses were a bunch of idiots, Walk was sort of a Top Forty kind of guy. While I'd always existed most comfortably in my head, Walker was most comfortable as the center of attention. He even had a dance named after him at IU, called the Walkman, which was a riot, and I wish I could describe it for you, but you may need to wait for the movie. While I'd distance myself from everything, Walker fully immersed himself and loved wherever he was. For example, he moved to Dallas, and immediately acclimated to the point where he wasn't at all averse to wearing Wrangler jeans and cowboy boots and he even frickin likes country music, which I'll never understand. For some reason, though, the chemistry worked then with us, and still does. Somehow we managed to complement each other. From the beginning, we were always able to talk and laugh about our lives, and trust and care about each other. And, not to be ignored is that he's always been really great to go drinking with.

And, so, "Waaalk! It's Seth."

"Goldie! Hey bud, what's going on?"

"For one thing, you need to get your ass down to Jamaica!"

"Huh?! You're in Jamaica?"

"Yeah, mon."

"What?! Goldie, what are you doing in Jamaica?"

"I don't know, bud," I said, noticing the waves lapping onto the shore, "everything seemed to fall apart back home and I needed to get away. You're not gonna believe this, because I don't, but I decided to move here. My feet are in the ocean right now."

"Get the fuck out of here! Goldie, you're joking right?"

"I'm serious, man." I told him the condensed story of what happened, similar to the version Alfred got. "So, I need you to meet me down here. My new palace has two twin beds, so you can stay for free. Use your miles and get down here. Can you do it?"

"You amaze me, Goldie. You just moved to Jamaica? Where are you staying?"

"Yeah, I moved here, get over it. I'm staying in a cabin at a place called the Blue Moon in Negril."

"Sounds like a dump."

"Excuse me, Ritz boy. What do you care? The way I see, you're going to bring down the property value wherever you go."

"Easy, there, Goldie, I'm gonna have to get you for that."

"Walk, man, so what if it is a dump...chances are you'll be spending the nights with some babe, and I'll be sleeping on the beach. Who cares what the room is like?"

"You're asking me to drop everything and come stay in some flea-bag dump in Jamaica. You can do better than that."

I knew he couldn't pass up the opportunity. He was one of the few guys I knew who would just drop everything to party in Jamaica for a weekend, but part of his character had always been to try to scam whatever advantage possible. In this case, it was that I had to admit that I owed him big. "Walk, you live in Dallas, I live in, well Jamaica, we don't get the chance to party together much anymore. We have to do this. And I'll buy your frickin drinks. Call the airlines and get down here."

Just then, Erika came over and asked if I wanted another drink, which

I did. Walker heard me and asked who I was talking to. Again fitting with his character, he needed to talk to her. I objected because of the cost of the call, but because I almost never won an argument with him—his persistence was too much—I gave him the phone.

I heard Erika say her name and start describing herself. I laughed when she said she had a nice tan and long blond hair. She laughed a couple of times. I'm not sure what he was trying to pull with her, but she was saying, "No...no...I don't know...maybe...yeah, I guess so...okay, we'll see...okay...okay... okay...okay, you too. Bye."

She gave me the phone back amused by their little conversation.

He said, "Sweet accent. I like her. Is she cute?"

"Yes, Walk, very."

"Does she have a nice tan and long blond hair?"

"The tan part is true."

"I figured that. All right, listen, I'll call and see what I can get. By the way, Erika will be going out with us, and she's gonna bring some friends. Call me tomorrow and I'll let you know, okay?"

"Cool! Thanks, man."

"Goldie, I can't fucking believe you moved to Jamaica."

"Me, either, bud, but I'm here, so let's get drunk."

"Yeah baby! Call me tomorrow, okay."

Erika was still around, so I apologized for whatever Walker had said. She said he seemed funny and harmless. I agreed.

Then I called my parents. I decided I wasn't in the mood to be brought back to reality, so I just told them I had come here for a vacation until the end of the month to regroup. They were, of course, concerned that I wasn't immediately looking for a job, and probably scared to death that I was going to be in Jamaica by myself for a month. I told them Walker was going to come down to hang out with me for a while, which didn't ease their concerns a helluva lot (though they love Walker, who never fails to charm them to bits), but it did get them to move on to a new line of questioning. Not that that was a picnic. They were stunned and dismayed by the news about Shulie and asked dozens of questions about that, the tone of which made it clear that it was all my fault. From there they moved onto what my hotel was like, what I was going to eat, if I had enough money, were the people nice, and if Jamaica was at war with anyone (just kidding.) I finally had to say the call was getting too expensive and cut them off, by saying, "Don't worry, okay, this is what I need right now." They said just to be very careful and to not forget to call. It was exhausting, but not enough to bring me down. Erika, on queue, came by with my beer.

"Hey," she said, "I was waiting until you got off the phone. Are you calling everyone in the states?"

"No, I just had to call my folks to tell them I was here."

I must have begun to look a little wrung out from the activity of the last twenty-four hours. She sat in her chair, and asked, "You okay, mon?" The concern in her eyes was touching.

"Yeah, I'm good. A lot's gone on in the last day. It's hard to believe I'm really here."

I was finding myself very curious about Erika, so before she had a chance to ask more about my story, I asked about her. She said she was going to school to be a teacher. She was working at the Blue Moon to pay her own way through school. Her parents had some money, but it was all tied up in the family business. I sensed just a tinge of bitterness, but rather than focus on that, I told her I admired her determination. Since there were no universities around Negril, she was taking college classes over the Internet at the University of the West Indies working towards a Bachelors degree in English Literature. Taking classes on the web seemed surprising, and incredibly resourceful. She told me about how she loved language and always knew she'd be an English teacher. I could tell by the way she spoke about things she had a passion for wanting to express her thoughts well, and I could tell there were going to be some lucky school children in her future.

She told me she lived free in the hotel, which meant she was, "available way too often to Dugan." Her younger brother Freedy also lived with her at the hotel, and also worked for Dugan, but she seemed hesitant to go into that. I couldn't tell if she was being short about it because of Dugan or because of her brother. She may have been trying to change the subject when she asked, "Can I ask you, what brought you to our island? I get the feeling it's not just a vacation."

Unlike with Alfred or Walker, I gave her the whole story. She seemed able to react on many different levels and we stayed up very late talking about Shulie and everything that had happened.

She concluded with, "I'm sorry, Seth, you didn't deserve any of that.

You talk like you do, but you're being too hard on yourself. Your only mistake may have been trying to make something work that wasn't right in your heart, but I can understand why you did that. My opinion, if you don't mind my offering it, is that she may not have been right for you. But she sounded nice, and I'm sure she loved you, and I know it must hurt." Looking down at the sand, I kind of nodded my head. Some of the pain was starting to sink in. After a long silence, she said, "But, I'm glad you're here, you know, it will be nice having you around. I think it may be good for you. And, for what it's worth, I admire you for what you're doing."

I looked up. "You do? I'm not just running away from my problems?"

"No, I think you're running toward your dreams. You're taking your life and making it what you imagine it can be. And I think that's great, Seth."

All at once, all the distinct emotions I was feeling washed over me like a wave from the ocean. I could clearly feel the bittersweet sadness of losing Shulie and the heartbreak of not being able to break through to success in my career. I could feel the apprehension of walking away from my old life into the unknown of my new. I felt pride in having the courage to leave and shame in the lacking the courage to stay. I felt confident in my abilities to turn it into a good thing, yet fundamentally insecure. I felt exhilarated and exhausted. And, at that moment, I felt tremendously grateful for Erika's kindness and understanding. It all finally got the better of me, and I felt barely able to put a thought together. I just said, "Thank you, Erika. I don't know how I got lucky enough to have you to talk to, but thank you." We smiled and just sort of sat there looking at at the water, until I said, "Listen, I really need to get some sleep, you know. Can I meet you here tomorrow night?"

"I'll be here."

"Good." I looked at her in the moonlight, and thought again of the first two stars I'd seen in the night sky. "Good night, my new friend."

"Good night, Seth," she said softly.

I looked at her—right at her—and there was a second there where it could have gone either way. I'm sure we both thought about kissing good night, and who knows where that might have led. Instead we ended up just awkwardly smiling at each other and heading to our respective rooms. Walking through the sand, I wondered what she was thinking. What I was thinking was that I needed a friend way more than anything else. She appeared to be a smart and grounded person and I had a feeling she was thinking exactly the same thing. In any case, I was kind of proud of myself for resolving to do the right thing, and briefly wondered—not for the first time—if there was some sort of cosmic connection between doing the right thing and getting rewarded for it. But the answer was way beyond my realm of normal thinking and too big to think about in the twenty or thirty seconds it would take to fall sound asleep.

25

"**J**ESUS CHRIST!" was my first reaction as I was rudely awakened to find it was four in the morning on, ironically enough, Easter Sunday.

I was startled awake, no more than an hour after leaving Erika to go to bed, by a crash in the room connected directly to mine. Through my grogginess, I got up to see if I could figure out what the hell was going on. Had I had a glass in my room, I would have done that TV thing where you try to hear better by putting your ear against the glass and the glass against the wall. Though, I'm not sure which end is more effective and for that matter, as long as there's a bottom to the glass, I don't know, it seems like kind of a flawed concept to me. In any case, the commotion became loud enough that the TV prop hearing device wasn't necessary.

I had initially been awakened by two intense sounds, and in my mind's eye, it seemed like someone crashing into the wall and maybe a picture falling and breaking. Now that I was clearly the detective assigned to the case, I immediately had to get my sleep-deprived mind around some very important questions. The first, of course, was if the second sound was, in fact, a picture falling from the wall, why the hell didn't I have a picture on my wall? Apparently at four a.m., not only was I groggy, but easily entertained. Other more pertinent questions arose as well, like how many people were involved, who was mad at who, was it just Domino's delivering way outside their half-hour window, and was I in an any danger? Because, after all, it's all about me.

After the crashing of the person into the wall and the picture to the ground, I heard some pained muttering and pleading of what sounded like an African-American with a Jamaican accent (which I very cleverly deduced might actually make him an African-Jamaican. Thank you very much.) Then some not very veiled threats of two other guys who had Spanish accents, and what sounded like it could have been a nasty punch to the stomach. One of the Hispanic guys in particular seemed to be doing most of the talking and most of the threatening, while the Jamaican guy seemed to be doing most of the gasping for air. There was some heated discussion going on between the two Hispanic guys in Spanish. That indicated to me that they a) spoke Spanish (I'm awesome at this, muchas gracias) and that b) weren't in full agreement on all of the operational aspects of their plan to accost the Domino's guy (who, by the way, for all you literal types or government workers, probably didn't actually work for Domino's.)

At one point, I heard the less demonstrative Hispanic guy call the other guy Sanchez. I think he was trying to get him to chill out a little. Catching his name was my first big break in the case, and I wondered where my little detective's notepad was when I needed it. Shortly after, another break as I distinctly heard Sanchez threaten the Domino's guy in English. Sanchez told the Domino's guy in no uncertain terms, "He pays or he pays." He seemed very much like he meant what he said. That was very ominous for Domino's guy, or whoever "he" was, and prompted a few thoughts, which is a lot for me. First, excuse me, "he pays or he pays"? What the hell kind of line is that? Apparently I wasn't the only one watching too much bad TV. Second, my neighbors were running roughshod over the peacefulness and tranquility of my little dream world. Third, clearly there was a story there that led up to that scene. It wasn't about a traffic incident or late pizza. Since it was happening right next door and interrupting my sleep, I felt entitled to an explanation.

Just then, the Domino's guy again was thrown into the wall, with an even louder crash, and I could almost feel his pain. But this time it sounded more like the wall nearer the door, rather than the one separating the two rooms. Sensing that might mean the scene was nearing its conclusion, I went to my window to see if I could get a look at the alleged suspects or victim. There was another threat and then the sound of Domino's guy being thrown out the door on his ass. In the time it took for him to get back to his feet, I got a good look at him. He scampered off and didn't see me. I tried to see if the Hispanic guys were in sight, but they had immediately closed their door after throwing out the pizza guy. I knew I'd remember the face of poor Domino if I saw him again. I kind of stayed awake for a few minutes to see if, like guys do, the two Hispanic guys would rehash the action or if perhaps one or both would also be leaving the room (so I could make an arrest?) But any more talking they did was in Spanish, and if

BLUE MOON

they did any leaving, it was after I had fallen back to sleep.

26

I awoke that next morning in the afternoon. Actually close to three, after sleeping nearly eleven hours. Birds were chirping outside my door and I realized it had been a long time since I'd heard those sweet sounds.

After showering and shaving, I put on a bathing suit and tank top. Still in the mode of working out regularly, I did fifty push-ups and sit-ups, knowing those days were numbered.

I headed to the bar and asked Spike to make me a world famous cheeseburger. Erika, who had been serving drinks on the beach, bounded up to me and broadcast to the beach people, "Hey, look who's finally up." Feeling a touch unnerved by her energy, I asked when she had started work. She told me, "I started at noon. Before that, I went to Easter services at church and then studied for almost two hours."

For some reason, I was beginning to feel slightly guilty for sleeping until three. I had heard that Jamaicans weren't the most industrious of people. As evidenced by the many unfinished and abandoned structures we passed on the drive to Negril, not to mention the hundreds of people I saw milling about for no apparent reason, it was as if their ambitions went for a smoke and never came back. They had their own "soon come" pace—which translates to "I'll get to it when I get to it, if you still happen to be here"—but Erika seemed to run on a completely different clock than everyone else. "Erika, don't you sleep?"

"I have a lot I need to do," she acknowledged matter-of-factly as she prepared her next tray of drinks. She was always doing something.

Since I had next to nothing to do, at least until I started my book, I told her, "I hope I won't be too bad of an influence on you."

"I still have to do what I have to do, no matter what anyone else is doing. You know." It was said without attitude, just a grasp on what it took to make her life into what she wanted it to be.

I smiled and said with sincerity, "I know you're going to get where you want to go."

"Yes I will," she agreed, with no false modesty or bravado. But with a nice smile. She was very easy to like.

Just then, she spotted her brother Freedy coming towards us, and said, "Seth, let me introduce you to my brother."

I looked over at a thin, relatively well-groomed guy walking in our direction and was stunned to realize that it was Domino's guy! I also realized that since I'd gotten up that morning, I hadn't given a second thought to the previous night, almost as if I'd hallucinated the whole thing. Now I was sure it was real.

He seemed to be walking slowly as if his stomach hurt a lot, though I could've been imagining it. When he got closer, I noticed that he also had a few cuts on his arms and hands, which I only saw because I was looking for some indication of last night's activities. Otherwise he had that not-all-there look of someone who had spent the night drinking too many different kinds of alcohol, though I knew that's not why he looked that way.

Erika, who may or may not have seen the cuts, did seem concerned looking at her brother. "Hey, little brother, are you okay? I tried to get you up for church, but you didn't budge an inch."

He smiled for show, kissed her and confessed, "I know, sis, I just couldn't get up this morning. Were mom and dad upset wid me?" He spoke softly and with the same cultured language as his sister, but seemed to lapse into the occasional street dialect, not unlike Oprah Winfrey, except that he wasn't faking it. My first impression was that he was someone who preferred to keep to himself and maybe lacked a bit of confidence, but I could clearly tell there was an intelligence lurking just beyond the surface. Actually, he kind of reminded me of me.

"No," Erika replied, "I told them you weren't feeling well."

"Thanks for covering for me," he said, obviously laboring.

"Are you sure you're all right?"

"Yes, sis. Stop worrying about me."

"I'm not going to stop worrying about my little brother." She kissed him and then introduced him to me, "Hey, Freedy, I'd like you to meet a new friend of mine. His name is Seth."

Freedy shook my hand gingerly, as if any movement was painful, said it was nice to meet me, and politely asked if I was staying at the Blue Moon.

I debated momentarily whether I should tell him the truth, but I wanted to see his reaction. "It's nice to meet you, too. I'm staying over there," I said, pointing at the cabins. "I'm in the first one closest to the beach."

I waited for it to sink in that that meant I was right next door while he was being accosted. He seemed to be deliberating with himself on what to ask me next. Finally, he offered, "I hope you like the Blue Moon. Did you get a irea sleep last night, mon?"

I gave him a look that tried to say, "I know why you're asking," but I just said, "I love it here and I slept just fine, thanks." Still I think my message was delivered. I had a feeling he might stop by later to see what I knew. Which, I was surprised to realize, is what I wanted him to do. I was finding myself drawn to figuring out what happened.

After a little friendly small talk, Freedy went to hang out with Spike. Erika went on her rounds, and I grabbed Spike's cheeseburger and ate it at one of the beach tables. I wouldn't say it was worthy of world recognition, but it did hit the spot and I felt like I was a character in the song *Cheeseburger in Paradise*. I could see Freedy and Spike over near the far corner of the bar, talking in hushed tones. By the reaction of Spike's eyes I could tell it was about the previous night's incident, and that it was kind of a big deal. I had no way of knowing what Spike's involvement might be, or if, as I suspected, he just had that Barbara Walter's gift of getting people to talk to him.

I decided it would be a good time to go have a chat with Dugan to see what he might know, or to at least let him know what kinds of people were staying at his hotel. I went to the office and found him behind the small counter. I looked him over. He looked very pale, even for a white guy in Jamaica, which didn't necessarily mean I suspected him of any crimes, just that I suspected he had no socially redeeming qualities.

"Hi, Dugan. Remember me, Seth Gold?" I began, being unnaturally cheerful on purpose, mostly because he seemed like someone who'd be especially annoyed by cheerfulness.

"Of course, I remember you," he shot back. In his tone was, "You just checked in yesterday, asshole."

"Yeah, well, Dugan, there's something I want to bring to your attention as manager of this fine hotel."

"I'm listening," he muttered as if he could not possibly care less.

"Well, last night, in the middle of the night, there was this huge ruckus in the room next to mine."

"A ruckus?" he repeated, like that word was somehow beneath him.

"Yeah, a ruckus, a commotion, a mosh pit without the concert."

"I know what a fucking ruckus is."

And I know what dialect means, asshole. "Good for you. Well, it sounded like the two guys staying next door had a late night visitor and roughed him up. They threw him against the walls and stuff and then they made some threats."

"What threats? What'd they say?" Suddenly he cared a lot, and this came out as more of a demand than a request.

"I heard one of them say something like, 'He doesn't pay, then he pays.' Pretty cheesy line, huh Doogs, but it sounded like he meant it."

"Did they say who they were talking about? Did they mention any names?" He was really on edge, and not just because I called him Doogs, which I thought was revealing.

"No," I replied, making sure to check his reaction, "they didn't mention any names. Why, what does that matter?"

His body language changed noticeably and he seemed like a weight had been lifted from his shoulders. I had the unmistakable feeling that the Freedy incident was about him. He said, "Oh, no reason. I just want to see if anyone here's in danger." If he was involved, and if the game was, in fact, high stakes, he didn't seem to be very good at it. His eyes and body language consistently gave him away.

"Listen, I just wanted you to know. You may want to have a talk with the guys next door."

"Yeah, I would, but they checked out this morning."

"They? Were there two of them?" I asked, trying to get him to admit he knew what was going on, thinking I was clever as hell.

"That's what you said, wasn't it, the *guys* next door?" Make that clever as shit.

My inexperience as a detective was becoming apparent, but I tried to cover myself by asking, "I meant how many signed in?"

"Usually only one person registers for a room," he lectured, again talking to me like a two-year old, though that time I deserved it. Shit, I thought. I suck at this.

180

Trying again, I asked, "Was the guy who signed in named Sanchez?"

That appeared to be a better question and Dugan seemed concerned that I was pursuing that line of questioning. I amused myself with the thought that he might suspect that I was some sort of law enforcement agent. He must have concluded there was no harm in telling me the name of the bad guy, especially since I already knew it, so he looked in the hotel register book and let me know, "Yeah, Sanchez Romerio," like congrats, dipshit, you still don't have squat. But then, as if I was an annoying loose end, asked, "What did you say you do, again, Seth? Are you a cop or something?" He laughed, trying to pretend he was joking. I considered letting him think I was a cop, but instead I just acknowledged, "No, I'm a writer working on a book. I'm just trying to see if I'm in any danger staying here." Actually, pretending I was a cop was no more of a stretch than pretending I was a writer.

Glancing down at the counter, I noticed a Post-it note with the name Alfred and a phone number. I thought about my buddy Alfred, the Rasta guy, and for a second wondered if it was him. Only because he said he was going to try to call me and since my room had no phone, the only way he could was through Dugan. Since I was standing here and Dugan wasn't mentioning it, I just as quickly dismissed that thought. Clearly the note was from some other Alfred.

"I run a very safe place," Dugan responded, sounding like a politician, which is about how much I believed him. "There's no need to worry." He said as if that was the final word and 'go away little boy.'

Again, I felt the urge to kick his ass or close with something like "Hey, mac, don't be leaving town, I got my eye on you." Luckily both thoughts quickly passed and I left it at, "Okay, Doogs, I'll drop it, I'm sure it is safe here. Hey, maybe we could get together for a drink sometime." Though I felt it unlikely I'd ever be able to fit him in my busy schedule.

"Yeah, let's do that," he responded with equal sincerity. I stepped back out into the bright late afternoon sunlight, put on my shades (like all the good cops do), and then rather than go for doughnuts, I laid out in the sun for a while. This had all gotten very interesting, and I thought that there might even be some sort of angle or start to my book here. Clearly Dugan was in the middle of something. I decided I'd see what else I could do to keep on the case. For one thing, I really wanted to know who Sanchez and his friend were. Plus, I was very curious what that weasel Dugan was up to.

That night, I met Erika to watch another magnificent sunset. I also noticed that we had settled into being firmly in the "just friends" category, which was perfect. There was no flirting or gratuitous touching, just some joking and hanging out like friends do. After the sunset, she went back to work, and I sat there with sinister plots and conspiracy theories running through my head.

The first opportunity I had to talk to Spike without Erika around was the next day. Taking a seat at the bar, I had to wait for him to finish a conversation with this dude named Dexter, a Jamaican guy who he seemed to be friends with. If I translated their conversation correctly, it was Dexter's birthday that day.

Dexter: Ah fi day today mon!

Spike: Wait dey ah yu birtday tiday. Dat Irea!

Dexter: Yeah, mon!

Spike: Con mon mek mi buy yu dey first beer mon!

Dexter: Yuh suh. Cheers, mon!

Spike: Soh, wah yu celebrate tinite…

Dexter: Mon! Ah bashment tonite trust mi pon dat!

I laughed at the way he said "trust mi pon dat." There was always a constant stream of Dexters coming through Spike's bar like colorful bit players in my new life. It had pretty much replaced television for me, and, if not more entertaining, was at least cheaper than cable. After Dexter wondered away, probably to scam more birthday beers from his other bartender friends down the beach, I eased into a conversation with Spike by asking where I could go to buy some food and snacks. He suggested I get up early in the morning and walk down the beach to a fruit stand. For a couple of bucks I could get some mangoes and pineapple and eat them all day. He said there was also a super market in the town center a half mile or so south. He said I'd probably want to get a cabdriver to drive me there and wait for me or go with Erika or Freedy some time. He didn't say it'd be necessarily dangerous to go their myself, but said I might be a fish out of water.

Then I asked how he liked working at the Blue Moon. He said it was kind of like a family to him, that Erika and Freedy and Emma were like his kids, and that Dugan was like an eccentric uncle. So as not to seem too much like I was focusing on Freedy, I asked who Emma was. Spike told me she was Dugan's daughter, a sweet and very bright young girl, who had come to Jamaica a few months ago to help her dad run the hotel. I wondered why I hadn't seen her around, but Spike filled me in that she had been in the states visiting her mother. He said he'd introduce her to me when she returned later that week. Like I said, I hadn't yet found a redeeming quality to Dugan and I briefly wondered what his daughter would be like.

"I look forward to meeting her," I offered without emotion, and then noticing that Erika was engaged in a conversation with one of her customers down on the beach, started to try to get some background info on Freedy. "Freedy seems like a great guy. Erika introduced him to me yesterday."

"Oh, yeah, mon. Freedy is a very good bwoy."

"Erika said he works here also."

"Yeah, Freedy is kind of de jack a all trades around ere, mon, elping Dugan out ere an der. He cover de desk when Dugan need im to, and rakes de beach in de mornin and keeps de native breddas from bothering de guests too much. He many time will drive ta pick up supplies fa de otel. Him kin of Dugan's personal assistant. Dem hard-working kids, Erika and Freedy."

I found Freedy's role being described as Dugan's assistant interesting. Not just lowly employee. I had a feeling those job responsibilities went beyond just the hotel, but Erika was returning and I didn't want to push it. "Sounds like a great group here, Spike."

"Oh, yeah, mon." I briefly considered Spike and all the presumably poorly paid Jamaicans who service American tourists for a living. He was always so friendly and up and everyone's best friend, but I wondered if the disparity of wealth between the locals and the tourists he served didn't lead to some below-the-surface resentment and dissatisfaction. Or maybe I'm just distrustful of anyone who's always up. They must be hiding something…or maybe I was just taking the detective act too far.

After thanking Spike for his advice and world famous cheeseburger, I laid out in the sun an hour or so, threw on my sandals and decided to wander over to the market.

No sooner had I hit the street than I was approached by several seasoned locals trying to help me out of my sobriety and a few bucks. "Ganja, fren?" one of them asked me. "The mushroom?" inquired another. The third offered cocaine with a facial expression that indicated the other two clowns were in the minors compared to the good time I could buy with him. I had to admire the one-stop shopping selection, like it was the Catch A Major Buzz Outlet Mall. I politely said no thanks and moved on to be approached at least a dozen more times by random people selling weed. The general rule of thumb seemed to be that if you didn't work as one of the three patrolmen who walked the beach in funny uniforms, or at the resorts, you had drugs and were open for business. And if you were white, it must have just really *really* looked like you needed some in a big way. Cars would even slow down to try to help me out in my obvious moment of need.

Honking is big in Jamaica. It means everything to Jamaicans—hello, goodbye, you're a putz, look at me I'm honking at you—sort of like shalom to Jews or aloha to Hawaiians. Almost every car that passed me honked and I finally realized they were asking me if I wanted a ride. It was hard to tell which were the legitimate taxis and which were the ones that decided they were driving that way anyway (or would be after making a crazyass U-turn) so why shouldn't they make a few bucks. But I wanted to explore a little, so I kept walking.

Nearing downtown, there were crowds everywhere. It was a little intimidating. The only minority I'd ever been was Jewish, which is something that's not that obvious to the general population, especially since I've always gone out of my way to not be stereotypical. The fact that I was still very white, I realized right away, was going to be a bit harder to hide, and I had never felt more like an out-of-place minority. Not that I wasn't going to work on it, but I didn't think getting a tan would help much. I wondered if I were in Jamaica long enough, if I'd ever develop the look or attitude of someone who wasn't such a tourist.

Down an embankment on the right was a shantytown of craft shops. I immediately regretted walking near it. So many people tried to get me to come take a look around it was like getting caught in a bee's hive. Like the guys selling herb on and near the beach, they were skilled salesmen and acted like your best friend. "Respect, mon" was their mantra. Like by not checking out their wares, I was disrespecting them. Saying, "No thanks, mon" eighteen times in eighteen different ways didn't seem to sink in. It was like the translation to saying no thanks to one guy's crap was that I clearly wanted the next guy's crap. I decided there was only one dignified thing I could do to escape. I made a run for it. I ran like hell, cutting and slashing, ducking and hurdling, and then nearing the end zone, I triumphantly stiff-armed some ninety year old women who tried to tackle me from behind. As I reached the other side of the street, it was clear the not-looking-like-such-a-tourist thing was gonna need more time.

In a Negril version of a strip mall, I found the supermarket. I went in, still sweating and breathless from my great escape, and picked out some Diet Coke and Ting soda, bananas and mangoes and pineapple, some bread and something that I hoped was sandwich meat and two twelve packs of warm Red Stripe. When I left the supermarket, a cabbie I had said no to earlier had apparently followed me to the store and waited there for me. He smiled a big smile and said, "Yeah, mon. Remember me? You need a ride?"

I said, "Yeah, mon." I didn't specifically remember him, but figured I needed a ride to carry my stuff and was thankful that the taxi actually said taxi on it.

He gave me the Jamaican shake that Alfred had taught me, put my groceries in the car and said his name was Vinny, though he didn't look the least bit Italian. He told me he was always out in front of the Blue Moon, so if I ever needed a ride, he was my guy. He was well-spoken, well-educated, well-groomed, and I wondered why he was driving a cab for a living. I felt bad for blowing him off earlier. It seemed that whenever I talked to the locals I was rewarded with a good story, a great character and almost always a philosophy on life. Like Vinny. He was great. While he imparted his insights into the Jamaican people, I found myself lingering in his cab. In fact, I ended up inviting him for a beer. He parked the car and we hung out for like an hour on the porch of my cabin. He talked about soccer and cricket and Michael Jordan and the famous Jamaican sprinter, Marlene Ottey, and life in Jamaica. He told me there was a lot of money in Jamaica, but it didn't circulate and there was little industry, and so most people had almost nothing. He said that's why you see waiters and waitresses, and cab drivers, that could be doctors or nurses somewhere else. He said this without shame or bitterness. I realized that I had been thinking about both he and Spike with too much of an American attitude. Back home, everyone's status is determined, more or less, by how much money you have. It was mostly different here. Certainly there was a class with some money, but almost everyone else was like Vinny and Spike, just trying to do what they could to provide for themselves or their families. There was no shame in being a bartender or a waiter or a hotel housekeeper or a cab driver. It was a way to make a living and you got to live in Jamaica.

He smiled while telling me, "And you know what, I could live in the states—I did for a while—but this is my home and it's nice here." He was happy about his life in the way that a lot of Jamaicans are—I ain't got much, but I'm here in Jamaica. I smiled at his life-affirming attitude and we did the Jamaican handshake because he had to get going. I asked if he was single, thinking maybe we could go hang out some time, but like many other Jamaican guys I'd meet, he had a girlfriend he lived with and two kids they'd had together. Apparently, the Jamaican fellas weren't big on the marriage idea. With pride, though, he showed me pictures of the kids, two beautiful little girls, names Shantae and Shantelle. He said, "If I can provide for them and give them a home to sleep in, then I've done good. You know, mon?" I smiled and said, "Yeah, mon," feeling that much better about the human race. I promised if I ever needed a cab, he was my guy.

As I walked Vinny back to his cab, I again had to fight through the Outlet Mall's enthusiastic sales personnel. But I was starting to like them too and my resolve was weakening. I decided they'd probably have a future customer.

27

There were no new developments in the Freedy case, so I spent the rest of the week getting to know the Negril beach. Early morning, a wonderful time of day on the beach, would be spent walking the beach, meeting the other morning people, buying fresh papaya or mango or sugur cane from a large, beautiful woman named Mable, and then heading back to my porch to eat it while sipping a cup of Blue Mountain coffee. It was not only my favorite coffee of all time, but two cups, I'd already had reason to notice a couple of times, would cure any hangover. Later I'd take long strolls along the white sand beach until I'd find a small bar or a tree to sit under or a shack selling jerk something or other and have a cold Red Stripe and do nothing. It was just me, the sand, the breeze and my thoughts, and frankly I had nothing to think about. At night, I'd watch the sunset with Erika and hang out with Spike and the cast of characters that came through his bar.

Seeking a bit more adventure, after Wednesday's sunset, I headed barefoot down the beach seeing who I might be able to meet. Negril attracts an exceptionally eclectic mix, from aging hippies to young topless European and South American women—they were probably with guys, I don't know— to handholding couples of all ages. My fellow vacationers, it seemed to me, were bound far more so by a state of mind than by nationality or demographics.

The first group I came upon was this motley collection of seven ugly dorky foreign guys. Back home in Bucharest or Budapest or some other city where kids weren't raised to wear matching clothes, one of them must have said, "Hey, we're all ugly, let's go to Jamaica!" And the rest must have thought that was a really great idea—probably made that guy their leader— because there they were, all walking down the beach together, all ugly, all presumably looking for a group of seven ugly dorky foreign girls. Everyone of them was wearing one of those red, green, black and yellow Rasta hats with five thin black strands which were supposed to look like dreads, but more looked like shoelaces, and I'm thinking, *that's* not gonna help you get laid. However, I liked that they were getting into the spirit of Jamaica and besides, I wasn't so smooth in the getting some department myself.

Just after that, in fact, this very tan, very cute brunette caught my attention. She had these sturdy, athletic legs, a tight tummy and solid shoulders and gravity-defying breasts all packaged nicely in this stylish navy with white polka-dot two-piece bathing suit. She had sauntered seductively into the ocean to drift on one of those cheap inflatable rafts.

She was lying on her stomach, with her backside sort of tantalizingly perched aloft as if some sort of invitation. Something about her being out there alone in the soft shades of the early evening got me going and I drifted out into the water and, managing to seize the opportunity, said hi. She looked over at me and gave me an appraising look I couldn't decipher. Then she turned over onto her back and reached behind her. In the semi-darkness I couldn't tell what she was reaching for and I briefly became alarmed it might be for a gun, though in retrospect that seemed a little misguided, her being in the middle of the fucking ocean and all. Then right there in front of me, she slowly undid her top. I watched with wide eyes as the bathing suit top took on a life of its own, tumbling down her chest, revealing one scintillating tan line, then another, and landing softly on her glistening, toned wet abs, before gaining momentum and falling lightly to the raft before sliding down into the water next to her. Gulp. I'm not sure if that happened in real time or if it took half an hour to be honest, though I checked and the sky seemed pretty much the same. In any case, there I am in the ocean insanely focused on the top floating in the water—praying I don't get a stiffie as I become aware of the waves pelting my groinular region—and I'm thinking she just might be sending me some sort of signal. But I'm not *entirely* sure because this kind of thing hardly ever happens to me in public. The night swimming must have put her in some sort of mood, though, because then she's saying, "Hi," like I'm the new lifeguard on Baywatch, and she puts her arm around my neck and gives me a kiss that would be considered wet even if we weren't standing in the ocean, and I'm now reasonably sure I'm not misinterpreting anything.

But, because I'm suddenly curious as hell as to who she is and why she's rafting at night in the ocean and, why the hell she has suddenly, inexplicably come into my life, somehow the one crucial line I need escapes me—the one that subtly implies, "Do what you want with me" or "Why don't we get drunk and screw" or "Forget getting drunk, let's just screw"—so I end up asking her where she's from and what she does for a living and, before I could stop myself, how she likes it, and right before my eyes, I watch as every last molecule of sexual desire is drained from her body. My odds of having sex with her are now roughly equivalent to me making the Jamaican national soccer team. As I stood there neutered, she ceremoniously puts her top back on and turns over, her derrière no longer airborne or inviting. *That* signal is clear enough, and I end up plodding back to the beach, thankful, at least, that it may no longer be emotionally possible to get a stiffie.

And then I'm trudging back down the beach briefly entertaining thoughts that I may soon need to try to catch up with the seven ugly dorky foreign guys to hang out with, if I only knew how to yell, "Hey wait up, guys" in Buchapestian, or whatever the fuck they speak.

Luckily, though, I was just passing the beach bar, Margueritaville, when I heard one of the bar's "social directors" yell a loud, enthusiastic "VOL-LEY-BALLLLL!" That sounded great to me and I gestured asking if I could play. The Jamaican guy, who said his name was Mr. Gumby Damnit (I'm not bullshitting over here, that's what he said his name was), called me over, and said, "Sure, come ya, mon." I played the rest of the evening and for every day the rest of the week—quite impressively actually against some generally drunken competition and the next day against some topless babes, which I only mention because they were topless—and had a really great time. Over the week, I became buddies with Gumby. He'd watch some of the games, play in others, but always kept up a running commentary on the action. He made fun of everyone for their volleyball mistakes or because a guy's shorts were too short, or a girl's breasts too bouncy for him to concentrate or that I jumped about a week early for a spike attempt. I was thankful he didn't know about my fiasco with the polka-dot bathing suit girl or I'd have never heard the end of it. He was volleyball guy at some bar in Jamaica, but should've had his own HBO special. I even started thinking about maybe fixing up Erika with him, not that she likely had free time for that sort of thing. Again, he had to make almost nothing, but he was on the beach in Jamaica, getting paid to play volleyball and have fun. It wasn't a bad life. For Gumby Dammit and for me, dammit, it certainly beat the hell

BLUE MOON

out of real life.

28

For some odd reason I was sitting at the bar early Friday afternoon, when I heard Walker's entrance to the Blue Moon before I saw it. He was honking the horn of his rental car and yelling, "GOLDIE." He jumped out of the car, raring to go, carrying only a small duffel bag with him. That was stunning for someone who'd never been known to underpack, or for that matter, to under-anything. He's visited me enough to know that he can bring up to three large suitcases for a two-night business trip, in addition to the largest briefcase I've ever seen and the biggest golf bag since Rodney Dangerfield in Caddyshack. With Walker, too much is never enough. In college, if his roommate Pablo had owned more than one pair of jeans, two button down shirts and IU tennis sweats, Walker may have needed to pay for a second dorm room just for his frickin sweaters. The last time he came to Chicago and stayed at my place, he choose to bring not one, but three pairs of cowboy boots. Like not only would someone in Chicago think it was cool that he was dressed like some shit kicker from Bonanza, but that they'd be doubly (or triply) impressed that he was wearing a differ-ent pair every night.

"Goldie!!!" He yelled, giving me a hug. "I'm here man, let's go! Where are the white women at?!"

I smacked him on the back and said, "I didn't think you were so dis-criminating, Walk. Let's throw your bag in the room first and then we're on our way. Hey, man, where are the rest of your bags? In the car?"

"This is it bro, all I'm gonna need." I looked at him waiting for the punch line. However, when I let him in the cabin, he opened his bag to reveal that not only had he left behind the boots, but everything but some very brightly colored clothes that said, "Hey island girls, I'm here for you" (not literally), and, in grand Walk style, two dozen condoms.

"Walkman," I wondered out loud in my typically bemused tone when dealing with him, "you sure you got enough of those babies? They all for you?"

"Goldie, Jesus, there's twenty-four condoms here and I'm here for two nights. Of course, they are not *all* for me," he said as if that was ridiculous. "I brought one for you."

"Thanks for thinking of me."

"How could I forget my best friend, Goldie?"

"You use even half of those, you'll forget me. You'll be staggering down the beach, trying to remember my name and where I'm staying, asking strangers if they've seen a really good looking Jewish guy around—named Brownie or Greenie or some other fucking Jewish color—because you need to find the rest of your condoms."

He laughed and shot back, "I'll be asking if they've seen a really deeky Jewish guy around because I need the rest my condoms. You're a deek," he yelled. *Yuradeek* was Walk's trademarked putdown and one we'd used since college.

I went with the local variation, "Yuradeek, mon." And added with sincerity, "But thanks for being here, bud. I appreciate it a lot."

"Of course, I'm here, Goldie. How many best friends do I have stupid enough to move to Jamaica?"

I play-acted thinking about it. "It can't be many. I mean, it's not like the number of illegitimate children you have."

"That's true, Goldie, I don't have enough miles for that trip." He laughed, then took another look around my sparse little room. "Hey, quite a place you got here. I love what you've done with it. Chicks must dig it."

"They haven't complained so far."

"Goldie! You've had chicks here already?"

"Well, no, but I've had no complaints."

"Oh, brother. So, where to first, bud?"

"Well, it's what 2:00? Let's sit at the bar and drink for nine hours and then go out and get drunk."

Walk, right there with me, replied, "If we only have nine hours, we better get going."

"Yeah, mon!"

"So, will my friend Erika be here?" Walker wanted to know.

"Yeah, Walk, but I'm starting to feel protective of her. Don't be getting her drunk or trying anything. You got that?"

"Goldie, come on," he said, like I had offended Mr. Innocent. "Do you really think I would do that?"

"What? Try to have sex with a very pretty girl after getting her drunk? Yeah, pretty much sounds like you."

"It does. Doesn't it?" he admitted, laughing.

"So, Walk, I hear my man Spike, the bartender, makes something called Spike's World-Famous Flaming Marley. I can picture a half a dozen of those with our names on 'em, and I'm guaranteeing right now, they'll be the best damn Flaming Marleys you've ever had."

"What the hell is a Flaming Marley?" Walk asked, but then answering himself, "Who the hell cares? Let's do it."

"Hey, a tip, Walk, if Erika starts looking like the white women, you may need to switch to beer."

"Oh, man. You just try to keep up with me."

"Sounds like nothing but trouble," I said in all sincerity.

"Yeah, mon!"

On the beach, I introduced Walker to Erika and Spike. Walk flirted with Erika, prodding her the whole time on making sure all her friends would join us that night and finding out what they looked like. He wasn't shy in asking about particular characteristics he likes most in women and suffice it to say, none of those attributes were more than skin-deep. With Walk, everyone knows what he wants, and I think that's the reason he attracts the kind of woman who wants the same thing. It's not uncommon for Walk to tell me the girl he's dating is a self-described nymph. I don't recall that ever happening to me—and, I have to tell you—I'm sure I would.

Walk also bonded immediately with Spike. They talked for hours about girls and drinks and Walk's past adventures, and Walk even negotiated with Spike to let Erika leave early for the evening. Meanwhile, Walk and I drank enough Flaming Marleys to sink the boat with the Jamaican flag. The drink is red, green and gold and then Spike lights it and you drink it from the bottom using a straw. I'm not sure what's in it, and I'm even less sure I want to find out. At about six, when Walker started talking to Spike about what shots to try out on me, I knew I'd be an early casualty, so I staggered over to the lounge chairs on the beach and passed out.

Walk woke me up at around nine that evening. Not long after I had hoisted up my white flag, he also decided to regroup by going back to my cabin to take a nap. He had since also showered and shaved and put on a new party shirt and had firmed up commitments from Erika and her friends to join us out for the night. I may have neglected to mention he woke me up by throwing a bucket of water on me, which, I have to say was pretty effective. Suddenly awake, I threw off my wet shirt, took a swim in the ocean and was ready for more damage to come.

As I was stepping out of ocean, I saw her…

Kicking her feet slowly through the sand, her white sandals carelessly dangling from her hand, her sandy short blond curly hair completing her adorably innocent look, was the girl I had been wishing for my whole life. I'm serious. Sometimes I know these things, and this time I knew for sure. I felt a connection like something had physically happened to my soul, like a magnetic pull I had no control over. My heart started beating fast and my palms, wet from my swim, still managed to feel sweaty. She was walking along the shoreline and I was walking back towards the hotel at an angle that, if neither of us were looking (though, boy was I looking), we would have walked directly into each other.

I knew I was staring at her, but I couldn't help it and didn't want to. I walked right up to her as she was about to pass, and with all the charm and wit I could muster said, "Hi." She smiled at me, which was on par with the Negril sunset as the prettiest thing I'd ever seen, and replied softly, "Hi to you."

Hi to you. My heart took those words like candy, and I knew whatever happened I'd always remember *hi to you.*

I don't usually notice eyes. I've dated girls for months and been surprised to find out her eyes were actually silver or burgundy or some damn thing. But, this girl's almost aquamarine eyes, like the sunlit Caribbean, seemed to be talking to me. Like she had seen the same thing in me I saw in her. They weren't, I was sure, declaring, "I want you now bad boy." It was maybe something more along the lines of, "There's something about you that reminds me of a favorite shirt that you can just throw on and feel just right. Or, of all the people I've ever met, there's so few that you can connect with and trust and want to be with, and have it be good—really good— but maybe I could do that with you." I wanted her to be thinking those things, so I couldn't be sure if I imagined it or not, but that's what I thought and hoped those pretty eyes were saying.

I stood there transfixed as she walked by. She glanced back at me once and gave me a smile like it was okay, she understood why I was standing there like an idiot looking at her walk away. Then, just as I was expecting her to walk into the night, she veered left to take a seat at Spike's bar. I could feel my face go flush. In my mind, I had already devoted the rest of my life to finding this girl wherever it was she was staying, or wherever it was she was from. But now, she had wondered into *MY* bar (…of all the Flaming Marley joints in all the world…), and I wondered if it was fate. I also realized with sudden distress that Walker was in striking distance. I practically raced to the bar, fearing that he was going to start picking up my dream girl, but when I got there, Walk was happily talking to Spike. I looked at him, knowing he never missed "talent" as he called it, but found he wasn't seeing it. Not understanding, it finally dawned on me that we had never competed for the same girl, and I realized that night, we never would. Whatever I had seen in this girl was lost on Walk, and I laughed to myself at what different taste we had.

Then, it kind of sunk in that Walk, Spike and dream girl were all looking at me, and I realized I was standing there inside the bar dripping wet and looking like a shaggy lost dog who had walked in from the rain. Walk and Spike made jokes about it and, embarrassed, I shot a look at the girl, who smiled, like I was kind of cute or something. When I smiled and said to Walk, "All right, bud, I'm ready to hit the town, how do I look?" she laughed a little (like dream girls do), and I felt great.

Just then, Spike said to me, "Hey, fish mon, me like to introduce yah to someone. Seth, dis is Emma. Emma, dis is Seth."

I absolutely got chills and hoped I didn't do that cartoon thing where your eyes pop out of your head. This girl was Dugan's daughter. Aside from the fact that I'd have to figure out how a shipwreck like Dugan could have produced such a treasure like Emma, I realized it meant I might see her everyday! I could feel my soul jump for joy.

Since I had more time to gather my thoughts so that I could say just the right thing to stir her soul, I quite cleverly stammered out, "Hi Emma," because, as you know, I kind of have a way with words.

She replied, "Hi to you, Seth." *Hi to you* was my new favorite saying by like a million miles.

Just then, Erika arrived with an army of girls, each prettier than the next.

"Showtime," Walker yelled.

Erika looked at me and asked, "What's going on with you, Seth, are you feeling okay?"

"Yes," I stammered, and it was never more true. "I'm doing great."

"Good. You had this look like, I don't know." Then she looked at Emma, saying hi to her, and realized, "Oh God, maybe I do know. Come on, Seth, let's get you ready to go and we can talk about this." She grabbed my arm and led me to my room. As I toweled off and changed in the bathroom, she said, "Seth, I saw that look. You have that look."

"What look? I don't have a look," I said looking in the mirror for a look.

"*That* look. Oh, yes you do. You have a ting for Emma don't you?" I loved that she picked right then to say ting.

I had just put on my frayed khaki shorts and came out from the bathroom to see Erika sitting on the bed. I took her hands in mine, sat next to her, and confessed, "Erika, I have to tell you. It's unbelievable. I saw her and the moon and the stars and my heart and soul all moved. Oh my God, Erika, she's the one. She's why Shulie would've been a mistake. Not for a second did I feel this way about her. Somehow, someway, Emma and I are partners. She and I belong together, Erika. We belong together."

"Seth," she said kissing me on the cheek, "my friend, then we need to work on making that happen."

"Thank you, Erika." I was tremendously relieved that she didn't bring me back to earth or tell me there's no way I could know that without saying two words to her. Actually I did say *two* words to her and I did know.

"But not tonight, boy, we are going out on the town with your friend and my friends, and we're going to have a bash. Put a shirt on, mister, and let's go. By the way, you haven't said anything about how I look."

She was wearing a short, tight dress with psychedelic colors in wavy horizontal stripes and looked amazing. *Trust mi pon dat.* There couldn't have been too many girls in the world that could've pulled off wearing a dress like that, but boy could she. I couldn't believe I hadn't noticed it before she pointed it out. "Wow, Erika!" was about all I managed, but I think answered her question.

She smiled at the compliment and offered, "I'm sure you'll want to walk by the bar again. C'mon, let's go." We did, but Emma was no longer there. I suddenly wanted to let Walk and Erika and her friends go without me, so I could find Emma, but Walk had come all this way because I said I needed a drinking buddy. I couldn't bag out, no matter how much I wanted to. We all piled into the Blue Moon van and headed out into the night.

29

Erika, her four friends, Walk and I turned into the dirt driveway of a place called Risky Business, the self-described party capital of Negril. If that wasn't an appropriate assessment before we arrived, it would be after Walker got done with it. The party was already in full swing both on its two inside levels and outside on the beach. Inside large and numerous speakers were playing reggae wonderfully too loud, and many on the lower level were already dancing. Outside a stage for a live band faced the water. The sign on the stage announced there'd be a live band at nine that night and a bonfire on the beach. I'd already learned there is time, Jamaican time, and reggae time, meaning the band showed up whenever they felt like it. I was sure they weren't gonna be starting anytime soon. I heard that Air Jamaica was the same way. The departure board doesn't list times next to flights, it just displays, *Soon come* or *Wheneverthefuck* and you understand.

We grabbed a table on the lower level just off the dance floor, and Walker ordered a bunch of food that he said he'd put on his expense report. He's the best salesman I know, but trying to convince his boss that Lobster Pasta and Risky Snapper from Negril Jamaica was a legitimate business expense seemed like a formidable challenge even for him. I knew we were in trouble when we ordered tropical-colored Appleton Rum drinks that arrived in fish bowls. The girls were getting a kick out of Walk and were in the full spirit of the evening, finishing their fish bowls and ready for more. Between the next round of drinks, which might as well have come in IV bags, we sloshed our way to the dance floor. The first song was Ziggy Marley's *Brothers and Sisters*, appropriate to our diverse little party group. Walk has always been a great dancer, the kind where the rest of the dance floor will stop dancing and form a circle around Walk and his date. Not to be too stereotypical, but Erika's friends, each dressed as fun as Erika, were up for the challenge. Before long, people were buying us drinks, and at one point Walk and all of Erika's friends were up on the bar as Walk taught them his famous Walkman dance. I was dancing mostly with Erika, but we also got caught up in Walk's showtime, and joined the rest of our group up on the bar. Most of the bar started doing the Walkman, and when we were done, we actually got an ovation from the other bar people.

In between dances—which were getting wilder and more erotic with Walk and the Jamaican girls—we drank every kind of alcohol they had, and at one point, I think they may have had to make a run to Barbados for more rum.

When the band started sometime after I had lost all ability to know where I was, Erika and I danced in the sand, and I noticed Walk leading a sing along with the people at the bonfire, who were now his best friends. I also saw him put on the hard sell, and briefly make out with one of Erika's friends, though I could tell she had it under control.

At some point, presumably much later in the night, I realized that we had outlasted Erika and her friends, and I had only a vague recollection of Erika giving me a kiss good night and a warning to not get in too much trouble. I had no recollection of where I got the cigar I was smoking or the spliff behind my ear.

Meanwhile, Walk found me still somehow on my feet and swaying to the reggae band. It was the first time in who knows how long that night that I'd been conscious of myself actually being there. A picture developed in my mind of myself flapping in the breeze like the Jamaican flag. Walk was accompanied by some new girls he had met inside the bar. They seemed quite attractive, but I couldn't focus enough to know for sure. Walker, though, assured me it was a "talent show." The girls, I was interested to find out were staying at Hedonism II. From what I understood from Gumby, it's just fuck, fuck, fuck all day long over there. Walk informed me we were invited back there with the girls. Though I had a vague thought of not particularly wanting to because of Emma, I was in no position to dissuade Walker. Even at my best, I was rarely in a position to argue with Walker.

It was sometime just before dawn when we got there. The last remnant of a toga party was actually still going on, with apparently only the most desperately determined partiers still going at it. There wasn't a lot in the way of clothes happening, and soon Walk and I were wearing only togas and the girls were wearing, um, less than that. The rest was just blurry, funky visions, like looking in a kaleidoscope. At one point, one of those visions, which I'd just as soon forget, was of Walker and the girls dancing the Walkman naked. That's the last I remember, until waking up sometime later that morning without my toga, an empty condom wrapper on the nightstand, and a wildly attractive girl in my—well, probably her—bed. I lifted up the sheets to find breasts that, like the night, couldn't have been real. Walk was coming out of the shower, like he was in an Irish Spring commercial, while two naked girls remained passed out semi-covered by their sheets in the other bed. I couldn't be sure that I had participated in any sexual adventure, despite the circumstantial evidence against me, and I wondered if it still counts if I'm not aware of it. I couldn't imagine that I could have been much use to anyone. Walker was whistling and annoyingly chipper, but was forgiven when someone knocked at the door with coffee he had ordered for us.

I got up slowly, grabbed my coffee and headed for the bathroom. I thanked Jah that one of the girls had a huge bottle of extra-strength Tylenol, and I took six to give them a fighting chance. I took a shower and after-ward, for the first time that morning, I thought I might actually live through the experience.

Through some quirk of fate both my wallet and Walk's were on a table between the beds, but our clothes were nowhere to be found. The girls were still very much out, so we put our togas back on and went down for breakfast, in what I was sure wasn't going to be a high point in my life. Prior to leaving the girls' room, though, Walk grabbed one of their cameras and took half a role of pictures of the three of them, and a couple of us—I guess to add insult to injury—and then laid the camera back down on the dresser. We left the room joking about how we just made the day of some photo department clerk at Walgreen's.

Hedonism II is an all-inclusive resort, meaning all of the food and drinks are included once you're there. Since we were there, we helped our-selves to what was left of the breakfast buffet. We each had an artery clog-ging breakfast of biscuits and gravy, bacon and eggs, and fresh fruit, to be healthy, which was more than I had eaten in the rest of my first week in Jamaica combined. We got a few looks from the other guests because we were still in our togas, but it appeared more in admiration than anything else. I was so proud.

I was more than ready to head back, but Walk said we needed to try and find our clothes—which is, I was sure, the opposite of what he wanted to do. I didn't know where we were earlier that morning, but I didn't think we left our clothes on the nude beach Walk led us to. Walk was ready to party au natural again. I looked at it as an opportunity to pass out face, and other stuff, down on the beach. If nothing else, I thought to myself, I could get a tushy tan to die for (not that I had any idea what that might come in handy for.) Walker was generous and didn't throw another bucket of water on me for another hour and a half. A new group of, not so much wildly attractive, as attractively wild girls was going on an au natural catamaran trip up the coast towards the Negril cliffs, and apparently we needed to join them. So, sometime that afternoon we went sailing and drinking, both of which after my nap I was able to do. Our route took us along the coast, passing the Blue Moon, until we anchored the boat, and maybe twenty naked people swam for shore to go to eat at one of the cliffside restaurants. Thinking ahead, I grabbed a life raft so I could make it through the water with a bag full of everyone's wallets and our togas in tact. We ate lunch with the crowd, then bid them adieu, which Walker did very grudgingly, presumably because he still had a few condoms to use. In our togas, we cabbed back to the Blue Moon. Walk complained the whole way back, and I realized that if ever a person had found his personal nirvana, Walk did at H2.

I paid the amused cab driver and we headed towards the Blue Moon beach when who's walking towards toga boys, but Emma and Erika. *Great.* I buried my head in my hands on the very weak chance that they wouldn't notice two idiots strolling in the middle of the afternoon in togas. I wasn't sure how Emma would react to me coming home nineteen hours after going out—after having lost my fucking clothes—but I didn't want to see it. Walk, of course, wanted to stop and talk, but I mumbled something about just doing our laundry and started to scurry away to my cabin. Then I realized I couldn't leave Walk with Emma to recount the previous night, so I went back, smiled at the girls and practically dragged Walk to the cabin. While I wasn't going to linger, I noticed that the pretty scent of Emma sure was. I took that back to my cabin with me.

Walk, wondering what had gotten in to me, said he was just making plans to go out again tonight—he was an even bigger freak than I had previously known—but I said no fucking way. He started to make an argument about not coming all this way to sit and do nothing, but I think he was just posturing because we both realized that drinking until we were dead seemed somehow counterproductive. He even offered the perfect solution of chilling for a couple hours, maybe getting Erika to watch the sunset with us and hanging out at Spike's. We agreed that over a few cocktails, I could catch him up on all the stuff that led me here in the first place.

We set up three chairs to watch the sunset, and Erika set us all up with Red Stripes. I noticed that Emma came out to the bar for awhile, but because I was a little embarrassed about earlier, and mostly because I owed it to Walk to hang with him rather than get hopelessly lost in Emmaland that night, I didn't try to include her.

Instead, after the wonderful sunset, which I was happy to see even got to Walker, we got caught up on each other's lives. Walk told a story about how he had gone out a couple of Monday nights earlier when he met an exceptionally attractive woman who, after taking her home and giving her his patented backrub, did all sorts of things to him that night (Walk didn't leave out the details, but I will.) Anyway, this girl then proceeded to call him several times every day trying to reach him, but she never left her number. With each call she appeared more desperate to talk to him. So, finally, she leaves him a groveling message saying, "I have to talk to you again, please— please—please call me." *And* she even leaves her phone number. But then she adds the kicker, "But if my husband answers, for God sakes, hang up!" I shook my head and laughed. That story is so Walk, and again, I'm out there and single, but can I just point out that that doesn't happen to me. Ever.

He again lamented the fact that he wasn't ever going to get married. He's dated seriously at least two really sweet, smart, fun, attractive girls (thrown in among the majority of bimbos), but always their ass was slightly too big, or some similarly shallow excuse was given. He doesn't cop to the fact that he's essentially looking for a superficial trophy wife, but rather says it's just very important to him that he never loses the attraction to his future wife, because he doesn't want to stray. Meanwhile, he isn't getting any younger, or thinner or growing more hair, and his likelihood of finding what he's looking for isn't getting any better. I hope he does, because he actually does treat the women he dates very well and does have the makings of a good husband. He lavishes them with attention and gifts and fun and has been single long enough to have become an accomplished housekeeper and cook. In the meantime, though, he's never hurting for stories, even if they are like the one above, and I don't think he's as ready to settle down as he says.

Then we started talking about Shulie. I told him she was sweet and very pretty, and that I had loved her, but it turned out to be more of a desperate attempt to find happiness by trying to be who I wasn't. I told him it was a lot more right in my head than my heart—and that I thought it worked out for the best. I said that it became clear to me that I shouldn't try to change, but rather try to make the most out of what I was good at by trying to write a book. I said it was a good dream and felt right, and that's why I had moved to Jamaica.

He thought about it for a while, and, clearly moved by my sharing my inner-most feelings and thoughts, put it in perspective quite nicely, "So, does she have a nice ass?" We may have been a little slap-happy, because we both laughed hysterically. Taking advantage of the opportunity, I grabbed the bucket the last round of Red Stripes had come in, filled it in the ocean, and, with a final bit of justice, soaked him with it. He yelled, "Yuradeek!" and tackled me in the water. We wrestled around in the ocean probably looking like a couple of lovesick homosexuals. It was late and we came out of the water with our arms around each other's shoulders. Without saying so, it was a perfect way to end his visit. Early the next morning he was on his way, honking his horn like, well, like Walk, waking up the rest of Negril, and I was left to begin my new reality.

30

Waking up that next morning I had two thoughts. One was that it was time to start my novel and my future. The second was, of course, Emma. In assessing which of the two had the higher priority, um, what was the first again?

After Walker left, I was enjoying various imaginary conversations with her, and had wandered out on my patio while brushing my teeth, when I saw her jogging down the beach. She was wearing ancient shorts that were probably the same she had worn in high school and a long gray tee-shirt. It was probably sexy only to me. I had a chance to yell, "Hey," or some similarly clever opener to let her know I had command of the language, but as I started to, I realized there'd be no way to do that without spitting toothpaste on myself. So, I ran to the bathroom, rinsed and spit, and headed out after her, under the guise of also going for a jog.

I even proudly hurdled the patio railing onto the beach before thankfully looking down to see I was dressed only in boxer shorts. Given that she had last seen me wearing only a toga, I felt compelled to turn around and change into, maybe, a normal person. Somehow diminished, I headed back for my cabin, tried to re-hurdle the railing, and was successful only to the extent that I hadn't fallen entirely on my head. My right foot clipped the railing and I needed my hands, my back, and the sacrifice of a good deal of my skin to avoid finding out what the Jamaican health care system was all about. This was all really excellent for my confidence. As is not uncommon for me after a little adversity in the face of a big challenge, I was all of a sudden in danger of being high school loser boy again. Rather than quickly regrouping and trying to catch up with her, I sulked around my cabin, slowly getting dressed and thinking maybe I'd see her later. Perhaps when I was cooler.

I grabbed my laptop for the first time and headed for a lounge chair on the beach. I was lost in space—probably dreaming of valiantly hurdling the railing, mounting my trusty white stallion and expertly riding bareback to scoop her up so we could ride gloriously into the sunset even though it was eleven-thirty in the morning—when I looked up and there she was. Emma had returned from her run and taken the seat next to me. She looked me over, smiled that wonderful Emma smile and said, "Hi, Seth."

"Hi, Emma." So far, a dolphin could've equaled the rap I had going.

"It's good to see you again, especially without your bed sheet," she said joking.

With a thoroughly embarrassed smile and not knowing quite how to get out of that with any dignity whatsoever, improvising like a madman, I went with, "Listen, Emma, you need to know that I was dressed like that strictly for religious reasons. I don't know if you know this, but Saturday afternoon was a Jewish holiday, and on certain holidays I can get religious as hell."

"I see," she said with a cute smirk. "And, your holiday tradition calls for wearing bed sheets?"

"Exactly. Okay, well, actually, no, some people were yarmulkes, those little beanie hats, but, from a fashion sense, I've never been able to make that work for me."

She smiled and replied, "Good choice. I though the toga was quite the fashion statement."

I could tell the embarrassment was never going to end. "Thank you. Not everyone can pull that off."

"I'm sure that's true. So, what holiday was it?"

"It's, um, you know, Passashanahanadah," I answered solemnly, doing that Jesus cross thing with my hand, except with the six points of the Star of David, realizing too late that Jews never do that because it looks ridiculous.

"Really," she said, trying not to laugh, "I'm not aware of that one."

"It's actually a little known holiday to celebrate the plight of the ancient Jewish tribe, the Macanudus, and their epic struggle against…um, static cling, and, you know, of course, the subsequent miracle of fabric softener." I should have just killed myself. It'd have been less torture.

With no semblance of pride left, I could barely look at her, but she finally let out the laugh she was stifling and let me off the hook with, "Sure, where would we be without Snuggle?"

I laughed, too, and with tremendous relief agreed, "That's the whole thing right there." I put my hand across my heart and said, "I'm so glad I can talk to you about this. Religion can be such a divisive subject."

"Especially when it comes to laundry products," she said with a smile and I knew for sure that my initial feeling about her was right on target.

I laughed, and said, "Oh please, I think we've all learned from the Six-Day Liquid Tide Fiasco of '73."

She gave me a smile and slight rolling of her eyes that said, okay, enough, laundry rabbi.

"I'm Emma Kelly," she said offering her hand.

I considered doing that thing where you kiss the back of her hand, but decided quickly that it was more corny than cool. Instead, I shook and said, "I'm Seth Gold, legendary unemployed beach bum."

"That's right, I thought I recognized you." She joked, "It's an honor that you would choose our little hotel to vegetate."

"I'm all about spreading joy and laziness around the world. But, I'll have you know, I don't just vegetate. For instance," I said in a shameless effort to insert myself in her life, "I can jog you know."

"Oh really? You jog?"

"No, but I know how."

"I'm impressed," she mocked, and then asked charitably, "Would you like to join me tomorrow morning?"

"I thought you'd never ask. It'd be my honor." I was being charming as hell, as far as I knew.

"So, what are you doing today?" she asked.

"Well, I hope to start the novel I came here to write." Then, hoping to get that out of the way in case she invited me to spend the day with her, I typed in the words Chapter One. "There, it's officially started."

"Wow. That was exciting. Congratulations!" she said. Then adding a little sincerity, "You're really writing a book? That's cool, Seth. Your first one?"

"Yeah," I said with pride, though I had nothing to take pride in.

"Is it something you've always wanted to do?"

"Kind of, but it kind of came in sharper focus for me recently."

She asked about that and we talked about the things that led me here. I focused more on the work angle, glossing over the Shulie relationship. I didn't want her to think it was too soon to get in another relationship, or that Emma might be rebound girl. Nothing could be further from the truth, but I'm not sure I was capable of explaining that to her. She was a sympathetic listener and we were bonding nicely. I was being self-deprecating, as usual, but so far, I thought that it was mostly charming, and that I hadn't yet embarrassed myself too much.

Everything was, in fact, very cool, until I asked what she was doing that day.

Then she hit me with, "I met this guy just this weekend and he asked me to have lunch with him today. Like a real date. There have been some hot-shot tourist guys that have asked me out, like I was going to be there vacation conquest or something, but there hasn't been anyone that I've considered going out on a real date with since I've been here."

Just this weekend! I just looked at her thinking, *Oh, isn't that just fucking neat,* having an internal temper tantrum. I loved my timing.

The conversation had taken quite a turn, and I wondered if there had been an audible sound as the air got let out of my balloon. I felt a knife in my heart when she shyly said that she kind of liked him. He was apparently gorgeous (I don't do a good job of competing against gorgeous) and had a wonderful accent, came to Negril often for business and blah blah blah. I got the impression that there was no 'kind of' about how she liked him. Evidently, I was her newest bestest girl friend—how did that happen exactly?—because she started asking for my advice and interpretations and friendship (as in *just friend* ship.)

It was a cruel twist of fate to be asked to help her out with another guy, but I was glad, at least, that she at least felt comfortable enough to share her personal thoughts and feelings with me. And, I decided it would at least give us something to talk about and maybe there was something to the idea of building our relationship without romantic or sexual pressures. So, I helped her with the best dating and fashion advice I had. I think it came off well, almost worldly actually (because I can be that way when it does me no good whatsoever), and she took my hands to thank me. She hesitated and then confided in me, "Seth, I had a feeling about you when I saw you on the beach the other night." She hesitated again, looking for the right words, "That you were somehow different and better than most of the guys I've met. And that I felt like we could be friends…good friends, you know. Now, I've met you and I feel that way even more. I'm really happy we met." The look in her eyes told me she meant it. She touched me lightly on the shoulder as she stood up. With a smile, she wished me, "Happy Passashanahanadah." And then with a bigger smile, "You're nuts."

Nuts about you, I didn't say. Though, pathetically, I did say, "Emma, I'll be around tonight, if you want someone to talk to…about your date."

"Thanks, Seth, that's sweet of you. I think I'd like that."

"Good luck." I tried to act like I meant it, but couldn't believe I said that.

She smiled, waved and walked away.

I sat there stunned, as if the competing feelings of ecstasy and depression were fighting to a draw.

I started banging into my laptop, starting my book by writing about Emma, rewriting the conversation we just had to leave out Accent Guy. It was going okay until I added the part about the horse riding down the beach. I deleted everything but the words "Chapter One."

Erika, who had apparently been keeping an eye on the whole conversation, suddenly materialized in front of me and sat down. "So, Romeo, how are you doing?"

"Didn't Romeo kill himself?" I asked looking maybe a little glum.

"Oh no, that bad?"

I told her all about it. It was perfect—everything I'd have dreamed, and she was everything I dreamed—until some other guy had rudely gotten to my dream girl first. That kind of tarnished the whole perfection thing. "I blame it all on Walker," I said, thinking that if hadn't come all the way to Jamaica just because I practically begged him too, Emma might never have met accent boy.

Erika, maybe just looking on the bright side, said that if I thought about it, it was great that Emma was the girl I had hoped. She said that was a victory not to be ignored because "what if she had turned out to be someone else…someone less than your expectations…wouldn't that be much, much worse?" It wasn't a bad point, I had to admit, not that I felt like celebrating. I also agreed with her that, at least, I still had a fighting chance, and that I wouldn't kill myself. Yet.

That night, Emma came and knocked on my door. It was bittersweet to invite her in my room and have her sit on my bed.

She looked simply beautiful to me. Her expressive face seemed filled with the wonder of a child and the sensitivity of a lover. It was understanding and sincere. It was that face that had given away fate's little plan that we were somehow meant to meet each other. She was tan and had those incredible eyes the color of the sea under a blue sky. Her smile always had a hint of shyness, with the tip of her tongue often touching the back of her top teeth. The smile was also almost imperceptibly asymmetrical, dipping slightly farther south on her right side. It was nearly impossible for me to look at her smile without smiling myself. And, under that was the imperfection of a little cleft in the center of her chin when she smiled big. It gave her face even more character and charm, and I found myself looking forward to making her laugh so I could see it again. Her body features were all just slightly understated to the point that if she walked by on the beach, wearing maybe an oversized tee-shirt, and you weren't paying close attention, she may not turn your head. But a more careful inspection revealed not a single defect. She was sort of the opposite of the Bulls' cheerleaders who were good from far, but far from good. The curls of her short blond hair were sort of an unmade bed: unfussed over, unpretentious, unglamorous and perfect.

His name was Diego, and he had an attractive romanticism about him. He seemed wonderfully interested in her and her family and was a good listener. To Emma, it was refreshing that he didn't just talk about himself like most guys. In fact, he didn't like to talk much about himself, so at times the conversation came close to dragging, but he was sweet and a gentleman and gorgeous (okay, whatever, stop with the gorgeous thing already!)

I asked what he did. He told Emma that he was a salesman for a wine distributor, and though he didn't provide a lot of detail, his job was to schmooze the restaurant owners to sell his wine. She told me a story he had told her and I was dismayed to find it was kind of clever and sensitive. Bastard.

I asked how it all ended, for the same reason, I guess, that people are drawn to a traffic accident or the sound of sirens. The news won't be good, but you can't not know. She said that he was a gentleman and asked if he could give her a kiss on the cheek. She told him that was fine, and told me she wanted him to give her more of a kiss than that. She asked me if I thought that was bad of her to think that.

Yes, Yes, Yes. I thought. "No, no, no," I said. "You had a good time and you like him. There's nothing wrong with that." What was I supposed to say? If I was going to be her buddy, she should at least like me. After all, no one appreciates honesty.

Diego told Emma he'd be in town again next weekend, and wanted to see her, but hadn't officially asked. "What do you think? Do you think that means he wants to ask me out or not?" she asked me.

"You know, Emma, one thing about guys is we're very literal when we speak. Women are always trying to find a hidden meaning in what we say. You know, or try to figure out what we *really* mean. That's giving guys way too much credit. We generally have nothing else going on in our heads. So, if he asks to kiss you and says he wants to see you again, I'm sure he wanted to kiss you and wants to see you again." And, I added, being quite literal myself, "I would if I was him."

That seemed to be what she wanted to hear, about Diego, anyway. "Thanks, Seth." She kissed me on the cheek, and said, "See you on the beach at seven-thirty tomorrow morning for our jog? I usually only go about three miles."

Seven-thirty?! Three miles?! Yikes. "Of course. See you then. Sleep well Emma."

"Good night, Seth."

I did mention that she kissed me, right?

31

Rising with the morning sun, I met Emma to go for a run (and I'm sorry, I didn't mean for that sentence to sound so much like Bob Marley meets Jessie Jackson.) Prior to that I had stretched for more than half an hour to minimize the likelihood of Emma having to carry me back home because of a debilitating muscle pull. Due in large part to the incredible adrenaline rush I got just being with Emma—and that she took it easy on me by cutting the run down to two miles—I made it the whole way. I even promised to be able to do it again the next day, not something she was likely to believe in that I had my face in the sand at the time. Like those marathon runners that come in last place out of ninety-two thousand entrants—but who heroically don't give up, despite obvious humiliation, and the likelihood they won't ever get laid again—I practically crawled the last fifty yards, and fell across an imaginary finish line, unable to move another inch.

I rolled over and asked if she wanted to have breakfast with me. Probably not just because that must have looked pretty unappetizing with my sweaty, sandy, lifeless body staring back at her, she said she'd like to, but had to get to work. She did, though, ask if I'd have a drink with her that night (presumably when I'd have a chance to make myself presentable.) I mentally checked my Day Planner and surprisingly, I had the evening open. Talk about a lucky break for her.

Fast forwarding to that evening—because, who am I kidding, nothing else mattered—we sat at one of the tables outside of Spike's bar. Emma went and grabbed one of the candleholders from the inside tables. As if a table with Emma needed any more atmosphere, the candle added a nice glow to the conversation, and the light shown nicely on her face. It kind of made it feel more like a date than just that we were hanging out. I looked closely at her face in the candlelight. If I was an accomplished painter, I could spend a career and never fully capture everything her face had to say, or at least had to say to me. She also smelled great again. I wondered if it was perfume or just her.

We each ordered Red Stripes. The only two choices of beer at Spike's bar, and indeed, at many places in Jamaica were Red Stripe and Heineken, which were both brewed in Jamaica. In the first of many things Emma and I found that we shared in common was a dislike of Heineken. It was, in fact, probably my least favorite beer not held together by plastic rings. I told her it was for people who needed commercials to tell them what they liked. Emma explained that her problem with it, aside from the skunky taste, was how much it reminded her of the people back home. She was originally from Greenwich, Connecticut, a beautiful, but very rich, preppy and snobby commuter suburb of New York City. I had been to Greenwich and that area a number of times for work, and commented that there didn't seem to be a thing about her that suggested she was from Greenwich. She smiled and said thanks. She told me she had a term for the Greenwich people: the bacon people, and had to tell me the story about where that term originated. Her animation as she spoke was infectious, but in truth, she could've been talking about advanced calculus theory and I'd have been into it.

"Okay, so it's lunch time in Greenwich, and we're at an overpriced deli at the Mill on the Byrum River, overpriced because you can see the Mill from the deli, and, of course, that makes the food taste better. Some of Greenwich, like me are just there for lunch, and some of us are over-dressed, over-perfumed, and over-jeweled for noon on a weekday in a deli, even if it is in Greenwich. My friend and I are standing behind this overdone woman in line at the deli. She orders the Dagwood sandwich, no bacon please, no bacon. They may not have heard her, so, NO BACON PLEASE!" Emma is getting into the story and doing a nice job with the bacon accent. "Anyway, my friend orders the Dagwood also, no omits, just the complete sandwich. Overdone woman is wringing her hands ahead of us inspecting the sandwich maker, impatient as hell, waiting for her no bacon sandwich. A tray pops up with a Dagwood. She can't get her hands over to the tray quick enough to start peeling up the layers of croissant, turkey, and AAAUGH! Bacon! She goes berserk. I think she's considering calling the police. She's really on a rampage. 'I said no BACON, I distinctly asked for NO bacon...NO BACON, blah-blah-blah-no bacon-blah-blah-blah'. The sandwich guy, evidently used to this sort of thing, barely looks up at her and says 'hey lady, that's his sandwich, *his*, WITH BACON.' I start laughing and my friend says to her, as the lady is wilting like uncooked bacon, please get your hands off my sandwich. I almost died. So that's why the bacon people are the bacon people, and that lady is the leader of all the bacon people."

I told her my view on people who wear Ralph Lauren Polo shirts and drive BMWs or drink Heineken is that the only thing those purchases say about them is that they have money. I said I'd much rather buy something that says I have style or taste. Emma was evidently happy with me and blurted, "Thank you. I love that you said that. Living there until I was twenty-one, I wanted to climb a building on Greenwich Avenue and yell out to the bacon people, *You're all the same and I'm not impressed!*"

I asked if she had dated much back at home. She said she had dated some bacon boys early in high school—because she didn't know any better—but had soon started seeing through it and wanted more. In high school, she had sung in a rock band, and had had a crush on the lead singer for almost two years. Then they started dating a while, but he turned out to be a druggie and a dick, and she realized a) just being different than the bacon people wasn't enough, and b) she was dating, more or less, her father. She said this with a sense of humor, not bitterness, as if she knew neither her dad nor her boyfriend had taken away from who she became.

However, when that led to a conversation about her family life, there was no mistaking a sense of sadness. Her mom and dad had divorced when she was four. Her mom, whom she loved more than anyone, remarried a couple of years later. Unlike the typical sob story of the abusive, drunken stepfather, Emma's step-dad, Michael, was a wonderful husband and the best father Emma ever knew. He was kind, loving, hard working, a good provider, and, to her, the funniest guy in the world. If he hadn't had the character flaw of dying of cancer when Emma was twelve, her mom, her older sister and she might have known nothing but good times. Instead, her mom turned lonely and drunk and committed the worst of sins by allowing her father back for chances he didn't deserve. Her sister, who was at the more vulnerable age of nineteen when Michael died and her mom got lost, went into a funk that eventually led her in and out of drug rehab centers. She was currently getting by, but it wasn't uncommon for Emma to hear that she had slipped again.

Having known nothing but a solid, loving family, I could still feel her pain. In fact, I've always been attracted to, and felt a bond with, people with troubled souls. I can always relate to the people who are working hard in the real world, putting a happy face on things, but who, when you dig a little, are fighting their personal demons. I'm sure it has something to do with the ghosts of my high school years, but, also like in the movie *It's a Wonderful Life*, I'm drawn to trying to fix the problems of the people I care for—so at the end everyone gives me money. Just kidding about that last part. Selfishly, there may also be something to that if they have no problems, they'd be less likely to slum with me.

Knowing it was obviously related to the conversation we were having, I asked why she had come here to Jamaica. She told me the unbelievable story of how her dad, Dugan, had won the Blue Moon in a card game from some drunk high roller in Las Vegas. Since Dugan had nothing else going on in his life, he came to Jamaican to manage the hotel. He was in the process of running it—or perhaps more accurately, not running it—into the ground, when Emma got a call from her crying dad. She had never heard him cry, but he had just been put in jail for a small-scale drug deal he had orchestrated. He needed her help.

Emma had been working at the American Cancer Society because she somehow wanted to make the Michael part of her life better by not letting his memory or life go to waste. Though she thought her dad, to a large degree, deserved what he got, she also looked at it as an opportunity to try to make that part of her life better, too. She decided it was worth a year of her life if she could make sure her father stayed above the law, and to help him turn around the Blue Moon. She owed her father, and herself, at least that much. When she got here, like I did, she fell in love with it.

I asked if what the Blue Moon needed was more and better promotion and marketing. She said she'd been here for three months and was mostly fixing all the operational problems—fucked up ordering of supplies, cleaning of the rooms and grounds, the reservations' system, the ability to do wake-up calls, you name it, everything there was to do with running a hotel was a mess. I asked if the flowers were her idea and wasn't at all surprised that the answer was yes. She said she hadn't had time yet for marketing, but that was kind of her next project. I told her I could probably help her out on that. She gave me the job and a wonderfully appreciative smile, which already made it one of the best jobs I ever had.

Then she asked if I wanted to take a walk on the beach. We walked in silence awhile, sipping our beers, probably both thinking about all the stuff she had shared with me. After a while, she looked at me and confided that she didn't normally open up to people like she did with me. That she didn't normally trust guys—they had a habit of letting her down—but she thought she might trust me. I told her she should and that I admired what she was doing for her dad and the Blue Moon.

I felt this surreal connection with Emma like I had with no one else. It was like we just understood each other, and dug the same things (except she liked the Knicks, which I felt was kind of a problem), laughed at the same things, and we're moved by the same things.

Ignoring the fact that I had no talent whatsoever, my fantasy had always been to be in a rock band. I told her probably the best night of my life was when my college friends and I won an "air band" contest at some bar. She pretended to be very impressed and I joked that we'd even cut an album, but that it didn't sell very well. We were still early enough in our relationship that she laughed at that. I asked about her band. She generally sang back-up, but her favorite song was the Stones' song *Gimme Shelter*. She used to love the solo line she had, "*Love, baby, it's just a kiss away.*" If she was trying to tease me with the "it's just a kiss away" line, she was doing a damn fine job. We talked about our favorite music. Her recent favorites were Dave Matthews, Keb Mo, Tori Amos and U2. Her favorite song was *In Your Eyes* by Peter Gabriel. As if by fate, her two favorite bands of all time were Bruce Springsteen and the Rolling Stones. I had worn out every Bruce Springsteen record, and probably a dozen Stones' albums. My college progression had been wanting to be Mick to wanting to be Bruce. Though, I've mostly moved on to more current bands, to this day, I still can't listen to my old favorites without singing all the words.

I had lived in Florida after graduating college, and I shared with her that one of my unfulfilled little fantasies back then was to sit on the beach on a warm breezy night, and bond with a pretty girl while listening to the album *Born to Run*. It's hopelessly melodramatic, as I am, but it's also passionate and poetic and beautiful. I told her that sharing that kind of thing with another person seemed so cool to me, like by extension, I also had the same kind of passion and poetry and beauty. Emma looked at me, took my hand in hers and with a wonderful smile started softly singing the first line of *Jungleland*.

"*The rangers had a homecoming in Harlem late last night.*" She had a really sweet voice. I didn't, but joined in with, "*And the Magic Rat drove his sleek machine over the Jersey state line.*" I was surprised I still remembered the words, and holding hands, we sang the whole song together...

Barefoot girl sitting on the hood of a Dodge. Drinking warm beer in the soft summer rain. The Rat pulls into town rolls up his pants. Together they take a stab at romance and disappear down Flamingo Lane.

I told her I'd like to take a stab at romance and disappear down Flamingo Lane with someone one day, and she smiled at me. I wanted to say "with you," but I'm never really sure when it's okay to say stuff like that. I hoped it was understood.

After the lines, *The midnight gang's assembled and picked a rendezvous for the night. They'll meet 'neath that giant Exxon sign that brings this fair city light,* she hoped, "Maybe I'll meet someone 'neath that giant Exxon sign someday."

We finished with a resounding, "*Tonight in Jungleland!*" and hugged in the middle of the beach. The only way it could have been more perfect would have been for Clarence Cleamons to have actually been there on the beach playing the sax solo as we walked by. I hoped like hell Emma and I would disappear down Flamingo Lane, or meet under the Exxon sign someday. We headed back, though I'm not sure that my feet actually touched the ground.

That night, when I got back to my room, I called and made flight reservations to come back for six more months. I had decided that Jamaica was my new home. For my dream of writing a book , for Emma , and for Flamingo Lane.

32

In my mind, the Magic Rat drove his sleek machine over the Jersey state line so often, I couldn't imagine he still had hubcaps. From bacon land to *Jungleland*, I replayed the previous night over and over in my mind and, if anything, it kept on getting sweeter and sweeter. I couldn't have written a better script, which, I admit, doesn't say much for my writing career. It was one of the best *dates*, one of the best *nights*, of my life. Only I'm not sure Emma would call it a date. (I am sure, though, that she didn't call it a *night* until it was nearly morning.) In fact, we were out so late, when we did go for a jog together late in the morning, she was moving as slow as I was. We jogged and joked, and this time she laughed more with me than at me.

Then a really sucky thing happened. As I was learning to get used to over the past few weeks, my highest highs were almost immediately followed by a Shu-lie to the ass or a Die-go to hell. My slightly conservative plan of celebrating my ten-year wedding anniversary with Emma ten years from maybe this weekend was dashed when that afternoon she shared the super happy news that Diego had called to ask her out again for Saturday. I waited for some indication that after our great night, she might have had second thoughts about Diego, but no. Just the same old excitement she had the first time she was talking about him. *Frickinmotherfuckingpieceofshitbastardasswipingtitsuckingdickwackinggoddamnfucking pieceofcrap!* Oh my God. I'm sorry, I really am sorry and ashamed. Please excuse the language. At the time, those were the only swear words I could think of.

So there I was, left with the unsettling thought that if that night was so wonderfully great that she shared the details of her whole life with me and we even, you know, impromptu hugged right there in the middle of the beach—*Tonight in Jungleland!!!* —how much of a loser must I be that she was so happy that someone else had asked her out? I guess that said it all.

I started thinking of people I knew from work who at the company holiday party would get a drink in them and suddenly the four-foot tall mailroom guy was dancing with the new babe from the Human Resources department. I was beginning to wonder, even to be convinced, that my view of reality was as similarly distorted as the mailroom guy. I had thought the door to my dream job was so close, when it turned out to be so closed. When I met Shulie, and then my dream girl, Emma, I thought the doors to their hearts led to a fortune just for me, only to find they led to a fortress, for which I didn't have the key. I wonder how that happens. I really do. That thing where you think you can get the babe from the Human Resources department and then realize you are the four-foot tall mailroom guy. I remembered back to my early days in college when I pretended to be Mr. Confident. Back then, I knew I was pretending. Maybe I was still just smoke and mirrors. Maybe, like Shulie pointed out to me, you can't change who you are. I don't know. I really don't. I just wished I could have trusted my own perceptions of myself.

Not sure of anything anymore, I decided to let Emma and Diego play its course. If she changed her mind, I'd be there. If not, I'd have to see what I could learn about the great loser stalkers in history.

That afternoon, unencumbered by visions of living happily ever after with Emma, we met to discuss how to get people to the Blue Moon. Unlike the majority of my meetings at Wright Star, I showed up without my shoes or shirt. But, despite my casual appearance, I was ready to get down to work—to regain some semblance of self worth.

We sat on opposite ends of a plastic-covered couch in the Blue Moon's lobby. I asked Emma what they were currently doing to promote the hotel. She asked if I liked the sign outside, because they weren't doing a hell of a lot more than that. She was being very cute, which I didn't exactly need at that moment. I asked what kind of budget we had. She joked that it depended on how Dugan did in his next card game. Very much like Wright Star, where we were asked to launch a new fund that wasn't in anyone's budget, clearly we were going to have to make something out of next to nothing.

I had been thinking about it, and thought I was up for the challenge. I separated out our objectives into two. One obvious one was to get more vacationers to stay at the hotel. Second was to make Spike's bar a larger profit center. I listed out a number of ways that we could do each, none of which required much of an investment. For the hotel, first we needed a nice direct mail piece to send to previous guests with some bribe or other to come back. Then we needed a web site, and probably an affiliation with an existing site that promoted multiple hotels. In our case, one that promoted the less expensive vacation spots (which would be, what, the all-exclusives?) I told Emma I was in charge of Wright Star's web site and suggested we could work (closely) together on the site design and then I'd create the HTML pages. To be honest with you, we had an ad agency do all this for us at Wright Star and I couldn't describe the difference between HTML and PMS, but I've been around the web enough to know there are a lot of morons who have designed their own sites. I figured I could be one of those morons. I made a mental note to buy an HTML for Dummies book from Amazon.com. Emma was excited, and if I cared at all, I'd probably have been somewhat excited that I managed to ensure we'd be working *together* every day, as a team, getting inside each other, motivating each other, challenging ourselves, spiritually bonding, sharing the wonderful thrill of accomplishment. So, it's a good thing I didn't care.

From there, we needed to create an affiliation with Air Jamaica Vacations and Fun Jet and Apple Vacations so that travel agents could package air and hotel deals to their clients. If we could, Blue Moon might have an advantage in that we could go lower than the other resorts, and grab a good chunk of the budget traveler business. You know how those bait and switch ads that say, "As low as $399 for seven nights…" (while the fine print says you have to stand on your head and your return flight is before you depart.) We'd be the one that would actually be $399.

Emma was getting pumped—this was much more fun than presenting to JT—and I still had my ace in the hole idea to come.

On previous treks down the beach, I had noticed places like Roots Bamboo that appeared to be just bars, but also happened to have hotel rooms. It got me to thinking that Spike's bar could become a bigger deal. It could be a business on its own. From there, the bar business could only help the hotel business.

My idea was to have a monthly Full Moon Festival at the Blue Moon. On whatever night the moon happened to be full, we could advertise the Blue Moon as *the* place to be. We'd have a reggae band and a bonfire, and a rented spotlight and maybe even a small-scale fireworks show. I had done the math, which believe me, wasn't easy without Microsoft Excel or a calculator, and found the profits could outdistance the added costs. I figured it would help business the rest of the month, too, and besides, it'd be fun. Spike could invent some World Famous *Moon*shine drink, and after that, you never know what could happen on a full moon. We could plaster the area with flyers and try to get some local press. We could put the Blue Moon on the map.

I also suggested that we put up a sign on the beach offering two for one Red Stripes to build traffic on a daily basis and get rid of Heineken and offer Guinness, which I'd found was also brewed in Jamaica. Plus, I'd recently had a great Belgian white beer, called Blue Moon, that would be fun to import and sell. As a marketer, I was all about building the brand, especially when it involved drinking really good beer.

That was my pitch. After presenting my case, I asked "So, Em, what do you think?" She was letting me call her "Em" and I was digging it.

In response, she gave me a huge hug…not that it aflected me…I mean aplectered me…um, affected me, at all.

Normally, I don't have use for a written marketing plan—it's typically a bureaucratic mess that no one looks at once it's created—but since it meant working through dinner with Emma, I was happy to do my part. We worked until the evening writing down everything we needed to do, and when Dugan kicked us out—ironically to have a card game—we got some dinner from Spike and went up to her room to eat and finish up.

When we finished the day's work, she said to wait there for a minute, she'd be right back. Four minutes later, she returned with a cold bucket of Red Stripes, saying, "Perks of owning a hotel."

Sitting on her bed, we drank beer and talked about everything. She had a CD player boom box and she put on a Van Morrison CD. She decided not to put on *Born to Run*, because (in her words), we couldn't top the night before. Without the pressure of trying to get her, or ever find happiness, because I had given up on both, I was relaxed and pretty much on. I saw the cleft in her chin—that one she gets when she smiles big—a lot.

She said thank you for helping her about a hundred times. I'm tossing around a new theory on Catholic girls. In my experience, when you are really and truly good—like coming up with a killer marketing plan or knowing all the words to *Jungleland*—they give you maybe more credit than you deserve. But the flip side is also true. If you are average, or phony, or undisciplined, or trying to hard, or take the lazy way out, or if, for example, you joke about writing a novel, rather than write one, they can be especially hard on you. That mostly shows up in the form of disinterest or indifference. For example, that girl in college that I was really into, and who was Catholic, didn't so much break up with me, as stop caring. At first, when I was good and funny and clever, she loved it. It was like she had this great inflated image of me that went beyond that I was being funny and clever. Like she saw all the good potential in me. When I couldn't keep it up, the bubble burst, and she just sort of moved on. She was nice about it, thank God, but moved on just the same. Even years later, if I did something really good at work or something—even though I knew it was something she might not give a fuck about—I still felt like it was something I wanted her to know about—because she'd *approve*. It was like a reflection of my conscience.

Maybe, as someone who has always considered himself on the edge of being good or bad—close to the bright side of the moon—I was in a unique position to notice something like that. I don't know. Maybe it has nothing to do with Catholic girls. Maybe it's just a fucked up struggle for self respect. Or maybe I'm just a freak. Nothing final yet, but if I come to resolution on this, I'll let you know. Maybe leave a business card.

Anyway, as the night progressed, Emma, after a few Red Stripes, got even more friendly and playful. Maybe it was my reward for being so good that afternoon. If I didn't know she didn't want me, I would have thought she did—we even had a tickle fight at one point, for chrissakes. Plus, Van Morrison kind of makes everything you're doing seem soulful. He could sing "I crossed the street to find a men's room" and it would sound like a make out song with religious overtones. It kind of made what we were doing seem significant. I guess she was just acting like good friends, maybe even best friends, but not kissing her was the hardest thing I'd ever done. And she smelled so good, have I ever mentioned that? Even knowing what I did about Diego, I almost went for broke.

There was a moment there—a moment I wished I could have had back—where she happened to be right there in front of me, face to face, mouth to mouth, and I wanted to kiss her so bad, but I couldn't stand the thought of her reacting badly and maybe losing her completely. So I just rolled her over and buried her head with the pillow, giving her little noogies while she giggled.

Feeling incapable of maintaining my discipline much longer, when Van the Man sang his last tune—sending *Glad Tidings* from New York—I excused myself and headed back to my now very lonely room to decide whether to think about nothing or everything. Neither one promised glad tidings from Negril.

33

While Emma was out dining with her dad that Friday evening, who did I happen to run into at the bar, but Mr. Gorgeous from Columbia. He was at first glance, I'll admit, exceptionally good looking in a girls-would-think-he's-handsome-and-guys-would-think-he's-a-dick kind of way. I appraised him self-consciously, in much the same way as a deer would appraise a rifle. He was muscular, tall and brooding, with this thick black hair and smooth dark skin. He had this physical presence that seemed to command attention, though, to his credit, he seemed oblivious to it. I got the feeling most of the attention he got from women was unsolicited. His look was casual and clean, like he had just stepped out of a Banana Republic ad, and I felt like a shmuck in my tee-shirt that said Beer is Food.

I introduced myself and asked if, by chance, his name was Diego. He was surprised, and eyed me suspiciously with these disconcertingly large, deep brown eyes and I felt like I was a kid walking up to try to get his autograph. When I said I was a friend of Emma's and that she'd told me about him, he lifted his perfectly formed chin as if to say that he was totally in awe of me, too. Well, maybe more like he might not make me run away crying.

Actually, the chance to talk about Emma seemed to take a bit of the edge off him and he even asked if he could buy me a beer. At the bar, he told me he was from Columbia, in town for business. When he asked, I told him my little story about why I was in Jamaica. He seemed interested and said he that envied me my freedom and the dedication it would take to write a book. I told him I'd let him know about that when I started it, which made him laugh. When I joked that Spike and Dugan—in that order— were likely the only ones that were going to make any money on my book, he smiled again and ordered a second round.

He said he hated writing himself, and I'm thinking that guys like that just appearred in the magazine and they hired people to write shit around his picture. But just when I thought I had the Mr. Shallow card to play with Emma, he told me a story in very measured words about how his father used to make him and his brother write up what they'd done every day as a means for his father to judge and keep tabs on his boys.

His brother was always getting in trouble and his daily stories were interesting and colorful and always positively reinforced by his father. The more harm he did, the more his father liked it. In fact, Diego said, he thought his brother started making up bad stuff for his father's enjoyment. Diego, in comparison to his brother, generally tried to do the right thing, get decent grades and that kind of thing and as a result his stories were always boring and his father told him so. I asked if his dad was always tough on him. His simple expressionless answer was, "Yes."

"Not on your brother?"

"No. My brother was the tough one. I was the smart one. My father liked his style more. Actually," he said with a confident smile, "I'm not sure if I was smart or if my brother was just a fucking idiot."

I laughed and complimented him on his English, while mentally noting the signs of depth, intelligence and sensitivity lurking beyond his perfect façade, and that, without question, I was fucked.

As the sun began its descent, Erika invited me to join her to watch the show and I invited Diego to join us. He accepted with a cool nod of his head, leading us down to the water. The setting sun that night was mostly blocked by the clouds, not unlike Diego blocking Emma from me. Ultimately, though, the sun once again triumphed, reflecting off the clouds to come up with new ways to inspire.

After Erika went back to work, we continued our little chat, and I was getting more and more annoyed that there wasn't anything to get annoyed about. He was guarded, I thought, but engaging. Edgy, but charming. You couldn't typically read his emotions behind the mostly protected exterior, but there seemed to be an implied tenderness and perhaps pain that was immensely likeable. I really hated to say that I really didn't hate him.

We talked about Emma and the bastard seemed to find her as uniquely attractive as I did. I was realizing, much to my absolute disgust, that I actually sort of liked him. And, when I started to accept that they were going to be together—I mean, Jesus, look at the fucking guy—I began realizing that I needed to work on liking myself as much as I did him.

The two of us were still hanging out when Emma returned from dinner and seeing her two guys said, "Isn't this cute?"

She put her hand sweetly on my shoulder and pulled up a seat on my side. We were all drinking and talking and Emma asked what we were talking about. I told Emma that Diego and I had just realized we were both gay and were going to run off to get married together. Diego, God bless the prick, played along with it, and said in that fucking unfair advantage of an accent, "Emma, we both want you to be the Maid of Honor." She cracked up, Diego smiled, happy with all of us, and we were all just one jolly, fun-loving group of friends, except that I was the only one no one wanted to sleep with.

34

After Diego had headed back to Columbia, that next night Emma came to my room and we sat on the porch and talked about their date. They again had gone out for lunch. They again got along great. It was a perfect afternoon, and she was even more sure she liked him and he seemed very much into her. She asked what I thought about him, and after considering all the possible ways of answering, finally just said that I thought he had a good heart. Her smile told me that she was really happy with that.

She said a funny thing happened. They both talked mostly about me. It was, I guess, our little triangle of life. I talked to Diego mostly about Emma, Emma and I talked mostly about Diego and Diego and Emma talked about me. Emma said it kind of filled in the gaps in their conversation at times. She kiddingly thanked me for that, and I thought, that even when I wasn't trying to, I was helping them along.

What's with that? Maybe I'm the real life George Bailey. Maybe after stupid Uncle Billy loses the money like he does every year at Christmas, everyone will gather around and talk about everything I'd done to make sure Diego and Emma got together. I could picture them and their six grown kids, one of whom ended up wiping out the common cold and another who managed to get people from Wisconsin to stop driving in the left fucking lane of the Illinois highways going under the goddamn speed limit. The other four, the lesser lights of the family, who averaged thirteens on their A.C.T.s, mostly ended up in the U.S. House of Representatives. And none of that would have happened if good old Seth hadn't helped them out every step of the frickin way. Go ahead, Uncle Billy, strike up *Auld Lang Zyne.*

I finally asked what Diego said said about me. It's one of those things where it's almost impossible not to ask. I guess Diego thought I was witty and that he respected that I had come to Jamaica to write a book and go for my dream and to be as free as I was. He said it takes a lot of guts to leave where you're from. I found that interesting and briefly wondered how much he was relating my experience to his own. Whatever. Anyway, then he said something that really got my attention. Apparently, he joked with Emma about me liking her. He was, she thought, jealous of me.

He, jealous of me? Right. I was willing to play along though and asked her what her response was. She looked right back at me with those Caribbean eyes and said, "I told him that I hope Seth does like me, because I like him."

I was stunned. I couldn't believe she'd say that to him—or me—and once again, I thought how perfect my life might be right then if Diego was Die-gone. I mean, I'd wish him well, just somewhere else.

"You said that to him?" My heart was on my sleeve as I asked, "How'd he react to that?"

"I really think that he wanted to clarify, 'no, that's not what I meant. I meant that he likes you, likes you,' but I don't think he wanted to push it. Instead he just kind of nodded his head and changed the subject."

For the first and only time I had doubts about Emma. Was she the type who would just use me like that? I asked her, "Emma, are you just trying to play me off against him? You shouldn't do that...to either of us."

"Of course, not, Seth," she said, stopping that thought in its tracks. "I was just being literal, like you say guys do. I hope you do like me, because I like you. And if Diego would've pushed it, I'd have told him that I'd have no problem with it if Seth liked me, liked me, because I like him, like him."

"You do? You do?" I asked I asked, my heart rate also doubling.

"Yes," she said quietly to let me know she wasn't just joking, "I do. I do." Then, "And while I'm on the subject, go ahead, Em, just say whatever you're thinking, what do you think of me?" Just like that. She wanted to know what *I* thought of *her*? I'd only been thinking about her non-stop since I met her. How could she expect me to answer a question like that, or to put a coherent thought together?

I'm not someone who is good at getting his thoughts out quickly so that it comes out right. I can easily end up saying I adore you, when I mean I abhor you, or vice-versa. This time, unable to think what the right thing would be to say, I let her know the truth, "I'm smitten with you. I'm in smit. I'm full of smit. I'm very full of smit. I'm so full of smit that..."

She laughed, cutting me off, "Okay, I get the point. Thank you."

She was about to move on, figuring that I was just joking again, when I asked, "Really, Emma, listen, what would you do if you had to choose between us?"

She could tell I wasn't joking, quite possibly because I was holding my breath, and starting to turn blue. "I don't know, Seth," she answered without smiling. "It would be a tough choice."

Oh my God, I thought to myself. Things had taken a very confusing turn. "Really? You mean that?"

"Really." And then it was her turn to ask the big question. "Seth, will I have to choose between you?"

This was the most important question anyone had ever asked me. I felt this confidence wash over me that somehow I'd screw it up. All of a sudden, there was a spotlight on me and the world had slowed down to wait for my answer. I saw people jogging in super slow motion on the beach, and small-time drug deals halted with both the money and buds in sight. Airplanes started flying lower and I thought I saw a dolphin lean in as if to hear what I would say. With the weight of the world on my shoulders I came up with, "I'm, well, actually, Emma—I'm just gonna say it—I think I really am in love with Diego and I want to have his lovechild. I'm serious about this. I think I'd look better as a woman."

The spotlight, the planes, and the dolphin were gone. Drug deals continued and joggers started running at their regular pace. The only thing that changed, besides that Emma was doubled over laughing, was that I had somehow managed to punt on the best opportunity I might ever have for true happiness.

While she laughed, I almost cried.

In the nights to follow I dreamed of ten thousand perfectly plausible and elegant ways to tell her that I loved her, and that it was the strongest feeling I ever had, and that I was the one that was right for her. Most didn't even involve the white horse. But I had blown my chance. How could I have done that? Was I afraid of competing, or of losing, or just of finally making a stand? It's one thing to be rejected. It's another, more devastating thing, when you reject yourself.

Oh, and I should tell you this. I had no way of knowing it at the time, but the only one more freaked out about Emma and Diego was Dugan Kelly. In fact, he knew something his daughter didn't. That Diego hadn't returned to Columbia that night.

35

In that next week, Emma and I made great progress in turning the Blue Moon into one of the foremost tourist destinations in the entire Dugan Kelly hotel empire. In fact, in my mind, it couldn't be too long before Robin Leach sat his pasty ass in one of the Blue Moon's soon-to-be highly sought after lounge chairs. I had sort of laid out the web site design on paper, and took the pictures that would be the star of our little corner of the World Wide Web. I got pictures of Spike with his big smile behind the bar, Erika looking lovely with a tray of Flaming Marleys, Emma welcoming visitors (and looking very cute if I may say so), the cabins featuring the fresh flowers, the sunset with a palm tree in the upper left corner, the hot tub with Diego (who modestly insisted on wearing a tee-shirt) and two babes who happened to be walking by on the beach (as if *all* of our guests were that good looking) and the little boat with the perfect Jamaican flag. We had pretty much everything but Dugan, since Emma and I figured that—*I won this fucking place in a card game*—wasn't exactly the marketing message we wanted to convey.

It turned out we were unsuccessful with the Apple, Air Jamaica and Fun Jet vacation folks; apparently we were a few amenities shy of their minimum standards. However, we were successful in securing a collaboration with a couple of local web sites, the most prominent of which was called Beingee's. It promoted a lot of the lower end hotels and bars, and did a nice job of capturing the real Negril. It had a hotel by price list table that tended to show up on search engines for the budget conscious Negril traveler. We'd be right there at the top of that list, since we were the cheapest, and it went in ascending order of price, which would be great for our marketing if not our margins. We also planned our first Full Moon Festival for April 30, the date of the next full moon. Unfortunately, I'd be on my way back to Chicago that day, but it was very fun planning it with Emma. We got a band, had Freedy rebuild a stage that the Blue Moon used to use, got an electrician so the band wouldn't have to do an "unplugged" concert, and taste-tested Spike's new World Famous Rum Moonshine drink until it was just right or we were too lit up to know the difference. Then we ordered A LOT of extra Appleton rum and A LOT of Red Stripes.

Emma was getting a kick out of the whole process, but wasn't quite as playful with me. In fact, we didn't have a single tickle fight all week. What kind of way is that to have a relationship? I guess I was out of contention to be Mr. Emma, because, as I may have mentioned, I'm a real big asshole.

I actually had assorted other opportunities to get it right with Emma, but I never matched the appropriate mood with the appropriate words. The closest I came was on the Friday night of the day before Diego and Emma were going to go out on their next date. This time they weren't just going out to lunch, but dinner, dancing and who the hell knew what else. That Friday afternoon, I had hung out with Diego for a while, before and after the hot tub photo shoot. I sort of encouraged him to ask out one of the hot tub babes, but he seemed pretty damn focused on Emma. When he talked, she was all he talked about, the disrespectful ingrate. He even confided that he was nervous about his dancing, for chrissakes. The two of us, were, in fact, kind of becoming buddies, which just shows I'm clearly too dysfunctional for society. In this society by the sea, you could say (if you had the time and inclination to think of dumbass stuff like that) I needed to be much more selfish than jellyfish.

That night, Diego, Emma and I had planned to build a bonfire and hang out. I had invited Erika to join us because, given the choice, I'd rather be the third wheel of a car than a motorcycle. Prior to starting the fire, while Diego was back in his room showering or something, Emma seemed very excited about her date. But then, as if just sort of throwing it out, she confided in me that her dad didn't really want her to go out with Diego. He said he preferred she go out with me. Huh? I wasn't aware that Dugan was so enamored with me that he'd single me out to date his daughter. My first thought was that maybe he didn't think I had a penis. Of course, at the time, I wasn't aware that there weren't too many people on the planet that he wouldn't have chosen over Diego.

Anyhow, whether she was aware of it or not, Emma had provided me another opportunity to tell her how I felt. Again, because I had only thought about her every second since the last time it had come up, I was completely unprepared. This was my big chance. But for some damn reason, while I should have been focusing on how to gather my thoughts to put together a compelling verbal resume of all my endearing qualities (not that I could think of any at that second), I actually started thinking about whether I could do that to Diego. I mean, I don't know, wouldn't it be some violation of our male bonding if I were to blindside the guy by asking out the girl we both knew he wanted (and, goddamnit, got to FIRST!) It wasn't so much that I decided I wouldn't do just that, it's just that I was wasting the opportunity to think about the right thing to say by thinking about the right thing to do. By the time I was ready to address her comment, Emma had probably forgotten she'd even brought it up.

In fact, when I finally blurted out, "Father knows best." She looked at me, like *huh?* I said it again. "Father knows best. Even your father."

Then, remembering what we were talking about, Emma anxiously asked, "Wait, are you saying that you think I should go out with you?" I suddenly had her attention, not that that's usually a good thing for me.

I tried to decide whether to launch into one of those relationship-defining speeches you might see at the end of a sappy movie right before the scene fades out with the happy couple kissing on the couch in forever-after bliss. The kind of moving, once-in-a-lifetime, we belong together kind of thing she'd never forget. The kind of thing where she'd probably gather our grandkids together one day in front of a roaring fire to spin tales about how old gramps, despite the fact he now has no teeth and mostly communicates by creatively breaking wind, used to be quite the charming Casanova. She'd tell them how I gallantly swept her off her feet with my poetic, stirring, romantic-as-hell words about destined love and true companionship and then onto a waiting white stallion—I know, that damn white horse again—to ride off into the perfect sunset. With those thoughts dancing through my head, I took Emma's hands in mine, looked her right in the knee and said like a dope, "Um, yeah, you know."

We were sitting in the sand, and she kind of excitedly got to her knees, and all kind of bubbly asked me, "Do you mean that Seth, do you? I mean if you had to choose between me and becoming a woman so you could have Diego's love child, you'd choose me?"

Not that it wasn't very cute the way she said it, but she shouldn't have done that. That joking around thing. If she had left it at "Do you mean that

Seth?" I would've eloquently replied, "Um, yeah, you know," because, among other things, that did seem to be working for me. Instead, because of the real big asshole problem I have (my apologies if anyone takes that literally), I was forced to answer, "I don't know, Em, it'd be a tough choice."

She smiled at the joke, said, "Touché," and then, before she could say something like, "no, really, be serious for a second, ya real big asshole," out of nowhere (or perhaps the shower because he did sort of smell better than he did before), Diego appeared ready for our bonfire. And that was that. We started the fire—the bonfire that is, because my fire had been doused—and it was beautiful, if you're in to that kind of thing. Erika joined me, and we held hands a while and looked at the flames of my life.

As usual, Erika was great. She knew what I was going through and why I wasn't being very talkative. She also knew that if she mostly just talked with me, it would've grouped Emma and Diego together. If she talked mostly with Em, Diego and I would've sat there silently wishing the other wasn't there. So, with her amazing talent to always be able to make people feel better, she started joking with Diego. He was digging the attention, too, because among other things, Erika's pretty much a babe. As they joked about who had the cooler accent—Emma or me—because, as opposed to us, they both spoke "normal," all the uncomfortable spotlights were turned off. By all appearances, we were just four friends enjoying a bonfire on the beach. I looked at Erika as if for the first time. She really was beautiful.

36

And then, just the next night, unable to contain myself a second longer, I found myself yelling out, "Erika. Sweetheart. Oh God. Oh my God. *Yes…ye-es… YE-ES!*"

Of all the dozens—hell, hundreds—of times, I don't think I've ever been compelled to actually scream before, but that night everything just felt so different. Every emotion was magnified. The highs were higher, the lows were lower. All the conflicting emotions washed over me, as I sat there breathing heavy, my face warm, skin tingling, senses alive.

My overwhelming desire had been satiated for the moment and I twisted at the waist a bit so I could look right at her, right in those pretty eyes. Despite what she must have been thinking, I gushed, "Wow, that exactly what I needed. I know it takes me a little while longer to recover than it used to, you know, but…maybe in a few minutes…if you're willing…I really want to do that again."

All the images stayed with me. The palpable anticipation in the moments just prior, the significance of the moment, the sheer enjoyment of the act itself—the not-so-subtly rounded curves, the bronzed coloring that attracted me in the Caribbean sunlight every bit as much as it did at that moment by soft candle light, the feel of my heart beat, the seductive tiny beads of moisture dripping slowly, tantalizingly downward (just barely a fleeting thought during, though a lasting image after), and how it had softened my hard edges. Those thoughts lingered in my mind and filled me with desire all over again.

Through all the combinations of events and feelings that had led me to be there with Erika that night, the only thing I really wanted at that moment—was *want* even a strong enough word?—was to drink another cold Red Stripe in the warm, breezy Jamaican night.

I had just savored my sixth Red Stripe that evening and caressed the little brown bottle—as if to say *thank you*—before reuniting it with its five buddies. "I love Red Stripe," I said, as I watched the sun set across the horizontal line of bottles on my table. "Sometimes, Erika, I think it's as close to contentment as I'll ever find."

Erika looked at me and wondered out loud, "What am I going to do with you, mister? You need an attitude adjustment." She set her drink tray down on my table and sat next to me, trying to decide how to handle me this time. "Seth, you know you don't got it so bad. You think you do, but it's not true. Listen to me, now, okay. You're sitting here in Jamaica breathing in the fine sea air, chilling with a soothing ocean breeze, feasting your eyes on the sun disappearing into the turquoise sea, you know, listening to the prophet Bob Marley jammin, mon. Beauty surrounds you here, it gives you peace. Your soul should drink that up and you should appreciate what you have. And, my friend, you have a lot."

She said that whole thing so that I might believe the last line. I smiled, marveling again at how Erika could entice you to feel her words, and then make a point in a way you hadn't seen coming. She's always the strong one, the rock, the calm in the storm. I've needed her a lot. I gazed at the brilliant red sun dipping into the Caribbean, and figured she was right as usual, at least about the night. It was hard not to be stirred by Jamaican evenings like this. And they were almost always like this. I still needed more convincing about myself.

"Erika, looking at your smile doesn't hurt either, you know. I've been thinking about this all day; will you marry me and, you know, support me financially forever?" As you might recall, I had asked her to marry me the first day that I arrived and just about every day since. It was kind of a tradition and as far as rejection goes, wasn't so bad.

She shook her head and laughed, "Marry you, baby, I don't even like you. I'm just being nice to you so you'll say nice stuff about me in that book of yours." Her big dimpled smile and light touch on my shoulder came with the comfortable feeling of two friends harmlessly flirting.

"So you'll think about it?"

"When you finish your book and you're rich and famous, you'll forget all about us little people."

"Oh please, sweetie, I *am* the little people. I'm about six weeks away from cleaning goat shit in the streets or something. Seriously, I already have the application."

"You're about six months away, my friend, from being the next great American novelist. I can see it now. When I get my teaching degree, I'll be teaching my class about the great Seth Gold."

"You're so sweet. You really are, but I may have dreadlocks by the time I finish this book. Best case scenario is that I become the next great *Jamaican* novelist."

She laughed. "I have faith in you, Seth. I know you can do it. No problem," she said in that accent that drives me crazy. Not that she ever would, but she could say, "Fuck you, mon," and it would sound soothing as the sound of the sea.

"And," she added, "I think you'd look cute in dreadlocks, mon."

"You think?" I took a moment with that, smiling at the thought of my mother seeing me come home in dreads. It wasn't enough to lift my sinking ship. Looking up at Erika, I said, "You know, you're always telling me no problem. You Jamaicans need a new expression for me." With the buzz I had going I knew it'd be a struggle to get the next thought out, but I took my time and worked my way through it. "I'm not sure if it's true or just how I start feeling when my dreams are fading away from me, Erika, but I don't think I'm worth any more than my dreams. You know, I mean, yes, it's true that I have these great dreams of doing what I'm good at and being exactly who I want to be, I'll give you that, but if I can't make them real, then what do I have? You know? Without that, what am I doing here? Except really wanting another Red Stripe."

"Seth, please stop drinking like that."

"I plan to be nice and passed out by the time Jamaica's most beautiful couple gets back from the date of the century. I guess I'll just have to wait until tomorrow to get the sordid details. It's a good thing I don't care."

"Uh huh," she said, knowing better. I think she wanted to be careful not to give me false hope—which, come to think of it, could be the title of my book—but she did say, "I've seen how she looks at you. How easily your relationship comes to you, almost like two little kids playing together on the beach. Certain things just need to play themselves out, because some things are too right not to happen. I can see that and I think maybe she can, too. Some things are worth waiting for, Seth."

"Erika, I hope so—more than anything—but, while we're waiting to find out, can I get another beer?"

Like she'd told me, some things just need to play out, including my moment of self-pity, so she moved on to make her rounds and probably get me one more beer (though I figured she'd cut me off soon). I tried to squeeze assorted dysfunctional thoughts out of my mind for a minute to focus on what I came here for, the inspiration to write something with my name on it. The decision to go for my dream, and run away from everything else, was either the most courageous or cowardly thing I've ever done. I hadn't decided yet, but I did feel certain that, quite literally, I'd be writing my own ending.

I'd actually had several story ideas that I thought had potential if I could just focus. I'd get close to getting on the roll, but my mind would keep going back to Emma and Diego, and I'd roll straight down that hill. Damn them. My newest, bestest idea, I thought while I was drunk, was to do a book about a Holden Caulfield-type character if he'd ever finally been in the mood to ask out old Jane Gallagher in *Catcher in the Rye*. Hell, if I couldn't ask out my dream girl, at least my character could. I thought about it more and decided the couple in the book could both be Jewish like Shulie and me, and I could call it *The Corn Beef on Rye*. Or, better yet, he'd be Jewish and she wouldn't, like Em and I, and it could be called *The Corn Beef With Mayo on Rye*. I did mention I was drunk right? I can only assume that's funnier after six Red Stripes. Anyway, I decided to give it more thought in the morning.

At some point, because Erika has always had my best interests at heart, she cut me off after I'd earned one too many Red Stripes. Since I don't seem to have my best interests at heart, I decided to visit my friends at the "Outlet Mall." I ended up buying a baggy with a ridiculously monstrous bud. If I remembered correctly from college, the thirty bucks they asked was an unbelievable bargain. I replied, "Okay," not unlike Opie Taylor making his first marijuana purchase, and they seemed surprised I didn't try to talk him down further. That told me all I needed to know about how plentiful the home grown shit was around here. Maybe because they felt like they had taken advantage of me, they threw in papers and a lighter. I went back and found a dark spot on the beach. Before reaching the oblivion I was seeking, unfortunately, I had time to evaluate my old life and my new life, and whether they were, in fact, sadly, the same.

37

Emma insisted on driving me to the airport even though our first ever Full Moon Festival at the Blue Moon was going to take place that night. I tried to tell her that Erika could have taken me, so that she could've attended to last minute details, but she wouldn't listen.

Since that night on the beach, we hadn't talked again about *us*, or what could have been us if I hadn't fucked up so many times. That night I had tried to tell her that she should go out with me—without benefit of a convincing argument or, for that matter, any argument at all—but then ruined it by making a joke when I should have just said yes. I had no way of knowing if she'd have actually chosen me over Diego—in fact, it seemed incomprehensible to me—but I didn't even give myself a chance to find out.

As if to rub it in, on the drive to Mo' Bay, Emma talked mostly about how things with Diego were going great. Well, except for the fact that her dad, for reasons she couldn't figure out, hated Diego and adamantly opposed her going out with him. That seemed very strange to me. What was there not to like? Back in my comfort zone, though, helping her get another guy, I told her a good rule of thumb was to not go out with guys until she received her dad's disapproval. She smiled and said she couldn't argue with that. Now that I had again reverted back to being her girl friend, she sort of quietly confided in me that Diego was pushing her a little into "taking the next step" with him. She didn't seem to be altogether opposed to that notion, and you'll be happy to know I at least refrained from giggling like a school girl at the exciting news. What I did was basically get too depressed to realize she was probably just trying to figure out a way to get me to make a fucking stand. To take Bob Marley's advice, "Get up, stand up. Don't give up the fight."

If she was just trying to provoke me—and I decided on the flight back to Jamaica that she obviously was, once again, getting a clue about a week too late—it wasn't the right strategy. At least not on me. I can lose my self-confidence like a pair of cheap sunglasses. When confronted with the love of my life talking about sleeping with another guy, all my systems shut down and I just get more self-abusive and more and more convinced of my unworthiness. Unlike my typical self-bashing, it's far more dark and annoying than humble and charming. When I get like that, I even want to slap myself, so I can imagine what a joy I am to others.

When we arrived at the airport, before I could get out of the car, Emma gave me a kiss—for the first time right smack on the lips—which wasn't at all unenjoyable. She made a great big deal of trying to make sure that I would came back, which caught me by surprise. To me, it was a given— I wasn't gonna just walk away from her—but she seemed very skeptical, even doubtful. I guess my blue mood of late had been showing more than I had thought. Trying to change the mood, I took out my camera and took a bunch of pictures of Emma standing outside her car, pretending to be Austin Powers—*YES! YES! YES! NO! And I'm SPENT.* It got her to smile only a little. I told her, in complete honesty, that I'd look at her pictures the whole time until I returned that Monday. But I think it only made her more doubtful that I'd come back. She had a really pouty face and said if I didn't come back, she'd come find me. It was very cute and touching. I returned her kiss, but *on the forehead*, like her goddamn big brother. I can't tell you how pumped I was to have another missed opportunity to mull over on the four-hour flight home. Some people read on planes, I just mull over missed opportunities.

At O'Hare Airport, back in Chicago, I called my friend Craig to come pick me up. I figured it was the least he could do since I gave him my damn car. He wasn't going to do it, though, until I convinced him I wasn't going to ask him for it back. The friendship between two guys is a special thing.

Craig and I had dinner at the Athenian Room—one of my favorite casual spots to eat in Lincoln Park. Being unemployed as I was, I should've just gotten the less expensive Gyros plate, but I had a taste for their skirt steak, maybe the best I've ever had, so I splurged and got that and their Greek fries. Yum. Yum. Yum. Connected to the restaurant is a neighborhood pub called Glascott's. After dinner we went there and had a couple of beers and Craig filled me on what was going on in town. Not much had changed, except the names of the girls and the names of the bars. Craig and I played that pop-a-shot basketball game, a sure sign of guys with no hope of getting laid, and he told me he missed hanging out with me.

Craig offered to drive me home but I only lived a few blocks away. It wasn't terribly cold, even though I was wearing the shorts I'd put on that morning in Jamaica, and my one bag was small, so I walked. It was the last day of April and the temperature was in the low fifties. May is kind of an in-between month in Chicago, a transition between two of Chicago's three seasons. Since there is some sort of city ordinance against having spring, at some point in May, the temperature goes from forty-five to ninety. Usually overnight. Then you know it's summer.

I began to recall past summers in the city. Chicago is a big playground in the summer with its lakefront, beach volleyball, beer gardens (the biggest of which is Wrigley Field during a Cubs' night game), parties on people's back decks or patios and citywide and neighborhood festivals. Most of the city's neighborhoods—probably all the ones you'd want to go to and some that you wouldn't—host big weekend-long summer block parties. The streets are lined, and the air fragranced, by food stands selling buttered corn on the cob, barbecued ribs, egg rolls, Chicago-style pizza, Italian beef sandwiches and various pig out foods unique to that neighborhood. They also have local bands, beer on tap and great people watching. And are all terrific reflections of the neighborhood.

The neighborhood I lived in had the Sheffield Garden Walk Festival. It was two blocked-off streets with the food and beer stands lining the streets and a stage at one end. As the name suggested, in addition to the festival, there was also a garden walk through the neighborhood, giving the local yuppies the opportunity to show off their gardens and their wealth, not necessarily in that order. I did kind of think it was cool how they'd take their postage-stamp size back yards and patios and turn them into wonderful flower and water gardens. If you could get past the obvious showing off of their wealth, it did add an element of character and fantasy to the neighborhood.

The festival itself was always a great place to see friends from college and drink and dance in the street. I'd even had a few successful dates at the Sheffield Walk. One year the temperature soared to like ninety-five degrees and I was on a first date with a girl who was rather hot herself. We were having a good time, but the heat really started to get to her. In fact, she looked just about ready to pass out until when I found this garden hose and hosed her down. The recovery was instantaneous. I think she considered marrying me right then and there, and I probably would have after judging the impressive wet tee-shirt contest. Lucky for her she didn't, because several weeks later she decided right then and there to dump me for some guy she'd dated in high school who'd called her out of the blue. What the hell was that? Did he just have a better garden hose?

Among my other favorite festivals were the Taste of Lincoln Avenue, a far more sprawling and eclectic mix of people and businesses, and the North Halsted Street Festival. The latter was more or less a homosexual celebration—it was their turf and their weekend—and always provided outstanding people watching. Every year, at a stage set up in the parking lot of a 7-11, we used to go to see my favorite local band, the Vanessa Davis Band. Vanessa was a party chick, and looked like an inflated Gary Coleman. A couple of things could probably tell you all you need to know about Vanessa and how good a time she had while performing. One is that when she switched to light beer, she dropped about forty pounds. The other is that once, at a show at the old Taste of Chicago at Navy Pier, she persuaded one of Chicago's finest officers to hold her joint for her while she finished up a song—and he did! The VDB was an unbelievable band and a great time, and it's exactly the kind of band that noone's ever heard of that makes you sick when you see a talentless, trendy, one-hit wonder on MTV.

One year, I was there with a big group of friends and there was this scraggly wisp of a black woman, wearing a red dress, red shoes, and a red purse, dancing in front of us to Vanessa Davis waving a nibbled-on bagel around her index finger. She wasn't gay that I could tell, actually I hoped she wasn't sexual at all, but even among the overly exuberant flamboyance of the queens parading at the festival, the bagel lady was strange enough to draw our attention. Waving her ever-present bagel, she kept trying to dance with this normal looking black photographer guy, while he pretty much wanted to concentrate on his pictures. But she kept getting behind him, and not getting the concept, was the back spoon in her version of a dirty dance. He kept swatting her away like a mosquito. She'd dance a while by herself, nibble on her bagel and, as if re-energized, go for it again. The guy, who'd been trying to be as nice as he could for as long as he could, suddenly couldn't deal with it anymore. He finally yelled, "Would you and your bagel leave me the fuck alone." Finally feeling rejected, she stepped back, wound up, and threw her bagel right square in the back of his head to much applause. It was very dramatic. She bowed to her new audience as if the whole thing had been a Broadway play, before dancing with three drag queens that just looked happy to be getting in on the attention.

I smiled thinking about the bagel lady and past summers in the city. In some ways the seven-mile beach in Negril was like Chicago. There was always something new to discover, and after you'd been there a while, there were places and people that became your own.

Walking back from Glascott's past the joggers and groups of kids heading to the bars, I looked around, as I always did, at the buildings in my neighborhood. I loved that walk through the brownstone three-flats and expensive single-family walk-up homes on the tree-lined streets. Very few buildings or homes had blinds of curtains—presumably because the twenty-something renters were just out of college where their lives were open books anyway and the yuppies in their million dollar homes wanted to show off their art and interior decorating. It kind of turned their front rooms into galleries and made the neighborhood into a museum of sorts. It was kind of amazing, really, how the just-out-of-college renters could fit so naturally on the same street as the people who could afford to buy homes in the area. It worked well for both, and was even a place where suburbanites could come and play. The neighborhood and the city still fascinated me, and I realized as I walked the steps of my old apartment, that wherever I would travel trying to find the place I was looking for, Chicago was my home.

I stopped off on the second floor—the door was open as usual—and was greeted enthusiastically by Bobbo, Javy, and, I was amused and happy to find, Darlene. We had some beers and shot the shit. I asked if they were enjoying my stereo. Javy said they didn't take it, because they were hoping I'd move back. I was kind of touched. I asked Javy about Alexa, but he hadn't heard from her. He did show me the latest Victoria's Secret catalog, though, and *ohmyfuckingGod!* I had the passing thought that if I could get a picture of Alexa walking out of the ocean and onto the beach at the Blue Moon, we'd never have another vacancy. Not that I'd ever exploit her like that, but I was thinking I would like to talk to her again some time. I hoped she had maybe found the person she was looking for. When I left that night, Bob, Javy and even Darlene gave me hugs. Bob said I'd better keep in touch or he'd "kick my fucking ass." I told him I would, and not just because I was afraid he meant it.

I knocked on Joe's door, and he came out in a tattered robe holding a huge drumstick of what must have come from some sort of giant mutant turkey. In his other hand he had what looked to be a metal goblet of wine. I was afraid to even think about exactly what kind of party King Joe was having in there. I commented on how trim he looked, which made him happy, though he'd clearly added a new wing to his already ample foundation. He proudly accepted the compliment and I wondered how someone like that could be filled to the brim with confidence and self-worth, when I, let's say, stopped at half a cup. He had rented my apartment, but the new renter wasn't moving in until that Sunday, so Joe said I could sleep in my place that Friday night. He was in a good mood because the new renter was a babe. He seemed slightly let down when I told him I wasn't expecting any babes of my own that night.

Joe took a drink from his silver goblet and asked how long I'd been renting with him. I told him I thought it was something like seven years. He shook his head and said he was going to miss me. Something in the way he said it made me believe him. I again appreciated the nice sentiment. What was going on here? I'd spent the last month believing I was some sort of misfit in Chicago, and now I was coming back to just short of a parade. Maybe they didn't realize how much they appreciated having me around until I was gone. Or, more likely, I was easier to appreciate when I was gone. Anyway, I told Joe I'd give him the keys in the morning. I thanked him, shook his hand (after he considerately wiped the turkey grease on his robe—which I thought made for quite a thoughtful parting moment) and wished him well.

I went out to my back deck and looked up at the full moon. It reminded me of a warm Sunday evening the summer before. I was drinking Watney's beer with a girl I'd been dating at the time, sitting on the deck in the dark and listening to a gospel choir belt out sweet sounds from the Baptist Church across the alley. The moon was like that night's and there was a heavenly summer breeze. It was one of those perfect nights that you get very few times in life and never in the suburbs. The kind of night that makes you love a city forever. I stepped inside, closed the door to that life—for now—and prepared my stuff for the next day's move. After sleeping that night in my bed for the last time, and getting the pics of Emma developed, I rented a U-Haul truck to move the rest of my stuff from my apartment to my parent's basement. I loaded my TV and stereo and dishes and clothes and stuff into the truck and headed back to my folks' house in Skokie.

I had dinner with my parents and my brother's family that night, and announced to everyone that I had decided to stay in Jamaica for a while. My brother and his wife thought it was really cool what I was doing, especially because it wasn't them doing it. My parents were less enamored with the idea. I lied that I was more than half way through the Jewish Holden Caulfield book and that I owed it to myself to stay until it was done. They knew I'd always been a good writer, so the excuse was at least plausible. On the other hand, they had like a thousand reasons why I was being irresponsible and reckless with my life. Unfortunately for me, I was now old enough to know that about eight hundred of them were pretty much on target, and I'd be saying the same damn things to my kids if they were as dumb as dear old dad. I just said it was something I needed to do. If they could've stopped me they would have, but they couldn't, so they did what they've always done. Tried to save me from me. My dad offered to give me money so that I'd have enough to live on. My mom was, of course, concerned that I'd never eat again so she baked me some cookies to take back with me. I'd gotten my mail from my apartment and included among the bills was a pretty good size tax refund from Uncle Sam. I figured that between the tax refund and the tremendous amount of pot I had (meaning I could potentially drink a lot less), I could go maybe the whole six months without needing more cash (unless my munchy budget got out of control.) For both reasons, I accepted the cookies but told my dad I was okay on money.

That Monday morning, after a cold, discouraging fifteen minutes of waiting, I saw her coming down the street long before she saw me. I had to be the last person she'd expect to see outside her office building so I was not surprised that it didn't actually register in her mind that it was me until I called her name. Especially, because I was wearing shorts, even though it was too cold to, and looking like I'd just been rescued from Gilligan's Island. She looked very professional in her designer raincoat.

"Shulie," I called out into the morning air.

Just down the street, she looked over at me, and it finally registered that it was me. She looked too uncomprehending to say anything.

"Seth?" was all she managed. She gave me a hug, not knowing what else to do. "What are you doing here?"

"I don't know. I wanted to see you."

"Here I am," she said accentuating how awkward the moment was.

"Yeah." And then, not knowing what else to say, I told her, "You look great." She did, too.

Her thoughts seem to come one at a time. Her first was, "I didn't expect to not hear from you."

"I've been out of the country. In Jamaica."

"I know. I tried calling you and the line was disconnected. One night I was out in your neighborhood, so I stopped by your building to see if I could find out what happened to you. Bob said they heard you had moved to Jamaica, just like that." She said it while absently sweeping some hair from her forehead, and I remembered the night of our first date at Sedgewick's when she had done that and some snow had fallen from her hair. It was a nice memory. I realized I had no pictures of her and decided I'd try to hold onto it.

"Yeah." I said, "I decided to leave. Actually, that same night I last saw you. I'm in town to get some stuff. My lease ended the other day." I pointed to my luggage, and said, "I'm heading back today."

In her voice was an attitude I didn't think was entirely appropriate in that she had left me. "How could you have just left? You just ran away, you know that don't you?"

"I don't know yet if I was running away from stuff or if I'm running towards other stuff," I said truthfully.

She looked away and then said, "But you just left everything behind. Your family, your career, your future…me. I mean, I don't know…maybe if you had…you should have at least…tried." Then, not wanting to finish that thought, she asked, "Seth, why would you just leave? I'm sure you didn't do this because of me. Was it because you had no job? You could have gotten another one easy. You're too good to be doing this."

"I don't know, Shulie, I think maybe I'm not. I thought about it on the plane, and it's hard to even imagine that someone would offer me a job like that. It's even harder to imagine that I thought I could do that job. I think I was just smoke and mirrors in that interview, Shulie. Maybe I had a few good ideas, or maybe not, I don't know, but I realized I'm lacking most everything else."

"What happened to you?" She looked at me like I was someone else. And I guess you could've had an easy time making that argument.

I shrugged my shoulders. "I have different goals now. Shulie, I'm trying to write a book. I think that's the life I want. When I was dating you, I knew I needed to change to make it work. And I wanted to. I mean look at you, look how much great incentive I had, but still I couldn't do it. I guess I'm thinking you can't change who you are. You said that about me. I think you were right."

She took a minute with that. I wasn't her project anymore, so she let it go.

"So, are you happy now?" she asked.

"I don't know yet," I said softly.

"Why are you here?" she asked again, still trying to understand.

"You meant a lot to me. I just wanted to…you should know that."

She seemed recovered enough to finally say what she wanted to say, though it seemed very difficult for her. She took a breath and said, "Seth, I've thought about you almost every day since…that day. I've been beating myself up—you have no idea—wondering if I did the right thing." And then after a long, tortured silence, she whispered, "I think I did…I think I did the right thing."

I closed my eyes, at once feeling her pain and mine. This time I did know what to say, "You did, Shulie, you definitely did. And I hope you get exactly what you want, you know, because you deserve it. That's really what I wanted to tell you."

She seemed on the verge of tears and I felt horrible. I mean, I guess I didn't think we were going to start cracking jokes about the Neal Diamond Christmas album, but I didn't mean for it to hurt. I went to hug her and she let me. Then, her head on my shoulder, she surprised me by saying, "Seth, I'll look for you in every guy I ever meet."

I pushed her away so I could see her, and told her that was the nicest thing anyone had ever said to me.

She wiped her eyes. "I have to go. I'll be late."

"Alright. Bye, Shu," by the time I said, "lie" she was gone. I was left on the sidewalk outside her building sort of waving goodbye to noone. I grabbed my suitcase, which didn't have much more than a couple of more pairs of shorts (I needed to replace the ones I'd lost at Hedonism II) and a few more short sleeve shirts (a little bit dressier this time, as if that would make all the difference in the world to Emma), and walked back to the train, feeling kind of lonely and sad. I wasn't sure if it was for Shulie or me or if it's just depressing when a promising relationship can't quite over-come itself. I started thinking about everything that had happened since I'd last seen Shulie. To that point, my Jamaican experience had been almost exactly what I wanted, but, really, nothing like what I needed. I hoped on my return trip I'd somehow get more of the latter. And, I knew, it was up to me. I needed to write my book and I needed to be with Emma. I had to start running toward my dreams, and not just away from my problems.

38

However, that plan was shot to hell almost immediately after my arrival. The Blue Moon van, with its insignia white crescent moon in a circle of blue, was waiting for me. I was surprised to see Freedy was driving, and not Erika, who I'd been expecting.

"Hey, Freedy," I said, as I tossed my stuff in the back of the van, pumped again to be back in Jamaica. "Everything okay with Erika?"

"Yeah, mon. She's fine. I told her I'd pick you up."

Jumping into the front passenger seat on the left side of the van, we did the Jamaican handshake and I said, "Well, thanks, Freedy, I appreciate you doing this. I owe you."

He mumbled, "No problem, mon."

I looked at him and he seemed intensely preoccupied.

"Freedy, you all right, man? Everything okay?" I'd only talked to Freedy maybe four or five times. I liked him, but he seemed to prefer to keep to himself, like he was keeping a secret. I hoped I wasn't prying into his life too much.

"Seth, bredda, mon, I need to talk to ya. It's why I came to pick ya up." I was surprised he'd call me brother. As I'd said, we weren't that close, and so it seemed so out of character. If he wanted a friend or confidant, that was cool with me, but alarms were going off that he wanted more than a friendly chat. He seemed very needy. Actually, desperate was the word that came to mind, and I was starting to get pretty worried about whatever he was gonna say. I was very glad he already told me Erika was okay. "What is it, man?" What's wrong?"

"Seth, a lot has happened. Some bad shit." I don't think I'd ever seen anyone so nervous. He'd started sweating even though the van had the air-conditioning cranked. "I'm sorry, mon, but I'm really scared. I don't know what to do."

He wasn't the only one who didn't know what to do. I figured I should probably get him to calm down a bit first. "Freedy, it's okay, man, whatever it is, it's okay. Take a breath and tell me what happened, okay. We have a two-hour ride to talk about this, so take your time." That had to have sounded condescending as hell, but I was getting kind of freaked out myself.

It did seem to work a little though. I watched him take a deep breath as I had instructed—he seemed grateful to have specific instructions on anything—and started telling me a story that built on itself until it became like a living, breathing monster.

"Seth, remember that day on the beach when my sister introduced us? You told me you were staying in the first cabin." He took a few long moments struggling to come up with the right way to ask me what I knew he was going to ask. Finally, he managed, "I got the feeling you were trying to tell me something…like you heard what happened in the cabin next door to you that night?"

"That was you getting knocked around in there, wasn't it?" I was kind of more direct that I'd meant to be, but he was struggling so much with how to ask me, I was just trying to let him off the hook.

He looked away, pained to hear that out loud, and quietly admitted, "Yeah, mon."

I took a breath and was going to ask who the guys were, but I wanted to let him steer the conversation and to go at his pace. He took a while to arrange his thoughts and then he started to tell me an unbelievable story; one that would change the life of everyone I knew at the Blue Moon.

"Oh God, Seth, I'm so ashamed of myself," he started out, trying to keep himself together, "I never shoudda got involved. I wish I could do it over again. Mon, I wish…"

"Freedy, it's okay, man. Go ahead and tell me what happened."

He took another breath and began, "I don't know if you know, but I kind of help Dugan out with a lot of things around the hotel. He lets Erika and me live there for free and always took pretty good care of us, you know. Then, about a month before you arrived, Dugan got involved in a business deal with these Colombian guys and said we were both gonna make a lot of money. These people, I never met them until that night in the cabins, they are not nice guys, trust me on that." There wasn't a trace of humor in his voice and I believed him entirely. "They approached Dugan about brokering this deal for them."

"Freedy, what kind of deal?"

"Drugs, mon. Cocaine."

Oh Jesus. That would've been my guess, I guess, but it still hit me like a punch in the stomach that Dugan would get involved with something like that. Especially after all his daughter was trying to do for him. Usually I'm glad to hear when I have a real reason to hate someone I already hated, but not this time.

"How'd Dugan get involved in this?" I asked, not doing a very good job of just letting him talk, though I did notice he had a much easier time talking about Dugan's involvement than his own.

"Dugan has a lot of contacts. Sometimes, they stay at the Blue Moon and I can't wait until they leave. Very shady characters, let me tell you. Dugan's been involved in some small-scale marijuana deals he set up and there's been some rumors of money laundering. Did you know he was sent to jail for a while?" he asked me. I shook my head yes and he continued. "I guess his name got out there. Jamaica, mon, is becoming a central transit point for cocaine on its way to the United States. We're about midway between South American countries, like Columbia, and the U.S., and becoming a more popular route."

I considered Dugan, and figured that the whole scenario made sense under the right set of circumstances. It would probably have to be a smaller scale Colombian drug family, some enterprising family startup; not the big cartels that I'd read about and didn't figure would bother with, or take a chance on, a loser like Dugan. Maybe they figured he could provide the contacts, and if it went very wrong, he'd be the fall guy.

Freedy waited for me and then continued, "Dugan knew some people from Miami who were interested in buying the cocaine. I was the go-be-tween, and he had me drive to a small bay between Negril and Mo' Bay and negotiate a deal." His voice cracked a little. He seemed thoroughly ashamed of his involvement, and I hated Dugan even more for putting Freedy in that position.

"We were going to sell the cocaine for $500,000. Ten kilos for $50,000 each. Our commission was supposed to be twenty percent. Dugan promised me twenty percent of that."

I did the math. The $500,000 deal would net Dugan $100,000. Of that, Freedy was in line for $20,000. That's a lot of money in Jamaica. I could see why everyone would be tempted, which is what I told Freedy.

His response sounded like a rationalization he didn't believe for a second. "I barely had to do anything. And I'd get enough money to help Erika pay for school and for me to get a future away from Dugan." There was a heartbreaking flicker of hope in his eyes, as he said, "I'm into computers— I use Erika's all the time when she's working—and I thought maybe I could use the money to go to school to learn how to…" He couldn't even finish the thought. I could imagine that the reality of his situation must have made it too hard to talk about how close he'd been to what he really wanted. I could see the flicker of hope replaced by a harsh dose of reality. It was profoundly sad and I really felt for him. Not wanting to break down, after a few moments he pushed on with, "Everything might've been okay, you know, except Dugan got greedy.

"The market temporarily pushed up prices. Like I learned in my economics class at school, I guess, demand exceeded supply," he said this with a slight smile, finding the humor in applying the lessons of his education to drug deals. He went on and, unfortunately, the smile quickly disappeared, "Dugan thought he could get more money, so he went looking for another buyer. He actually found some guys who wanted to buy five kilos for $350,000. $70,000 each! He was so happy, he had this crazy look in his eyes, when he explained that we were going to sell five kilos at the higher price to the new buyers and the remaining five kilos to the people from Miami. It worked out that we'd be able to pay the Columbians their $500,000, collecting our $100,000 commission, and because we'd be selling the whole lot for $600,000, pocket another $100,000 for ourselves. He acted like he was the king of the world for thinking of it.

"So, I had to go tell the first buyers their deal was cut in half. They weren't happy—they were scary looking guys and looked like they wanna kill me—but they eventually agreed to do the deal. I guess after coming all that way, they didn't want to go back empty-handed. So, that night I unloaded the van onto this dark beach and they loaded the five kilos into their speedboat. Dugan told me to threaten them that their boat would blow up if they fucked with the deal in any way. Could you imagine me threatening these lunatics their boat would blow up? Seth, you have no idea how scary that was…there's no way that night was worth $20,000 to me." He took a second and then said, "Thank God, though, they paid me the money they owed, $250,000, and I got out of there as fast as I could. It took hours before I could breathe normally again.

"Then, later that week, just like that, the market dropped. Dugan heard there was a huge new infusion of cocaine from the Cali cartel. Our second buyer dropped completely out a site. Maybe they thought we were trying to rob them at $70,000 per kilo. Dugan was panicked and went back to the Miami people to ask if they wanted to come back for the other five kilos, at $50,000 per kilo, or whatever he could get, you know, but they just started swearing at him. I don't blame them. You take a big chance smuggling that big of a shipment by boat. It's not something you want to chance too many times. So, Dugan was left with no other contacts with that kind of money. And, of course, he still needed to come up with another $250,000 to pay off the Colombians.

"So, that night in the cabins, I delivered them only the $250,000 we got from the Miami deal. They grabbed me, demanding the rest, and started throwing me around the room, punching me. I told them if I had $250,000, I'd give it to them. I offered to return the rest of the cocaine, but they wanted their money. They gave us one month to get them their money or we'd pay. I knew they meant it."

"I know, Freedy. I heard them that night and I could tell they meant it. Did you see the guys?"

Freedy looked straight ahead and said, "No, mon, they were wearing ski masks?"

"Do you know where the remaining five kilos are?"

"No. I've wondered about that a lot. Dugan has it hidden somewhere. I think the Colombian guys may be snooping around for it in case they don't get their money and have to do what they said they'd do...kill us both."

"Oh my God! That's what they said? I mean, they included you in that threat?"

"That's what they said." He closed his eyes and through clenched teeth added, "And this weekend they said it again."

"What?! What happened this weekend?" I demanded, not proud of how unnerved I'd become.

The van swerved, not all that uncommon on that fucked-up road, but I started to get nervous he wouldn't be able to control it. "Freedy, pull over, okay. Right here. Pull over right here!"

He stopped the van on the side of the road and nearby there was one of the ubiquitous thatched-roof Jamaican "lemonade" stands selling Red Stripes and fruit and assorted Jamaican junk. There were two plastic chairs behind the hut, on a small patch of sand, facing the ocean. I told Freedy to grab a seat, and I went in and bought us two Red Stripes. I figured if he didn't want one, I could use two, but he grabbed the one beer from me and finished it in like two seconds. I felt compelled to give him my second one. He took that, and I told him to take relax and take his time (with the story, not the beer.)

When he seemed ready, I said, "Okay, Freedy, tell me exactly what happened this weekend."

"Seth, they both came in ski masks again and shoved Dugan and me into Dugan's hotel room. They were standing over us with a gun and we were sitting in these two chairs in the dark. They said we had two weeks to pay or they'd kill us both." I waited for Freedy to be able to get the words out. When he finally did, I thought I might get sick.

"They grabbed Dugan and held him over a table. They turned a small desk lamp on. One guy held him there and the other one…" Freedy was really struggling to get the words out and keep himself together, "this guy, Sanchez—he's the craziest motherfucker I've ever seen—takes out this fucking machete and chops off Dugan's thumb. They cut off his fucking thumb, Seth, and his blood splattered on the walls, the lamp…on me. His blood splattered all over me, Seth. Dugan was screaming this sickening scream I can still hear at night, and I…I thought they might do the same thing to me."

Freedy was practically hyperventilating. I put my hand on his back for a long time and gave him a chance to let his fears and emotions drain out of him. He started to sob with his head in his hands, while I sat there thinking my head was going to explode. I didn't much care what happened to Dugan, but I cared a lot about Emma. I started thinking about what Dugan would say to her, how he would say it. I knew it would be devastating for her to find out she came all this way to make that part of her life better, and then find her asshole father was in deeper shit than ever. I also thought about sweet, wonderful Erika and the kind of trouble her brother was in. I wondered if she even knew. And, then, of course, poor Freedy, who was shattered to the core and in way over his head.

I got up, went into the hut and bought a six pack of Red Stripes. When I returned he was standing on the beach. I gave him another beer. We both looked out over the water for a while. He started talking so quietly I could barely hear him and I was standing right next to him.

"Dugan has a plan," he said.

"What?"

"Dugan says he has a plan to get us out of this."

39

"**O**h God, Freedy. I'm afraid to ask, but what plan?" I asked as if there was not a chance in hell it would be a good idea.

Freedy shook his head, like even talking about it would lend credence to it that he didn't feel. "He's convinced himself that he can buy and sell enough ganja to make $150,000 to pay off the Colombians."

"Doesn't he owe them $250,000?" I asked, careful not to include Freedy in that obligation.

"That's what they say, mon. They said we can forget our commission, but Dugan is convinced they'll be satisfied and go home. I don't know about that. What do you tink, mon?"

"First, Freedy, where the hell is he gonna get that much bud to sell? And, then, where is he gonna get a buyer?"

"He says he has a supplier, a Rastaman from the hills named Alfred, and..."

"Wait a second! What!?" I didn't want to believe what my gut was telling me. I was suddenly sure that it was my Alfred; that the Post-it note I'd seen on Dugan's desk with Alfred's number on it was originally meant for me. I thought about Dugan getting a call from Alfred, and gently easing into a conversation, like, "My fren (suddenly Mr. Jamaican), if we work togedder, I think we can both make some money, mon." I wasn't sure how I'd find out if it was really him, or, if it were true, how I'd feel about it. In any case, I may have startled Freedy, who didn't need startling. I asked him to slow down and tell me if he'd ever seen Alfred.

He said, "Yeah, mon."

"Freedy, I need you to describe him for me. I need to know what he looks like." Freedy's face couldn't hide his confusion, but he went on to describe Alfred to a T.

I guess I knew in my heart it was him, but I left myself the hope that Alfred's was a fairly common description in Jamaica. Alone it was incriminating but inconclusive. I'd have to find out for sure some other way.

I just told Freedy that I knew I Rasta guy named Alfred, but that he didn't match that description.

Freedy repeated his earlier question, "What do you think? Do you think they'll let us off the hook for the $100,000 after all this?"

I thought about it. What the hell did I know about a Colombian drug family? My dad's an accountant. But, to be honest with myself, I didn't share Dugan's conviction. Freedy's tone revealed that he didn't either. Because of Dugan, the Colombians had to spend the last several months tangled up in that mess—pissed off, plotting strategy, making at least a couple of otherwise unnecessary visits to Negril. I guessed that sometime on the insane drive from Mobay to Negril, they certainly would've vowed vengeance against Dugan Kelly. There was no way they were going to let him off the hook for $100,000.

"I don't know, Freedy," I said indicating my skepticism, "but I think it'd be a good idea for you to get out of the line of fire. Either way, you know?"

"Yeah, mon. I know that." In his eyes I could see a plea for help. I wasn't sure how qualified I was, but I thought to myself, I'd do my best.

"Freedy, does Dugan have a buyer?"

"He says he does. One of his Vegas pals, I think. His plan is for it to all happen this month at Negril Carnival."

"Negril Carnival? What's that?"

"It's a big deal. It's held every year in May. You know where the craft stores are as you near downtown? It's held down there near the river. It's for five nights and they have bands and drinks and food. Everyone comes— the natives and the tourists. It's very exciting."

"Why'd Dugan pick there?"

"There's always so many boats and people near the shoreline it should be easy for a deal to go unnoticed."

"When is it?"

"It's May 11 to 15. I think Dugan's thinking Friday the 14th, because that should be the most crowded night."

That was less than two weeks away. Clearly it had moved from ill-conceived theory to ill-conceived plan.

"And the buyers will be coming in by boat?"

"Yeah, mon."

"Did Dugan ask for your help?"

"He's not saying. It's making me nervous."

"What do you mean?"

"Seth, I think he wants to do the deal himself. Believe me, I don't want to ever get involved with that shit again, and normally I'd be happy to stay as far away as possible, but there's only one reason I can think of he'd want to do it himself." He paused for a moment and said, "He's planning to take the money and run."

Oh Shit! The consequences of that hit me immediately. "He can't do that!" And, almost to myself, said "Then they'd go after Emma." It had suddenly become a nightmare, a monster no longer just Freedy's and Dugan's, but Emma's and mine. Yes, I *wanted* to do everything I could to protect Freedy, but I *needed* to protect Emma. And, of the two, I was pretty sure Emma was in more danger. It had just gone to a whole new fucked-up level.

"And me," he said, reminding me that his neck was also on the line.

"Listen, Freedy," I said, trying to calm us both down, "let's think about that. If he leaves, what incentive would the Colombians have to come after you?"

"Cause I'm there."

"Yeah, maybe, but, no offense, they're not going to think you have $250,000, or even $150,000, sitting around. And, revenge against you, when you're clearly not the main guy, seems worthless."

"And, what if they think they can get Dugan back by threatening to kill me?"

"Freedy, believe me. I'm not trying to minimize the danger you may be in if Dugan were to run, but I don't believe these guys would think for a second that Dugan would give himself up to save you." I didn't say so, but I knew that Emma was a different story and a whole lot more leverage.

"What about the remaining cocaine that Dugan hid? They may think I know where it is."

"That's a harder question. I think if it came to that, you'd be able to convince them you don't have a clue where it is, and if you did, you certainly wouldn't risk your life trying to conceal it. But, let me see if I can work on something a bit more reassuring, okay."

Freedy was again shaken. "What should I do? I need help."

I looked Freedy in the eyes and promised to help. "Come on, let's drive back. It'll give me a chance to think of something." I hoped that all my years of being analytical was finally gonna be worth a damn. I better not fuck it up. Just outside of Negril, I thought I had a plan.

"Freedy, listen up. Here's what I think we should do." I stopped to go over it quickly in my head one more time before saying it loud. "First, Freedy, I'd suggest trying to find out what Dugan is up to. Whether he's planning to have you do the deal, or if he will. If he commits one way or the other, we'll be better prepared. If he says he's going to do it himself, or if he stays non-committal, I think we should assume he's planning to run. If so, press him for a phone number where he might be after the deal. He'll know what you mean. Convince him that it's for his own good that he can be reached in case something were to happen to Emma or the hotel. I can't imagine he'd completely turn his back on his daughter if she were in danger. He doesn't need to give an address, just the number." I just wanted to make sure that if they got to Emma, we could get in touch with Dugan.

Freedy thought about that for a minute, and asked, "What good does that do me?"

"I think it may keep you alive. If Dugan disappears, and you know how he can be reached, they have reason to keep you alive."

"But what if they threaten me and force me to give up the number? Then they wouldn't have that reason any more, and, I've seen how they try to force you to see things their way. Remember, what I told you about Sanchez. He's fucking crazy."

It was a good question and one I'd also considered. "Here's the rest of it. After the deal goes down, however it goes down, I'd like you to hide out for a while until things blow over. Somewhere only I know where you are and only I can reach you. Can you think of anyplace like that?"

He shrugged helplessly and said, "No, mon, not really. Anywhere I could think of to hide, Erika would be able to find me. And, I don't want to involve her or any of our friends."

"Okay, I don't blame you. Actually, I may have the perfect place for you to hang out a while where no one could find you. You'd be safe there. Let me contact him and set it up, okay?"

He nodded without hesitation as if his load was already lessened immeasurably. Staying the hell away from the Colombians must have felt like a mother's hug.

"We need a way to get you out of there fast. Assuming the Colombians have an issue with the payoff being $150,000, rather than $250,000, I don't want you to be the first person they see. I may have an idea on that. Once you get out of there, we'll get you to my friend's place and I'll let you know when it's safe to return. Sound okay to you, pal?"

He nodded his head and gave me a small trace of a smile. I think safe was the only word he heard.

I needed to contact Alfred. He was going to have a visitor. Unless I was badly off base, he owed me that much after contributing to this fucked up mess.

"Oh, one more thing…"

It started off innocently enough, but Freedy's, "Oh, one more thing," as we were parking the van who the hell knew how many hours after I'd arrived back in Jamaica, was followed by another grenade.

"Oh, Seth, one more thing. Erika told me that you are pretty close with Emma." He hesitated and then said, "I'm sorry to tell you this, but you should know that the other Colombian guy is Diego."

My heart almost fucking stopped. "WHAT DID YOU SAY?" I yelled at Freedy.

Freedy, who appeared to just realize how that news might affect me, had an apologetic look in his eyes as he repeated, "Dugan told me that Sanchez's partner is Diego…the Diego that's dating his daughter."

"Oh Jesus, that can't be," I said, and it must have sounded no stronger than the wishful thinking it was.

I knew that Dugan didn't like Diego, actually hated him according to Emma. I also knew that Dugan was enough of a weasel to make up a thing like that to try to break them up. If so, the fact that Diego was admittedly Colombian would make for a convenient bit of evidence against him.

On the other hand, if Diego were involved, it would certainly explain the previously inexplicable dislike that he had for his daughter's new boyfriend. And, of course, he was fucking Colombian, which seemed incriminating enough. There was something else about Diego I was trying to remember—one of those fleeting thoughts that's there and gone. I felt like it would shed some light on my thoughts, but I couldn't put my finger on it.

I was left with the sincere hope that it wasn't him. I really wanted to not believe Dugan and I was willing to give Diego the benefit of the doubt. Still, though, I had to carefully consider how, or if, I should approach the subject with Emma. How did my life get so complicated all of a sudden?

Freedy was looking at me. Now that I was the one shaken, he put his hand on my shoulder to comfort me. I thanked him for his understanding and then asked him one more question. "Does Erika know about this?"

He gave that look of shame I'd seen earlier and said, "No, I can't tell her. She'd be too disappointed in me. You can't tell her either."

I gave him what I hoped was a somewhat reassuring smile and said, "Don't worry, bud. I won't. I'm on your side, okay."

He gave me one of the least assuring smiles of all-time and said quietly, "Yeah, mon. I'm glad I came to you."

My feelings on that were decidedly mixed.

40

I threw my bag in my cabin and looked around at its stark lack of character. Except for some new fresh flowers, no doubt from Emma, nothing had changed. I was glad for that, because it sure seemed like everything else had.

I grabbed a Ting soda and some pineapple from the fridge and briefly considered how to approach Emma.

I found her on the beach, and savored a moment of looking at her before she saw me. She looked as beautiful as ever, but I thought, without the same spirit, like a light inside her had gone out. She sat at the edge of a lounge chair, her shoulders bowed a bit, her hands clasped, just sort of thinking, or maybe, trying not to think.

"Em," I said quietly, trying not to jolt her, as I touched her shoulder as gently as I could. I looked at her face as her eyes found mine. Unsaid was everything else I was thinking. How bad I felt for all the emotional hits she'd taken in just the few days I'd been gone, how great it was to see her again, and how much I wanted to help her regain her old spirit. But I think she heard all those things anyway. She touched my hand and I held it there on her shoulder as she closed her eyes, all her pain and relief an open book. I could see a slight smile inside her that told me she was glad to see me.

I sat down next to her and just said, "Em, I'm here sweetie, I'm here."

She started to cry, but I sensed it was more of relief and hope than of despair. It was obvious she'd been trying to deal with too much by herself. I held her close to me. She finally said, "You came back to me," and I was surprised and moved that her tears were at least partly because of me. I wiped away a remaining tear and kissed her on that spot.

I'd had too brutal of a ride in with poor Freedy to be able to offer any more help at that moment than just holding her, so I asked her, "Listen, Emma, why don't you and I go to dinner tonight. There's this place on the beach. We can talk about things, or not, but it will be a good chance to be together and maybe start making things better." I hadn't intentionally used the term 'make things better', but I realized after saying it that I didn't think anything could resonate with Emma as much. It was why she worked at the cancer society when her step-dad had succumbed to cancer and it was why she came to Jamaica when her dad needed help.

"I'd love to, Seth."

Sometimes, it's the impromptu stuff that's better.

That night, I walked with Emma down the beach to the Charela Inn. I'd noticed the place a few times before as I walked by. Of all the hotels on the beach, it struck me as having a character all its own—elegant, but without looking as if it was trying too hard. Right in the middle of their nicely maintained beach was a glass-enclosed sign that had their restaurant's daily menu, and I'd looked a few times, always thinking everything sounded great. The restaurant, just off the beach, had two sections, a large outdoor patio and an adjacent open-air indoor room. The inside room, though it appeared not used that often except for the row of tables nearest the beach, was appointed nicely and included ceiling fans, plants and a fountain. It was another beautiful night, though, and we chose a table for two outside. We split a lobster pizza, along with a Red Stripes for Emma and me. For some reason, the waitress loved us immediately, and offered the first round on the house.

Fitting with how the setting was helping to lift our spirits, they also had a band playing that night. Their first set was Jamaican folklore songs in Patois. The singer, who had the most heartwarming and brightest smile I'd ever seen, would explain the songs afterwards in a way that was very cute, because it didn't explain a thing. He'd say, "Dat was the song, *The River Runs Deep*," and would go on to explain its meaning to us tourists by saying, "It's about the river runs deep." Emma and I looked at each other and blurted out a laugh. For the first time, her smiles were starting to come a little easier. When smile guy was going to explain the song *Matilda*, we both looked at each other and almost on queue with the singer, said, "It's about Matilda." So far, we hadn't talked about anything, but we were both starting to feel better.

Besides the smiling singer, the band included three dancers and a Rasta-looking guy who played bongos. The dancers also sang, and beautifully at that. There was one thin guy in sharp royal blue pants and a long Hawaiian shirt, and two heavy-set, but beautiful women, in Jamaican costume dresses. They sang the Harry Belafonte line, *When daylight come, I gotta go home,* and if old Harry had made that song into a video, the two women singers would have perfectly fit the part. The band was so low key and unassuming, and I couldn't imagine that they could make any kind of real money doing that, but it was one of the most charming and beautiful sets of music I'd ever seen. Gentle Caribbean rhythms filled the night. Sometimes music can hit you just right and make you feel just perfect. I could tell Emma dug it too. She seemed to be making the band hers. And ours.

Between sets, after we had finished dinner and some ice cream for dessert, we sat in the beach chairs just on the ocean side of some hedges that separated the beach from the restaurant. We sat there on the lounge chairs, our legs touching, while looking up at the most magnificent sky. It's hard to imagine anything more like Eden than staring up at a night full of stars through the leaves of a palm tree in the Caribbean. Except for maybe looking at Emma's face as she looked up at the stars through the palms. Sometime in our reverie, we noticed the band started to play again. The three dancers had taken their leave and the singer with the smile and the Rasta guy with his drum played mostly Bob Marley songs. We had settled into a comfortable sedation and neither of us got up until Emma asked me to dance during *Three Little Birds*. It was the same song I'd sung with Alfred on my way to Negril, and the words *Don't worry about a thing* took on new significance. I'm sure we were both hoping, more than believing, that was true. In any case, Emma and I again felt like a perfect fit. We danced slowly in the sand, my chin grazing her forehead, my left hand cradling the tenderness of her right hand and my other hand around her waist. Dancing together seemed wonderfully intimate without trying to be. I wanted to kiss her, but waiting felt like the right thing to do. When we did kiss—really kiss—for the first time, I wanted to make sure it was the real thing for both of us.

Meanwhile, the two-man band started grooving, and out of the blue, the waitresses had one by one gotten up to sing and dance along with the band. If you didn't know, you'd think they were part of the show. The food service stopped entirely, but no one was complaining. I got the sense the band had planned on leaving, but the staff wouldn't let them and they didn't disappoint. Emma grabbed my hand and we walked back up the sidewalk towards the music. We were kind of dancing off to the side, when our waitress, the one who loved us, came over and pulled us over to dance with them.

It was just the waitresses and us dancing to *Could You Be Loved.* One of the waitresses, this tall, beautiful Jamaican woman started singing and anyone who heard the beauty of that voice felt like they were in a better place. It was a voice that belonged to the heavens; not one you'd ever expect to hear providing backup vocals to a band no one ever heard of in front of maybe a dozen people eating dinner. To those of us lucky enough to have been there that night, it gave an unexpected gift of grace and charm to a night that seemed to be all about that. When it was done, everyone stood and clapped—us, the staff, the customers, the rasta bongo guy and the smiling singer—at what a special night it became. We hugged our waitress and the waitress with the amazing voice and the smile guy and the bongo player and joked about all of us going on tour. We promised to come back and see them again and Emma and I looked at each other and smiled. The night had embraced us and made it ours.

We sat back down under the palm trees, feeling that life was somehow better and that, sometimes when you needed it, our little blue planet could be a tender and giving place.

After a while, I asked how she was doing.

"A lot better now. Thanks Seth, tonight was wonderful."

"It was, wasn't it."

I took her hand and said, "Em, Freedy told me what happened. About your dad. I'm so sorry."

She looked up at the stars again, as if for inspiration, and said, "I just wish I could hate him more. I mean, so what if he's my dad? That gives him no right to have my love, you know. He's such a jerk and he deserves everything he gets, but he's still my dad, the only one I have. And I still feel like I want to make things better for him, whether he deserves it or not." And then, as if laughing at herself, "I just wish I could get over that." I laughed with her, feeling very in love with her.

I looked down and said, "And he told me about Diego. All I can say is I hope that's not true." And, letting her know I was on her side, "I don't think it is."

Without emotion, as if she had thought about it until it had drained every bit of emotion from her body, said, "It's not Seth. It can't be. My dad's just saying that because he doesn't like him. You know, it's the first time he's been around when I've dated someone. He probably just doesn't want to lose me, you know. I mean, I kind of feel sorry for my dad when I think about it."

I gave her a smile and said, "Don't feel too sorry for him."

She laughed a little, and said cutely, "Don't worry about dat, mon."

"Hey, Em," I said, thinking our perfect night may have survived talking about her dad and her would-be boyfriend, "how was our Full Moon Festival?"

She lit up again. "Seth, it was so great. I wish you were there. It seemed like all of Negril was there, and the night, with the moon, was so beautiful. You would have been so proud. Our little place just looked great. I bordered the beach with candles in paper bags I'd filled with sand and it looked so amazing. The band was wonderful and everyone was dancing and Spike sold about a million *Moon*shine drinks. It's the new hit in Jamaica. If we advertise the next one a little, it could be even bigger. Everyone came up to me and said what a great idea it was. And I think we should do your fireworks idea."

She looked at me and I gave her a proud smile. I said, "Hey, we're a pretty good team, huh?"

"The best," she said with a bursting smile and even dumbshit me could tell we were having a moment.

I picked her hand up in mine, and we both sat there looking at each other as time stood still. The kiss was soft and perfect and the taste of her held on my lips. But for the promise of more, I'd have been completely satisfied to continue savoring the first, to turn it into an everlasting memory. Its affect was almost overwhelming. I looked up at her to make sure a second was okay. She smiled an angel's smile that told me how she felt about it, and I gave her a kiss that told her everything she needed to know about how I felt about her.

After what could've been ten seconds or an hour, I wasn't sure, she rubbed my cheek and gently pushed me away. *Oh my God*, I was thinking, *what does that mean?* I was too aware of how recently every time I had a great moment, it was followed be an equally crappy one. I didn't feel too much better when she said, "Seth, I have to tell you something."

I'd never felt so exposed. I was naked and full of raw nerve endings trying to imagine what she might tell me. I was mentally ready to bury myself like a crab in the sand if it was as bad as I was expecting.

"Diego," uh oh, not a good start, "told me he loved me." Not getting any fucking better, either.

I just looked at her. She finally said, "And I believe him." I was sinking further into my personal quicksand.

And then she said it.

"But, Seth," she said with quiet sincerity, "I have these feelings for you. I missed you so much when you were gone. I really didn't think you were coming back, and I knew I wasn't going to be able to handle it if you didn't." A tear came down her cheek. It was for me and it was beautiful. I looked at her and with my eyes encouraged her to keep going. "I mean, Seth, if I had to choose between you... I don't know...I..."

I put my finger on her lip to stop her, satisfied for the moment that I was very much back in the game. My body, which had been expecting the worst, seemed unable to recover. My spirit wanted to soar, while my body wanted to finish falling apart. Emma, unable to read my reaction, said, "Seth, are you okay?"

All at once, thankfully, it began to come together. I knew the game wasn't won yet, but it suddenly became full of possibility. "Emma, I've never been more alright." Then with conviction I hadn't known possible, I said, "Please choose me. I want you more than anything I've ever wanted in my life. More than anything in the world." I was proud of myself for finally getting it right after so many false starts and missed opportunities.

"Do you mean that, Seth? Really?" She seemed so happy.

"Oh yes," I said. "Oh my God, yes." And I picked her up and kissed her for a really long, really great time.

When I put her down, she said, "Seth, will you help me get through all of this?"

"I promise, I'll do the best I can. Nothing means more to me."

We walked back down the beach, and trying to take advantage of the time I had, I stopped to kiss her in the moonlight about as regularly as we were approached to buy ganja. When I told one sales guy, "I'm all set," more optimistic words were never spoken.

I didn't even have time to consider what an amazing day I'd had. It was that morning I'd talked to Shulie and felt like that door had closed for good. That afternoon, I'd talked to Freedy, who'd opened up way too many dark, scary doors. That night, for the first time, Emma had opened up her door for me and thankfully I had pushed it more open than closed. I didn't know where any of these doors might lead, but I knew this was the story of my life.

41

I had kissed Emma outside my door. Slow and sweet and like new lovers. That morning, I awoke without Emma in body only. Otherwise, she was with me in every thought I could put together and in every feeling I had, as if all my senses were still having a party. Her scent still danced before my nose. The taste of her lips still embraced mine. The touch of her still made me tingle. I could still hear her say how much she missed me, and, as if it was happening at that very moment, I could look at her face as she looked up at the stars.

Not everything had gone right, of course—she still had not chosen just me—but, for a change, nothing had gone wrong. True feelings replaced bad jokes. Real emotion replaced sad escapes. Ever since that first kiss with Emma, my soul carried my body, instead of the other way around.

That morning, feeling exhilarated and ready for whatever the new day might bring, I bounded out my door and right the hell smack into Freedy's chest. I knocked him to the dirt with an unflattering thud. For the second time, I stood looking over Freedy laying on his ass just outside the cabins. In fact, he fell not too far from where I'd seen him get thrown out of the cabin by Sanchez and a guy who may or may not have been Diego.

"Jesus, Freedy," I asked helping him up, "you okay?"

He smiled, or as close to a smile as he could get given all the shit he was going through, and answered, "Yeah, mon. Then shaking his head cracked, "That's no way to welcome a visitor."

"It's my new high-tech security system," I joked, still basking in my Emma euphoria, "what do you think?"

"I don't know how much good it will do. The really dangerous people are *inside!*" he retorted quickly and with a wry smile, and it was very funny.

I slapped him on the back, appreciating his sense of humor and invited him in. Since I had been on my way to go meet with Emma to work on the continued marketing of the Blue Moon, I sort of had the marketing stuff on my mind. Seeing Freedy, I made a mental connection that led to a great idea.

"Freedy," I said, with some excitement, "I just thought of something. Emma and I want to build a web site for the hotel. We've taken pictures, and I've laid out the links and how I'd like it to progress. I also have a book at home about how to program an HTML web site. What would you say if we hired you to build it for us?"

Freedy gave me a look like I had just given him a new life.

"YEAH, MON! That would be great!" He couldn't have been more thrilled.

"Have you ever developed a web site?" I asked after I'd offered the job, probably not a sign of a real quality interview.

"Well, no. But I'll learn it in no time. You'll see. You won't be disappointed."

"I believe you, bud. I think you're gonna do a great job. Can you finish it by Carnival?"

"I better get started," he said like a kid who couldn't wait to open his birthday presents.

"I'm on my way now. We can get you all set up," I said, and then remembered he must have come to my door for some other reason than he expected a job offer. "Freedy, what's up? Did you want to see me about something?"

He looked at me and then remembered why he'd stopped by. He frowned as if he'd also remembered he wasn't carrying good news.

"Yeah, mon. I talked to Dugan last night. You know, about the deal."

Apparently because we were talking about drugs, we had to talk in code.

"And, what about *the deal?*" I asked.

Freedy fidgeted with his hands, and finally looked up for a second and said, "I asked him if he wanted me to do the deal for him. He wasn't answering and I could just see he was planning something, you know. So, I told him that. I told him that I thought he might be thinking of running. He seemed stunned that I'd think of something like that and he got all uptight about it. You know how he gets. To calm him down, I told him it was fine with me, whatever he wanted to do. But for his own good, he needed to leave a phone number where he could be reached. He weakly tried to insist he wasn't leaving; that it wasn't an issue. So I said, 'Okay, IF you would ever even think about leaving—even to get away from Sanchez—you need to make sure that I could reach you, just in case anything went wrong at the hotel or with Emma.' I think mentioning Emma might have made the difference. He said again that he wasn't going to leave, but gave me the number of a friend of his that could reach him…just in case. I'm surprised, you know, but I think maybe I caught him off-guard."

"Good work, Freedy," I said duly impressed. Outwardly, I wanted to keep things light. Inside, though, I was disgusted by Dugan and his selfishness. If he ran away without paying the Colombians, he'd be jeopardizing everyone and everything he should have cared about—Emma, especially, but also Freedy and the Blue Moon. There was no getting around the fact that, very soon, Emma could be in an awful lot of danger.

I realized that the key to Emma's safety would be to not let the bad guys know that they could reach Dugan. Without access to him, they couldn't blackmail him or force him back, and so there'd be no point in endangering Emma. Suddenly, I wasn't sure if my bright idea of getting Dugan's number was so bright. As long as that number was available to someone, it meant they could find Dugan.

"Freedy, have you memorized the phone number or is it on a piece of paper?"

"It's written down. I haven't even looked at it yet," he said, fishing in his pocket for a piece of white paper folded neatly into a little square.

"Listen. I'm really not sure if this keeps you safe, like I originally said, or puts you in even more danger."

"Whattya mean?"

"Okay, if they want revenge, they might want to come after you. If they did go after you, having the number might be the only leverage you have. But if they're thinking about playing a ransom game with Emma, it would only work if they thought they could reach Dugan. And the only way they could reach Dugan would be to get that number. Do you understand what I'm saying?"

"Yeah, mon. Perfectly."

I thought for a minute and decided what I needed to do. "Freedy, let me hold onto that number. It's for Emma and me more than you."

"No, Seth! I know you care about Emma and that you're trying to protect me, but this is about me, not you. I got myself into this mess, and I'm not going to let you take a fall for me." He held up the folded piece of paper and said, "I don't know if this will keep me safe or not, but I *know* why it's so important to have. I'm taking it and I'll take good care of it." In his voice was no uncertainty or room for compromise.

I wished I knew the answer to how it would all play out. There was a chance that Freedy keeping that number on him would keep him safer or I would have insisted on taking it. In retrospect, it was clear. At the moment, not at all. All I could say was, "Hide it and don't tell *anyone* you have it! Got it?"

"Got it."

"Freedy, you're a good guy." I said and meant it. "Let's go build a web site."

42

In the few minutes I figured I had, I made sure no one was looking and snuck into Dugan's small private office. It was a fucking mess. There were papers everywhere, some facing up, some down, some sideways and some stained with spilled coffee. There was one file cabinet, which I opened mostly expecting to find what was there. Nothing. Except for a dirty coffee mug. He hadn't bothered to file a single piece of paper. Yet, somewhere in this pile of junk, I had to find a Post-it note. Not helping my cause was that I decided not to turn the lights on, because Mr. Stealth was pretty much a chicken shit. There were no windows in the inner office, so the only light came from the setting sun as it filtered in from the outer office.

I pushed some papers around on top of the desk, being careful to not make more of a mess than was already there, until I decided that wasn't possible. I looked furiously, but there was no yellow to be found, except for an old copy of a local Connecticut paper with a picture of what looked to be a ballet recital. The star of the show, I saw reading the caption, was eight-year old Emma Kelly of Greenwich. It was under some dusty glass on the desk, and I it took every bit of self-preservation I could muster to tear myself away from the picture. She was thin then as now, but I could see the makings of the beautiful woman she would become. Her pose looked like she was trying hard not to mess up, but her eyes projected the same sense of wonder and a mischievous sense of confidence. Knowing Emma, I imagined that if it didn't go exactly as planned, she was still going to have fun, make the best of it, and improvise like crazy. It was a face you couldn't help but love. The camera certainly did, and even her dad, with his under-developed sense of what was beautiful and what was right in this world, couldn't miss it. It was, in fact, the only spot on his desk not completed covered by papers and food wrappers. Maybe somewhere he did have a heart. It's only because of that picture that my negative feelings towards Dugan weren't absolute.

I realized that I had probably been staring at Emma's picture for more than a minute. I had only allotted myself maybe two minutes of looking around. I grabbed at a drawer in the lower left of the desk and it was locked. That seemed strange enough for me to focus my remaining half a minute on that drawer. I pulled at the drawer directly under the center of the desk, and it opened. It was the drawer that usually holds pencils and assorted paper clips. Dugan's contained pencils and assorted paper clips and a small silver key. I grabbed the key and trying to open up the drawer on the lower left, the key fell to the ground. I scampered around on a fairly disgusting linoleum-tiled floor until I spotted it on the other side of the desk. I strained as far as I could and just barely was able to reach it and grab it in my hand. Rushing to regain the lost time, I banged my head into the corner of the center drawer of the desk. I resisted the almost overwhelming need to yell, "*Oh shit!*" I grabbed my forehead, over my right eye, and wasn't really pumped up to see there was already a spot of blood on my hand. If it was bleeding already, it might be a pretty significant gash. It hurt like hell, but all I could think about was how I was gonna explain it to Emma, and more importantly, how bad was I gonna look. After all, I was trying to get the love of my life, competing against some gorgeous foreign guy. I needed to be at my best. That wasn't gonna help.

Interrupting my thoughts, lucky only in the sense that they were were completely inappropriate at the moment, was Dugan's voice. *Shit.* I heard him shouting something to Spike on his way back to the office. I figured I had about fifteen more seconds. I prayed that he'd stop off and talk to Spike for a minute. If he didn't, I was caught red-handed in his private office without a remotely plausible story. I looked at the key and suddenly my curiosity got the best of me. Hell, if I was gonna get caught, I was gonna get caught. I might as well go for it. So, I unlocked the drawer, listening for the sound of Dugan's footsteps entering the outer office. No sound yet. The drawer came open and I looked over the desk to see if he was coming. It was difficult to tell how much time had passed, but I guessed he must have stopped, at least for a second, to talk to Spike. Not sure what I was expecting, I looked down into the drawer, and found enough dangerous shit to make a state militia proud. The first thing I saw was a handgun. If that didn't get my heart racing, the library of books he had about wiring explosives certainly did. I remembered Freedy saying that Dugan had threatened to blow up the boat of the people who had purchased the five kilos of cocaine from him had they fucked with the deal. Clearly, it was a personal interest. He had every militia-endorsed book but, *How the Government Fucks You in the Ass* and *I Did it McVeigh*. I moved the books aside and saw a collection of timers and wires. Jesus, he wasn't just reading about this shit. That's when I heard him approach. I looked in vain for a closet, even though I knew I wouldn't have time to get to one without him seeing.

I slid under the desk, which was gonna be a really great place to hide if he happened to sit down at his desk. What would I do then, offer him a blowjob? Say I was just looking for his thumb? The latch to open the door to the outer office turned, and about two seconds before I would certainly have had a coronary, I heard, like my guardian angel, the voice of Emma calling her dad. She came into the outer office, asking her dad about some bills he was supposed to pay. Listening, I tried to decide if it was safe to breathe again. I also had to consider whether I could close the drawer without being heard. A voice in my head kept saying, "Take it outside, Emma, take him outside." As if on queue, she said, "Dad, come on out here. I need to ask you about…" The whatever it was about was muffled by the sound of the closing door. Then, a second later, it closed again, as Dugan followed his wonderful daughter out the door. I slowly eased myself out from under the desk, in case he suddenly changed direction. I was just about to close the drawer with the frightening little look into his life, when I saw a Post-it note attached to the side of it. Not even taking the time to read it, I grabbed it and finished closing the door, locking it with the key that was still in the latch. Once locked, I went to put the key back in the pencil drawer when, once again, I fumbled the key out of my hand and to the floor. I reached around in the darkness under the desk for a second until I heard Dugan and Emma closer, and decided I didn't have time to find it. I scrambled out of the private office and into the outer office just as Dugan returned. Emma, after saving my ass, wasn't with him. Had I made it to the other side of the counter, I could've escaped clean, but no. "Gold," Dugan demanded, wondering what I could possibly be doing behind his counter, "What the hell are you doing? And what the fuck happened to your head?"

Just as Dugan was searching for an explanation, so was I. I finally came up with, coincidentally, the truth, "I banged my head and it feels like it's gonna explode (pun intended.) I was looking for some Tylenol, you got any?"

He took a second, deciding if the explanation was plausible, before politely letting me know, "This isn't the fucking nurse's office and I don't have any fucking Tylenol. Get your own."

My goodness. "Good thing you're not in the *hospitality* business, Doogs. You know, some service businesses are actually known for providing some service."

He gave me a look like, "Okay, whatever, Mr. Business School."

Our relationship had become openly hostile, which didn't bother me a whole lot, but I thought if that was how he spoke to the guy he'd endorsed to date his daughter, he must really fucking hate Diego.

"Hey, Gold, since you think so highly of service, why don't you watch the desk for me for a few minutes? Emma's got me running around trying to keep up with her new cost-cutting program. She's driving me fucking crazy with that stuff." That last part seemed like his way of saying please.

Relieved that I appeared to be out of the woods, I spit out, "Sure, but don't take too long, I got a fucking headache," which was my way of saying "Sure, but don't take too long, I got a fucking headache."

He was out the door before I finished the sentence. I walked to the front of the office to make sure Dugan wasn't playing some game where he was gonna sneak back and try to catch me at whatever he suspected I was doing. But the coast appeared to be clear, I thought, wondering if people still said that.

I went back behind the counter and took the Post-it Note from the pocket of my shorts. There on the unfolded note were the letters and numbers that spelled out Alfred's name and phone number. Since I'd found what I was looking for, I just needed to find out if it was my Alfred. I'd do that when I got back to my room.

Standing behind the desk with nothing to do while I waited for Dugan to return from a meeting with his CFO and daughter, I remembered my thought about how much he must have hated Diego.

I thought back to the date of my first night in Jamaica. It was Saturday night, April 3, and two guys had victimized a poor Jamaican guy in the room next to mine. The victim, I knew, was Freedy. One of the attackers was Sanchez. I had heard his name that night and again through Freedy. The question is who was his partner in crime? When I had asked Dugan

275

about it, he said the registered guest was Sanchez something. Romerio, I thought. I took a look at the hotel register book in front of me on the desk and decided it was worth taking a peek. It was likely the registered guest was, in fact, Sanchez. On the other hand, Dugan could have just been telling me a name I'd already mentioned to him.

The book was closed, but a bookmark opened it to that day's date, Wednesday May 5. I quickly turned back through the pages. Following a thought I'd just had, I took a quick glance at some of the weekend dates I knew Diego had been around. On all those dates I saw the name D. Romerio. Knowing that's how Diego registered, I turned to April 3rd. Right there in front of me in cabin number two…D. Romerio. My heart sank. There was no longer any doubt. Diego was involved up to his Columbian ass.

I went back to May 5th and paged ahead looking for the next D. Romerio entry. It was for that Friday, May 7. Shaken by the magnitude of what that might mean to Emma, I closed the registration book and practically ran out of the office back to my room, forgetting I was supposed to be there to man the desk.

Suspecting one would-be friend of wrongdoing, I had found another would-be friend had done wrong. Way wrong. Back in my cabin, I thought about Diego and remembered the thing that was bothering me about him. Emma had told me how he didn't like to talk about himself anymore than he had to, and that he he seemed to leave out a lot of the details about his job and his life. I'd also found that to be true. Suddenly, not only did it make more sense; it became a whole lot more significant to Emma and me than an occasional lull in a conversation.

He wasn't going to be back until that Friday. That gave me a couple of days to figure out how to approach Emma about it. I wanted her to choose me, of course, but I didn't want it to be because my competition was a thumb-chopping, Colombian drug dealer. More than any of that, though, I suddenly felt very afraid for her. I had found myself trusting him. How vulnerable might Emma be if she trusted him? He had even expressed his love for her. What might she be willing to believe if she were also blinded by love?

In addition to the pain of my head wound, this was giving me an even bigger headache. I really wished I'd had some of those Tylenols I'd asked Dugan for.

I sat there on the bed awhile and realized I also had the Alfred Post-it note. Already feeling like it was the day to find out the people I knew were not the people I knew, I dialed Alfred's number, hoping like hell the number wasn't his. If it was, I'd be all but sure he was, in fact, Dugan's supplier. It would explain how Freedy was able to describe him in detail and why Dugan never passed on the number to me. I guess everyone has to make a living, and who the hell am I to pass judgement on him, but I hated the thought of Alfred also being corrupt. That day, of all days, I wasn't in the mood.

I would just say, "This is Seth Gold calling for Alfred," and see what Alfred said. If he responded, "Who the hell are you?" or more likely, "Who da ell are you?," I could rest at least a bit easier. If so, I'd still have to find out my Alfred's number some other way in order to hide Freedy, but I'd be relieved to know that he wasn't going to be part of Dugan Kelly's dirty, corrupt little scheme. "Who da ell are you." That's what the ell I hoped I'd hear as I listened to the phone ring. A voice on the other end said, "Yeah, mon." I took a deep breath, introduced myself and waited for the response. "*Star, bout time ya ring me. Wat tek sah long?*" I closed my eyes and set my head in the palm of my hand.

"Hey, Alfred, my friend," I said dejected, but trying not to show it. "I just got your number." I decided against bringing up Dugan's name and that he hadn't given me the message.

"*No problem, mon. Gud tah hear from yeh. When ya ginna cum get yah belly full wid me?*"

"That's why I'm calling," I said, sounding far more cheerful than I felt. "I need some of that pure food you were talking about."

"Yeah, mon. Good to see you finding religion. I'm going to make you a Rasta after all," he said laughing. "*I and I do a bashment tomorrow night, Star, mon?*"

With that, we planned for Alfred to pick me up, to grab some dinner, and then he'd show me his *yard*. I agreed to head out into the hills of Jamaica to a different world, and quite possibly a different person, than the one I'd known.

43

Alfred's Bluebird sailed around traffic and potholes as if with an entirely different paradigm than the rest of traffic, which generally limited itself to the streets. I realized it was the first time I'd driven with Alfred not stoned senseless and I vowed not to make that mistake again.

Thankfully, in Savannah La Mar, near the road that headed up into what were actually referred to as "The Hills," Alfred pulled over at a roadside stand/restaurant under a sign advertising I-TAL food. I looked at the handwritten menu, and quickly realized nothing seemed remotely edible. Alfred's plea that I try it was based mostly on that much of it was actually cooked with ganja—which presumably giveth and taketh away the munchies at the same time. I held tough and was glad that Alfred didn't mind too much my going to another stand across the dirt lot to get some beef patties. There were maybe forty people crowding around the beef patty stand, but none were actually in line. Actually, none were actually doing anything. Apparently they called each other and said, "Everyone's gonna be at the beef patty stand tonight. We're gonna stand around and do nothing. You in?" The beef patties were the equivalent of like three for a buck, and were clearly priced for the locals. The one guy in front of me in line seemed really upset that there were no chicken patties left, apparently they sell out early in the day, but the beef patties hit the spot nicely for me, and were easily the best value I'd had in Jamaica. I had to resist being a total pig and getting three more.

Wid dem bellies full, to again quote Bob Marley, we got back in Alfred's car and turned off Norman Manley Boulevard and headed up into the hills. I guess I'd been expecting to see nothing but poverty as we moved farther from the beach, but was surprised to find that we were passing some really big, modern houses that would've looked at home in the affluent suburbs of Chicago. It wasn't hard to guess how these people made their living. One interesting difference, though, between the houses in the hills and the houses in the Chicago burbs was that these houses were on some really horrible roads. Apparently, the owners, were selling drugs, and the government wasn't. The comparison of the homes and the roads made it clear who was better off financially. Alfred's perspective, though, was that it was just a case of the government trying to get even.

Proportioned between the larger homes, as we wove our way up the road, were numerous unfinished structures apparently awaiting some new, and it seemed, unlikely financing in order to add a second floor and/or a roof. And some smaller, completed houses that looked only marginally more livable, where people sat outside on chairs that looked like they came from 1920s Mississippi, staring out at nothing in particular. At the bottom of the lane that led to Alfred's house, we passed this Rastafarian guy sitting cross-legged up against a post. Alfred said he was almost always there. I guessed he wasn't getting paid a lot for his contribution to society, but had almost certainly attained an altered state of consciousness.

Entering the steeply inclined, poorly maintained street that led up to Alfred's place, he was telling me how his house was cleverly situated so that people couldn't easily find it. Passing roosters and barking dogs and a row of lower and middle class homes that were all shaped just like Monopoly houses, I couldn't yet spot Alfred's. Not until we got near the top of the hilly road could I see the top of his house and then the road turned a bit, and there it was. I'm not entirely sure what I expected, but I certainly hadn't expected anywhere near the scale of his house. It had to be five to ten thousand square feet. It was made entirely of cement and had this incredible porch that wrapped around the whole house. Looking out over the ridge that Alfred's house was situated on, there was a stunning view of the ocean, only about a third of a mile away. People looking up from the beach could easily make out Alfred's house and I laughed to myself that it wasn't as cleverly situated as he thought.

Amazed by the porch and the view of the ocean, I noticed there wasn't a single chair or piece of furniture on the porch. I asked Alfred about it and he said he'd grown up there and the ocean was just kind of always there, no big deal. He was no more interested in looking at the ocean than I might be looking at a parking lot. I was thinking most people would work their whole lives to be able to afford a house and a porch with a view like that so they could sit and think about their lives. Alfred, on the other hand, had no use for it. The crowded streets of Chicago captured his imagination far more than the amazing blue ocean sitting outside his door.

There were three cars and two vans parked outside his house. Alfred had been telling me that in the hills everyone knew everyone and most were also related somehow. He said you had to be careful who you dated. I laughed until I saw from his expression that Alfred wasn't joking. He rattled off the other major family names who owned most of the land up there—the Hogs owned about half of it, the Jacksons owned a great deal and the Parkinsons were another major family. His was the only Rastafarian group.

And a group it was. I asked about the abundance of cars and Alfred said most were his, but that there were always people staying at one another's houses, for a day, a week or even months. Anyone lived with anyone and nobody cared. It was free for all and pretty much a free for all. Most didn't work, they were just there. It could be a cousin or it could be a friend of a cousin you didn't know.

Alfred brought me into the house and introduced me to his wife, who was named Lexus. She was a big old woman who could have kicked my ass every day of the week. Apparently in the hills, bigger was better. In fact, when this one really cute and thin girl walked through the room, someone made the comment that she'd be good when she got bigger. She seemed pretty hot to me, but by their standard, Alfred's wife was stone beauty.

The house was immaculately clean—the women cleaned the house from top to bottom every day—but very stark. The floors were cement and there was no carpeting, except for the occasional throw rug, without any padding. The furniture was at a minimum.

No tour of the house was offered. I was given the first seat at the table and was basically expected to stay there. Alfred told me nicely that it was impolite to, for example, wander into the kitchen to check it out, like Americans all tend to do, trying to get closer to the food. Their notion of entertaining, as a matter of fact, didn't include serving you food. They had a TV and a satellite dish, but their life didn't revolve around it like it did for most people I knew. Entertaining meant hanging out, sitting and talking.

Various friends and relatives joined us. They were friendly, and had great white teeth, but were pretty much a stoic, stone-faced bunch. They asked me no questions and, thinking I had to make conversation, their answers to my questions were short and inexpressive. Thinking about Diego, I wondered how much that had to do with the drug culture and not wanting to give away any information. Even Alfred got more stoic than I'd known him now that he was up in the hills.

They didn't talk much about the marijuana they grew, of course, but it wasn't hard to gather that all of the money up in the hills came from drugs. And, I got the impression it was very much a community effort, both the harvesting and the not talking about it.

As friends came and went, it eventually dwindled down to just me and Alfred and he asked if I wanted to *brown-up*. I asked if he could do that in the house and he looked at me like I just landed in a space ship. He got busy rolling some massive spliffs, and then we both got busy losing consciousness. I really could have used a nice bowl of nachos and dip or something, but no one was offering and I wasn't allowed to leave my chair. Jeez, how did their women get so fucking big? Were they sneaking Twinkies while we smoked ourselves into oblivion? There was no limit to what I would have paid for a beef patty.

To keep circulation, I finally got Alfred to go for a walk with me. We walked down the lane to near where the Rasta guy was still sitting there cross-legged. He hadn't moved in hours and I wondered if I shouldn't poke him with a stick.

Alfred looked at me and asked, "Different world out ere, mon?"

"Different world out here," I agreed.

Alfred asked if I was disappointed in him for being involved in the Dugan deal. I thought about it a minute and said that it wouldn't be right for me to judge them. They were just making a living and it was their way of life, probably the only life they'd known. He nodded and I couldn't tell if he was agreeing or merely considering what I was saying. "But," I said, "any business deal with Dugan is rotten, and I was disappointed when I found out you were involved." His expression didn't change and we walked a while in silence, before he explained to me that he was *The Don*, the guy responsible for everyone else. I said, "You should be you," like he'd told me the day I'd met him, and he gave me a less than stoic smile. "And," I added, completing my evaluation of his life, "you should sit on your porch and look at the fucking ocean once in a while."

He flashed the big smile again and said, *"Be seen. I shud sata a lilly bit. Gi praise an thanks to da lord."*

"And it will feel alright," I said completing his thought and a line in Bob Marley's song *One Love*.

"Yeah, mon."

It soon became apparent I wasn't going home that night (or eating), so before I might have decided to eat my right arm off or fall asleep next to the cross-legged dready freak, I asked Alfred if I could spend the night.

"*Yeah, star, mon. I yard yah yard.*"

I'd have preferred 'I beef patty yah beef patty,' but I smiled and thanked him just the same.

Walking back with Alfred, past the chickens and the dogs and the Monopoly houses, it felt somehow enriching being friends with someone from a world so entirely different than my own.

44

I arrived back at the Blue Moon late the next morning a little groggy and somewhat worse for wear. I knew I'd have to factor in some recovery time if I decided to visit old Alfred again.

Trying to rejoin the living, I longed for a cup of coffee like a guy lost for days in the desert longs for two beautiful lesbians pouring water on each other, or maybe that's just me. Walking up to the bar, I saw Emma sipping a cup of coffee. Looking at her, then the coffee and back again, trying to decide which I wanted more, I hoped neither was a mirage.

Sounding like the big shot I wasn't, I offered Spike $50 for a coffee.

"US or Jamaican, mon?" Spike answered with a smile.

"Damn, Spike, you're onto me," I said, whipping out $50 in Jamaican, worth about $1.35. Since I lived at the Blue Moon, it had sort of become a thing for Spike to not charge me regular tourist prices. If he had, I might've run out of money or had to stop drinking Red Stripes a long time ago. As it was, he just sort of charged me whatever I felt like paying or happened to have on me. It was never a lot, but everyone at the Blue Moon, except for dear old dad, kind of treated me like family.

Spike took my fifty and poured me a pot of Blue Mountain and threw a cheeseburger on the grill for me.

"Looks like you cud use a whole pot, der, mon."

"Spike, could you not mention the word pot to me right now?"

"Be seen," he said laughing, "yah been sampling Jamaica's natural resources."

The look in my red eyes was answer enough. He laughed again and headed back to work.

I sat next to Emma who smelled far better than I felt. Course mothballs smelled better than I felt. The first sip of coffee I had seemed to reduce the years I felt from 140 down near social security age. Nearing the end of the pot of Blue Mountain and after my world famous cheeseburger,

I began to feel myself again.

After I'd eaten, she gave me a good-natured, conspirational smile and asked, "So, Inspector Seth, find anything good in my dad's office?"

I'm sure my face did a pretty rotten job of hiding my surprise. "You knew?"

"I thought I did. I saw you kind of look both ways like you were a detective in a bad late night movie and then scurry in to my dad's office. I was just about to come find out what was up when I heard my dad. So, I acted quickly," she said like a corny TV narrator, "using my wits to get you out safely. Did you like my performance?"

My first thought was to give it two thumbs up, but quickly realized that'd be a poor choice, given Dugan's inability to give two thumbs either way. "A lot. Thank you. You saved me." Then using my own bad TV voice, said, "The bumbling, yet oddly attractive detective saved by the beautiful heroin. Now there's some good late night TV."

"Beautiful?" she teased, twirling her hair. "Oh my, do you really think so?" Her old-time movie acting was a little over the top, but I'd have given her my Oscar, which, by the way, wasn't a sexual reference, so please get your mind out of the gutter for a second.

"Very beautiful," I replied, and unable to resist, "Here's looking at you, kid."

She seemed very happy with my shameless flirting.

"So, detective, did you find any incriminating evidence?"

What incriminating evidence didn't I find? Other than anything linking Dugan to the Dallas murders of J.F. Kennedy and J.R. Ewing (who, the FBI has never really proven conclusively weren't done in by the same person.)

"Well, yeah, actually I did find out some stuff," I said hesitant to come right out with it.

Perhaps sensing my hesitation, Emma said, "Hey, I've got an idea. Why don't you and I go to dinner tonight? We can go some place special. It would be great to go out to the cliffs to Rick's Café or X-tabi. We can watch the sunset and get a nice meal and some drinks. And," she said with about the cutest, most disarming grin I could imagine, "it's on me. I have something to tell you." She seemed up to something. "And then you can tell me what you found. The suspense will be kind of fun for both of us," she said playfully.

With what I knew about Diego, I couldn't quite match her playful mood, but dinner and a sunset with Emma sounded great. And, I knew, I had to tell her sooner or later.

She very gently touched my head and asked what happened.

"Well, babe," I said, reverting back to my bad TV voice, "I can't tell you everything...it'd be too dangerous, you understand...but I got in a bit of an altercation while on my most recent undercover assignment."

"By that you mean crawling around my dad's office?"

"That's classified information, mam. I can't tell you anymore or there'd be consequences."

She laughed. "You banged your head on the desk, didn't you."

"Uh huh."

"You poor thing," she exaggerated, "let me make it feel better."

She returned from behind the bar with a wet cloth. Even thought it didn't hurt that much anymore, when she started rubbing my forehead, I acted like I had just found religion or sex (the language, if you think about it, being almost identical.)

Maybe I overdid it, because she looked like she wanted to give me another head wound. "I think you like this patient/nurse game a little too much." Then, pointing to some accounting ledgers she had in front of her, said, "I need to get some work done. Dinner at six. We'll get your friend Vinny to drive us. And, if it's not too much trouble, wear a nice tee-shirt."

It was a little joke we had, since we agreed that wearing anything more than a tee-shirt in Negril seemed wildly overdressed. Dates, though, she had let me know called for a clean tee-shirt and preferably one that didn't say something funny.

"See ya then, gorgeous," I said, resembling Bogie likely as much as Rick's Café would resemble Rick's Café. Then, I went to my room for a four-hour nap.

We walked outside the Blue Moon just before six and fought off numerous offers to drive us while we looked for Vinny. I always used Vinny, and the people I fought off knew it, but still wouldn't cut me any slack. Even though I'd made it clear none of them were going to drive me, a near fist-fight broke out among the would-be drivers just as I spotted Vinny running from his cab across the street.

"Vinny, you sleeping over there?" I asked, teasing him. "You need to be quicker than that."

He seemed thrilled to see us. On previous cab rides, I'd told him all about Emma. One time, he said he had to see her, so he parked his car and walked back to the beach with me. Emma had been sitting at her "office" at the bar and from across the beach watched us as we both rudely pointed at her. She hadn't got mad or uncomfortable. Instead, she was immediately in on our joke of exaggeratedly inappropriate social behavior, and just waved back at us sweetly. It's kind of what made Emma Emma to me. Just another little thing that made my heart fill up to double its normal size whenever I thought about her. Vinny couldn't have been more happy that we were going out together, and that he was chosen to drive us, like he was the guy who drove the horse carriage in Chuck and Di's wedding or something.

We decided to go to Rick's Café, partly because of all the *Casablanca* talk, and so we could drink at the bar during the sunset before having dinner. Vinny would pick us up at nine, though I had no doubt he'd be there at least a half-hour early so he could hang out with Emma and me.

I hadn't been to Rick's before, though it was probably the best known of Negril's restaurants. It was sort of divided into three parts. When you first arrived, to the right as you faced the ocean, was the open-air, covered bar area. Just across the bar from the ocean was a stage for the reggae band that was playing and the mildly sloshed crowd that was dancing. On the patio on the other side of the bar, along the ledge that separated the bar from the cliffs and then the water were set up dozens of plastic chairs. People were relaxing, keeping their prime first row spots, kicking their feet up on the ledge, waiting for the sunset. From there, just the Caribbean in all its majesty, until the sun made its regal appearance.

In the middle was an outdoor section for elegant sunset dining, or as elegant as you could get with most of the patrons wearing swimsuits. To the left of that were cliffs, where groups of tourists waited for the next crazy sonuvabitch to dive from the cliffs to the water. It was sort of a two-level affect with the bigger schmucks diving from the higher cliff and the less inebriated ones choosing the safer, shorter dive. Alcohol and peer pressure seemed to be an effective combination, and of course, the largest guys and shapeliest babes got the majority of the encouragement and applause. Probably the majority of the alcohol as well.

We walked over to the cliffs and were part of the encouragement for the mother of all jumps…a fat guy and a bouncy, trashy drunken babe. She had on a bikini that didn't look like it would survive the jump, which didn't hurt the crowd's enthusiasm. I'd seen her type before at the Indy 500. The one that'd be staggering around in a seemingly lost, braless jiggle as a group of guys formed around her encouraging her to, "Show us your tits." That was a popular refrain among the trailer trash who showed up at the race with their rebel flags in heavily-armed recreational vehicles—often sporting giant *Show Us Your Tits!* signage—cranking Lynyrd Skynyrd, and eventually passing out in the infield during the race. Not that the girl at the race appeared to be especially considering their request, just that she had the look of someone who might just giggle, "Okay, I have no brains," and off would come her skimpy little tee-shirt.

Emma and I were captivated by the impending drama of what might happen if, as it appeared they were considering, both jumped hand in hand. After a raucous build-up, several false starts, and a dramatic draining of a couple of Banana Daiquiris, they just went and did it. Their form was actually impressive, because at that height, if you didn't hit the water feet first, you could be opening up orifices you had never intended. Her splash was lost in his whale-like approach into the water. When the water cleared, the big payoff. First he emerged, looking like he had just knocked out the heavyweight champion, and she emerged dramatically a few seconds later, also in an arms-up victory pose. However, what little material her bathing suit had brought to the party was sacrificed in the effort. Since EVERY person at Rick's had brought their camera for the impending sunset, I'd never heard so many clicks in my life. Or so many guys getting slapped by their dates. She swam to the steps and still basking triumphantly in all the attention she was getting, she still hadn't noticed her clothing problem. The big fella, her diving partner, emerged from the water just behind her, but failed to point out to her that not only was she topless, but her bottom was less, too. To her credit, when she found out—hearing the laughter as she neared the top of the steps—she acted like that's what she intended to happen. If anyone hadn't had a photo op while she was coming up from the water, they certainly did as she exuberantly danced and posed for several more minutes. Finally, her boyfriend, who seemed to be enjoying it as much as anyone, offered his tee-shirt, returning the programming to R-rated. Later, another triumphant diver actually emerged to a huge ovation with her bottom in hand. As if bringing a treasure to the queen, he ceremoniously climbed the steps with his new riches, and dropping to his knees, bowed his head and offered up the bottom of her suit to her on both hands. She accepted it with a big kiss that only temporarily halted the party her boyfriend was having. There was great applause and everyone felt okay about the future of the world. Like that was hard drinking rum drinks, waiting for the sunset in Jamaica.

Our night off to an eventful start, Emma and I held hands and walked over to the bar. There seemed to be something about the two of us together that made everyone go out of there way to make sure we were happy. Were we that cute together? I thought so, I guess, but I was still surprised and thankful when a group of four rowdy couples said they'd scoot over so that Em and I could get good plastic seats up front.

Feeling a bit giddy, I bought the group of our new friends the next round of drinks. They seemed ready to name a new religion after me.

Em and I started with Pina Coladas. Everyone sitting near the bar was lit wonderfully by the dusk sun, not to mention their tropical drinks. By the time we got our drinks, the sunset was only a minute or two off. We clinked our glasses and watched as almost surrealistically, the horizon exploded into the brightest, most intense orange I'd ever seen. Emma told me that the Crayola people were going to have to get busy on a new color to try to capture that. When the sun made its exit, everyone at the bar, at their dinner tables or over by the drunken diving cliffs, dropped their cameras and started to applaud. Emma and I applauded too, though inside, I was going through something. Some feeling of pure and complete joy I had never experienced. Emma put her hand out for me to hold and I grabbed it while she gave me a priceless smile. I looked at her and she seemed a picture of contentment.

Then, our new best friends around us started throwing cameras at us. We had to take pictures of them in every conceivable combination and every conceivable angle as they stood with their backs to the evening sky. They each insisted on taking a picture of Emma and me—with their own cameras—for what reason, I couldn't guess. We finished our drinks and our party buddies bought us a couple of more before heading out with hugs and promises of Christmas cards and keeping in touch. Because, of course, we had shared so much. "Hey, remember that round of drinks you bought us? That was so great."

Emma gave me a cute look, probably wondering what the hell I was thinking, and asked me, "So, should we break the suspense now or save it to later?"

"I can wait a little longer," I said showing for her how much longer I could wait with my thumb and forefinger nearly touching. "You?"

"I can wait a little longer, too. It'll give us a chance to talk about stuff."

"Stuff?"

"Yeah, you know, stuff," she said, clarifying for me nicely.

"What stuff?"

"I don't know. Stuff. There are things I should know about you. You know?"

"You're absolutely right," I agreed. "For one, we need to resolve the Bulls-Knicks thing."

"That's true." She thought about it like it was the one issue preventing a huge corporate merger, before proudly declaring, "How about we just agree that they both suck?"

"I guess I can't argue with that. That was easy. I say we should get married."

She laughed and said, "Wait, I have more questions."

"Oh, really." It was starting to feel like a job interview. But, I really wanted the job. "Shoot."

"What do you think about kids?"

"I don't think I'd be comfortable if they played for the Knicks."

She hit me in the shoulder, which, I thought, remembering Shulie, was either a sign I was being funny or was about to get dumped big-time.

She summed up for me, "So you'd *want* to have kids. They just couldn't play for the Knicks?"

I thought about that, making sure I was comfortable with all the ramifications and said, "Right."

It seemed to be satisfactory to her. "Okay, a few more, sir."

"Shoot."

"Religion?"

Uh oh. "I don't know. What do you mean?"

"I mean, I don't know, I'm Catholic and you're Jewish. If hypothetically, we were together, do you think it could work?"

"No chance." I said with a straight face.

She laughed and said, "No, really, asshole, do you think it could work with us?"

"If the food was better, I'd think we should both be Rastafarians. Erika thinks I'd look cute in dreads, you know."

"I think so, too," she said, rubbing my buzz cut. "Okay, let me try this again. Hypothetically, we have kids and they don't play for the Knicks, okay, what religion would they be?"

"What time did the other train leave Boston?"

"Seth!" she yelled. "C'mon. Be serious, this is important…stuff."

"Okay, Em, here's the thing. I personally think religion has caused a good deal of the problems we've had in the world. I would never let it cause a problem between me and you. You should have exactly the religious freedom you want, and I should have exactly the religious freedom I want."

"So, if you want to celebrate Rosh Hoshanahanadah, you should be able to." She said with a smile, and I really liked that she didn't like me to stay serious for too long.

"Yeah, though it's Passashanahanadah. And if you want to celebrate, what was it called, Christmas, you should be able to."

"That seems fair enough. And what about the kids?"

"They just can't play for the Knicks."

She laughed out loud.

"Can I ask just one more?" she wanted to know.

"Of course, but then we have to talk salary and bonus."

"Of course. So, where would you like to live? I mean if you didn't stay here?"

"I love cities. I love Chicago. It'd be great to show you Chicago and my favorite places. But I could probably also live in Manhattan or Boston or San Francisco." I thought for a second, trying to be as inclusive as I could be so I didn't answer it wrong. "I also like the desert. I've been to Phoenix and Santa Fe. I think I could live there, too. But, you know, Em, I really want to finish my book and then travel the world, finding all the cool stories and all the cool places to write about. That's what I'd really like to do. And, you know, I'd love to do that with you."

She beamed a big, beautiful smile and I knew I hadn't answered wrong. In her eyes, I thought she might be starting to share my dream.

"Em," I said, "I have one question for you."

"Shoot." She said with a smile.

"Do you want to eat?"

We got the best table they had, right by the water—again getting the feeling of being Jamaica's first couple.

Our waiter introduced himself, his name was Romeo, and took our drink orders. I was considering a Guinness, which Romeo told me, "Puts lead in de pencil," but thinking that'd be putting the cart before the horse (if you'll pardon the expression and delusions of grandeur), I just ordered a Red Stripe. So did Emma. We also ordered dinner, with Em getting the Ahi special that Romeo recommended and I got Lobster Fettucine. My dinner was amazing, but apparently not as good as Emma's. She followed one, "Oh my God," with another, and I had to tell her I was envious of her multiple "ohmygodisms." Luckily she thought that was funny.

We watched as the hour-after-sunset orange did its heavenly thing to the sky, like a perfect Hollywood set for our little date. It was absolutely spectacular and impossible not to be in love with Jamaica. We ate dinner just enjoying the night and each other and the really great food. I was beginning to wish I didn't have to bring up the Diego stuff, but I knew that wasn't possible.

After dinner, we ordered Iced Cappuccinos and it was time to talk. "Okay, Seth, who should go first?"

"Em, maybe I should."

"Uh oh, you're turning serious."

"Can I just tell you that I had about as good a time tonight as I've ever had. It's been a perfect night and there's nowhere I'd rather be than right here with you. I wish I didn't have to bring this up, but I think I have to."

"Seth, I've had a wonderful night, too. What is it, you're making me nervous?" Her alarm at my change in behavior was readily apparent.

"I found out a couple of things. Neither are good."

"Shoot," she said, and I smiled that she would offer up that little joke under the circumstances.

"I've told you about my friend Alfred. The guy I had dinner with last night and who drove me from the airport?"

"The cool out your ed, guy?"

I smiled again. "That's him. A while back, I'd noticed a Post-it Note

291

on the hotel's front desk with the name Alfred and a phone number. At the time, I remembered thinking it might have been for me, because Alfred said he was going to call to ask me to have dinner with him. But your dad didn't give me the message, so I assumed it was a different Alfred and forgot about it, until recently. This is the hard part. Freedy has told me that your dad is planning to do another deal to pay back the Colombian guys who did the thumb thing. I'm sorry, Em, but I think he sees it as his only chance."

"When is his deal taking place?" She said "his" putting full blame on him.

"A week from tomorrow I think."

Her look was a mix of disgust and exasperation with her dad, but she didn't say anything else, so I continued.

"He's going to sell ganja. Freedy told me the supplier was named Alfred. So, on a hunch, I needed to check if it was the same Alfred. I was looking for the Post-it Note. I found it and turns out it is the same Alfred. I talked to him last night. He asked that I not judge him harshly. He was just trying to make a living and feed his family."

The news about Dugan seemed to be just about all she wanted to handle for one night, but she bravely asked, "What else?"

I didn't know if she was ready for this. I tried to set the expectations.

"Em, I'm really sorry about this one. This may hit you even harder. I wish like hell it wasn't true."

"What?"

"It's Diego."

"Diego?"

"I'm sorry, Em, but he's one of them. The bad guys. The Colombians that did what they did to your father."

"What? How do you know that?" She was still fighting to not believe it.

I told her the story. "I looked through the hotel register at all the dates where Diego has stayed at the Blue Moon. Every time, there was an entry for D. Romerio. The first night I was in Jamaica, two guys next door to me accosted Freedy. I looked in the book for who was registered in the cabin that night. It was D. Romerio. I know it's him, Em, it's gotta be."

She was too shaken to speak. All she managed was to mutter a weak,

"Oh God," under her breath.

"Please believe me, Em, I am so sorry."

"Why can't I ever trust guys?" She asked rhetorically, and I felt like she was slipping away from me. I thought about her old boyfriend, her dad and now Diego. She may have even included her step-dad Michael, who she trusted to stay alive and keep her family happy.

"You can trust me," I said, and she let me hold her hand, though she suddenly seemed unsure of anything. I couldn't blame her.

She told me all the things Diego had said to her and I could tell she was really beating herself up for believing him. I told her I really trusted and liked him, too.

I asked her, "I also saw that Diego is going to be here tomorrow. Asking you this isn't about me, please believe that, but are you planning to see him?"

"Actually, he asked me out for Saturday and there was something I was going to tell him. It might be even more appropriate now."

"Just be careful, okay. Try to stay near other people. And…"

"I can handle it, Seth," she said cutting me off. "But thank you for worrying about me."

When she mentioned having something to tell Diego, I remembered she had something to tell me. "Hey, what did you want to tell me, Em?"

She thought about it for what seemed like forever, staring at the ocean as if for an answer, and finally said, "It'll have to wait, okay, Seth?"

"Yeah, sure," I said and gave her hand a light squeeze to know I was on her side.

Not long after that, Vinny showed up and oblivious to our newly somber mood, regaled us with stories. He told us excitedly about the garden he had grown in his yard. He said it was his personal Eden and his favorite thing was to reach out his kitchen window and grab a fresh mango in the morning. He said it was important for Jamaicans to give thanks for such things, and he had even written a song about it, called, *Give Thanks Jamaica.* Emma and I obviously had come way down, but we couldn't help but be stirred a little by Vinny's infectious enthusiasm. He told Emma about how he'd also lived in Connecticut, but to him, Jamaica was home and even though he had less here, in many ways he had more. To Emma's credit, she was genuinely friendly and engaging with Vinny, and I could tell the two of them liked each other.

Vinny drove us back and on the way, Emma asked him to sing us some of *Give Thanks Jamaica*. I looked at her and smiled, finding an overwhelming feeling of love and admiration for her. His voice was soft, wonderful and unwavering. The stunning lyrics were beautiful and heart wrenching. As he looked straight ahead and drove his cab, his words floated back to us and took us with them on a ride through his Jamaica. Emma took my hand and squeezed. When we got back to the hotel Emma gave Vinny a kiss and a hug. I gave him the Jamaican high five. Neither of us had to tell him how beautiful or meaningful his song was to us.

Emma and I found ourselves outside her room. "Seth," she said, "will you stay with me tonight?"

"Really?" I asked, not expecting that at all.

"Yeah, I really need you to hold me and to feel that I can trust someone."

I could tell she meant just that. "Of course, Em."

"Seth, I didn't say so before, but I do trust you. You may be the only one." She took me by the hand into her room.

We slept all night in each other's arms. Holding her, she very much felt a part of me that I never wanted to give up. As I drifted off, enjoying her touch, I asked myself what it was she had planned to tell me.

45

I woke to a kiss on my forehead and another on my cheek as Emma was leaving. I felt a little uncomfortable lingering in her room alone, only because I realized I had the opportunity to go through her things or something, and didn't want to be the kind of guy who realized I could go through her things or something. So, I put my shirt back on, and headed back to my room doing what would have been the walk of shame had I done anything shameful.

It was Friday and there wasn't a hell of a lot on the old agenda. I'd help out Emma and Freedy on their marketing and web efforts, and I'd take another futile stab at my book and pretty much have the other ten daylight hours free.

That is, though, until I saw Diego carrying his suitcase past my cabin.

I went to my patio and watched him enter cabin number three, wondering what it was he might be thinking about. I sat on my bed figuring how best to approach him. Since I couldn't think of anything that made more or less sense than anything else, I walked over to his cabin and knocked on the door. Waiting for him to answer, I had visions of him opening the door with a gun in each hand waiting for me. "I'm onto you, Gold, you're a goner." Or he'd whip off a mask of his perfect face and suddenly be someone scary like, I don't know, Hannibal Lechter or Elmer Fudd or something. Instead he opened the door and greeted me with a smile and a warm handshake.

"Seth, it's been awhile, amigo, you finish your book yet?"

"You'll have to go away a lot longer than that," I joked, thinking that going away for a while now had a different meaning.

"Diego, can we talk?"

"Sure, have a seat. I'll run to the bar to get us some beers."

"That's okay. Maybe later." I sat down and we faced each other on opposite twin beds.

I was kind of fidgeting around—never having accused a friend before of being a drug runner and thumb chopper offer—when I finally decided I better say something. "Diego, I don't know any good way to say this, so I'm just gonna say it. Listen, " I said after taking a deep breath, "I know. I know about you."

"What?" was his initial reaction, but I could tell it quickly set in what I meant.

"As hard as it is to say this to you, I know that you and Sanchez are involved in all sorts of illegal shit with Dugan, and that you accosted Freedy in the cabin right next to mine, and that the two of you chopped off Dugan's goddamn thumb. I know that you lied to me and you lied to Emma, though I'm not gonna focus on that—I mean, I'd lie too if I were you—but at the same time, I don't know who you really are. I don't know if you're going to take out a gun and shoot me right now. I don't know how someone as cool as you could be involved in some of this shit. Seriously, man, what the fuck is going on?"

When I'd finished, I saw a guy thoroughly disgusted with the reality of what he'd done.

He wasn't saying anything, so I pressed on with, "Is it true?"

He looked at me with heavy eyes and then, scaring the shit out of me, got up and punched a hole in the wall with a huge fist.

I was still looking at the hole in the wall, when he said, just above a whisper, "Everything."

I didn't say anything. I couldn't. I just stared blankly as he absently rubbed the fist he had put through the wall. At that moment, I think I had heard everything I needed to. My mind had stopped, like I just wanted out. But there was more to be said, and he had to say it. In the end I needed to hear it.

"I am in love with Emma, and I'm ashamed to look her in the eyes anymore," he said, fighting himself to get the words out, "She's all that's right in the world, you know, and I'm…," after a deep breath, "I think I was that kind of person once."

He put his hands through his thick black hair, and it reminded me that I had forgotten all about the imposing physical stature and cool exterior that no longer seemed to fit him. He pressed on quietly and quickly, like purging himself in a dignified way was what he had to do. He wanted me to know why he was involved, what they'd done, what was gonna happen next and what he was going to do. The way he was talking didn't make it seem like he was trying to make me believe him. More like he was relieved to get it off his chest.

He looked up at me and asked, "I've told you about my father, right? You may think you have a good idea what he's like, but no, you don't. He's much worse. Look at this, man. Look at what he does to someone who messes up." He said it with controlled hatred in his voice. He slowly took off his shirt, and turned around. I stared in disbelief.

"What is that? Were you whipped?" I asked, never having seen that before in person. It's not an easy sight to take.

He looked at me with that face that had once seemed so inpenetrable, and nodded yes. He also had scattered small acne like pockmarks on his back. He told me they were from his father's cigarettes. He certainly wasn't making up the pain he'd endured. He said, through clenched teeth, that it was because he didn't measure up. It was proof that he wasn't good enough.

Looking down he told me a story. "Our village is about one hundred and twenty miles outside of Bogota. It's lush green country, with hills from two mountain ranges and trees and streams and not a lot of roads. Every year in the valley, we'd gather all the village families together for a festival and sporting competition. I was thirteen. There was this girl I liked that I had asked to go to the festival with me. We made a picnic and ate it down near the stream that ran along our property. We rode horses and we danced together. I remember thinking it was the best day of my life.

"Then, though, the competition started. It's always late in the afternoon, before a big dinner and celebration. The competition was meant just for the kids to have fun and to have something to do. But not to my father. He had to have his family win. I was very fast. My brother, Sanchez, was also a good athlete, but not quite as good and it ate him up. My father had felt so confident his boys would win, he bet one of the other men from the village. The last race was a downhill run that was kind of my specialty. I'd been doing it with the kids in the valley my whole life and since I'd been nine, no one had beaten me. The race started and I got off to a good start. But then, my brother Sanchez, who was running at full speed, with no effort at pacing himself, caught up and pushed me from behind. It was a steep hill and off balance, I fell maybe one hundred meters until I was stopped hard by a tree. From where I was I could see the finish line. I tried to get up but couldn't put any pressure on my leg. My ankle had been broken. I yelled for my father. I saw him running up the hill for me. But when he got there…he started yelling at me for not winning. 'Do you realize what you cost me?' And then he started walking back down the hill. I yelled, 'I can't walk, I need help.' He stopped in his tracks, turned around and said, "If you want to come back to my house, you have to do it yourself."

Then he was gone. My leg ached and the pain was shooting through my body. With one leg there was no way I was going to make it down a steep hill. I thought I'd be stuck out there all night until my dad or brother would come for me. But I heard the music from the dinner celebration begin and I thought of the girl I was with wondering where I was. Her name was Leticia. I decided I was going to get back somehow. I found a branch and used it as a crutch. I started slowly and had gone maybe fifteen meters when I lost balance on the hill and fell again. My leg was in agony and I screamed. Ten minutes later, I heard Letty's voice. She cried when she saw me, but she helped me get back down the hill. When I got there, all eyes from the dinner tables were on us. I defiantly looked right in dad's eyes. I wished I hadn't. He yelled at me in a rage, 'I told you to come back by yourself. You are weak. How could you be my son?' Then, he came and grabbed me away from Letty and into the house. I don't know what hurt more, the humiliation of being dragged away or the first whipping I ever got. She came back to see me, but I couldn't face her anymore."

He waited for his rage to get back under control, and said, "That, is what my father's like."

I looked at him, his face still clenched in anger, and could feel the nearly unbearable pain that was in his voice and in his heart. "I'm sorry, man. I really am."

Then after a long silence, I said what I had to, "It was horrible what you've been through, but it doesn't explain the things you've done."

"I know. And, man, I wanted to do this deal. I really fucking did. I wanted to take my share and get away from my family forever. It was going to be fuck-off money."

"How'd you get involved?"

"I have always worked for my father. There's never been a choice. There are two factories in my town. My father's and another. They compete for everything. That's the guy my dad bet in that race when I was thirteen. My father's factory has been mostly losing lately and everyone knows. He feels disgraced. He can not keep up. He decided to try to make it up another way. He gathered us around the table one night, Sanchez and me, and told us we were going to sell cocaine. We would start very small and build up. We were to help him do it."

"How did your family find Dugan?"

"We had no contacts or buyers set up, so we needed someone who did. Jamaica is a popular route for drugs from my country to yours. My father didn't trust any Jamaicans. So, when we heard that Dugan had been involved in some activity like this, and was a white American, my father approved using him to broker deals for us. This was our first deal."

"So, you're telling me, you had no choice? Your father said you had to sell drugs, so you go sell drugs?"

"We had no choice. I know nothing but my family. We've always been expected to do as my father says."

"Wait, I don't get it. You're in Jamaica, now, probably fifteen hundred miles away from your family. You could just as easily be anywhere. Why don't you just leave? The money?"

"No, man. Not any more."

"What then?" And then I thought about it and it dawned on me, "Emma?"

"Si, amigo. I want to protect her. I'm afraid of what my brother might do to get back at Dugan. He's crazy. You should be very scared of him. I can't even fucking believe he's my brother, that my mom had him. He's all my dad. One hundred percent. We used to be close, you know, when we were very young, but than he realized the tougher and crazier he acted the more my dad gave him his acceptance. My father says this is what I need to prove myself. But I don't need to prove myself to him. Fuck him. I won't do it anymore and I won't do it fucking selling drugs. Not long after I came here, I decided to leave for good. But I keep coming back because I need to stay involved."

"Because of Emma."

He nodded, yes. "My first few trips my job was to snoop around for the cocaine Dugan hid. At first, I wanted to find it, sell it myself and use the money to buy a whole new life. I also used those trips as excuses to get away from them and to see Emma. Now, it's just to protect her. It's more important than even my future. I'm in love with her. I've never met anyone so genuinely good." He lifted his eyes to look at me, took a breath to make it easier to talk about and softly asked, "You are too, aren't you? I mean, in love with her?"

"Yes," I said, more certain of the answer than if I should say so.

"Good," he whispered, covering his mouth with his hand, "I think you'd be good together." It seemed like the hardest thing he'd ever had to say, and I took a moment and then nodded my head to sort of recognize that I appreciated the sentiment and how hard it must have been to say.

Feeling like I needed to move on to something else, I asked, "Does Sanchez know what you are up to?"

"I don't think so. He's relentless, but not a very smart guy."

"Does he know about you and Emma?"

"No, I never told him that. But, he knows who Emma is and he knows who you are."

"What?! Fuck, how does he know that?"

"On one of his trips to the Blue Moon, he asked around and found out that Emma was Dugan's daughter. He watched her one night and she was with you."

I suppose a part of me recognized that I was now in danger, but the only concern I felt was for Emma.

Diego must have read my thoughts. "All I want, before I get out of this for good, is to make sure Emma is protected. Know what really keeps me up at night? It's that Dugan will run away from here. I know that Sanchez will never stop looking for him. More on principle than for the money. Just like that race when I was thirteen, he can't lose. He knows how our dad treats losers. But if he doesn't find him, he wouldn't hesitate for a second to use Emma to get to him. If he does, all I want is to be there to save her from him. He's bad, Seth, you have no idea."

"Nice family you got there, amigo."

He shook his head as if to underscore that all that had happened in his life was incomprehensible to him. "If Dugan doesn't run…if he lives up to his end of the bargain…I'm telling you right now that Sanchez will kill him anyway. It'll probably happen that night."

I was suddenly very tired of playing cops and robbers in international drug deals, with its plots and counter-plots, and talk of people getting killed. I closed my eyes and said, "It's hard to measure what impact that might have on Emma, but really, goal number one, two and three is to protect her. Number four, which I want to talk to you about, is to protect Freedy. I've gotten to know him. He's a really good guy, with a good future. He'd do anything to not have been involved with this mess. He needs to be protected. Dugan's safety may not make my top ten list."

"I like Freedy, too. He is as out of place in all this as me. I will do what I can to protect him. You have my word." He then looked me right in the eye for the first time. "Do you believe me? You know, about all of this?"

"Yes, I do," I said without thinking. All I could do was trust my instincts, and they told me he was telling the truth. Plus everything he told me fit with the opinions I'd formed of him. That he was bitter about his family and that the reason he couldn't elaborate on any of his feelings was that it was stuff he couldn't talk about. And that he was a good guy.

"Seth, you don't need to be involved. You're a tourist getting in the middle of some dangerous stuff. All I want is protect the people who are innocent. Emma, Freedy…and you. If you trust me, I volunteer for the job. You don't need to be involved."

"No. Trust has nothing to do with it. I'm in, bud. Protecting Emma is the most important thing in my life."

"Me too," he said. "Let's figure out the best way out of this."

"We are going to work together on this?"

"Si, amigo. Together."

I wouldn't have expected it when I walked in, but there I was shaking the hand of the guy partly responsible for every rotten thing that was happening at the Blue Moon.

At eight that night I saw Emma and told her about Diego. His admitted involvement, his family history, his whippings and burn marks. And because it had to be said—so she'd fully understand his intentions—that he loved her and his only objective now was to protect her. She was horrified at the things his dad had done to him, yet was also horrified at what he had been a part of. She wasn't ready to just roll over and say all was forgiven out of sentimentality for what he'd been through. She asked a lot of questions and we went in detail into what he'd told me, trying to poke holes in his story. But clearly, at the end of that night, we both believed what he was saying was true.

I asked Emma if she was still going to go out with him that next night. She said she had to. There was something he needed to know. I wanted to give the "be careful" speech, but there was no point. I'm sure she heard those words even thought they weren't spoken.

Trying to gather my thoughts, feeling like I had to say something, I told her, "I once told you that I thought he was good at heart. I still think so." She was looking at me, I thought, though she didn't respond. She was far away and I could only guess what she might be thinking.

46

Emma and I went to Carnival together on its second night, two nights before her dad's Friday rendezvous. People were everywhere and the spirit was festive. We drank beer, shared jerk pork and danced one time to a reggae band under a tree decorated with white Christmas lights. It had all the makings of a really nice night, except that neither of us was enjoying anything. We were there to get a feel for the place. A feel we got.

We walked down by the shoreline and scouted out where the deal was going to happen. Freedy had told me that a boat was going to pull up and the ganja was going to be unloaded from the van into the boat. A marina of sorts was down in the water, with assorted glass-bottom tour boats and fishing boats in various degrees of disrepair. Also, just off shore were nicer boats of all kinds. People with money docking to enjoy Carnival. The sea seemed to be as frenetic as the carnival grounds. It did seem to be a good place to have a drug deal go unnoticed. Down near the water, there was a large hibiscus tree with beautiful pink flowers and branches that jetted out over the water. At its trunk was where Emma and I decided we could sit under cover and watch Friday night's festivities. Just a romantic Friday night watching what might be the last act and last night of her father's life.

Then, like an unexpected storm front, we saw Sanchez walking towards us...

Earlier in the day, Freedy had knocked on my door. He was with Erika and had decided he was going to tell her everything. He was going to be going away for awhile and she deserved to know why. He wanted me there while he did it, I think to show that there was someone on his side. They were both grim-faced as Freedy sat her down and told her his story. He didn't leave out anything. Again, Erika was the strong one and did everything she could to comfort her brother. At least outwardly, she never made things about her. It was about her brother, his safety and his absolution.

The more I knew Erika, the more I marveled at her inner resource of strength.

Taking the cue from Erika, I also tried hard to make the moment theirs, not mine. It wasn't until tears had flowed and comforts had been made and we were all sitting there wondering what to do next, that I spoke. I asked Freedy if he'd learned anymore about Friday's deal.

"I talked to him earlier today," Freedy said, referring to Dugan. "Get this, Seth, he told me that he wanted me to handle the deal for him."

"Really?!" I said stunned and suddenly somewhat hopeful that Emma was in less danger than I'd feared. "That's a good sign. I guess he decided not to run."

"I know, but now I'm right in the middle of it. Not exactly where I want to be, you know?"

"We will get you out safely. I've talked to Diego. He's on our side. I'll tell him to be right there with you. As soon as you get the money, they get the money. Then, I've talked to a friend about getting you out. I'm confident you will get lost in the shuffle. He'll then drive you out to his place. You haven't told Erika where that is, have you?"

Erika and Freedy looked at each other. Almost apologetically, Freedy said that he hadn't. I told him that was good. I told Erika that if she didn't know, no one could use her to get the information. She understood. She asked if Freedy could call her. I said that it was fine as long as he didn't say where he was.

"Freedy, as soon as I think it's safe, I'll get you back here, okay?"

"Yeah, mon," he said without looking up, as if he had lost all control over his life.

"I'll stop by your room Friday for the latest. It's gonna be all right. You will get out okay."

"Thanks, mon. Hey, Seth," he said, suddenly with some pride in his voice, "check out the Blue Moon's new web site. It looks good."

"You finished it?" I went over and he took me through the site. It was exactly what we needed.

"Yeah, mon, www.bluemoon.com."

"Freedy, that's great, that is so great!" I said and shook his hand. "Your future looks good to me, partner," I said, hoping like hell he'd have a chance to have a future.

An hour later, Diego was on my porch. Ice cold bottles of Red Stripe sat between us as we kicked our feet up on the railing and looked at the turquoise blue water. Quite a nice scene as two friends enjoyed a beer to beat the heat in the Caribbean. Except we were talking about how to keep our other friends alive.

"Can you convince Sanchez it's best if you tail Freedy?" I asked him. "So you can get the money right away?"

"We already talked about it. He even brought it up. I think it's so he's free to tail Dugan."

"He's going to kill him isn't he? Can't you talk him out of it? Tell him that means the cocaine is gone forever if he's dead?"

"His plan is to torture him first. To get Dugan to tell him where it is. Knowing my brother, I think he will be successful."

"Poor Emma," I said and he nodded his agreement.

We both polished off our beers and then Diego said, "I guess this is it. Sanchez is arriving in Negril in about an hour. He's going to check out the Carnival grounds tonight. So we probably can't talk again before the deal."

"Stay as close as you can to Freedy and let him off the hook as soon as you can, okay?"

"I promise."

"Hey amigo," I asked, suddenly remembering something, "What does Sanchez look like? He's seen me, but I've never seen him."

His expression changed as if thinking about it was like revisiting hell. "His skin is darker than mine. He's an inch shorter, but stockier, and it's all muscle. He usually wears short-sleeve muscle shirts. He has a giant red rose tattooed on his right bicep. And barb-wired on his left. You will know who he is."

"Not someone I want to meet in a dark alley?"

"No." That was all he had to say.

He was fifteen yards away, walking in our direction, towards the shore. It was me who had spotted him, and instinctively, I had yanked Emma to hide behind some people waiting at a Red Stripe tent. I covered her mouth and waited with dread for the moment where we'd find out if he'd spotted us or not. I had seen his expression, if only for an instant, but couldn't be sure if it was one of recognition. Three steps more and we'd find out. We inched closer to the tent. I held my breath and my heart went still. Three, two, one…and then he moved past us like a cold wind and I noticed my skin suddenly had goose bumps. I started breathing again, and slowly removed my hand from Emma's mouth. Combined with the fact my skin had gone cold, all I had to say to her was, "Sanchez."

He walked alone with purpose that was unmistakable. He definitely wasn't someone you wanted to accidentally bump into. He wore thick black work boots, black jeans and a black, skin-tight shirt that didn't hide a single ripple. His arms seemed to involuntarily flex and you could see the red rose bob and weave. Probably trying to escape. Even after he'd passed, Emma moved close enough to me that I could feel her shudder. She asked me something I had also been thinking, "How could her father *know* who this guy was and still decide to fuck with him?"

Even hidden behind a tree and several food booths and like a thousand people away, I didn't feel comfortable. He walked down to the shore, but because we felt safer at least knowing where he was, we moved out to follow him, staying way the hell back. Passing through a clearing between two booths, we had been momentarily exposed before I grabbed Emma and moved her behind a "Craven A" stand just before he abruptly turned and looked back to where we were. I don't think it was possible he saw us, but we looked at each other, and with no pride whatsoever, I said to Emma we should get the fuck out of there. I got no argument.

When we found Vinny, who was, as usual, early to pick us up, we were breathing hard and our shirts were sticking to our backs, wet with sweat. I'm not sure if it was more from the run or just seeing Sanchez in person. "Step on it, bro," I directed Vinny, the urgency obvious in my voice.

Our engagement at Carnival was only two days away. The tension filled the cab and even Vinny felt it and was keeping quiet. I was more thankful than ever that Freedy was going to be with Diego and not the monster that was his brother.

47

All the preparation was done, the countdown to Friday night at Carnival had started and my stomach was holding up poorly.

I talked to Freedy early in the evening and told him the signal to look for when he was to make his escape. He'd told me he had loaded the duffel bags of ganja into the Blue Moon van. Dugan had made a big point of having Freedy open the bags and confirm that the goods were there. I guess, since Freedy had accused him of planning to take the money and running, he was assuring Freedy that it wasn't his plan. The drop point was going to be just to the right of the hibiscus tree that Emma and I had spotted two nights earlier. Not too far from there, Emma's car was already parked in the dirt soccer field turned parking lot as close to the water as possible. Dugan would be in Emma's car waiting for Freedy. When Freedy pulled up in the van, Dugan would pull out and Freedy would take his parking spot. At ten, Freedy would open the door of the van and carry the duffel bags the remaining ten paces to the shore. He'd then trade the skipper of the boat the drugs for a briefcase with $150,000.

We had decided I was going to watch the proceedings without Emma under the hibiscus tree by the shore. At precisely 4:00 a.m. the previous night, Emma had emerged from her room. I stood lookout as she snuck over to Erika's room. As far as I could tell no one was up or looking. Emma knocked once and Erika was there to immediately let her in. It was my idea to keep her hidden from Sanchez should he decide to use her to influence Dugan. She'd seen Sanchez up close and provided no resistance whatsoever. She was to stay in Erika's room until I called to tell her it was safe and was not to open the door for any reason. Freedy was staying in my other bed that night. Erika, for her part, once she left her room in the morning was not to go back. When Freedy left to discuss last minute strategy and logistics with Dugan, he gave Erika the key to my cabin.

With all the pieces in place, I gave Alfred a final call to make sure our timing was synchronized. The deal was set for ten p.m. At 10:05, enough time to exchange the money for the duffel bags, Alfred's friends were going to break into a planned impromptu party. It was the diversion I had planned to allow Freedy to get out. At a spot twenty yards south of the drop point, on a sandy spot just off the shore, guitars and bongos and snare drums would appear from nowhere. Along with the newly assembled band, a very enthusiastic audience of crazyass dancers—all friends and neighbors of Alfred—would assemble. I'd described Sanchez to Alfred. As many as his friends as possible were going to stop him to offer drugs or other wise get in the way. This was Alfred's idea. I told him I wasn't sure if it was such a good one, but he said, no problem, his friends knew how to handle themselves. It was crude, but I hoped the distraction of the suddenly raucous party would provide Freedy the momentary cover he might need to get out. I offered Alfred a twenty dollar bill to each of the fifty or so of his friends (as much as I could afford), but he flat out refused. He said his buddies—most of whom were profiting from the deal—would be glad to help if he asked them to.

I sat in my room watching the clock, which had decided to start going really slow. I wondered, for about the millionth time, exactly how I had gotten involved in this shit. Friday night back home the guys were going to the bars to try again to get laid. Here I was in the frickin middle of an international drug deal, trying to keep alive people I didn't even know two months ago. Now they were more important to me than anything. Finally the digital clock in my room hit 9:15 and it was time for me to roll. Vinny was out front, as I'd asked him to be, and drove me over. I wore an army green v-neck tee-shirt and khaki shorts, as close to camouflage as I had available. Vinny dropped me off and offered to wait for me. I gladly accepted. It was Friday night and, probably because of the weekend, the crowd was even more raucous than the other night. A band was playing at the main stage a few hundred yards away and people were loitering in and around food and beer stands everywhere. I made my way down the shore, offered drugs by almost all of the ten thousand people I walked through, and settled in under my tree. I was armed with nothing but the darkness provided by the tree. I sat there and waited.

I quickly spotted all the key areas. Over my right shoulder sat Dugan waiting in Emma's car, where the van would pull up. Straight ahead was where the boat would dock and just to my right was where the exchange of money would take place. Satisfied I could see all and had my bearings, I spent the rest of the time looking out for Sanchez, like a guy in a swamp might keep his eye out for a gator or snake.

Except for Dugan, none of the cast was yet in place. I looked at my watch and it was ten minutes to ten. Looking at the water, I spotted a boat meandering its way around the docked sail boats and pleasure boats of Carnival's more fortunate visitors. The boat—the only one out there heading for shore—held my attention and I guessed it was the boat sent to make the pick up. When it spun around to dock, facing back to sea, I was surprised to see only one person on board. The thought briefly crossed my mind that the boat didn't seem large enough to cross an ocean. But then I saw the name on the boat. It was called "Slut Machine" and I had no doubt it was owned by one of Dugan's obviously classless Vegas buddies.

Momentarily captivated by the little drama of the docking boat, I almost missed Diego take his spot. He was standing in the shadows just to the right of a dock directly to my right, ready to get the briefcase from Freedy as soon as the deal went down. He looked over to me under the tree just for a second and made a small, barely noticeable gesture. It was five minutes before ten. I looked once and hadn't yet spotted the van, but when I looked again a minute later, Emma's car, driven by Dugan, pulled out. The Blue Moon van pulled in. I saw Freedy park so the back of the van faced the water.

I went to look at my watch again and just for the briefest moment saw it was 9:59. Then my vision went momentarily blank. My head got jerked violently back and I found myself wrapped in a vice-like headlock and staring up at the tree, feeling the butt of a gun-like gun. Without comprehension of what was happening, the vision of a large red rose tattooed to a massive arm, stuck in my head, as if to say, "Do you get it now?" I did. Sanchez, the monster, had found me. I don't know a lot about guns, so I can't tell you exactly what kind he had, except that it was that kind that was pointed at my fucking head. I was pretty focused on cold metal against my cheek, but I quickly realized I had a more immediate problem. Sanchez was squeezing his forearm into my neck. The thick-veined muscles of his left arm were rippling into my skin and breathing was becoming difficult. Struggling, which was my instinctual reaction, was pointless. My only other option was to try to stay as calm as possible to let him know I was no danger. And that the gun was NOT going to be necessary. But his grip was unrelenting and I began to have the very real fear that he was going to kill me right there under the tree. And that no one would know.

With the little air I had left, I stammered out that I wasn't going anywhere and "fucking ease-up." He gripped harder, as if insulted that my larynx had room enough to talk, and demanded, "Where's Emma?" He pulled up on my neck and his grip was getting unbearably painful. I wondered how long I could last without air. I pointed with my right hand to my neck to try to express that I couldn't talk if he didn't let go. He did enough for me to breathe in as many quick breaths as possible and say, "I don't know. I'm here alone." I heard him mutter, "You'll have to do." I started to figure out all the ramifications of that—and none of them were good—when we both noticed the scene taking place right in front of us.

Three duffel bags lay on the beach, but no one was moving to put them in the boat. Diego was choking the boat guy like a madman. Freedy was standing there looking bewildered. Sanchez grip momentarily got tighter as is anger intensified. I felt a sharp pain in my right eye and I think I came within a moment of losing consciousness. As Diego started swearing something in Spanish (even a choking-to-death American could tell he was swearing), the grip around my neck relaxed entirely. It took a second for it to sink into my head that I was free. Sanchez had started running toward Freedy and Diego and the boat guy. Seeing the opportunity, I didn't hesitate. I ran like hell back through the crowds. I saw him look back at me pissed, but unable to kill people in two places at one time, he decided the drug deal had taken priority. Just then, as if from nowhere, seemingly hundreds of Rastas came from everywhere and set up a make shift concert on the beach. Freedy immediately recognized his signal and eluded Sanchez who had been a second too late in realizing what was happening. In the crush of people, Freedy immediately made himself lost.

Over the embankment that led to the main road, I spotted both Vinny's Toyota, and about fifty yards away, Alfred's Nissan. I told Vinny to pull around and meet me across the street, facing in the direction of the hotel. I ran to hide behind Alfred's car. When Freedy got there, just as planned—but out of breath and practically out of his mind—I grabbed him and pulled him down with me behind the car. Huddling behind Alfred's car, trying to suck up some air, he tried to tell me what happened. He said that Dugan had switched the bags. Alarm bells went off in my head and I barely heard the rest. The words started flowing from Freedy's mouth. Dugan had filled the fake bags with file folders and paper and sand. The guy from the boat had been in on Dugan's scam and laughed that Dugan was already gone and the deal already done. That was apparently when Diego started choking him. Freedy had seen the Rasta guys and ran faster then ever. Sanchez lurched for him but missed. And, not that it needed to be said, he was really glad to see us.

That fuckhead Dugan had actually duped everyone. He'd set up a phony drop point to hide that he had done the deal himself somewhere else and run with the money. Part of me was impressed. He was more resourceful than I ever gave him credit for. Most of me wanted to kill him. The night had become a fucking nightmare. At least, though, Freedy had gotten out okay. I opened Alfred's door, got him in and told him to get going. Alfred and I briefly made eye contact and I mouthed, "Thank you." He stepped on the gas and they were gone. At the same time, I ran over to Vinny's car and his tires squeeled as we raced back to the Blue Moon.

My heart was beating wildly. I might have had a heart attack had my heart not been confused as to what to be most concerned about. For now, though, Freedy was safe, Emma was safe and I was safe. For now. After that, all I knew is that one pissed off, scary lunatic Colombian drug dealer was out there. I struggled to keep myself together.

Vinny didn't charge me for that one. Or maybe he didn't get a chance. Before the car had stopped, I was out the door and back to my cabin.

I scrambled getting the key in the lock. By the time I got in, Erika, who'd just fallen asleep in my other bed, was instantly awake. I held her and told her that Freedy had gotten out as planned. She hugged me hard, which also helped calm my nerves a bit, and I could tell I'd just killed a thousand nightmares she'd been having. I shrugged off her effusive thanks, smiling reassuringly, like I didn't have a care in the world, and told her we could talk about it the next day. She seemed overcome with relief and I held her awhile as she fell asleep in my arms, content her little brother was okay.

When I was sure she was out, I put a dresser in front of the door. I laid awake thinking what to do next and praying that Sanchez wasn't going to come right back after me. How did he find me? I guess he could've followed me over or just happened upon the tree. Obviously, he knew that getting me was leverage to get Emma. If he had Emma, he had Dugan. Sleep was not going to be possible.

I knew Emma would be a wreck until I called. I'd promised to, but I didn't know what to tell her. The story of her fleeing dad, and that she and I were both in potentially immediate danger, wasn't exactly going to lead to sweet dreams. On the other hand, I didn't want to lie to her. I mostly wanted to just go and hold her, but I knew I couldn't take a chance. Sanchez could be lingering for just that sort of opportunity.

I decided then that she had to leave. Get the hell out of Dodge. She could go anywhere a crazy Colombian monster wasn't looking for her. It might be the only way to keep her out of danger. Emma was all that mattered to me and I couldn't think of a meaningful downside. I gave her a call and she answered before the first ring had rung.

"Seth?" she answered and I could tell her heart was racing.

"Hi, Em, it's me. Are you okay?" I tried to put a smile in my voice.

"Am I okay? Are you okay?" she asked incredulously.

"I'm fine. I'm back in my room," I said leaving out the story of the gun to my head.

"Oh, thank God. I was so worried about you. Did Freedy get out okay?"

"Yes. He left with Alfred, but Emma…"

"Oh God, what happened?"

"Dugan. He pulled a scam on everyone and ran."

"Did he make it out okay?" she asked, her concern taking shape before her shame or digust.

"Yes, but if I see him again, I might kill him."

Her relief for the safety of her dad was replaced by an immediate grasp of the situation. "He put us all in danger, didn't he?"

"Yep. That's what I want to talk to you about. Em…I don't think it's safe for you to be here. You have to leave Jamaica. Sanchez knows the only way to get Dugan back here—if he finds him—is you. We can't let that happen. I can't let it happen."

She was smart enough to know what I was saying was true, but it was a lot to absorb at once. "Where would I go?" was her first question.

"It doesn't matter. Arizona, maybe, or maybe it'd be better if you went someplace obscure that he couldn't find you if he tried. And you couldn't tell anyone where you went."

"Not even you?"

"Especially not me."

The other end of the line went silent. It was for long enough that I started to get worried.

"Em, you there?"

"Yes. I'm here. And I'm staying."

"But, Em, you can't..."

"Seth, I'm staying. Three reasons. One is the Blue Moon. If my dad's gone, and even Freedy's gone, there's no one left to run it. We've worked really hard to make it someplace I'm proud of. I can't just let it go. Two is that Sanchez can't use me as bait, so to speak, if they don't know what lake the fish is in. No one knows how to reach my dad, right?"

"Well, Freedy does, but no one but you and I know where Freedy is and only I know how to reach him."

"Does anyone know you know that?"

"Only you."

"And I'm not gonna say anything. So, if Freedy can't be found, my dad can't be found. What I'm saying, Seth, is that without a way to find my dad, he has no use for me. And he has no way to find my dad. Right?"

"I think that's all true. But what if he tries to threaten you to find out what you know?"

"I'll play like I'd love to tell him where he is. That he abandoned me after all I'd done for him. That he should kill him. That I would myself if I had a chance. That I'd tell them where to start looking."

I admired her ability to think under pressure and I had to admit, it was pretty clever.

"That's not bad, Em. I think it could work. If we see Diego, we can have him embellish your story. Say that you're bitter and really hate the SOB."

"I already thought of that," she said with a smile and some pride in her voice. I couldn't help but smile.

"Sorry, I'm a little slow," I said letting her have her moment.

"Well, you better stick with me then," she said sweetly. "That's kind of the third reason..."

BLUE MOON

"What is?"

"The third reason is," she said quietly, "I love you."

It wasn't a good reason to stay, but I liked that third reason a lot.

48

We were lucky in that Sanchez had made a pact with himself to never again stay at the Blue Moon. It's not that Dugan would have been insane enough to make a guy who cut off his thumb pay for a room, it's just that being in the same place as Dugan was enough to send Sanchez flying into a rage. I was, of course, completely in favor of him trying to maintain his mental health. Had I known any of that I might have been asleep. And the knock on my door might not have scared the shit out of me.

"Amigo, it's me, Diego."

It sounded like him, but having reason to be paranoid, I asked, "How do I know it's you?"

A moment later, I heard, "We're in love and we want Emma to be maid of honor," which under the circumstances included nearly getting killed, being afraid of imminently getting killed and having my dream girl tell me she loved me, seemed really funny. I moved the dresser as quietly as I could and let him in.

As Diego stepped in my room, Erika turned over and we both hoped she'd stay asleep. Diego whispered, "Where can we talk?"

Under my breath, I said, "I don't know, where's your brother?"

"He's not staying here. But we should still be careful."

"No shit," I said responding to the understatement of the year.

I thought for a moment and said, "Let's walk down the beach."

I grabbed some Red Stripes, thinking there'd be almost no way to enjoy my impending tortuous death without cold beer. I opened the door and poked my head out. With no obvious signs of a homicidal lunatic outside my door, I gingerly stepped out. I made it to the beach without breathing and clung to the shadows as far from the water as possible. It was a moonless night, which helped keep us under cover. Maybe too much. Every shadow looked menacing, every darkness a trap, every outline was Sanchez. He had materialized out of the shadows once before, and frankly, that was more than enough for me. Two months ago, I was a Database Marketer, and as a point of reference, we hardly ever get ambushed at gunpoint. Even the ones who send the same damn credit card offer twenty-seven times in a month and deserve it.

Four or five hotels down the beach, out of sight of the Blue Moon, we sat next to each other in the dark on a walk-up step of a closed bar. Someone would have to be within a couple of yards of us to know we were there.

I took out my bottle opener and took the tops off two squat little brown bottles of Red Stripe. Having a post-near death experience moment, I decided I loved the squat little brown bottles. They were so cute and never hurt anyone. Suddenly feeling an emotional attachment, it almost hurt to give one up to Diego.

"Here's to family, amigo," I toasted in a loving tribute to Diego's and Emma's fucked-up families. Diego blurted out a laugh and we clinked our bottles and took long, satisfying chugs.

"So, what the hell happened tonight?" I asked now that the tension had been broken a bit.

Diego told me he was as surprised as anyone when the bags turned out to be fakes and the sleazy boat guy told them what had happened.

"I don't know what got into me. All of a sudden, I am choking the hell out of this bastard, even though I knew he was just the messenger. Just a big, fat and ugly messenger." Diego laughed at his own joke and I could tell I wasn't the only one feeling a little loopy.

"The message pretty much sucked, huh?"

"Por que?"

"Sucked. You know, suck, sucks, sucked. Remember it, it's a great word. It means really not good."

"It's great to learn English from you Americans," he mocked.

"De nada."

"Si, the message sucked," he said smiling and chugging down the rest of his beer. I bid a silent so long to another squat little bottle and handed it over.

"I wasn't really able to enjoy it as much as you, Diego. I was too busy thinking about your scaryass brother choking the shit out of me. I can be self-centered that way."

"He did what?!" Diego asked stunned. He just kept shaking his head, like if he did that enough, the fact that they were in the same family would go away.

Normally, I'd embellish a story like that (like all the other times I've nearly been choked to death), but in this case, I couldn't think of how. "He came up from behind me, out of nowhere, and put his arm around my neck and his gun to my head. If he would have squeezed any longer or harder, I'd be another casualty of the drug wars, instead of enjoying a cold beer with you at 5:30 in the morning." Thinking of something that struck me as kind of funny, I added, "Actually, come to think of it, you may have saved my life by choking the poor boat guy, which is ironic if you think about it. Did your mom teach you guys that choke hold before bedtime or something?"

"I'm sorry, amigo, I shouldn't have let you get involved."

"Oh, sure, then I wouldn't have the cool, getting-choked story to tell Emma."

He looked up and said, "I don't think you need the help."

"What do you mean?" I asked. I could tell it made him uncomfortable, but of course, I was eager as hell to hear all about it. You can't really get enough of hearing that your dream girl loves you.

"I don't know if it's right to say these things."

"C'mon, Diego. Before your brother kills me, or I kill you, tell me what you mean."

"You know that I went out with Emma on Saturday. I was going to tell her that you and she would be good together, as much as it would kill me to say that. But she beat me to it. She told me that she was in love with you and that she was really happy. That it felt just right. She said that choosing you had nothing to do with the stuff I was involved in. That she was happy that she had the chance to get to know me. So, I guess this is congratulations, Seth." Like a gentleman, he offered his hand and I shook it, admiring him. If I had lost Emma to him, I'm not sure I could have handled it so graciously.

"Did she mention how good looking I am?" I asked, tongue in cheek, though probably pushing it a bit.

"Yes, she did. But don't worry, amigo, she said it's what's inside that counts." Diego's smile showed his pride in giving me the slam I deserved.

317

"Oh man, you gorgeous guys are all the same. Let's go, right now," I said, putting up my fists.

"Sit down, amigo, you won already. Must have been that phony story about being an author. One more beer, Hemingway?"

"Diego," I asked opening the last two bottles of Red Stripe, "if this had gone down as planned, what would you have done?"

"All I wanted was for this to be over, you know, for Emma to be safe. I think I might have headed for Rio. But now, I can't leave. It's not over and Emma is still in danger."

"What would you do in Brazil?" I asked, curious about the life he dreamed of.

He took a swig of beer, and with perfect timing said, "Become a drug dealer, probably."

I laughed my ass off. I almost couldn't stop. "When did you get so funny?"

"I don't know. I think I learned from you. I think that's why Emma chose you." I must have looked hurt by that, because scrambling to recover, he said "Sorry, I didn't mean it like that. You're a great guy, really. But you're also always making Emma laugh. When Emma and I were together she would always repeat the stuff you'd say to her, laughing again. That's not so easy to take on a date. You know, amigo, if I didn't like you, I'd fucking hate you."

"Same here, bud." We smiled at each other, our bonding complete and clinked our last two bottles of Red Stripes.

"You really want to know what I would do?" he asked, turning serious about his future.

"Yes, I would."

"I want to finish school and then teach. I know Portuguese. I could teach Spanish or English. Mostly, I just want to get out on my own, you know. I want to teach people to be their own person. And to be my own person, without my family, you know. Hey, is sucky a word?"

"Sure, sucks is not only a great word, it's also very flexible."

"Then, without my *sucky* family." He laughed, but it was definitely without joy.

"I think that's a great plan, amigo. You'll be good at whatever you do, you're a good person." We sat there a while finishing off our beers and looking at the big ocean. I looked at him and asked, "Do you think you will miss Columbia?"

"Columbia is my home country, the only home I've known. It's a nice place with good people. You probably don't know that most of the country has never seen cocaine and doesn't know we have a bad reputation. And, Seth, it's really beautiful," he said, "but, will I miss it? No, my memories are not good."

49

It had been so pretty the way she said it. "I love you, Seth." I couldn't decide if I liked her words more or they way she said them, though that was kind of like deciding between the stars and the moon. I could picture the shy smile, the tongue just slightly pressing gently against the back of her top teeth, her smile just dipping slightly lower on one side, the dimples getting deeper, her cheeks getting flush and her heart beating a little faster when she said it. More and more I felt able to feel her feelings. More and more she was becoming a part of me.

We lay in her bed feeling every wonderful cliché of true love come true. I had felt nervous walking over to her room, but once there, nothing I'd ever done felt more natural or right than making love with Emma. It had taken me more than a month and a half and several thousand day-dreams to get to that point and I wanted to make sure it lasted. It was graceful, intimate, satisfying, irreverent and we shared laughs and smiles and understandings. It was us. The world was ours.

She had told me that she'd wanted to tell me how she felt earlier—it was what she wanted to say that night at Rick's—but hadn't because she didn't want me to think it was because of what I'd told her about Diego. She said she'd been imagining saying, "I love you," ever since. I told her I'd been saying those words in my head since that night I walked out of the ocean and saw her walking down the beach. I joked that if I'd said it then, she probably would have run away. She smiled and said she probably would have. I touched her check and said that she got it just right. She replied, with a deep blue smile in her eyes, that we should both keep practicing, and I agreed. "Seth, I love you. Nothing's ever been this right."

"I love you, Em, nothing ever has."

From there a kiss, a look in the eyes and then the sweetest embrace in history.

The next couple of weeks were the best there would ever be. We realized we were in two great places, in love and in Jamaica. So we went parasailing together while drinking Red Stripes in the air. We spent a day at YS Falls, just one of the most beautiful places on the earth, where barefoot we walked over slippery rocks to a rope swing, letting go to submerge in one of the cascaded pools. We shopped at the craft market, played volleyball with Gumby, went to Vinny's house to meet his family, and had another great dinner at the Charela Inn. We went there on a night the smiling guy band was playing and got the waitresses to sing again, which wasn't all that hard to do. Between sets, smile guy asked our names and said he might like to write a song about us. Walking back, we joked that the song *Emma and Seth* "is about Emma and Seth."

I even started writing my book and had given it a name, the *Blue Moon*.

I thought about all the stuff that had happened to me since the beginning of the year and realized there was plenty of self-deprecating stuff to write about. I began with Shulie and Wright Star and Capricorn and would get to the blue moons over Chicago and the blowup at Passover dinner. I outlined the rest, including Alfred and Erika and Freedy and Diego and Dugan and Vinny and Sanchez and *the* Blue Moon and, especially, Emma. A lot had happened—my life had suddenly become interesting—*and I felt like I was living the book's happy ending.*

I'd write during the days when we didn't have plans, and at night, we'd get together in one of our rooms and she'd read the next chapter. I'd nervously look over her shoulder awaiting her verdict. She could have been Evelyn Wood and she couldn't have read it fast enough for me. I'd pace the room like a dog waiting for a treat. About two chapters into the book, Emma told me that after the good chapters, we could make love. Talk about incentive. I'd write and re-write like a frickin madman until I thought she'd approve. She was an excellent editor, always adding the right touch or perspective, but she'd always ultimately approve.

I also helped Emma prepare for the next Full Moon Festival. After the promising turnout we had for our first in April, we could both feel the excitement of May's. Gumby Dammit knew some guys who were in a really great reggae band, and we were able to hire them for a relative bargain. With the rest of the money we'd budgeted, we decided to go nuts and have a small-scale fireworks show as well. We mentioned fireworks and the radio stations loved it. We got press mentions we could've only dreamed of. It

321

was being billed as THE PARTY IN NEGRIL. We were handling calls asking about it from people in Mo' Bay and Ocho Rios and even Kingston. The fireworks were part of it, but there was something about the full moon that seemed to capture people's imagination. Encouraged by the radio mentions and the calls we were getting, we even decided to have a second bar built to cover the other side of the beach. We hired Gumby and some of his friends and some of Erika's friends to do the serving. I don't think I'd ever been so pumped for a party.

Two nights before the big night, we checked our list of to-dos for like the fiftieth time and decided there was nothing else we could do. We were as ready as we could be, so we decided to celebrate.

That night, Vinny drove us out to X-tabi, an outdoor cliffside restaurant not far from Rick's. We could have taken Emma's car, but Emma liked Vinny. We got there a few minutes before the sunset, and being somewhat off-season for Jamaica, Emma and I were the only ones there. We got a table and drinks and found stairs that headed toward some underground caves. I took a camera and got some wonderful pictures of Emma framed by the silhouette of the cave's walls, the ocean and the setting sun. There were these magical pools you could dive into and go for a swim. I asked Emma if she wanted to go for a swim.

She said, "Maybe after dinner, we could fool around down here." I raced her back up to the table.

We held hands during the sunset. During dinner she asked about my parents. I told her they were loving and caring and if a bit overbearing, it was only because they worried about my brother and me. I told her my dad was pretty much the opposite of hers. That he's never put himself before his family. She said, "They sound great, but it's funny that you mention the comparison with my dad."

"Why's that?"

"My dad called me today," she said it looking a little shaky.

"You're kidding? What'd he say?"

"He said that he was in Las Vegas and didn't think he could come back. But he said that if there was ever a situation where I was in trouble he would be there for me. He wanted me to know he really meant it. I told him that I believed him, but I don't."

"Em, I do. I mean I think I do." I told her about her picture on his desk and how he'd cleared a space to always be able to see it. "I think if you needed him to, he'd come back. His heart may not be very big, but I think you are in there."

Emma looked ready to cry, but that she really didn't want to. Like he didn't deserve her tears.

"I told him that I'd come all this way and changed my whole life so that I could come down here and help him. He didn't really apologize, but did say that he was so thankful that I'd come to help with the Blue Moon. That it really meant a lot to him. He talked about ownership of the hotel and faxed me some papers to sign and fax back. He's giving me the hotel."

"He is?! Is that what you want?"

"I don't know yet. I mean, I think I want to make that decision with you."

Every day since we had gone shopping at the craft market, there was something I'd been carrying around with me. I decided at that moment what I wanted to do.

"Emma, sweetie, I want to make every decision together. I want to be with you the rest of my life."

"What are you saying?" she asked, and I could tell she was moving to the edge of her chair.

"I want to marry you."

She put her hands over her mouth, but I could see her smile shining through.

I went down to one knee, looked up at those amazing eyes, and asked the girl of my dreams, "Will you marry me, Emma?"

"Do you mean that, Seth? You're not just joking with me?"

"Of course, not," I said, laughing that she'd think I'd joke about something like that, "I don't know how I got lucky enough to meet you, and I don't ever want to lose you."

"Yes, yes, YES. I will."

"Thank God, my knee is starting to kill me down here."

"Come here," she said, taking my hand and helping me up. She stood up, too, and we danced slowly together even though I'm not sure there was any music. I guess we made our own. The waiters, who were having a slow night anyway, gathered around to watch with goofy smiles.

"Oh," I said, remembering what was in my pocket, "this is for you. At least until I can get back to the states and get you a real one." I put on her finger a little wooden ring I'd bought at the craft market for $100 Jamaican when Emma hadn't been looking.

She put it on like I'd given her the rock the size of Gibraltar. "Seth," she said looking in my eyes while hers got misty, "this is real enough for me. I love it." She just kept touching it, and smiling and looking at it like it was a ring worthy of the attention of Shulie's hideous friends. "When did you get this?"

"When we went to the craft market last week. I didn't really have a set plan on asking you to marry me, but knowing me, I didn't think I'd be able to stop myself. I just know that I always want to be with you."

"Me too, Seth. I love you."

"Em, so, hey, how bout that dip in the ocean you mentioned before?"

"I got a better idea."

About fifteen minutes later, after one of our waiters brought us complimentary drinks to celebrate our engagement, Vinny showed up to drive us home. He was so excited to hear we were getting married.

"Hey guys," he asked, "where are you going to go on your honeymoon? You are already in paradise."

Em and I just looked at each other. We couldn't think of anything. Vinny was right.

At the Blue Moon, Emma told me to put on my bathing suit and meet her on my porch. Ten minutes later, she was there in her suit and a small white cover up and carrying her CD boombox.

"Where we going?" I asked, knowing that every possibility I could think of was great.

She took me by the hand and led me to the hot tub, which was more than great, it was inspired.

She said, "Why don't you go get us some drinks and I'll set up here."

I raced over to Spike, ordered two Flaming Marleys and was back. Not that I was anxious to join Emma in the hot tub, or anything, but the whole drink-getting experience took about twelve seconds.

"I'm back," I said, out of breath.

"You are very cute," she said, making fun of me.

She had started the stereo, softly, to not attract attention, though no one seemed to be out and the hot tub was off a sidewalk that was off another sidewalk, and completely secluded by the plants and trees. The CD was by Dennis Brown, who I'd heard a number of times on IREA-FM, until his recent passing, had been one of the top Jamaican reggae stars. "Is *Moonlight* on this CD?" I asked. I'd heard it a couple times before. It was the most romantic song I'd ever heard.

"Uh huh," she said with a sparkle in her eyes.

I got in and the water felt great. We took our time, getting used to the water and each other's wet touch. By the second song, we were slowly kissing. By the third song, our clothes were off. She had been wearing a two-piece white bathing suit. First she took her top off, and, under the water, I removed my suit, and she took off the bottom of hers. She sat on my lap, her back to my chest, and stretched her lean body over me, as I kissed her neck and mouth. The moon just barely peaked through one of the trees and her breasts looked like islands coming out of the water lit by the moon. I held one in each of my hands and rhythmically caressed each one and then her flat stomach which faded downward as I faded deeper into the music, the moment and the night.

She momentarily interrupted my reverie, which was nearly dreamlike, to turn over, sit facing me on my lap, and ask, "Are you ready?"

I slipped into her as the music to the fifth song, *Moonlight*, began. The song was so right for the moment that I got goosebumps and had to grab my head with my hands to try to keep it together.

"*You…me…and the mooonliiiiiiiight. All through the night.*"

We made love to the rhythm of the music.

"*Don't you know that the nighttime is surely the right time for love.*"

We repeated the song three times.

"*It doesn't have to be a fancy place, just as long as it is cozy.*

Anywhere with you is fine, I'm really not that choosy.

Love is in de air, your company I'd love to share

As long as I'm with you, we could go just anywhere.

"*You…me…and the mooonliiiiiiiight. All through the night.*"

When we were done, we held each other a long time, not wanting the moment to ever end. The song, the night, the moment were pure bliss. If ever there was an exclamation point on a relationship, this was ours. We could live our whole lives together—we were going to live our whole lives together—and it'd be great, but never quite reach that summit. Sometimes those moments happen and you don't realize it. We both did, though, and wanted to sit at the top of the mountain and hold onto it as long as we could.

We spent the night in each other's arms. At least until the phone rang jolting us from our fantasy.

50

Emma picked up and I could tell from her wrinkled brow that it was something important. She handed the phone to me. It was Diego.

I didn't have a phone in my room, so he took a chance that Emma might know where I was. He didn't say so, but I could tell when he said my name that it wasn't easy for him to find me in Emma's room. He had a much more pressing issue, though, and didn't waste any time getting to it.

"Sanchez found Dugan."

He hadn't yet said, "Hi," and the news was slow to register in my head.

"What did you say?"

"Sanchez called home. He said he found Dugan."

"Oh my God."

Emma looked at me and in her eyes I could tell she knew what was happening. I held her hand, looking at Emma's digital clock, it was 4:40 a.m.

I had too many questions to ask at once and because my mind was mush from the lack of sleep, and frankly, because I'd had sex a few hours earlier, I couldn't prioritize them.

"Start from the beginning, amigo."

"Sanchez didn't give all the details, but, he was proud of himself, so he let on a bit. He tracked down Freedy and then the number for…"

"What?! Oh my God," I said, my head about to explode in horror and disbelief (and the fear that it might all be my fault), "how? No one knew where he was but me and I would have fucking remembered telling him."

"He got it out of Spike."

"Spike?! Oh shit. Goddammit, Freedy! I told him a hundred times not to tell anyone." My head was beginning to ache.

"Spike was not helpful, but Sanchez forced him to talk. I guess he wanted to keep his thumbs. He told him about Alfred's house and where he could be found."

"Is Spike okay?"

"He didn't say, but I think so."

"So, has he contacted Dugan?" I looked at Emma, who's head fell slightly at the mention of her dad's name, which pretty much confirmed her fears.

"Si. He told him he could kill Emma whenever he wanted and would if he didn't come back." Those words, even spoken hypothetically, were enough to make my stomach constrict and my heart pound.

"Is he coming back?" As if I wasn't already shaken enough, I began to worry that Dugan's selfishness and lack of courage would win out over his feelings for his daughter.

"He is coming back tomorrow night. Eleven o'clock. With the money he owes."

"Jesus, nice timing. Right during our Full Moon Festival."

"I know. I'm flying in."

"Diego," I asked with my heart in my throat, "did he say what happened with Freedy or Alfred?"

"No. I have no idea."

"Shit! This really sucks."

"Si, amigo. And, Seth…he's going to kill Dugan."

"I know."

I hung up, ignoring Emma for the moment and ran to my room to get Alfred's number and ran back.

I dialed as quickly as my fingers could dial.

It rang once, twice, then again, and my heart began to sink. A fourth time, then again and again and again. No answer. I was close to tears.

I looked at Emma, who seemed conflicted by one too many emotions. She was sitting there as if in a trance.

I held her and said, "I'm sorry, Em. They found him. He's coming back tomorrow." She just shook her head back and forth. "Listen, we are going to bring you to Erika's room. Same drill. Do NOT open the door for anyone for any reason. Okay?"

Gathering a bit of strength, she said, "Let's go."

We knocked on Erika's door. We quickly told her that Emma needed to hide out in her room again. Erika, without even questioning, took Emma inside, held her and brought her over to the other bed. I held Emma's hands and said I needed to go to Alfred's.

"I know. Be careful, and Seth, I love you."

I smiled and quickly went back to her room. I could have taken Emma's car, but I was going up in the hills at night and thought it'd be better to go with Vinny. I'd have to call him at home and wake him.

Ten minutes later I was in the front seat of his cab and he was driving like a madman through the Jamaican night.

I told Vinny the whole story as a way for me not to think about how scared I was for Emma and for Freedy and Alfred. It didn't help. I really wanted to be pissed at Freedy—he'd promised me he wasn't going to tell anyone, and he had to go and tell Spike—but I was too scared to even think about what happened to him. The poor guy had made one mistake, got in way over his head, and I didn't want to find out what price he was going to pay. And Alfred and his wife. Oh God. No one had answered. "Vinny, can you go any faster?"

We pulled up and I was out the door before the car stopped. I knocked loudly, then tried the door and it was unlocked. What did that mean? I didn't have time to think about it.

I knocked again as I opened the door, but I heard no sounds in the house.

I walked slowly through the kitchen area to the room I'd stayed in. My heart was beating almost out of control. With each step, I was braced for Sanchez to leap out at me or to trip across a body of one of my friends.

I reached for the door and pushed it open. I could make out a shape on the bed. I was practically in tears when I touched his shoulder. No movement. Again, with both hands, I rocked him. Nothing. "Freedy," I practically yelled and shook him hard. I turned his body slowly over and when I did I saw his eyes were open. He was looking up at me.

"Freedy!"

"Seth?" Until that moment I'd thought he was dead.

"You're alright?" I hugged him hard.

He smiled, like he was proud of himself for something, and said, "Yeah, mon, why not?"

"Why not?!" I asked incredulously, "Wasn't Sanchez here, threatening your life and getting Dugan's phone number from you?" Something in his attitude didn't compute.

"Yeah, mon," That smile again. "No problem, mon."

"Freedy, what the fuck? Get up, I'll get Alfred and we'll talk at the dining room table."

Just then, coming up behind me with what I'd guess to be was a cricket bat was Alfred. Just in time, I said, "Alfred, it's me Seth," or he might have knocked my head for a wicket, or whateverthefuck they call a homerun in cricket.

"Star, mon, what are you doing here?"

"Well, if someone would answer a frickin phone or say something when I bang on a door, I wouldn't have to be sneaking around here like a tief." I nodded at Alfred and he approved of my use of the word tief.

He put the bat down and I gathered everyone at the dining room table, including Vinny, who'd been waiting outside in his cab.

"Freedy, if I wasn't so happy you were alive, I'd kill you. You know that Sanchez found you because he talked to Spike don't you"

"I, ah, it's…"

"Freedy, I frickin told you not to say anything."

His coy smile of earlier was gone. "You're right. I was wrong. I talk to Spike about everything. I didn't think it would hurt."

He knew he had screwed up, so any more lecturing would be pointless. "So, what the hell happened tonight?" It seemed like I was asking that question a lot lately.

Alfred started, "That Sanchez a scary dude, but he's no match for my boy Freedy here."

Freedy's smile was back.

"What? What are you talking about?"

Freedy, modest long enough, told the rest of the story.

"Around midnight, we hear all these gunshots coming from just outside the house. My heart almost stopped and I just about died right there. Then, the door slams open and it's Sanchez, and I thought for sure my heart will stop. Alfred came out to see what was going on and Sanchez grabbed him and he's got his gun to his head. He wants to know where Dugan is. Tells me that he's going to kill us both if we don't tell him."

Alfred rooting him on, said to Freedy, "*Gwan, bwoy*, get to the good part."

Freedy, glad to oblige hurried the story along. "I didn't wait to see if he was bluffing. I said that I had the number. He points his gun right at my head and says to give it to him. I smiled and said no problem."

"You did not just smile and say no problem."

"Yeah, mon."

"So," I said shaking my head, disbelieving and impatient, "you gave him the number and he just left, just like that."

"No, mon. Even better. I told him if he wanted the number he'd have to go get it, because it wasn't here. He said to not fuck with him. I said I wasn't. So, I told him where the number was. He said he should just kill me right there. I said, you can if you want, but if you can't find the number, then you are out of luck."

Beginning to understand, and to be very impressed, I asked the only remaining question, "So, where was it?"

"In a locker at the Mo' Bay airport."

"No way."

"Yeah, mon." He said, with the biggest smile I'd ever seen from Freedy.

I got out of my chair, went straight up to Freedy, and kissed him on the cheek. "You still fucked up, but I love you."

Alfred, again the comedian, offered, "Would you boys like to be alone?"

I got up and hugged him too. "I am so happy you guys are alright. I thought for sure…"

"You shouldn't underestimate us Jamaicans," Alfred said.

"I never will again, my man. I promise." I looked over at Freedy in awe, and asked what he was going to do next.

He said, "I was planning to get a good night sleep until you came. Then I was going to find someplace else to stay."

On queue, Vinny piped in, "Stay with me. My lady and I would be happy to have you stay with us a while. It's no problem, mon."

Vinny and Freedy did the Jamaican knuckle five and the deal was sealed. I gave Alfred another hug and thanked him for everything. He asked, "Everything cook and curry, mon?"

"Yeah, mon," I said, "all cook and curry."

"Cool runnings, den, mon, and don't forget me arite?"

"I don't think that's possible. I'll keep in touch." Then thinking of something, asked, "So, why didn't either of you hear the phone? Maybe a likkle celebrating, Alfred style?"

331

BLUE MOON

They just both looked at each other and laughed.

51

The moon was huge and sort of right there like a spotlight you could reach up and adjust if you wanted. Not that anyone wanted to. It was the main attraction of the Full Moon Festival, not only as something to look at, but how it elevated people's spirits. Gumby's friend's band was playing and definitely livelying up the place, to quote Bob Marley. Not that it needed much livelying up. Our beach was packed and I'd rarely seen a group of people so intent on having a big time. In fact, probably as many people had Spike's world famous *Moon*shine or world famous Flaming Marley as had Red Stripe, which gave you an idea of the buzz they were seeking and the sense of adventure they brought. And, whatever they chose to drink, they also came smoke enabled. Daniel Burnham, who designed the layout for the city of Chicago once said, "Make no small plans." This group was saying, "Catch no small buzz."

Em and I couldn't have been more proud of our creation. In fact, we were becoming small-scale local celebrities of sorts in that we were the hosts of THE PARTY IN NEGRIL, as dubbed by local radio. People everywhere congratulated us and I could hear a few people tell their friends, "That's them" as Em and I walked by. People were dancing everywhere. It didn't take much for people to catch a groove and go with it. I shook hands and schmoozed and danced and shared the occasional toke from one of the many who offered. One time, an enthusiastic group of dancing, drunken tourist girls got me in a circle, which seemed to keep getting smaller around me. I was laughing and dancing and thinking of a way out when I spotted Emma. She laughed at me and pointed to her ring and then pretended to be mad until I wiggled my way out and went over to her and gave her a kiss. A really nice kiss.

"What a night, huh, Em?" I yelled above the band.

"It's amazing." She gave me a very proud look, like "yep, we did this."

We'd been so busy making sure everyone was sufficiently entertained that we hadn't had a lot of time for ourselves. I took her hand and we went and sat down in the boat with the Jamaican flag. I remembered back to my first night in Jamaica, mesmerized by that flag, wondering what the hell I was doing here.

To that point in the night, we'd pretty much ignored what we both knew was going to happen later and I wanted to see if she was holding up okay, "So, anything interesting going on in your life?" I asked, easing into it.

She laughed a little and said, "Just regular stuff. You know, I just got engaged to a great guy…"

"You did?!" I asked hurt, "Is he taller than me?"

"It's too close to call."

"Hmm. Well, is he good in bed?"

"I think he needs more practice."

"Really? So you're saying he's not the most amazing lover you ever had?" I was just kidding. I'm not really a "So, was it good for you kind of guy."

"I didn't say that. I just think practicing would be fun." She rubbed her shoulder against mine and I briefly considered scheduling a practice right then.

"Okay, I know it's none of my business what you do with your fiancé, in bed, or you know, in a hot tub, for example, but," I whispered, "have you ever called out my name when making love with him?"

"Actually, a couple times the other night," she whispered back, and we both smiled thinking about our perfect night.

She did that shoulder thing again and I howled at the moon, which you'd be surprised to hear, I'm not compelled to do that often. She looked up in the sky and beautifully, softly sang the words. "You, me and the moon-light," stretching the syllable light as long as she could.

I looked up and the moon seemed to be smiling at us.

"So, you got any plans tonight?" I asked, still thinking about the hot tub and some more practice.

"Well, I thought I'd throw the best party in the history of Jamaica, hang out with my very handsome, very tall fiancé, then maybe watch my dad get killed, then…"

"Em."

I put my arm around her shoulder and held her quite a while. Humor can ease a lot of pain, but it can't always hide emotions that close to the surface. I asked how she was holding up. "Seth, I'm petrified for my dad. I just wish this would all just go away, go somewhere else, be over, so I can look forward to our great future together." She smiled at the thought of our future, but then thinking about her dad, became subdued again and said, "I know he's not a very good person, you know, and he asked for this over and over, but he's my dad and he came back here for me. That counts for something, doesn't it?" I nodded.

"Do you think there's any way he could walk away from this?"

"I really don't know, Em, I hope so."

"Seth," she said, putting her hands in mine, "I've never had a guy I could count on to be there for me," and then a pause as she struggled to maintain her composure, "until now. If I haven't said so before, thank you…for everything." Emma, she'd told me once before, wasn't a crying person. She'd already cried once in front of me and was trying hard not to again. I held her head to my shoulder so she could if she wanted to. I looked briefly at my watch and saw it was a quarter to eleven, fifteen minutes before her dad would meet his fate. It felt very much like the last night of a death row inmate, though Dugan at least still had a chance. I thought about what she said, and knew she was, in her mind, already accepting the probable outcome. She was subtly removing her dad from her expectations and her life. I knew that I had the opportunity, and responsibility, to become the male figure she'd always wanted. I think we both took great comfort in the fact that I'd do everything I could to never let her down. I looked up at the full moon and told her, though I wasn't sure she was listening, how I used to always look up at a half moon and feel like I was on the dark side. But, because of her I would never feel that way again and I'd always try to make sure she never did either. She looked up at me and kissed my cheek and said our life would only be full moons. She smiled a little and wiped away a tear and said she was ready.

I told her she should stick with me the whole time, that I wouldn't let anything happen to her. She promised she would. We kissed in the boat under the moon and my heart felt heavy with the joy of being with her. I started to get up and she tugged on my hand to sit me back down for a second.

"Seth, before we go, I just wanted to tell you something. I've been thinking a lot about our future together and I can't wait for it to happen."

I was surprised to find how happy those words made me feel at that moment. It wasn't like it covered new ground, but it filled me with happiness. I realized one of the things I loved about her is that she also had this great romantic fantasy life in her head, just like me. With both of us thinking that way and being together, we'd actually be able to make our fantasy life real.

She was in love with all the stuff our future might bring. "It's going to be so cool. So perfect. You know what I think, Seth? I think your book is going to be a best seller and we're going to get to travel the world together as you write your next one. You are so good. You knew that about yourself, didn't you? You knew it and had the courage to try to live your dream."

I didn't respond, but it was starting to feel like what she was saying was true. I mean, I guess, I pretty much did believe in myself, but she was taking away all my doubts. She gave me that Emma shy smile—that one that is all her own —and said, "I think all your dreams our going to come true, Seth. And, being together will be like living a dream," she said putting words to my exact thoughts. "I think about it and I can't help smiling."

Even under the circumstances, I couldn't help smiling either. For just the briefest of moments I thought about running away with her. Just running down the beach and ignoring all the crap that would happen in a few minutes. Ignoring the reality that was infringing on our fantasy. Instead, I looked at her and said, "You've already made my dreams come true." She smiled big and I saw that small cleft in her chin that I loved so much.

Through an opening in the crowd, we saw Diego. He hadn't seen us yet and was frantically searching the crowd for us. We laughed and Em yelled, "Hey, over here."

Diego, understandably, wasn't sharing in the light moment Emma and I were having. The strain of the moment was very apparent in his face. "Emma, your father's here. The plan is he's supposed to give my brother the money in the parking lot outside his office in ten minutes. Are you guys coming?" We nodded yes and stood up. Diego stopped, looked at us both and said, "Guys, I don't know when I'll see you again." He bent down and gave Emma a kiss on the cheek. Then he looked over at me, said "Amigo" and shook my hand.

The band was throbbing out reggae rhythms, people were dancing or drinking or smoking or kissing their date. It was an amazing party and I'd have certainly preferred to join it then to be going to witness the impending train wreck between Sanchez and Emma's father. Dugan was the littler of the two engines and I didn't like his odds much. I told Emma one more time as we made our way through the crowds to stay with me whatever happened. She said I wouldn't be able to get rid of her that easily.

With a few minutes before the meeting, we saw Sanchez. Though Emma and I were sticking to the shadows of the back of Spike's bar on the other side of the parking lot, he spotted us and gave me a look like, "If I get another chance, you won't get away." It gave me shivers and I found myself ready to run with Emma if he made a move our way. I certainly didn't envy Dugan, who gave him many legit reasons for being pissed.

I was standing face to face with Emma, holding her as close as possible. If anyone was going to get at Emma, they'd literally have to go through me. Emma flinched a little as she saw Dugan step into the parking lot holding a briefcase, his eyes darting everywhere and again looking like he had to pee. You can manage expectations and rationalize all you want, but you can't really prepare yourself to watch your father on the verge of possibly losing his life.

Out of nowhere, we heard the sound of sirens. Everyone in the parking lot kind of turned to acknowledge hearing them and soon it became apparent they were headed our way. Lights flashed on Norman Manley Boulevard and a police car started pulling into the driveway. "Who the hell called the police?" I whispered to Emma. I wondered if it hadn't been Dugan to try to save his life. He had proven at Carnival that he was ready with a trick up his sleeve. Was this another of his tricks? Actually, I was hoping it was. Walking away in cuffs was the only way I could see that he could walk away at all.

Sanchez had been listening to the sirens and saw the lights of the police car approaching and, being a person of action, decided he just couldn't let this whole thing end with Dugan going to jail and keeping the money. In slow motion, I saw him pull his gun and aim it at Dugan. The shot did not happen in slow motion. Before I knew it Dugan was laying on the ground bleeding and motionless. Stunned, I hadn't noticed her instinctively run to her stricken father until she had gotten away from me. I tried to recover and went after her. But Sanchez, with a head start, moved quickly. He grabbed

Dugan's briefcase before the police had gotten out of their cars and turned to run to the beach. Seeing Emma coming his way, he grabbed her, scooped her up onto his shoulder like a sack and ran towards the beach and its crazy mass of people. Most of the crowd must not have heard the gun shot over the sounds of the band, so no path was formed and Sanchez had to fight his way through. It worked to his advantage.

My momentum when I'd ran toward Emma had taken me past where he'd picked her up and I had to come to a skidding stop, my hand touching the ground to keep me up, before switching directions to go after them. Through the madness of the beach, I couldn't tell which way they'd gone. Panicked, I tried to look everywhere at once. I was yelling, "Emma," which was pointless in a crowd that had just muffled a gunshot. They weren't anywhere. I was going out of my frickin mind as I bulled my way through the crowd. I ran and pushed myself south until I got to the end of the hotel's property, but when I got there, I didn't see anyone running in that direction. I didn't have time to go on a wild goose chase that way, so I switched directions and ran back through the crowd the other way. Running into people, knocking over drinks, I heard people shout, "C'mon, respect mon," from the locals, or just "Hey, fucking watch it," from the Americans. I finally broke through, cutting through a group that was dancing in a circle. I had been ready to try to catch him from behind and haul him down, but facing north, I didn't see them that way either. I felt completely helpless. I noticed the shadows to the north of the property, where I'd hid that night with Diego, and tried to decide if I should risk everything by trying to find them in there. But, I knew they could be anywhere, and my chances of finding them remote at best. Not knowing where to turn next, I went towards the only other border of the property, the water. I ran along the outskirts of the crowd on the north border to the shore. My eyes immediately went to the boat and I knew before I saw them that it made sense for Sanchez to try to escape by boat. I ran closer and saw two figures getting aboard the aging wooden craft. I had no doubt it was them.

For a moment I had held out hope that Sanchez wouldn't be able to start the boat; that he probably didn't have the keys. Then, though, I heard the engine turn over and catch and I realized he had planned his escape in advance. Almost at that same time, three things started happening. The boat started to slowly pull out through the shallow water. Diego, who still had most of the great speed he had told me about, ran like lightning from the beach in pursuit of the boat. And just at that very moment, the sky lit up with fireworks. The crowd on the beach all turned at once in ecstasy to watch a fireworks show on a perfect full moon night during one of the great parties of all time.

They were oblivious to Diego, but I saw that he had caught the boat and deftly pulled himself aboard. I entered the water giving up at least fifty yards in position to where the boat was struggling to get to deeper water. One advantage I knew I had was that the water was shallow for probably a quarter of a mile, which might give me a chance to catch them. I ran, having trouble spotting them in the dark, until in the intermittent light of the fireworks, I saw the outline of the two brothers on the back of the boat. Then maddening darkness, then the light of the fireworks, and then I could see that Sanchez had definitely realized Diego had become a traitor to his family. They had begun to scuffle, and from the intensity of it, were quite possibly trying to kill each other. Behind the two of them, I could see that Emma was still on board. I yelled, "Jump Em, jump," but there was no way she could hear me over the din of the fireworks, and it looked like it was possible that Sanchez may have had a hold of her arm. Like watching a movie where the frames of the reel don't quite connect, I had trouble following it all. Diego, who wasn't a small guy, was still severely overmatched against his psycho brother. From what I could tell, it looked like a hockey fight, with Diego desperately trying to hold onto his brother's free arm, so he couldn't get off a good shot.

I ran through the waves as hard as I could hearing the fireworks go off above my head, my heart beating wildly. I was gaining on the slowly moving boat a bit, I thought. Twenty-five yards away, then only twenty. My spirits sank, though, when I saw Sanchez rip loose his massive right arm and wind up and connect with a powerful shot to to the side of Diego's head. I could hear Diego cry out, just as the blow knocked him to the side of the boat. Sanchez moved quickly after him to the side of the boat where Diego had been staggered, and he grabbed him with both arms and threw him off the far side of the boat. In the light of the fireworks, I could see Diego flailing helplessly into the ocean. I could feel the pain as if Sanchez had hit me. It was now entirely up to me and I put my head down to make a final push with everything I had. I was making progress, and for a moment thought I might catch them...until the force of the explosion threw me clear back to near the edge of the beach. I landed on my back and was rolled over backwards twice to stop my momentum. I momentarily lay dazed in the shallow water considering if I might be dying. I saw no blood, so I was encouraged to try to get to my feet. Getting up slowly to make sure nothing was broken, I had the disoriented hope that the explosion had something to do with the fireworks. When I looked up, though, the boat was in flames.

I remembered yelling, "Noooooooooooo!" and, running into the ocean like a crazy person. I swam trying to find any reason to be hopeful. The waves were small, but it seemed to take forever to get near the boat. I swam and swam and swam, expecting to be there, but no boat. Finally, feeling the heat, I realized there was no boat to find. It was gone. It was fucking gone. My head was spinning, and I fought to think of some logical explanation that would involve letting me see Em again.

That's when I saw the body. I thrashed my way around pieces of metal and wood, some still on fire, until I could see Diego was floating in the water. He had a tenuous hold on one of the boat's seat cushions. His hold on his consciousness may have been even more tenuous. He was bleeding from his head, hit hard by pieces of the shattered boat, not to mention by the vicious blow from his lunatic brother. My head aching, and my heart beating so loud I could hear it, I had to make a decision that had no right answer. If I abandoned Diego to continue to search for Emma, he'd lose his grip on the floating seat that was saving his life. If I went to try to rescue him, by the time I got back, Emma would be that much more gone. I wanted to scream.

Diego looked up at me, in agony, and with most of the strength he had left said, "Where's Emma? Save her."

Treading water from where I was, I looked around one more desperate and futile time before answering, "I don't know. I don't fucking know," and I was crying because I realized that that was my answer. I didn't know. I had to force myself to admit I had no idea where she might be. She could be anywhere or nowhere anymore. Diego, though, was right there in front of me.

I heard him say, "No," as I wrapped my arm around his chest, and, as fast as I could, but way too damn slowly, made my way through the ocean's obstacle course and back to the beach. I'd never swum carrying someone else and I felt exhausted by the time I dragged him to the beach. I dropped him off there, took his hand and implored him to keep fighting. Then I yelled for someone to help him. I briefly saw the police come running in his direction.

Dazed and spent, I ran back into the water and desperately flailed around as long as I could stay afloat. I would think I'd see something that might be Em—what was that?!—but then just find a piece of wood from the shattered boat. I looked everywhere she could conceivably be and then again. My lungs, along with my heart, were ready to explode.

Looking up in near total despair, I saw the big full moon, which gave me a jolt of irrational temporary hope, and followed the moonbeam down to the horizon. There, in the light of the moon, I thought I saw her! I had been bobbed and tossed around so much I couldn't be sure where I was. Nor was I sure what I saw. But in that glimpse, *if it was her,* it was nowhere near where I thought she could conceivably be. I started in that direction, filled with new hope and new strength, but also the very real fear that I might drown before I'd be able to swim the two or three hundred yards to where I was headed.

Forcing myself to continue kicking, arm after arm punching through the water, I pushed myself far past what I thought I had in me. Allowing myself to look up every dozen strokes, I finally saw a floating tube only yards in front of me. Even as close as it was, I barely made it. The life preserver was dancing on the water, and I grabbed it with my left hand to save my own life. The arms and shoulders hanging onto the floating ring belonged to Emma. I put my right arm around her to make sure we could both stay aloft. I desperately touched her expressionless face and called her name and begged her to open her eyes and come back to me. No response! She was out of it. Oh, God! Emma, be alive!

Cursing myself for not knowing how to check someone's pulse, I used my free right hand to check my own. Fuck! I had no pulse! Where was it?! Finally, I put my neck back and found it. I reached for Emma's neck in the same spot, and it was there. I could feel the precious beats of her pulse.

It was the most draining thing I'd ever done, not knowing if Emma's heart was still working, but I made it back to near where the ocean met the land, and Gumby and Spike ran to drag us from the water. There was still a crush of people around Diego, though it felt like I'd left him there hours earlier, and just as suddenly around us. I saw Erika, always the strong one, and I saw the fear and uncertainty in her eyes. She was making sure that only the people that could help Emma were standing around her.

I had used up far more energy and adrenaline than I had stored up. I was aware that, in this, the biggest moment of my life, I probably should have had some heightened sense of consciousness, of needing to be up and strong and ordering people around to make sure Emma got what she needed, but instead, I was used up, entirely exhausted, and laying there motionless with my back in the water and my hand reaching out to touch hers. I was conscious only of that she was getting help. Not knowing if she was going to make it or not, I briefly lifted my head to look at the moon, and I felt like I knew the answer.

My thoughts, like the ocean, came in waves of memories and images. We're in the boat—*the wave of the Jamaican flag*—we're going to be married—*the little wooden engagement ring*—we're talking about our future together—*the smiling singer*—we're talking about our dreams coming true—*the full moon*—all our dreams are coming true—*her pretty face*—we can't wait for our future—*kicking back with a Red Stripe*—we're working on the Full Moon Festival—*her hug*—we're together less than half an hour ago—*she's singing*—we're in the hot tub—*our song*—we're dancing on the beach—*her kiss*—we're laughing and flirting—*she believes in me*—and then—*and now*—

52

The night was kind to us. The sky clear and soft, the breeze gentle and soothing. We gathered on the beach at sunset for the service.

Erika, of course, was there. So were Freedy and Spike and Alfred and Vinny. Diego was still in the hospital. When it was time to give a eulogy, the words were chosen carefully, and all that was left was to get them out. It was, after all, her father. And, he had, in his own misguided way, come back to try to save her. Emma was weakened, but still strong. Her words were touching and appropriate, only alluding to her father's shortcomings, and finding the characteristics she could memorialize and keep with her. If nothing else, he had, we had all concluded, loved her deeply.

When she was done, I held her hand, not wanting to ever let go again. All of us held each other and watched the setting sun.

Emma had seen Diego approaching the boat, and even though Sanchez had a grip on her arm that cut through her flesh to her bones, she knew what she needed to do if she got the chance. Sanchez had been startled to see his brother, and had originally welcomed him on board. In didn't take long for him to realize that the reason Diego had boarded was to do anything he could to stop him and save Emma. Sanchez had been able to fight off Diego, even with just his right hand, while holding onto Emma with his left.

When Sanchez's punch had sent Diego sprawling across the boat, without thinking he let go of his grip on Emma, because he needed both hands to throw Diego overboard. When he did, she didn't hesitate. She grabbed the life preserver from the boat on her way out, held it out in front of her, and dove for her freedom. It must have been in midflight, we determined later based on how far away she had landed from where the boat had been, when the explosion happened. She recalled nothing beyond leaping for her life and briefly considering her entry into the water. She had escaped with only that split second it took her to jump off the boat to spare.

She had lost consciousness and stayed out for many long, harrowing hours, though from the litany of MRI and x-ray images, had somehow escaped any serious injuries. I sat vigil, with alternating visits from our friends, until sometime early that next morning, when finally, from my restless sleep, I heard her stir.

"Seth," she said in a searching voice just below a whisper.

I bolted towards her bed, and took her hand. "Em, it's me. I'm here."

I thought I felt her squeeze my hand, and thrilled beyond reason by that small act, was almost startled to see her Caribbean blue eyes looking at me.

"Well, hi," I said, ever the dope.

"Hi, to you," she said back, and more welcome, wonderful words had never been uttered. At least not to me.

"You're going to be okay, Em, you're gonna be okay."

She closed her eyes a second, as if gathering strength, and looked back up at me and said, "I'll be better than that. Seth, we're going to have our life together."

Diego was slightly drugged but awake and thankful to have someone to talk to. He had his right arm in a sling, broken, and he sported bandages across his cracked ribs and covering the top of his head. In the explosion, he'd suffered a pretty severe concussion. His face wore the imprints of his late brother's knuckles. Just another reminder of his family. I looked him over and said, "It's good to see you in so few pieces."

"The rest of me is in the room next door," he said, and the three of us laughed.

Emma got up from the wheelchair they insisted she use, gave him a kiss on the cheek, and said, "You saved my life. I'll never forget what you did."

"I mostly just got hit in the head," he joked with envious timing, and Emma had this huge smile, while wiping a tear from her eye. Diego strained to look over to me, and said, "But, your man here saved my life. Seth, thanks, amigo."

"Stop it, bud, you were the real hero out there."

Again, we had formed our little circle of life.

The next week Emma received a Fed Ex package. The return address appeared to be a law firm. She read through it, thoughtfully, I could tell, but without emotion because whatever she could muster had been used up at the funeral service, and then handed it to me. It was Dugan's last will and testament. I made my way through the legalese—cursing lawyers for justifying their jobs by writing like assholes—until I got to the gist of it.

Dugan was doling out his estate. You could tell a lot about Dugan from his will. Dugan's was the will of a gambler and a thief. He left Emma the Blue Moon and $50,000. He left her sister a small house he owned in Nevada and $50,000. His ex-wife got some money from a pension plan at a company he'd worked for from 1977 to 1979. It had been compounding for over twenty years and was worth the staggering sum of $24,000. Of his estate, my guess is that was the only amount that was earned legally. I had a feeling the $100,000 he was leaving his daughters was the $150,000 he owed Sanchez less the money he'd put in the exploding briefcase. A gambler and a thief right up until the very end. The will was dated May 27, the week before. Em was the new owner of the Blue Moon.

Diego was released from the hospital and spent a week at the Blue Moon getting stronger, going over everything that had happened and deciding what to do next. One day, at my encouragement, Emma and Diego had gone out to lunch together. They both now shared the common bond of having lost family members, as it were, and both having just barely survived the night. He had also bravely saved her life, and I could never repay him for that. I wanted them to have a chance to have their personal so longs and thank yous and laughs.

On the day Diego was going to leave, he and I sat along the shore and slowly slipped from our Red Stripe bottles on a day so strikingly beautiful it was hard to believe anything bad had ever happened on this beach.

I told him I had had a visit the day before from Spike. He had come over to my cabin, which I thought was unusual, because it was one of the only times I'd not seen him behind his bar. "He came over to apologize because he felt horrible for what happened to Emma and you. And, get ready for this, my friend, but he told me it was he who called the police that night."

"What?!" Diego said, with the same surprised reaction I'd had. "Why?"

"He wanted to get back at Sanchez for roughing him up the night he got Freedy's phone number. He was going to make sure Sanchez never got his money. Then he started to say something else—and this was really weird—he just abruptly stopped and said he had to go. I'm not sure what to think about that."

"I have an idea," Diego said. "I overheard part of a conversation Spike was having with one of his beach buddies. I can't keep up with the Patois, but I got the feeling Spike was bragging about coming into some money soon. Amigo, I think it's possible that Dugan had Spike hide the cocaine and that Spike knows where it is."

"Jesus. You know, if that's true, that could be the real reason he called the police."

"What do you mean?"

"If Dugan and Sanchez would have been arrested, guess who gets to run away with $250,000 worth of coke?"

"My God. Spike? I didn't think he had that in him."

"I don't know, man, he always struck me as being a little too happy. Maybe he just got tired of always serving all the rich foreigners and decided it was time to get something for himself."

Diego seemed dismayed, but then thought about it and said, "Actually, you gotta give him some credit for his plan. If you think about, he probably figured that no one would get hurt except Sanchez and Dugan and the idea of them torturing each other in prison forever does have its appeal, don't you think?"

I chuckled briefly, seeing the humor in that, but just said, "I hope it's not true. It seems like almost everyone I've met has tried to make some dirty money from this fucked-up situation."

"Yeah, quite the group of associates you assembled here, amigo," he deadpanned.

Now, that made me laugh out loud. "I know. I love everyone here, but I'll be lucky to survive you people."

"Speaking of surviving, did you find out anything about the explosion?"

"I have no evidence," I said, "but it had to be Dugan. I think the cowardly piece-of-shit wired the briefcase with explosives and timed it to go off when he knew Sanchez would have it. It was his way to save his butt, but it could've killed a lot of people, depending on where Sanchez went after he got the briefcase. You know, in Dugan's desk drawer I found a bunch of books about explosives. It just fits. Dugan wasn't very smart, but he kept trying to outsmart everyone."

"In the end, all he did was get himself killed, and nearly his daughter."

"And your brother."

"The only thing Dugan did right. Good riddance," he said, raising his Red Stripe to finish it off, the bitterness of his words hanging in the air.

I also finished my Red Stripe, and we sat in silence looking at the water until Diego turned and looked at me suddenly with the eyes of a child, and asked, "Seth, can you do me a favor? Tell me about your family. What's it like to have normal parents?"

I sat up in my beach chair, turned toward him and told him all about my family. I told him how my mom had baked me cookies and my dad had offered money before I'd come back to Jamaica. I told them how much they worried about me. And, not a drug dealer or lunatic in the bunch. I thought to myself that I might just go ahead and read the Passover questions next year. In fact, I told him I might invite him to Passover dinner.

"Oy vays," he said, auditioning for the role. "How was that? You think I'll fit in?"

"It needs some work," I said laughing, patting him on the shoulder and standing up, because it was time for him to get going. "Of course, I may not be the one to talk to about fitting in."

He had decided to visit some friends in Mexico for a while before heading to Brazil to pursue the career and the life we wanted. I shook his hand, gave him a hug, and told him I could never thank him enough for what he did for us. Emma gave him a kiss and a long hug and her unspoken thanks. He took one last look at the Blue Moon before getting into his car, and said, "Even after everything that's happened, I'm still going to miss this place." Per Jamaican custom, he honked his car horn and drove off.

Three weeks later, Spike drove up in a new Mercedes and handed me his old uniform. I was mostly disgusted with him, but he'd been really good to Emma, and like a father to Erika and Freedy, so when he offered his hand, I took it and wished him well. We replaced him that week with Gumby, who had become quite smitten with Erika since they'd met at the last Full

BLUE MOON

Moon Festival. Gumby was amazing with the customers, and no one was more pleased with the Blue Moon's new bartender than Erika.

53

I finished the book in the middle of that summer and sent it to a literary agent with a letter telling him, not about the book, but all about Shulie and Emma and Erika and Diego. He later told me he was touched by the emotion of the letter and felt compelled to read the book, which he thought was funny and poignant and wanted to represent. I got a small advance from a publisher and didn't start making some real money until it hit the bottom part of the *New York Times* best seller list. Writing the book had been so wrapped up in the fresh memories of all that had happened to us, I didn't realize until later that I had actually accomplished what I had come to Jamaica to do. It wasn't the overwhelming feeling of success that I thought it'd be, but it felt like an accomplishment and that I'd be able to make a career doing what I enjoyed doing. And I felt great to live up to the belief that Emma had in me.

Business at the Blue Moon had increased considerably. We were getting a ton of emails from Freedy's web site and the Full Moon Festival also helped. I had just assumed we wouldn't continue the Full Moon Festivals thinking the memories from the last one would be too painful. But the staff loved it, it was great for business, and Emma was too proud of what we had accomplished together to let it go. In the end, I was glad they all talked me into continuing them.

Emma and I spent Thanksgiving with my family. They completely loved Emma, and I was never more proud of myself, of her, or of my parents. I showed her the Chicago that I loved, and I could tell she was falling in love with it, too.

When we returned, we told the staff we had decided to sell the hotel. Not that it needed to be said, but we told them that we loved the Blue Moon and Jamaica and each of them, but that it was time to move on. The hotel was on a roll and we got a lot of interest. By mid-December, we had a done deal, and sold the hotel for far more than I would have expected. Because we wanted to show our love and appreciation for all our friends—and because my book was doing nicely—we chose to split it up and gave most of it away. Erika and Freedy got $100,000 each and Gumby got $25,000. I could tell by how they'd been together recently that Gumby's might some-day be combined with Erika's. She had graduated last May, but was hanging around allegedly to help us with the hotel. But I think she was really waiting for Gumby and her to decide on taking the next step together. While Emma and I were in Chicago, I received a birthday card that said she'd gotten a job teaching English in Kingston and that she and Gumby were getting mar-ried and we better be there. Being a Jamaican guy he had put up some resistance to the marriage idea, until, I'm sure, Erika kicked his ass and made him see the light. I wrote back that we wouldn't miss it for the world.

Freedy was using the money to go to school. He was going to design and program web sites and told me he felt like a new person. I had to force it on him, but Vinny finally relented and took $25,000, an outrageous amount for he and his family. We also forwarded some money to help Diego make a life of his own. I thought about giving some to Alfred, who I considered a good friend, but he wasn't hurting for money, had already profited enough from the drug deal that got us involved in this whole mess, and I didn't think he would take it anyway. Still, though, I went to dinner with him again, thanked him for everything and promised to stay in touch. Then we gave a large donation to the American Cancer Society in Emma's name.

We had an emotional, but really great going away party just before Christmas. Erika and Freedy and Vinny and Gumby and Alfred had be-come our extended family. It was hard to leave, but Emma and I knew we'd be back. In fact, we already had the date in mind.

Epilogue

I've had a lot of time to think about my experience in Jamaica. I've long since decided that I couldn't imagine having ended up with anyone but Emma...someone who felt so totally right in my heart. Because of her, I think I've changed and grown. I now know true love and happiness are, in fact, possible. I've also found that now I believe in myself more than I ever had.

Choosing to go to Jamaica, I think, also made me a better person. I took stock in my life, explored who I was and wanted to be and decided to change the direction of my life. In much the same way as the Jamaican people focused on the things they had rather than things they didn't, I was able to put my life in my hands, using the few materials I had to work with, and sculpt it into something I wanted to be. It made me finally appreciate my life, the touch and feel of it, and to not want to waste a moment of its possibilities. For the positive vibrations, for Emma, and for being the perfect place to be me, I give thanks, Jamaica. And as Alfred said, "Yah should be yah." I should be me. That, looking back, was probably the whole point.

I returned home somewhat of a celebrity. Thanks to Freedy, *Blue Moon,* the book, had a web site so I could get the people's comments and questions. The ones I remembered most were from people I'd known growing up. Friends and acquaintances, in grade school through college, who, I noted with some amusement, were now treating me as if I was higher on the food chain than they had remembered me. I got fun notes from my brother and Walk (saying he wanted to play himself in the movie) and from Bob and Javy, who wanted me to know they were stunned to find out I was interesting. I got one from my college love who told me she was happily married and expecting her second child. She enjoyed my book and, giving me a dig, "approved." I answered every comment from friends and strangers.

Late one night, at our new apartment in the city, I checked my emails and there was a note from Alexa. Alexa was going to be in Milan the next week for a photo shoot and was really tired because she'd stayed up the entire previous night finishing my book. I smiled thinking about that. She said she'd been so happy for me reading that I'd met the right person. She still hadn't, but was glad to find out what it was like. She also said that she was thinking it was time to get out of modeling, that she had other talents and dreams of being who she wanted to be. That I had help her realize that whatever your talents, you're only here a finite amount of time, and that you need to move in the directions of your strengths and passions while you can. In fact, she wanted to go to school to go into psychology. It warmed my heart. I called Emma over to read it, too. When she did, she gave me a big proud smile and told me it was really cool to be able to touch someone's life like that. She also asked me to email her back and get an address where we could reach her. She wanted to send Alexa a wedding invitation.

Under another brilliant full moon, Em and I said, "I do," on the beach in Jamaica with a lot of our family and friends, including Alexa, Diego, Bobbo, Darlene, Javy and Walkman.

Emma and I danced our first dance to *Moonlight*, sung beautifully by our friend the smiling guy singer and the waitresses from the Charela. Vinny and his girlfriend and their two beautiful little girls were there, and Vinny sang another astonishing version of *Give Thanks Jamaica*, which made Em and I have to wipe at the corner of our eyes, as if there weren't really tears there.

At some point much later and much looser in the evening, everyone was dancing in one form or another with someone on the beach. Erika and her new husband Gumby, Bobbo and Darlene, Freedy and his new girl-friend, Alfred and his wife, my parents, my brother and his wife and Walker and Javy with some of Erika's hot friends. Walk was leading everyone in his famous Walkman dance, when I pointed out to Emma that Diego and Alexa seemed to be hitting it off at one of the candle-lit tables back by the bar. Emma and I smiled at the possibilities, looked at each other and high-fived. It was her idea to have them sit together at dinner.

"Hey, Seth," she said, looking at her new wedding ring, which she wore with the old cheap wooden one I'd given her when we got engaged, "I'm now Emma Gold."

"I know. I like the sound of that. How does it feel?"

She thought about if for a second, and said with her shy smile that lights me up, "Like everything I ever wanted is now possible. How about you?"

I shrugged and said, "My name's always been the same."

She laughed and punched me under my left shoulder. "That's not what I meant."

I looked at her beautiful eyes looking back at me, touched her face and said, "It feels like everything I ever wanted is now real."

Since I had time to plan it so it'd finally turn out right, I even rented a white horse for Emma and me to ride off down the beach into the sunset, even though it was after midnight. Walker gave me a bottle of champagne and Emma two glasses for the ride, and everyone cheered for us as the horse with the "Just Married" sign started making its way down the beach with the happy couple.

It was beautiful and perfect and the moon shown down upon us, and the horse was galloping through the shallow water, and, never having been happier, I lifted my arms up in the air, in sheer joy, to wave to our friends. Then I uncorked the bottle of champagne and when I leaned left to pour some into one of the glasses Emma was holding out to me, the horse leaned right, and I fell off the damn thing into the ocean. Emma turned the horse around and I could hear her laughing. When she saw me sitting back in the water with my legs crossed at the ankles enjoying some champagne, she just shook her head. She jumped off the horse, ran to the water, threw the glasses over her head, went to her knees, knocked me down and, all at the same time, grabbed the bottle from me so she could take a swig. And then, she in her wedding gown and me in my tux, held each other and rolled around in the surf like it was all meant to happen just like that.